A SUMMER BEFORE

- Croc Brothers Romance Series Book Two

Donna Munro

Warm Witty
PUBLISHING

Warm Witty Publishing

Sunshine Coast ☺ Queensland ☺ Australia

A SUMMER BEFORE

- Croc Brothers Romance Series Book Two

Donna Munro

Warm Witty Publishing

Sunshine Coast ☺ Queensland ☺ Australia

First Published – 2018 - Kendwa's Secret
This edition published 2022 by Warm Witty Publishing
Sunshine Coast, Qld Australia
www.donnamunroauthor.com

The National Library of Australia Cataloguing-in-Publication

Creator: Munro, Donna, author.

Title: A Summer Before / Donna Munro.

ISBN: 978-0-6452629-2-6 (paperback)

Subjects: Romance fiction.
Australian fiction.
Contemporary women's fiction.
Adventure Romance

Typeset in Times New Roman 12pt by Warm Witty Publishing.
Cover artwork by Donna Munro.
Printed and bound in Australia by Ingram Spark.

A catalogue record for this book is available from the National Library of Australia

Other books by Donna Munro:

Books by Donna Munro:

The Zanzibar Moon (2017)
Kendwa's Secret (2018)
Elephant Creek (2020)

The above series, now titled

A Summer in Paradise
A Summer Before
A Summer of Hope

Non-fiction:

Dad Love (2011)
How to Self-Publish in Oz (2021)

Chapter 1
2001

The sun hung high in an azure sky, blazing down on the scene below. Sweat poured from the men, dripping down grimy faces and creating wet patches on their armpits. It was chaotic; long grass, mud, tough men and one angry crocodile.

The documentary crew filmed from a safe distance. A cameraman's eyes shifted to the leech attached to his leg. Jumping at shadows, the well-dressed producer took his frustration out on the unfocused camera and the man holding it, yelling a tirade of swear words. Adrenaline surged through the female anchor. Fear gripped her but so did respect.

'It's a well-practised drill,' yelled the head crocodile wrangler, looking up at the camera momentarily before rallying the five men surrounding the croc.

The ancient leather body spun with claws and tail thrashing, splattering muddy water over the men holding the rope tethers. On each side of the beast, a lassoed rope held the ugly jaws tight. Muscles tensed, swear words flung through the air like mud. The beast slowly stopped fighting.

Head wrangler nodded at the boy. 'Mate, you get on her now and strap that gaffer tape on.'

The tall boy with the body of a man, all sinewy muscle, but the face of an angel, didn't hesitate. He straddled the nobbled back of the beast, effortlessly wrapping the mighty jaws in silver tape. His bicep flexed, showing sinewy veins as he snapped the end of the roll with a tight pull.

The reporter couldn't take her eyes off him. She motioned with her hand for her cameraman to zoom into his face. He was an extraordinary-looking male.

The wrangler slapped his thigh, nodding his approval. The young man grinned widely, revealing bright white teeth in a muddy tanned face.

The wrangler said, 'Geeze, Kendwa. Mate, you're a natural. Okay, boys, let's get this croc on the truck and move her up to Thompsons Landing.'

Six Territorians lifted the docile croc onto the flatbed truck. The wrangler patted Kendwa's shoulder as he got into the passenger side of the truck. 'Top work, Mate.' Tapping the tin sides, he sent them on their way.

The reporter straightened her black bob before running a finger over her lip gloss. With the croc gone, the goose bumps that had popped along her arms disappeared. Reptiles terrified her, though watching the wild men catch it also made her horny. Particularly the young man. His gorgeous image remained in her head. First, she would interview the head wrangler. Second get the segment in the can, third – *seduction*.

'Wow. That was quite impressive. How big was that crocodile?' she asked the wrangler.

Shrugging, he rubbed his dirty hands down his brown trousers. 'That mumma 'd be 'round 600kg and 'bout three metres. She's been scaring stock and the farmers around these parts, so we'll move her on.'

'Why did you let the young man wrangle her? It's such a dangerous job. He looks like a schoolboy.'

'Why not? Did you see how good he was? He's old enough.'

'Yes, he did seem to know what to do. Must have been with the team for a while, then? Is he an apprentice or something?'

'Na. Two weeks. Fastest fella to eva' catch on. Most are shit scared. Oops, sorry, lady. Peeing their pants on their first wrangles. He's fearless and skilled. It's uncanny.'

'So, how did he come to you with so much skill?'

A fly sat on his crooked nose. 'Damned if I know. He and his dad got in touch, asking if he could do some work experience. Most kids will head to the beach and bludge this time of year.' Taking his hat off, he shooed the flies away. 'Just wanted the outback experience and tough work. Kid doesn't talk much, but he's lived all over the world. He's a Yank but originally from Africa. Maybe he was brought up with wildlife or somethin' A bit of a Tarzan if ya ask me.' He scratched his thinning head and then his groin.

They ended the interview by agreeing to meet at the local pub in the small outback town for a post-production beer. Going by the wrangler's lurid looks, she could tell that he wanted her for more than a shared beer. She had other ideas. *Seducing young Kendwa.*

People spilled out of the hotel onto the dusty red dirt street. A couple of kangaroos bounced past, probably searching for water. They stopped metres from the patio, alert ears twitching for a few moments, then bounded off into the distance.

There were wolf whistles as the reporter sashayed across the timber floorboards, short heels tapping a beat in time with her swinging hips. Ignoring them, she entered through the open doors and let her eyes adjust to the darker inside, scanning the shiny timber bar.

He had his back to her. Broad tanned shoulders, in a navy Bonds singlet, tapered down to a trim waist. Denim jeans sat snuggly across his firm bottom, unlike the saggy bums of some of the other men. Restraining her hands from patting his jeans, she shoved them in her own pockets.

The camera crew tried getting her attention at their corner table, but she only had eyes for Kendwa. As if he sensed her, he turned smiling, raising his glass of beer. A dimple dug into each cheek, one deeper than the other, in dark copper, flawless skin. *A perfect smile.* As she neared, she realised his eyes were bright aqua, not the blue-green they'd looked with mud around them. *Amazing eyes.* She caught her breath at his beauty, leaning against the bar so she wouldn't swoon.

'I'll shout you a beer,' he said in an almost-man voice. It wasn't Australian – a mix between English and American.

'Thank you, Kendwa. I'm Abi.' He passed her a cold glass of beer. Their fingers brushed. Electricity shot to her womb.

During her career, she'd met plenty of sexy, powerful, interesting men. None so hot as Kendwa. He had more charisma than a movie star. Something undefinable, putting her a little on edge in an excellent way.

'You're welcome, lovely lady. Abi for Abigail?' He angled his head towards the crew's table. 'Your mates want you over there.'

She didn't look towards them. Instead, she held Kendwa's mesmerising gaze. 'Uh huh. I prefer Abi, and I'd rather drink with you.'

'I'm glad.' He clinked his beer glass against hers, taking a sip.

Abi watched his luscious thick lips and the beer foam on his thin moustache. His beautiful eyes drank her in, even glancing at her exposed cleavage.

Catching her tongue in her throat, she managed to ask, 'How old are you, Kendwa?'

'Eighteen, but people tell me I have an old soul.'

To hide her smile, she placed her hand over her mouth. *OMG, old enough for sex.* Fidgeting with her hair, she squirmed on the bar stool. 'I'm sure you are. So where do you stay here?'

'Out the back of the pub. There are some dongas. They're small but fit a single bed, a desk and a wardrobe. We share amenities.'

A single bed. Abi grinned, imagining how close their bodies would be. *Him naked.* There was no turning back after that thought.

'I've never seen inside a donga before. I probably should—while I'm here.' She lied easily with raised eyebrows.

He gulped, his Adam's apple bobbing. 'Research?'

'Of course.' Abi rose from the bar stool. Kendwa knocked his half-full beer over. The beer drenched the front of his singlet. He dabbed at it. Through the fabric plastered to him, she eagerly noticed his chest, nipples and muscles. *Yum, yum!*

'You mean right now?' His voice broke a little.

Abi nodded, smiling seductively, tilting her head towards the door.

He cleared his throat. 'Okay.'

Ignoring the wide eyes and leers of mostly male pub patrons, she followed Kendwa. At the middle donga, he pulled a key from his pocket, quickly opening the door. She stepped inside, glancing at the bed and back at him with seductive eyes. Their bodies nearly touched, with barely enough room to swing a cat in the tiny room.

Heat radiated off him. Reaching for the door handle, Abi pulled the door closed with a soft click. An air conditioner hummed above the bed, sending cool air washing over them, making her nipples erect.

Kendwa stood like a rock. He didn't look ill at ease; he just didn't seem to know what to do next. *Was he letting her decide?*

4

Almost clutching the pheromones in the air, she inhaled the intoxicating male sweat. Inching closer, she placed her hand on his cheek, feeling the soft bristles. Slowly she drew his face to hers. Their lips touched. He proved he wasn't a boy, returning her kiss with experienced lips and a tongue that explored where she wanted it to. His arms went around her, trailing down her back, over her hips pulling her close.

'You have done this before?' she asked, as his erection pressed against her leg.

'Mmmm,' he mumbled, kissing her neck. 'Only with girls, though. You're all woman.' His hands told her so as they cupped her breasts.

'Oh, don't worry, honey. You're all man. You just don't realise it yet. Besides, I'm only twenty-six.'

Turning her around, he quickly unzipped her dress, letting it fall to the floor.

'Show me what a woman likes,' he said, grinning, as he pulled his singlet over his head, revealing a trim six-pack. He unzipped his fly. His package bulged for release in his underwear. Slipping the denim jeans down his hips while his eyes raked her almost made her combust.

Flicking her panties and bra, she edged onto the bed facing him. Her eyes devoured every inch of his sculpted naked body as he stepped closer. *Wow! If he still had some growing to do, he would be extraordinary in a few years.*

'You are so beautiful,' Kendwa said, his astonishing eyes raking across her body in appreciation. Bracing himself above her, he kissed her deeply. It didn't last long before he crushed his body against hers. There was no denying he was a man when he entered her. A scream of ecstasy escaped her lips. The pub patrons heard it. Some raised a glass, mostly enviously, to Kendwa.

Abi and Kendwa didn't leave the donga until the following afternoon when they both had to return to work. Abi's next assignment was waiting in the city. Kendwa had more crocodiles to relocate away from people and stock. Their paths would probably never cross again.

Kendwa discovered that he enjoyed the long conversations they'd had between the bouts of sex. Perhaps he had some sort of gift when it came to women, just like the talent he had with wild animals.

5

The lessons Abi taught him in the tiny donga, in the heart of the Australian outback, would remain with him. He liked to think that he had imparted something too. By the look of her satisfied smile and smudged lipstick he had.

After Abi left, the wrangler jibed Kendwa. 'You surprised me, mate. Didn't think you had it in ya.' He lifted his hand for a high-five.

Kendwa left him hanging. 'My business and hers. None of yours,' he said, his jaw tight, facing the wrangler with a steely gaze. 'You need to treat women with dignity and respect.'

The wrangler took a step back, raising his hands. *I'll be.* The young guy had more integrity than most grown men. The wrangler wasn't scared of crocs, snakes, cattle or most blokes, for that matter. He decided young Kendwa was someone he didn't want to cross.

Chapter 2
Ten Years Later

It was Kendwa's twenty-eighth birthday. The day should have been a happy one, but he knew future birthdays would suck forever. Instead of celebrating, he was heading down a Miami sidewalk towards the morgue. Each step was a stab to his heart.

His phone buzzed in the pocket of his board shorts. Fishing it out, he realised it was his friend, not the police and answered on the second ring.

'Toby. Man, is it good to hear your voice. No, can't you deal with the gator? I have to be somewhere—' his voice trailed off. He stared vacantly up the bustling street full of holidaymakers and locals in various forms of hardly-dressed.

A pretty blonde girl in a yellow Brazil-style bikini, with more bum showing than a Kardashian, bumped his hip as she skated by on roller blades. Grinning mischievously, she winked, though he didn't notice.

He ran his free hand through wavy brown sun-streaked hair. 'Toby. I'm—yeah, okay. Where?' Nodding, he listened to Toby's instructions about an alligator in a backyard pool, then put his phone in his pocket, sighing.

The medical examiner would have to wait for him to come in later. His parents couldn't get any deader.

He knew he was putting it off. Sometimes, even he couldn't face death, especially when it came to family.

Family. The thought burned through his heart. He was orphaned, with no other close family, just floating like the expensive boats in the harbour; no anchor, drifting.

7

Striding back to his jeep, he slid onto the driver's seat, slamming the door. Putting his foot down, he drove the ten miles dangerously fast to the address Toby had supplied. *Probably a little self-destructive, but what the hell.*

When he skidded at the back of a massive house, a security thug with a meaner snarl than a crocodile allowed him through. The lush gardens wafted with floral perfume. Immaculately trimmed hedges lined the tiled pathway. Kendwa wondered how many gardeners they employed to keep them that way. Fancy people chatted and lounged around the luxury eighty-two feet pool. Wealth had never impressed Kendwa, so when a woman of about fifty, adorned in jewels and some sort of flowing kaftan, rushed towards him, he eyed her with disguised censure.

'You must be Kendwa, the gator guy.' She gushed.

'Yep.' He glanced at the pool, yelling at his friend, who was reaching into the water with a large metal hook. 'Tobes, what's the go with this gator?' He neared the edge, striding past the woman and the others sitting at café tables around the pool.

The woman touched his shoulder with a long silver polished nail. In a ringing voice, she said, 'I thought you'd like to meet my daughter, Beatrice.' She waved to her right.

A lady of indeterminate age (fake contours, bursting tits, plastic face, huge pouty lips, too much makeup) lifted her designer sunnies eyeing him from a deck chair and blew him a kiss. Even with all those enhancements, she was on the ugly side of pretty.

'Tobes?' Kendwa demanded, ignoring the lingering glances of the women.

Toby had sweat dripping down his handsome face from under his peaked cap. 'He's just so fast. I can't get a good grab of him. He's a big one,' confirmed Toby in his Australian drawl.

They'd been mates since meeting in Australia's Northern Territory ten years earlier. After that, they enjoyed stints as rangers in Africa before moving to Florida, forming their business *Two Gator Guys*. It was perfect for them. They were adventurous but eco-warriors, sharing the same passion for moving reptiles safely away from humans rather than killing them.

It was only surprising to them they because semi-famous. The local women were fascinated by the handsome duo. This kept them booked

8

solid as gators encroached the suburbs near the glades and new housing estates.

Kendwa took the hook from Toby, picking up the second rope, ignoring the women's unchecked sighs. 'I'll move over there. You try that angle.' He pointed. 'We should be able to back him into that corner.' Kendwa whistled at the alligator. 'How'd such a big one end up in here?'

Toby rolled his eyes. 'Don't ask.'

Kendwa glanced back at the people around the pool cabana, slowly realising there was a party going on. 'This is their entertainment?' Kendwa incredulously shook his head. 'Are these people serious?'

Toby chuckled. 'Hired Rambo's mob to put it in the pool. Hired us to get it out. They probably knew not to ask us to put it in because we sure as hell wouldn't have done that.'

'Damn straight. Serve them right if we left the poor guy here.' Kendwa took a firm stance, calling, 'Now,' as he reached the alligator with the hook, lifting its head high enough for them to lasso either side of its long jaw. 'That's it. Pull tight.'

The gator thrashed around, but the men kept the rope taut, gaining control of the agitated reptile, expertly hauling it over the side of the pool coping.

Sounds of the ancient reptile sliding from the pool were lost to the round of applause and shrieks of delight from the partygoers.

Toby smiled at the women, attempting a slight bow. 'She's kinda cute,' he said of one of the girls.

Kendwa didn't even look. 'I hope you don't mean the one called Beatrice.' He had an uncanny memory, even when he didn't appear to be listening.

'Nah, that one sounds as posh as she looks. The short, sweet-looking one in the yellow dress,' said Toby while he straddled the gator, wrapping its mouth with tape. Kendwa placed a bag over its head so it wouldn't get stressed. He didn't glance back at the women.

'Done. I'll haul it to your truck. You can clean up since you clearly want to seduce miss-not-so-posh-as-the others.' Kendwa lugged the gator over his broad shoulders. He strode towards the truck, waving at the near-fainting ladies as he left.

9

Once back on the road, he glanced at his watch. They'd probably have the shits down at the morgue. He drove in that direction, his stomach feeling like it had dropped to his feet.

Early in his life, his grandparents and other family members died. He'd witnessed plenty of stomach-churning events in the wilds of Africa, even wrangling crocodiles in Australia, but nothing could compare to finding his parents dead. Brushing the tears pooling in his eyes, he swallowed the lump in his throat.

It had been two years since he'd returned to America to spend more time with his folks. *How fleeting that time.*

At Miami Dade Morgue Bureau, they'd been waiting for him. He filled out the necessary paperwork, then was shown to the viewing room. Trying to ward off the bile rising, he took his time before lifting his gaze to the bodies.

When he finally looked, he beheld his beautiful mother with translucent blue skin and a small hole in her otherwise perfect head. On the gurney beside her, his dad still looked huge, but sallowness tinged his dark skin. A larger wound to his temple, where his tight curls matted with bits of blood and— He turned away, his jaw set firmly, eyes brimming.

The forensic guy spooked him when he suddenly spoke. 'You know it's murder-suicide?'

'Yeah. I know.' Kendwa sighed, wiping a thumb under his eye. 'Mom had terminal cancer,' he said as if that explained everything. And it did to Kendwa, but also it didn't.

He left the morgue as the sun dipped past the horizon, creating an orange glow to an ink-black sky sprinkled with stars. To drown his sorrows, he needed a drink, even though he wasn't a big drinker.

He rang Toby. 'You free? Feel like a beer or ten? Meet you at Wood.'

Returning to the tiny apartment he shared with Toby. He showered until the hot water ran out, glad to have stripped off the clothes he'd worn on the worst day of his life. He'd probably burn them later. The scent of death still lingering on them.

Slowly, he strode towards the little arty tavern bar, trying not to think about his parents and how they had left him alone. There was a hole inside him that would never close over.

Toby waved. Kendwa half-smiled until he noticed the others. He frowned, disappointed to see there were two girls with Toby. A beer, just with Toby, was preferable if he wanted to talk about his parents. He had no wish to discuss them with total strangers.

For Toby's sake, he tried to lift his frown when he reached the table. 'Hi,' he muttered, 'I'll get myself a beer,' noting their glasses were full.

As he turned to go to the bar, Toby said, 'They have table service. You look like shit. Take a seat. This is Katie and Deana.'

Katie wore a yellow dress. The girl from their pool job. Kendwa gave a weak smile, shaking the girls' hands. He had to give it to Toby because she was a stunning girl, in a next-door-kind-of way. Deana was on the pretty side of plain. Kendwa had a rule. The outer beauty might draw you in, but it was the inner beauty that counted. He decided to try and enjoy their company to forget his horrible day temporarily.

He took a seat next to Deana. She shifted her chair close to him. Their thighs brushed. 'We've never met gator catchers before. Have we, Katie?' she said. 'You guys must be brave.'

Toby motioned to a waitress for a beer for Kendwa. Kendwa nodded before saying, 'It's like any job. Risk assessment, the right equipment and skills. Go in and do what you have to do.'

Katie sighed, running her hand down Toby's arm. 'Toby says it's real dangerous. You're downplaying it.'

Toby winked at Kendwa. Kendwa half-smiled. 'I guess we have our moments.' He went quiet, caught in his world of grief. The conversation flowed around his ears, not entering, like a tiny flock of swallows. Soon the girls excused themselves, heels clattering towards the ladies' room.

Toby leant across the table. 'Kendwa, what's wrong with you? You're never rude to chicks. You're not even talking.'

Kendwa brushed moist eyes, looking up from his beer.

'Shit. What?' asked Toby.

Kendwa took a breath. 'It's Mom and Dad. They—they're dead.' His Adam's apple bobbed. Toby came over to him, placing his arm around his shoulder. The girls were walking back but backtracked towards the bar when Toby shot them a give-us-a-moment look.

Kendwa brushed his tears, gulping down the last of his beer.

Toby shook his head. 'Mate. I'm here for you. I loved your folks. Such kind people. God, I'm shocked.' He bowed his head.

11

'Me too.' Kendwa shifted Toby's arm off his shoulders. 'I'm okay.' He took a big breath. 'I'll have to be. I have no choice.'

'What happened? An accident?'

'Something like that. Hey, let's drop it. I want to forget it for a while. It's too soon. Maybe I should be nicer to Deana. She seems like a sweet girl. I could use a little distraction.'

'Why don't I suggest them coming back to ours?'

'Yeah. That'd be good. I don't want to break down in public again,' he said with no embarrassment, shooting a weak smile.

'Kendwa, you have every reason. Let's get out of here.'

They arrived at the modest walk-up. The girls poured wines and made themselves comfortable on facing sofas. As the boys retrieved beers from the fridge, Toby glanced at his best mate. 'Are you sure you want them around at a time like this?'

Kendwa shrugged, raising his moist eyes. 'What's the alternative? Wallowing in my own misery?' They joined the girls. Toby, giving Kendwa a reassuring slap on the shoulder as they sat down.

Toby proceeded to tell stories about their early days catching crocodiles in Australia. It helped Kendwa forget for a while. He loved those memories. There were lots of funny tales of the crazy Aussies. Kendwa even laughed once or twice.

'What about when old Ricko lost his hand?' Toby shook his head at Kendwa, laughing.

By then, Katie was sitting on Toby's lap. He had his arms around her waist, kissing her bare shoulder. Deana sat close to Kendwa. Her perfume wafted enticingly. Though his thoughts were scattered and cold, the proximity of a woman was heating him.

'It would have been hilarious if it hadn't been so stupid,' said Kendwa raising his beer, sipping.

Toby laughed. 'Who tries to feed a wild crocodile a live turkey with his bare hands? Of course, the croc snapped his hand clean off, turkey and all. I remember him just looking at the stump pissin' out blood, then back at the croc and swearing his head off. He was yelling, 'bring my bloody hand back, ya thievin' bastard'.'

'He was still yelling at it while I stopped the blood flow with our shirts and rope as a tourniquet.'

'He was such a stupid shit, wasn't he?'

'He sure was,' said Kendwa, turning to look at Deana who stroked his thigh with soft fingers and nails painted pink. Feeling sick with grief but oddly excited, he stared at her hand.

Katie and Toby began kissing with loud slurps as they found each other's tonsils, oblivious to the other two.

Kendwa grabbed Deana's hand. Wordlessly she stood, following him into his bedroom. He shut the door with a click and said, 'I can't promise anything, but I've had the shittiest day, and I'd like to have sex with you but—.'

Putting her finger to his lips to silence him, she smiled. 'I'll try to make the end of your day better than your start,' she said as she stripped. He watched each garment drop, penis twitching. She had a nice curvy body. Reaching for her, he pulled her close, kissing, fondling her breasts and moving down over her hips to cup her bottom. He picked her up and practically threw her on the bed, then tore at his clothes.

Grasping for his erection, Deana stroked it smoothly. She didn't seem needy, but she gave every indication she wanted to fuck. Fumbling with a condom, he entered her quickly. He usually enjoyed more foreplay, but it wasn't an average day.

A fast fuck. Then sleep in oblivion, forgetting the day ever happened.

Caught up in her own needs, Deana sighed and groaned as he pumped into her until they both came.

Not long after, she began snoring. Untwining himself from her embrace, he folded his arms behind his head, willing sleep to come as he stared at the ceiling. Instead, his mind churned with grief. Images of his parents slid through his mind like a movie of memories. Tears filled his eyes. He didn't bother wiping them and stifled the sobs forming in his throat, wishing he were alone in his misery.

When he awoke in the morning, only an imprint on the sheets and the overpowering scent of her perfume remained.

Kendwa felt worse than the day before if that was even possible. His gut felt heavy with sorrow. He shut his eyes again, wishing, like his parents, he would never have to wake up.

Chapter 3
Borneo Orangutan Sanctuary

The baby orangutan curled his fingers through Sharli's long ebony hair. Cuddling the orangutan to her chest, she smiled. He was so human-baby-like with a wizened face and orange fur. Big soul-filled brown eyes kept her gaze, hands circling her neck, clinging tightly. She sighed, smiling. *Was it possible to feel any happier?*

A yawn escaped her lips. The furry baby copied her, which made her giggle. Lack of sleep didn't dull her contentment. Working all night feeding the babies and tending to their needs was what she'd come to the sanctuary to do. The other volunteers had long gone to bed. They didn't take their roles as seriously as she did, but each to their own.

An Indian-African from Zanzibar, off the Tanzanian coast, she was among a mixed worldwide bunch of volunteers. It was nice to make new friends, though some were kinder than others.

With Zanzibar's literacy rate low, many of her contemporaries didn't receive the schooling that allowed her a good education. The opportunity to work overseas would have been impossible if she hadn't been one of the lucky ones fortunate to learn English. Though her first language was Swahili, good schooling was her stepping stone to the world outside Africa.

Sharli sorely missed Zanzibar, family and friends. At least she could help her community with skills of nursing when she returned. Her goal wasn't about selfish travel. It was a selfless quest to learn enough to go back home and never leave.

Carefully she untangled the baby from her neck, placing him in a crib with his orphan siblings. 'Be a good boy now, Bibby.' She glanced

15

towards Suellen, the veterinarian. 'I need a few hours' sleep.' She stretched her arms wide then clamped a hand to her mouth.

'I should think so, Sharli. You've been up all night and most of the day. I'll make sure someone is rostered on and stays up for it. Don't worry about it.' She gave her a measured look through her black-rimmed spectacles. 'Though I know you will.' She went back to filling her medicine cabinet. 'I don't want to see you until morning.'

'Okay. Okay. Goodnight, Suellen.'

She strolled towards the small shack she shared with three other girls, one from Utah, USA and two New Zealanders. It was late afternoon. The hot sun was sinking in the western sky. Volunteers worked in various parts of the sanctuary, building bridges, cutting up fruit for the feeding area, relocating orangutans and other duties. *Let them.* She could barely move her feet along the moist dirt track. Her eyes were heavy when she stepped inside the shack.

As she lay on the simple single bed, a raucous monkey fight screeched outside the room, waking her. She stared at the rattan ceiling, thinking about her lonely life. The other young travellers often partied in town. They had sex with strangers and bragged about how much fun it was. For Sharli, though she longed for companionship and probably a little sex— eventually, only she couldn't be that casual about it.

Her Hindu upbringing was part of it. She wanted to make her family proud. Getting distracted by the backpackers around her would not help in her crusade. Besides, she didn't seem to be attracted to most men. Call her fussy, but she needed something more. There hadn't been many who had piqued her interest. She was in no hurry to find a boyfriend, though there was a longing to be held. Hugging her arms to herself, she tried to picture what the perfect man would be like.

Then, of course, having grown up in a primarily Muslim country, she was always aware of how she behaved around men. Flirting wasn't in her nature. It was frowned upon in her native country. She screwed her nose up, baffled how the other girls did it.

Nights out with her friends made her feel boring and out of touch. They knew how to flaunt their sexuality, and they weren't afraid to show a flash of boobs or bottom. Sharli hid her body behind baggy clothes. She told the other volunteers the attire was comfortable. She had grown up wearing the African sarong, the kanga and draped saris, so she was used to covering up.

She was a petite woman with a beautiful shapely body. Her ebony skin was smooth, unblemished; it glowed. Friends in Borneo teased her about what she wore, but she felt more comfortable without the attention of men.

There was a tick-tock to her biological clock. It seemed to be drumming relentlessly. At twenty-six, she felt more like thirty when it came to her desire to start a family. *A baby.* Stupid thing was she had to find a man to get one. Finally, she nodded off with the now-familiar noises of the Borneo forest providing a musical chorus.

Sharli awoke with a start, glancing at her wristwatch. It was four am. She rubbed the sleep from her eyes, watching Rachel slip into bed. 'Where have you been?' Sharli asked, sitting up.

Rachel giggled. 'OMG! I met the cutest guy at one of the bars in Sandakan.'

'You sound drunk. You'd better go to bed. I'll cover for you. I was getting up anyway.'

'Sharli, I don't know why you never come,' Rachel's Utah accent slurred slightly. 'You'd just click your fingers, and the guys'd be all over you. You're the most gorgeous girl. Hair to your waist, a Kendall Jenner body, olive skin and beau'ful eyes. I just don't get why you don't use what God gave you.'

Sharli was thinking up answers. Before she could reply, Rachel's soft snore betrayed that her friend was asleep. Sharli laughed. 'Night, night, Rachel.' She got out of bed, stretching her arms high. Chainsaws screamed, like scraping chalk on a chalkboard. They were only a few miles away, sawing down trees for palm oil and destroying even more of the orangutan's natural habitat. Wishing the sound wasn't ruining the natural noises of the forest, she frowned.

After taking a quick shower, ever mindful of how much water she used, she ambled towards the kitchen shack. Holding a torch, she lit the muddy path, wet from a tropical shower overnight. The jungle was alive with noises of various monkeys and birdlife. There was a temporary reprieve from the horrid buzz of the palm farmers.

After pouring a bowl of muesli, she took it to sit on the high timber deck facing a creek. The orange sun slowly rose in the east, casting silhouettes in a purple-pink sky. Last night's rain pooled on the lush foliage, glistening like pearls on oysters. It was dank, pungent and beautiful. When the palm farmers stopped for a break, it was tranquil.

Sharli pictured a time in the future when they wouldn't have to rescue the orphans. It would be a day the Palm Oil plantations finally halted for good. A time when people were banned from using animals for entertainment or keeping them as pets.

The glorious sunrise made her smile. She was glad she had decided to come to Borneo instead of heading straight back to Zanzibar. Her studies in Australia finished earlier than expected because she handed assignments in early and completed every module. It enabled her a small respite before the rest of her life.

A love of environmental causes began in the forest back home, where the Red Colobus monkeys struggled to survive. The human population, particularly the resorts, infringed on their trees in the forests. Working with the bigger and more human-like orangutans was a dream come true for a primate-monkey-lover like Sharli.

Leaving the kitchen, the dampness seeped through her sneakers on the path to the wooden bridge. The dispensary sat on the rise. It was early, but some of the babies would be hungry. They were housed in a glassed-off nursery beside the veterinary hospital or dispensary, as they called it. That way, tourists could watch them but not interfere with their rehabilitation. She found Suellen already at work.

'Hi, Suellen. Are we still taking them climbing today?'

Suellen looked up from the assessment bed and the small orangutan she was checking. He had his fingers curled around her hand.

'Hi, Sharli. I thought you'd need to sleep in.'

'Rachel woke me. I'm glad, though. The sunrise was magical.'

Suellen smiled. 'It nearly always is. Hey, Mitto, stop moving. I need to check your ears.'

Sharli stepped beside her, holding the cute little ape down on the gurney. It was good practice for nursing. With a cheeky face, he gazed up at her. She giggled. 'Hey, little man. Keep still, and you'll be able to learn to climb today.'

'Done. Thank you, Mitto.' Suellen nodded at the ape before scribbling notes on a clipboard. Sharli reached for Mitto. He wrapped his hairy arms around her neck. She lovingly stroked his wiry fur, carrying him to the nursery. Boisterous, happy baby orangutans greeted her enthusiastically. Eight babies were ready for climbing lessons. She organised the motley group.

Suellen rounded up her four charges. They clambered in a wheelbarrow. Sharli's did the same with her four, with a little more difficulty as Mitto kept climbing out again. They took the path towards the clearing readied with ropes, bridges, platforms and trees.

Umar was already there with two of the teenage orangutans. They climbed the trees and swung down the ropes, screeching and grunting in joy.

'Morning, Umar,' she called.

'Selamat pagi, ladies. Are the little ones ready to learn to climb?' Rubbing his hands together, he grinned, showing perfect teeth in a wide face. A Malaysian with smooth olive skin, black hair and eyes, he had worked at the sanctuary for over fifteen years and adored his orange charges.

Sharli laughed as Mitto curled his body around her ankle. 'Mitto may be a bit slower than the others.'

The young orangutans watched the older ones climbing. Their expressive eyes took in the set-up for their lessons. There were lower ropes and higher ropes crisscrossed over them, with timber bridges and dangling tree branches. They would help them learn without being afraid like they would be if in the jungle alone.

One baby, Suria, had been caught in a snare. Her foot was severely damaged. However, she had been in the forest long enough to know how to climb. The rest were stolen from their mothers as babies and caged. They never had the chance to learn how to survive in the forest, let alone climb or forage for food.

With Umar's urging, the youngsters to tentatively grab the tree or the ropes. Some climbed, others tumbled and fell the short distance to the soft bed of leaves, set to break any fall. They looked uncoordinated but were all trying, except Mitto.

Sharli lifted him to a rope. 'You can do it. Follow the others.' She glanced sadly at Suellen. 'He must have been mistreated in captivity. He's scared of everything.'

'Yes, I can't believe people think it's right to trap them and then use them for their own entertainment. It's sad. It makes me angry too.'

19

'At least this lot get a second chance. It could take a while for them to fend for themselves in the wild again. Oh, look at Suria. She remembers how to climb. Even with her injured foot, she's keen to get higher.'

'She does look happy. I'll tend to her foot afterwards, but it seems to be holding up alright for the moment. I'm struggling to treat it properly, though. I'm going to seek some advice on getting to the infection. I heard there's an African vet in town who's worked with primates who poachers had trapped.'

'Hopefully, she'll be able to help, and Suria will leave the bandages on. It's so funny how she keeps taking them off.'

'You'd think she'd know by now that they are helping her heal.'

'Up, up,' called Umar as two of the babies ventured higher on the ropes.

After a couple of hours, the orangutans were bored and trying to escape the climbing area. After ten am, their food would be out. Suellen returned to the dispensary. Umar and Sharli took the orangutans to the feeding platform, a big deck at the bottom of a huge tree. Some of the volunteers had cut up watermelon, papaya, bamboo shoots and bananas.

Tourists watched from a nearby viewing platform, taking photos and trying to get closer, waving to the orangutans.

Rachel sheepishly strolled to Sharli. 'Sorry about this morning. I didn't mean to wake you.'

'That's okay. I got to see the most beautiful sunrise.' Sharli passed Mitto another slice of watermelon. The feeding platform was now a mess of food and happy apes.

'I hope you caught up with your sleep. You promised you'd come out with me tonight because Dee went home.'

Sharli scratched her head. 'Oh, the guitarist at The Lake Bistro?'

'Yes. It's not like you must go into Sandakan. We can walk over. Come on, you promised.' Rachel placed her hands together in prayer.

Sharli couldn't remember promising anything, but she loved the sound of a guitar. She smiled at Rachel. 'Okay. What time are we going?'

Rachel hugged her. 'Be ready at six. Do you want me to help you with your make-up?'

Sharli shook her head. Rachel was kind, but the question annoyed her. *I can do my makeup, or lack of, just fine.*

When they arrived at the lakeside bar, locals huddled at tables near the kitchen, mostly tourists, filled the bar tables and the majority of the bar. It had a hipster vibe with lots of timber, plants and hanging lanterns. The serene outlook over the lake contrasted with the noisy chatter and music. The solo guitarist strummed a country tune in the corner.

Rachel giggled, elbowing Sharli. 'See how hot he is.'

The guitarist's blond ringlet curls fell to his shoulders. He had a handsome face with freckles over his nose, like he'd suffered one too many sunburns. He glanced up at them, smiling. They took seats facing both him and the water view.

Rachel ordered them a big bowl of nasi goreng and a Bintang beer each. Animatedly, they chatted about their days at the sanctuary.

Rachel soon asked, 'Why are you here, Sharli? You're not the typical backpacker type.'

'I've been studying nursing in Australia. I'm on my way home, but I've dreamt about the orangutans and luckily had time to stop by.'

'You won a scholarship, didn't you? I was never smart enough to be offered one of those.'

'Yes. I was fortunate to be offered it and have the chance to fulfil my studies at such a wonderful university. I hope there will be a job for me when I get home. I've been applying, but it seems they need to meet certain quotas of applicants from the mainland. Hopefully, my experience here will help with that a bit.'

Rachel smiled at the guitarist, tilting her head in a provocative gesture. 'I can't tell if he likes you or me.' She flicked her auburn hair.

'He likes you, Rachel. I haven't even made eye contact with him.'

'I hope so.' She lifted her beer, sipping as she watched him.

Soon the singer took a break and strolled to their table. 'Hi ladies, can I sit down?' Before they could answer him, he pulled up a chair and sat on it backward with his arms folded over the back, which made his tight biceps flex.

'Oh, you're from the Mid-West too,' said Rachel, delighted.

'Beaver Mountain. Y'all?'

'Salt Lake City. Fetch yeah! Ya, probably snowboard. We used to holiday at Beaver Mountain. I'm Rachel, and this is Sharli.'

21

'Heck yeah, I live for tha snow.' He took her hand and shook. 'Tom.' He turned to Sharli. 'Where are ya from, Sharli? Ya, look exotic 'n' sexy. My guess, tha Maldives.'

Rachel shot Sharli a fake-angry look.

'I'm from Zanzibar.'

He whistled. 'Knew it. That's effin' awesome.'

Sharli moved her chair a bit further away from him. He was invading her personal space. Glancing at Rachel, she said, 'You should know that I'm gay, but Rachel isn't.'

Rachel hid her smile by sipping on her beer. Tom's eyes widened as he glanced from one girl to the other, his mouth agape. He stood, nearly toppling his chair. 'Um, I betta get back to playing tha guitar.'

Rachel laughed, holding her hand over her mouth. 'OMG! His face was priceless when you said that.'

'He's all yours.'

'I don't know if I want to be the second choice. Besides, he's a bit of an urban redneck.'

'You said you love rednecks.'

'It's that good-old hometown-accent, I guess.' She shrugged her shoulders.

Sharli rubbed her temple. 'I think I'm getting a headache. I might head back.' She caught Tom winking at Rachel. 'You might change your mind. He is cute, and you are a sucker for guys with curls.'

'You go. I think I will stay to flirt with Tom.'

'Just don't wake me up tonight, Rachel.'

'No, my dear bro-dette. Maybe I'll stay wherever he's staying.' She winked at Tom.

Sharli chuckled, kissing Rachel's cheek. 'See you tomorrow.' Rachel grabbed her face and kissed her lips before grinning mischievously at Tom. 'Rachel, stop teasing him. Bye.' She waved.

Sharli strolled back to the compound, feeling a little envious of Rachel possibly being in Tom's arms tonight. It wasn't that she was attracted to him. Being held in someone's secure embrace was overwhelming.

Perhaps she needed to get back home and find herself a nice Zanzibari man to settle down with. Homesickness lurched in her stomach, making her wrap her arms around herself. It was time to move on.

Maybe she should give herself a few more weeks. For some reason, she knew she couldn't leave just yet. She had no idea why.

Chapter 4
Miami, Florida

Two dark-stained wood coffins sat side-by-side, both polished to a reflective gleam and adorned with cascading white flowers. A tiny tattered teddy bear sat on top of the smaller coffin. The Pentax SLR camera's lens faced the congregation as if photographing their grief.

A minister informally dressed in a suit with no tie rather than robes dropped his eyes directly at Kendwa. 'Would anyone like to speak before we send the dearly departed on their way?'

Kendwa shook his head, staring at the coffins, his jaw set firm and his tears at bay. Ironically, thick blood-red curtains slowly closed. Kendwa's tears came. He let them drip. The knot in his stomach twisted tighter.

The hundreds of people at the service honouring his parents started to trickle out of the chapel. Some ventured near Kendwa, kissing his cheek, or patting his shoulder, saying their condolences and how sad they were.

Truly admirable people or such a waste of two lives, most said.

It seemed to take forever for them to leave the hall. He could hear the sniffles, nose-blowing, sighs and whispers. A couple of elderly people shuffled his way, noticed his slumped body and thought better of it.

After some time, when he could no longer hear anyone in the room, he stood. Bowing his head, he took one more glance at the ugly curtains and strode out of the crematorium.

The minister nodded, and Toby and Katie, silently waiting, stood and followed Kendwa, arm in arm.

They found him, hands against a brick retaining wall as if he were about to headbutt it.

Toby touched his shoulder. Kendwa flinched. Toby paused. 'Kendwa. If I can do anything, mate.'

Kendwa slowly nodded. His body shook as he sniffled. They silently walked towards the car, leaving him to his grief for a while.

Later, someone called the boys to a job to get a gator away from a swimming hole. It had a large jetty. Children often dived off it and swam during the summer months.

'Are you sure you want to work today? You should be holding a wake or something,' Toby watched the water for the gator while driving the aluminium boat through the shallow reeds.

'Yeah, I'm sure. It will keep my mind off things.'

The water swirled near the boat. 'Get your mind on it then. That was the gator. This isn't the sort of job you can lose concentration, Kendwa. I could have got Reese to come with me. Seriously, mate, you really need to get your head together. You've had a tough fortnight. I wouldn't be working if it were me.' He shot a worried look over his shoulder. 'Let's set a trap and get out of here so you can clear your head.'

Kendwa knew, deep down, that his friend was right. He'd never missed the tell-tale signs of the reptiles. It was dangerous to let your guard down. Over the years of wrangling, Kendwa tried his hardest to keep his skills sharp. He did not want to let Toby down, no matter how shitty he felt.

When they'd returned home and cleaned off, they relaxed on the porch with a beer. Kendwa confessed, 'You're right, Toby. I probably wasn't up to it today.'

Toby clinked beer bottles with him. 'Yup, but it was your call to make. I trust you.'

'You're a good mate, Tobes.' Rubbing his forehead, he paused. 'I do think I may need a break, though. I have some stuff to sort out.'

'Have you thought about what you're going to do with your folk's estate? May they rest in peace.' Toby raised his beer bottle to heaven, taking a swig.

26

Kendwa did the same. 'Not totally sure, but Dad always had a dream about ecotourism in Africa. Perhaps, I'll finish that dream off for him. I miss Africa. It would be good to get back home.'

'I loved Africa, but it was your heritage. You totally looked comfortable, much like a native, particularly when we were getting rid of those poachers and protecting the wildlife. You should go back. Mate, your dad would love that.'

'He would, wouldn't he?' Kendwa smiled. 'I think Mom would too.'

'Hey, I understood the camera on your dad's coffin. His love of wildlife photography, but what was the teddy on your mum's? Yours?'

Kendwa's mouth opened, but he couldn't form words. He snapped it shut, frowning with his eyes closed to the brimming tears.

'Sorry, mate. Did I say something wrong? I know you're—raw.'

Kendwa shook his head. 'It's nothing. It's something she treasured. Anyway, I couldn't have done today without you. Thanks. You're more than a best mate. You know that?'

Toby turned to Kendwa, grinning. 'Speaking of best mates. You'll have to promise to come back for my wedding.' He beamed.

Kendwa rose his eyes, his brows creasing in the middle. 'Are you for real? It's only been a couple of weeks.'

'You know when you know. I'm saving up for a ring Katie will love. I'm going to get all romantic, set something up to pop the question.'

'Wow, mate. Cheers.' They clinked near-empty bottles. Kendwa stood. 'I'd better get another beer since you've given me something to celebrate instead of—well, instead of feeling sorry for myself. I can't believe it. You, getting married?' He slapped Toby's shoulder.

'Me neither, but it feels right. She's the most beautiful girl I've ever known.'

Kendwa passed Toby a bottle and sat, putting his feet up on the rail, watching the stars in the sky. 'I'm sorry to leave you in the lurch when you're going to be planning a life with your future bride.'

'No worries. I've been thinking about that too. Reese keeps asking to buy-in. I can't see myself working with anyone full time other than you. I thought if he got a partner, we could both sell out.' He evaluated Kendwa to gauge his reaction.

Kendwa was still gazing at the stars. 'You've been talking about going back home too. Maybe it's time for both of us.'

27

'Katie always wanted to return to Australia, so she's pretty keen. She did an exchange year and reckoned it was awesome.'

They talked into the night about their plans and reminisced about Kendwa's parents. Toby got him laughing at some of the dumb dad jokes his father made.

Though the day still sucked, having a friend like Toby made it easier. He would miss hanging out with the larrikin. Deep down, he knew they both needed to move on with their lives.

The problem was Kendwa wasn't afraid to move on. Going back to Africa was in his heart, but it also stirred memories he'd been trying to forget all his life. Africa held the land and wildlife that were a part of his soul. It also harboured secrets from his past that he'd been running away from his whole life. *It was nearly time to return home.*

Chapter 5
Borneo, Malaysia

Meowing broke through the rainforest cacophony of birds, frogs, monkeys and waterfalls. The guide stopped paddling. Placing a finger to his lips, he eyeballed the people in the boat to make them understand the signal of silence. A litter of forest cubs were somewhere in the scrub. He scanned the banks of the Kinabatangan River, hoping it was the illusive carnivore, the Sunda clouded leopard.

After a few minutes, he spotted the beautiful dark-spotted cat high in a tree. It watched the water with intelligent eyes. The small wild leopard's litter would be hidden safely below, waiting for a feed. Blood dripped from the cat's chin, though he couldn't see the kill.

He savoured the moment to himself before speaking softly. 'Keep very quiet and still. There's a Sunda clouded leopard up in that tree.' He pointed. 'Her young must be nearby. That's the meowing we can hear.'

They obeyed him, watching the exquisite wild animal. Suddenly the skinny guy, with a camera bigger than his head, took some rapid shots, whooping with delight. That, of course, sent the clouded leopard scooting off the tree and down to wherever the stashed cubs were.

The guide swore to himself, taking hold of the oars, paddling in an angry rhythm. Though he could have gunned the engine, he needed the exercise to burn off some irritation. Hoping the next bunch of tourists were better than these was probably futile. Accepting the river guide job was to discover more of the waterways and ecosystem of Borneo. Dealing with people in his current headspace was tiresome.

The large canoe neared a long timber jetty. Ably he tied thick ropes to the bollards like an experienced riverman. The chatting tourists disembarked. In long strides, he walked to the booking desk, signed off. Reading through his next list, he ran his hand through his hair. It was a long day. *Six more annoying people.* Then he could go to his room at the resort. He'd write down his notes for the day. Perhaps have a nice meal and go to bed.

He turned to the tourists waiting on a bench seat. 'Selamat Tengah hari,' he said in Malay. 'I'm Kendwa, your guide for today. We'll be travelling about ten kilometres up the Kinabatangan River. Hopefully, we'll get to see some of Borneo's big five.' They followed him towards the boat. He turned back to them. 'Does anyone know what they are?'

They shook their heads. A young woman took off her large straw sunhat, revealing a beautiful olive face and exquisite golden eyes. In a honey-smooth voice, she answered him. 'Orangutan, proboscis monkey, crocodile, rhinoceros hornbill and the pygmy elephant.'

He smiled. The woman was way more than beautiful. Glancing at his list to find her name, he looked back into her eyes, melting. 'Nice that you know. You must be Sharli, I take it?'

'I am.' She was light-headed as his brilliant blue eyes bore into her. Fanning herself with the hat was out of nervousness, not need. It was a sweltering day. *Ouch, he was hotter than the humid air. A scorching as hell but heavenly hot,* was how Rachel would have put it.

He spoke to the others in a deep voice. It sounded slightly African and American, stirring feelings of home, but it held a funny twang of maybe Australian. The family of five were from Bolivia and seemed to speak limited English, let alone Malay. Only the mother seemed to understand English. He read off their names in his tantalising deep voice, then climbed aboard the boat, holding his hand out to her, which she refused.

Kendwa couldn't concentrate on the boat as he lifted his eyes to Sharli, willing her to sit near him. *Where was she from?* She looked and sounded African, possibly even Zanzibari. What would the chances be of him running into someone else from his original home? Exotic and intriguing and without even trying to; pushing all his buttons. Her

30

refusal of his help onboard made him assume she was independent too. *Hot damn, she was adorable.*

Sharli sat at the front of the boat as far away from the intimidating man as she could get. She'd never received an instant response in her life. Something shifted her symmetry when she first locked gaze with Kendwa. *Wow, he was so uniquely sexy.*

It wasn't his rock-hard, sinewed muscular body. *That was only the start.* The bright blue eyes held soulful depths, like pools of water in an aqua lagoon. It didn't hurt that dimples dug in his bristled cheeks, and it was a dazzling smile to boot. Ineffectually, she tried to switch thoughts back to why embarking on the tour was important.

After requesting time off from volunteering to see more of the wildlife, she intended to do so. Why was she letting a guy distract her? He looked a little wild with his mane of windswept hair and stubbled chin. *You tell yourself that while you watch him, thinking about wild things with nothing to do with wildlife.* She fanned her face.

Pulling the motor cord to sputter the engine to life, his muscles rippled and bulged. She stared at his arms and shoulders. Trying to keep her jaw from dropping, she quickly recovered, pursing her lips and turning to the river.

With the engine buzzing, the long boat puttered off at only a few knots. The youngest boy of the three, about eight years old, spoke Bolivian to his mother.

'He wants to know, why aren't we going faster,' the middle-aged mother asked Kendwa.

'It's so I can spot the wildlife. Like, for instance, those crocs on the bank to your left.' He pointed.

They gasped, and the father took photos with a camera. The oldest son held a mobile phone in front of his face, then turned to take a selfie with his brothers in the background, grinning.

Kendwa watched Sharli stare at the large reptiles with a big smile on her beautiful face. No camera or phone—nothing distracting her from the wildlife. Something softened in his hardened heart.

She was astonishingly pretty with a tiny nose and sweet lips, but she didn't seem to know it. She wore a long-sleeved tan shirt and brown

31

trousers covering her body, though they did nothing to mask her curves. Kendwa imagined her body was smoking hot. She fanned her face with her hat as he admired the long silk-like black hair tied in a low ponytail. He thought about running his hands through it. *Mate, where is your head at?*

Shaking his head, he tried to concentrate on his job. 'This river is over 560 kilometres and has one of the most diverse ecosystems on the planet. As well as the two from the big five, there are over ten species of primates alone.' Cutting the motor, he took the oars in each hand to row slowly closer to the banks.

'There'll be even less if they don't quit with the palm oil plantations,' said Sharli, turning to face him. *Why did he have to look so manly as he rowed?*

'Yeah, that is a concern, but for years Indonesians and Malays have trapped wild animals and sold them for either entertainment or pets, and it takes a worse toll than the plantations.'

'It all needs to stop.'

'At least the government is finally wise to it. They are trying to make changes by outlawing it.'

'You have no idea how badly some of the orangutans have been treated and the injuries and hardship they endure.' Wiping moist eyes, it annoyed her that he'd sided with a government who allowed these things in the first place.

They were interrupted by squawking noises in the trees. The Bolivians pointed, turning to Kendwa expecting an explanation.

Still pondering why Sharli seemed upset, he scanned the bush. *Had she seen these things first hand?* She wouldn't be so concerned about reading them in some tourist brochure.

'Hornbills. See all the colours on their huge beaks?' He pointed upriver. 'Around this next bend, we saw a clouded leopard earlier today. We'll need to be quiet on approach,' he said, hoping to impress Sharli with the wild cats.

The family looked a little scared, but Sharli smiled and nodded. 'I hope we see it too. Do you come across the pygmy elephants at all? I know they're shy and hard to spot.'

'I know a place they may be.' He grinned. *Anything for you, sweetheart.*

The canoe swooshed through the meandering muddy waterways. They slowed to the area where he'd last spotted the mother clouded leopard. He made a point of letting them know how important it was not to spook her. 'She has her young nearby.'

They waited for about five minutes with eyes darting. Then the mother leopard appeared near the same branch as before. Her dark eyes followed the boat as a collective sigh escaped their lips.

Sharli turned to Kendwa. Where he'd seemed stern, even cranky before, his handsome face melted at the wildcat. It softened his looks, making him seem vulnerable. A deep affinity with wildlife seemed to pump through his veins. With smiling eyes, he watched the leopard. A half-smile on his delectable lips, a deep dimple in one cheek. Sharli was unsure of whether to watch the native cat or the wild man.

Water lapped the boat. Bird whistles piped through the air, blended with the soft meows of the cubs. Sharli carefully edged towards Kendwa's end of the boat to sit beside him. She whispered in his ear. 'Have you spotted any of the cubs yet?'

'They sound too young to be venturing far yet. Perhaps we'll see them in a week or two.'

'That's a shame. I haven't got that long.'

Kendwa's heart tensed. *Only weeks.* He inhaled deeply of the scent of flower shampoo in Sharli's hair. Coconut oil glistened on her olive skin. Drinking her in, the essence of everything womanly enveloped him. Dainty fingers clutched the brim of her hat, stopping it from blowing away in the soft breeze.

'I'll head round there to a clearing where the elephants sometimes come to pick at the papayas and grass. Maybe you'll get to see your little pygmy elephants. Make up for missing the cubs?' He winked. She smiled back, a perfect smile. *Man, you're in trouble with this one.*

Kendwa pulled the motor cord. The engine sputtered to life, humming up the river to where he'd last seen the elephants. They had to find them soon because they would need to head back. He couldn't have them on the river when the sun went down. The crocs may have been part of his comfort zone, but the people in the canoe weren't the same as him. Though perhaps Sharli would appreciate the ancient reptiles.

'Where do you come from?' she asked, watching the banks like a hawk, trying to spot the unique little elephants.

'My namesake Kendwa, in Zanzibar.'

She laughed, taking off her hat. 'No way. I am too. It should have twigged with your name, but you don't sound Zanzibari. You sound American.'

'I've lived mostly in the USA lately, but I'm definitely African. I'm going back there one day. What town are you from?'

'Stone Town, but my family now live on the eastern side of Unguja.'

'It's a small world, isn't it.' He stared at her in wonder. *A beautiful girl from home.* She couldn't get any better if she tried. 'Hey, do you want to have dinner with me and talk about Africa? I haven't been back in a long time.'

'I can't. I'm on night shift tonight. Maybe another time.'

'Can't you get out of it?' He frowned.

'No. The babies depend on me.'

'Babies?' He raised his eyebrows.

She laughed. It was like a beautiful tinkling bell. 'Orangutan babies. I work at the small sanctuary close to the Sepilok Rehabilitation Centre.'

'Oh, those babies. I'd like to see them myself. They are amazing animals. I've hung out with the gorillas in Rwanda and the Congo, but I'm fascinated by those orange guys.'

'They are so much like us. I love them like children.'

Breaking into their conversation, the three boys pointed and excitedly talked at once.

'Ah, there they are,' Kendwa nudged her shoulder, 'as promised, Pygmy Elephants.'

The small herd of pygmy elephants stood in long, flattened reeds at the water's edge. Their ears were bigger than Asian elephants but had shorter, stumpier bodies, with rounder bellies and long tails touching the ground. They looked like baby elephants who would never grow up. Larger ones pulled the grass from the ground so the little ones could eat it. Others used their trunks to pull pawpaw bits from the broken fruit.

'Wow. They are so cute.' Sharli placed her hat on her lap, moving closer to the edge of the boat.

Kendwa leaned towards her, gently lifting her hair to whisper in her ear. 'I was kind of hoping they wouldn't be here, so I had an excuse to bring you back.'

Turning to him briefly, she shifted away from him. 'I'd be disappointed if they weren't. Let me enjoy these cute animals. I'm here for the wildlife, not the wild men.'

'What does that mean?' It wasn't often he had a rebuff.

'It means I don't need or want a man in my life, even if he happens to come from home. Not even for dinner.'

Woah! Where did that come from? 'Okay, back to the facts then,' he said, trying not to sound bitter. Raising his voice so the others could hear, he asked, 'Did you know they can outrun any man? They reach up to 45 kilometres an hour. That's about 28 miles.'

'We heard tigers eat them,' said the mother. The boys nodded eagerly.

'True, but not often. There hasn't been a tiger in this area for years. Unfortunately, they are practically extinct in Borneo. Humans, poachers kill more elephants, though. They have ivory tusks like African and Asian elephants. The poachers kill for the tusks, and then they catch the babies to sell as pets.'

Sharli looked forlorn at this, turning her head slightly to frown at him. Kendwa continued, 'The conservationists here are finding better ways to protect them. Government rangers now issue fines and even imprisonment for poaching them. The numbers are back up to around 1,000.'

'That's still not many. I think animals are mostly nicer than people,' Sharli said, looking back at the elephants, her sweet lips turned down.

'I totally agree,' said Kendwa, thinking of the poachers in Africa that he would shoot, given a chance. His fist clenched.

When he reluctantly turned the boat around, Sharli moved back to the front. He was perplexed. They seemed to be getting on, and then she'd suddenly turned cold. *Women! They often surprised him, but he didn't like this revelation.*

He'd been looking forward to dinner with her, had been anticipating how delightful it would be with her. Bedding her wasn't even on his mind, only her sweet company. *A kiss, maybe.* She had transfixed him, enough for him to want to get to know her first.

Sharli didn't speak on the way back. It was a magical afternoon with perfect weather. The incredible wildlife and the lush beauty of the forest from the water would stay with her. She'd even met a gorgeous Zanzibari man. *So why did she blow it?*

Of course, she could have got someone to cover for her at the sanctuary. She was always covering for them. Why didn't she say yes to dinner with Kendwa?

It was simple. She was terrified. The man was faultless. But how could he be? Perfect men didn't exist. He was sexy, stunning, cared for animals and came from Zanzibar.

There was a logical side of her brain telling her to keep away, but her heart was winning. It whispered, she should give him a go. Firmly she told herself, it didn't matter. She was leaving in a fortnight and would never see him again. Rubbing her cheeks of the flush she felt beneath them, she frowned. *Kendwa had stolen her heart in mere hours on the river Kinabatangan.*

Chapter 6
Borneo, Malaysia

The rattan fan spun over the top of Kendwa, creating a slight relief from the humid heat. Thinking of Sharli, he watched the rotors clicking around in a blur, wishing she was in his bed, like the dream he had woken from moments before. Languishing longer, he tried to keep the sweet vision with him.

They'd been making out—kissing and exploring. Clutching the sheets, he willed his mind to return to sleep so he could feel her soft, exquisite lips blending with his again. Glacing at the erection tenting the sheets, he groaned. *Sharli, sweet Sharli—an instant obsession.*

Perhaps Toby was right. True love could happen quickly. God, he'd barely seen Sharli's face, hidden by the huge hat, or her body, covered in long clothes, but he knew she would be flawless naked. The fact she also came from home was a bonus. In all his travels, he'd never come across a fellow countryman. It seemed to be destiny that their paths crossed.

Kendwa usually didn't need a strategy when it came to women. He'd never been the chaser. But, hey, Sharli wasn't like any other woman.

Even when she'd sat next to him on the boat, she wasn't flirting. She asked questions about the wildlife, with no idea what her proximity did to him. She seemed oblivious to her beauty. To him, it made her even more delightful.

Now he needed to figure out a way to get her attention. He realised with only two weeks until she left Borneo, he must think and act fast.

At the sanctuary, Sharli was already tending to the babies. They were all mischievous for some reason. Perhaps it was the full moon due that night. Laughing at their antics, she turned to the sound of a clearing throat behind her.

Kendwa smiled. Sharli nearly dropped the rope ball she was about to throw for the babies.

'Hi, Sharli. What a surprise,' he said unconvincingly. 'I'm looking for Doctor Suellen Price.' The orangutans tumbled towards him. Mitto climbed up his leg. Kendwa picked him up with a dimpled smile.

'What are you doing here?' she stammered.

'Nice to see you too.' To the orangutan, he said, 'Hey mate, you should tell Sharli that I won't bite.' He grinned wickedly.

Ignoring how cute he looked doing that, she wrung her hands. 'You shouldn't pick them up unless instructed on the process. You're not involved in the project.' She threw the ball to get the orangutans away from him, but they seemed to like him and stayed. Only two vigorous males followed the ball. Mitto stared at him with wide eyes as if Kendwa were a god.

Kendwa grinned, raising his eyebrows at her, shrugging broad shoulders. 'Hey, he climbed up my leg. What am I gonna do, swat him off?' He gently placed the orangutan on the ground. 'So, the vet? Where is she?'

He stepped closer, and she felt the heat of his breath. *Oh, my God, he was delectable.*

'Up in the dispensary. That way.' She pointed, trying not to make eye contact so she wouldn't drown in his beautiful turquoise eyes.

'Thanks.' He turned to leave.

'But, what…why?' Looking at him, finally, she shielded her eyes from the sun with her hand.

'She needs some advice on a leg wound.'

'Are you a vet?'

'Maybe.' Chuckling to himself, he walked away.

Sharli watched the babies playing with the big ball of rope. Usually, she'd be giggling at them. Her mind was on Kendwa. *Why did he have to look so damn handsome?*

Seriously! He strolled in like he owned the place, wearing khaki shorts and a tight brown t-shirt that did nothing to hide his sexy

38

physique. And he kept smiling. Those dimples were doing her head in, seriously!

Another thought crossed her mind while she absently scuffed her shoes over the damp ground. *He was heading to the dispensary.* Suellen was gay and wouldn't even think he was sexy, but Bianca and Rachel positively would. They were up there helping Suellen with an operation.

Sharli placed her head in her hands. She'd knocked Kendwa back. Both young women knew how to lure a man quicker than a shark to burley. Clutching her chest with one hand did nothing to contain the aching beat of her heart. Within days he'd probably bed with one of them. She realised that thought stung her. Did she want to be in his bed instead?

As she shook her head and sighed, Mitto grabbed her hand. Following him to a new play area, she tried to forget Kendwa and the lingering glances the girls would be giving him. *She had her chance and blew it.*

About an hour later, Rachel ran towards Sharli. Rachel's happy face was a dead giveaway that she'd indeed met Kendwa and was smitten. She considered blocking her ears with her hands.

'Sharli, have you seen the new vet? OMG, hottest guy on the planet. Seriously!'

'You say that about a lot of guys, Rachel.' Sharli rolled her eyes.

Bianca sidled up behind her. Bobbed brown hair, big green eyes and a body like Gisele. Bianca was the envy of many women, though not usually Sharli. 'I have dibs on him, Rachel. Keep your hands off.' She narrowed her eyes at Sharli. 'That goes for you too.'

'His name's Kendwa, Bianca. I already met him yesterday,' Sharli said, tempted to add, and I have first dibs on him. She held her tongue.

Rachel placed her hands on her hips. 'Why would you not mention that, Sharli? Did you see those eyes and dimples, Bianca? Not to mention the buff body.'

'Oh, yeah.' Bianca said, 'He kept looking up, smiling at me during the operation. When I held Suria's foot for him to insert the needle, our fingers brushed more than once. I'm sure it was on purpose. He even winked.'

'He did not wink, said Rachel. 'I watched his eyes the whole time. He enjoyed working with Suellen, not smiling because of you. He's like amaaaaze balls at what he does. Even Suellen was impressed.'

'Why did he have to help, anyway?' Sharli asked, trying her dandiest not to sound too interested.

'Suellen's been struggling with the bone fragment? Kendwa's has more experience with trap injuries than her. He's worked all through Africa, Australia's top end. Even with alligators in Florida.'

'You learnt all this during a one-hour operation?' Sharli sighed. There was no hope with Kendwa now. She needed to ignore her attraction to him. *Harder done than said.*

Bianca laughed. 'We grilled him. The only thing we didn't ask is which position he prefers during sex.' She winked.

'Don't be so crude,' said Sharli. 'He's come to us as a professional. You should be treating him that way.'

Rachel looked closely at Sharli, holding her shoulders. 'Oh wow. You like him too. No way.'

Sharli felt like she was turning beetroot, but she didn't blush because her skin was too olive. Running her hand over her flaming forehead, she forced her flustered feelings away. 'No, I don't,' she denied adamantly.

Rachel's eyes rolled, seeing right through her. Bianca skipped up the track. 'Good, you're out then. I took dibs, so drop out, Rachel. I can't wait to get him in the sack and—' She stopped mid-sentence with wide eyes.

Kendwa strolled towards them. Moving like a wildcat, they hadn't heard his footfalls. 'Hi, again, ladies.' He turned to Sharli, who tried to ignore him, but his magnetism was an impossible force. 'Sharli. That dinner we talked about?'

The girls watched them closely. Bianca held manicured fingers over her big mouth.

'The one I said no to?' Sharli glanced at Bianca, holding the smirk taking her lips hostage. Lifting her eyelashes to him, she hoped she wasn't blowing her chances further by reminding him she said no.

'You didn't say you'd never go out to dinner with me, just not last night. I'd say you wouldn't be rostered on tonight as well.' He checked the sports watch on his wrist. 'I'm hoping you'd be free to join me.'

40

Stepping closer, he bent his neck down. His cool breath somehow warmed her cheek. Muddled thoughts slipped around her brain, but self-preservation kicked inside her gut. *Was she going to be one of those girls who fought for a man or a shrinking violet?*

'Okay. I'm free tonight.' She couldn't believe she'd said yes.

Giving her the thumbs up, he grinned. 'I'll come by and get you around six.' Waving with a dimpled smile, he strolled up the narrow path.

Bianca turned to Sharli with a curled upper lip. 'I said I had dibs.'

'What does that even mean?' asked Rachel, shaking her head. 'Besides, he likes Sharli, and why wouldn't he?'

Bianca huffed, storming back to the dorms like a cyclone circled her head.

Rachel patted Sharli's shoulder. 'Are you sure you want to take on a guy like that? He's beautiful but rather intimidating. You are kind of a novice when it comes to guys.'

Sharli didn't know. 'I guess there's one way to find out, and that's to have dinner with him. It's because he comes from Zanzibar. We both miss home. It's not a real date.'

Rachel winked. 'It could be a match made in heaven, I reckon.'

Sharli rolled her eyes. *Or a match made in hell.* 'I'm going to the dispensary to check how Suria is.'

Later, while Sharli dressed, Rachel pranced in to sit on her bed. Sharli had white slacks placed on the bed beside a flowery blouse. She held a low-back, soft yellow dress with shoestring straps, tentatively in her hands. 'Which one?'

'You have to wear the dress. Plus, it's too hot for trousers.' Rachel pushed the dress closer to Sharli. 'You know you want to wear it. Yes, it will show that you have great boobs, but that's the point, isn't it?'

Sharli chewed her bottom lip. 'I don't want to look like I want to go to bed with Kendwa. We're having dinner only.'

'That dress is pretty and feminine. It is not an I-want-to-fuck-you dress, Sharli.'

'Are you sure?'

'Of course. Put it on. I'm even excited about seeing you in a dress for once.' She giggled. 'Imagine how thrilled he'll be.' She slapped her thigh.

41

'Don't.' Sharli shot her a fake angry look, slipping the dress on. It slid over her hips hugging her curves. Biting her lip, she glanced at her wristwatch. 'He'll be here soon. Do my hair and makeup look okay?'

'Seriously, Sharli, you have no idea, do you? You look gorgeous. I'd be envious if we weren't such good friends.'

There was a knock on the closed door. 'She's coming,' yelled Rachel, holding Sharli's shoulders. 'Okay. Go and enjoy that fabulous man's company. Don't go all quiet and shy on him. Talk about home. You know Bianca's waiting like a crocodile to snap him up if you fail?' Sideways she clapped her hands together like a jaw.

Sharli nodded, tucking her hair behind her ear, trying to keep her nerves at bay. *Why was the thought of seeing him making her so nervous?*

Rachel shoved her towards the door. 'Go. Enjoy!'

Slowly opening the door, she found him pacing with his hand raking through his neatly combed waves of thick hair. Dressed in denim cut-offs and a button-up shirt in pale blue, he couldn't have looked better. The shirt accentuated dark olive skin. It was a bit too tight around his upper arms, where muscles bulged.

She couldn't take her eyes off him. Butterflies fluttering inside her belly did not help. A wayward curl hung, masking one of his beautiful eyes. He forced a finger over his forehead, revealing eyes raking over her. An appreciative smile spread across his handsome face. In that instant, her nervousness evaporated.

'Wow,' he said.

'Wow, yourself.' She tilted her head.

'You look more than beautiful. You're flawless.' There was a catch to his deep voice.

Her heart skipped a billion beats. 'Thank you.'

Kendwa took her hand, and his large fingers curled into hers. They strolled towards a rent-a-car.

'Where are we going?' she asked.

'Ba Lin Rooftop Bar. Have you been there?'

'No.'

'You'll love it.' He opened the passenger door for her.

'You're pretty sure of yourself,' she said as she got in the car.

A lopsided dimpled smile was his reply to that.

They arrived at the Sandakan hotel overlooking the bay. 'Not much to see outside the old Nak Hotel, but the upstairs, the rooftop bar has the best views. We're in time for sunset and full moon rise.' Music filtered down the stairs.

Grabbing her hand again, he led her up the narrow stairs. She more than liked the feel of his touch. A waiter showed them to a table for two close to the balcony. Sharli rested her chin on her palm, staring at the water view across the hotel roofs. There were dozens of boats of all sizes bobbing in the water. The sun cast an orange-purple glow across the smooth bay.

'You like it?' He asked, facing her

'It's magical. I love it.'

'I'm glad.' '

'What's the food like?' She picked up a menu, opening it.

'There's some Indonesian and Persian, then hearty food, Pizzas and Western dishes, plus they have a good choice of vegetarian as well.'

'In case I'm a vegetarian.' She smiled, glancing up from the menu. 'I'm not, but I don't each much meat. A little chicken and seafood.'

'That's good we have it all covered then. I love a steak myself, but I pretty much eat anything.' Surveying the menu with enthusiasm, he chuckled.

A waiter arrived, taking their order with a toothy smile. Both declined an alcoholic drink, asking for coconut water instead. Kendwa because he was driving and Sharli, so she could keep her wits. Considering his proximity was almost making her combust, adding alcohol would be a risky blend.

'So, you miss home?' he asked.

Glancing at the water as if she could see Zanzibar, she said, 'Very much.'

'Your family?' He looked down at his meal, his eyes soft. Something flickered in his eyes, sadness perhaps.

When she spoke, he looked up, smiling weakly.

'My ma isn't well. We lost dad to Typhoid ten years ago, and I have a sister. Ma faced a lot of stigma being a single mother in Zanzibar, even though she was a widow.' She frowned. 'My best friend works with a shelter for widowed mothers because of it.'

'At least things are changing. They're not as narrow-minded as they used to be. This old guy I know, Jambi. He was a friend of my dad's. He's kept in touch over the years to let me know what's going on.'

'Your parents aren't there anymore?'

As if he was weighing his words, he went quiet, chewing the inside of his cheek. 'Nope. We moved to England when I was about ten, then the states in my teens. We came back but usually quick visits and didn't spend much time on the island. Dad's cause was getting rid of poachers, so we did a lot of game warden stuff when we returned to Africa.' He paused, something flickering across his eyes again. They seemed to have a mist across the aqua. 'Let's talk about what you did in Zanzibar.'

'But what about your parents, where are they now?'

Putting down his cutlery, he raked his hand through his hair. Eyes were downcast, his jaw firm. Then he looked away, composing himself. 'Look, the moon's huge.' The glowing moon rose in the darkening sky.

'Kendwa, are you okay?' She turned slightly, taking the full moon in, waiting for his answer.

'Yup. Don't ask about my folks, please. It's um—. Is your meal okay?'

So, he had some things he wanted to keep to himself. Sharli could understand that. She could avoid the subject of his parents. Instead, she told him funny stories about growing up in Zanzibar. He seemed to cheer up, adding a few of his own. It was surprising they hadn't crossed paths until now, though he was four years older, and it might be why.

They enjoyed each other's company so much neither realised they were the last diners until waiters began stacking chairs nearby. 'We'd better go,' she said unconvincingly, not wanting the night to end.

Taking her hand, they strolled to the car. She wished the ride would never end.

Pulling the car up at the gates to the Sanctuary, he took the keys from the ignition. 'I'll walk you up,' he said.

A protest died on her lips when she saw his expectant face. She was used to being independent but decided against it. 'Okay, thanks.'

Taking her hand in his again, it felt natural and lovely, running the tips of her fingers across his callouses, feeling his warmth.

Halfway along the track, he tugged her hand to spin her around to face him. Wrapping his muscular arms across her shoulders, he brought his lips to hers— a soft brush. Pulling back, his blue eyes questioned her.

When she nodded with a small, breathless smile, he kissed her again, this time deeply, hungrily. She surprised herself by responding. His body crushed against hers, so solid. Hands explored down her back until he cupped her bottom under her dress. The soft cotton of her underwear did nothing to block the heat of his hands.

Picking her up, as if she were as light as paper, he straddled her legs around his waist. Her hands twisted through his thick hair as they continued deep, delicious kissing. The undeniable hard erection prodding between their clothes forced her to come to her senses. *And practically cum too.*

Foggy with lust, her brain barely functioned, but she wasn't the kind of girl to act wantonly. She rarely initiated sex after a month of dating. *And here she was practically having sex with Kendwa through their clothes.*

Squirming from his grasp, she pulled her lips reluctantly from his and immediately felt the void.

Kendwa's eyes searched hers with questions, but he put her down. His fingertips lingered on hers. 'Sharli, I didn't mean to—'

Rubbing bruised lips, she moved back a step, dropping her fingers, so they were no longer touching. She wanted to tell him that she enjoyed every moment. *I love your company more than you'll know. But sex is out of the question.* Instead of saying anything to explain how she felt, she fled. Before he could even protest, she ran to her room, shutting the door quietly so that the girls wouldn't wake.

As she got into bed, Bianca opened one eye, watching Sharli's flushed face. Bianca smiled, shutting her eyes. Sharli wasn't the type to sleep around, but she figured a man like Kendwa couldn't wait forever. Now Kendwa would be hers. Slowly she reached her hands down, slipping them into her pants. Kendwa's image behind her closed eyes, she rubbed the sweet spot.

45

Chapter 7
Borneo, Malaysia

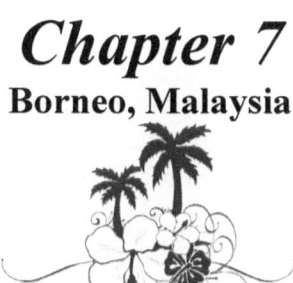

Kendwa couldn't figure out what went wrong, even after sleeping on it. *What spooked Sharli?* They clicked. He knew that for sure. Laughter came easily, and the conversations flowed smoothly. It felt comfortable, and it was probably cliché, but it was like he'd known her forever.

Perhaps he shouldn't have gotten so amorous. *How could he help himself?* Her sweet lips, a drug he couldn't get enough of. Her body pressed against him—a release from the darkness of his heart.

Working on the river distracted him somewhat but not enough. Last night played on loop in his brain, and he found himself staring into the bush or water but not seeing anything.

After five long hours taking tours through the river, he ran back to the sanctuary. He'd promised Suellen he'd come back and check on Suria. Suellen was a fine vet. She mainly worked on Australian domestic pets and wasn't a specialist in primates. Though studying them through an online university, her degree was incomplete. And with more experience, she would make a fine primate vet. With so few volunteers taking on roles in the sanctuary, it was better to have a vet of any qualifications, but a bonus if someone with his skills could help.

Mostly, if he were honest with himself, he wanted to make sure Sharli was alright. Though he'd tried to reign in his intense feelings, it wasn't easy when she showed such tantalising responsiveness when he kissed her. He needed to apologise, but he wasn't sure what he had done.

Bianca sashayed towards him on a narrow timber bridge. She flicked her hair but didn't look up at him, though he knew she'd seen him.

Bumping into him, she pressed her large breasts to linger on his chest. Fingernails trailed his biceps.

'Oh, sorry. I wasn't looking where I was going.' She blocked his way.

Sure, you were.

'Can you let me through?' Trying to edge by her only made her push closer to him. She was as tall as him. Their faces were close. He could smell last night's whisky on her breath, which turned him off even more than her blatant come on.

Sliding hands down his arms, she rested them on his chest and down to his stomach. 'You have a six-pack.' She smirked. 'Of course, you do.'

Taking her hands off him, he grabbed her shoulders. 'I'll physically move you if you don't get out of my way, Bianca.' His voice held a controlled menace.

She shrugged. 'You'll never get in little-miss-frigid's pants. So why even try? If you want kinky, glorious sex, come to me, Kendwa. You won't be disappointed, and a guy like you must be horny as hell.'

Kendwa turned away from her, gritting his jaw tight. *How dare she speak about Sharli like that?* Sharli wasn't frigid. She just wasn't brazenly wanton like Bianca. She must have her reasons for running away. He planned to find out what they were. He strode away to the sounds of her laughter.

After helping Suellen source a tooth problem in one of the older orangutans, he washed his hands, thinking about Sharli. He was about to go in search of her.

He didn't need to go looking because she rushed in crying, holding a baby orangutan. 'It's Mitto. He was trying to climb after the others and got stuck by the neck on the ropes. Umar said he only turned his back for a moment, and Mitto had gone blue.'

Kendwa got to her first, taking the baby orangutan, placing him on the table. Suellen reached for the oxygen, fastening the mask over Mitto's face. Kendwa gently checked the injury to his neck. They worked on the little orangutan calmly but quickly.

Suellen and Kendwa spoke medical jargon in hushed tones until they got the little guy stable, giving each other concerned looks across the table.

Kendwa wiped his brow, glancing across to see tears streaming down Sharli's face. 'Hey, he's going to be alright. You did a great job getting him here quickly.'

Suellen added, 'See how his colour is coming back and his breathing is deeper. Good signs. Thanks, Kendwa. I've got him now. You go clean up and look after Sharli. She looks a bit shaken.'

Sharli held her finger to her bottom lip. Kendwa thought it was about the most adorable thing he'd seen in a long while. Wobbling on her feet, she clutched the wall with her face turning sickly pale.

He reached for her before she fell, enveloping her in his arms.

Twisting her fingers into his shirt, she clung to him, burying her head to cry.

He held her until she stopped. With solemn moist eyes, she glanced up. 'I was so worried.'

'Come on. You need to sit down. You've had a shock.'

Nodding mutely, she let him take her hand. He led her to the kitchen veranda, directing her to sit on the long timber bench seat.

'I'll go inside, wash my hands and change my shirt. Will you be okay?'

'Mmmm. I will.'

At the sound of his footfalls, she looked up. Broken from her sad thoughts, she nearly slid off the seat. A dirty shirt in his hands, he was shirtless. Broad, muscular chest narrowed to a trim waist. The six-pack stomach rippled as he moved. It was so chiselled it defied physics. Scrunching the shirt in a ball, he fished around in his knapsack for a spare. Flapping the clean black t-shirt, so it unfolded, he turned it in the right way, put his massive arms through the sleeves. Poking his head through the neck, he stretched it down with his hands, over taut muscles, until it fit him like a glove.

Noticing her staring, he asked, 'What?'

'Um, nothing,' she said, hiding her smile. *How could watching a man put on a shirt be so mesmerising? Way to go, Kendwa. This girl is no longer sad.*

He sat next to her. 'Do you feel better?'

'Yes.' *Understatement!* 'Sorry I was so upset. I thought Mitto was going to die, and he's such a precious little guy.' She wiped under her eyes, but the tears were dry.

'I promise he'll be fine after he rests up for a while. Looks to be no permanent damage.'

'Good.' Her hands rested in her lap. Averting her eyes from his gaze didn't stop her from smiling or wanting to touch him.

'Can we talk?' Gently he lifted her chin with a finger.

'Kendwa, don't.' She brushed his hand away.

He raked his hand through his hair. It only flopped over his confused eyes. 'Sharli, I like you—a lot. I'm not pushing you for anything. I only want to see you until you go home, and hopefully when we are both back in Zanzibar.'

Puzzled big golden eyes blinked at him. Long lashes fluttered, mesmerising him.

'Kendwa, I like you too, but I don't know what to do about it. I'm going in over a week, so what's the point?' She shrugged her slender shoulders.

'This is the point,' he said, leaning in to kiss her. 'There's something between us. You can't ignore it.' He puckered to kiss her again, but she placed her finger on his lips.

'Maybe, but we don't have enough time to figure out if there is, and when I go home, I have too many duties. I wouldn't be able to start anything there either.'

Slowly he took her hand, squeezing it. 'Sharli, I'm asking you to spend time with me until you go. I know there's something you're not telling me. I'm sure you have your reasons, but I need to talk to you, hold you and kiss you. No more.'

It sounded too nice to be true. How could a bloke be so rugged and wild but kind and soft? He was breaking down the barriers she'd built around her heart, brick by brick, wall by wall. Shifting closer, she smiled coyly. 'Kiss me, Kendwa.'

There was no need for further prompting. They kissed on the bench like newlyweds. Picking her up, he placed her on his lap, never breaking the deep kissing.

50

'You taste so delicious,' he said, groaning between breaths.

'We can't do this here. What if someone sees?' Pushing his chest with her hands, she broke the kiss. Both breathless, the steady rise and fall of his chest seemed exaggerated by her words. *God, he felt so good.* Her womb twisted, creating urges she'd never felt for any other guy. Trying to snap herself out of dangerous thoughts of sex was difficult. Every nerve ending in her body betrayed her.

She squirmed off his lap, but his hands around her waist held her firm. 'We can go somewhere more private.' He raised his eyebrows.

'No. That would be even worse.'

He lifted his hands, letting her climb off his lap. 'Why would it be worse?'

'Because then I might want to have sex with you.'

'I have no problem with that.' A crooked smile played at his lips as he tried to make light of it.

'I do, Kendwa. I have a big problem with it.'

'What aren't you telling me, Sharli?'

'It doesn't matter. I can't do this.' Turning from him, she walked away.

'I was joking about the sex. We don't have to make love. I'm not an animal. I can control myself.'

'I'm sure you can, but maybe I can't,' she yelled from the path. *Kendwa said, make love. Not have sex or fuck. Love?*

Kendwa rubbed his chin. He was genuinely baffled by what was going on with her. It didn't concern him. He could fix whatever it was. All he wanted was to love and protect her.

'I'll see you tomorrow when you're in a better mood then,' he yelled, not quite sure if she would hear him.

That night Sharli called to Rachel from her bed. Bianca was out for the night. 'Rachel, are you awake?'

'Yep. Are you wondering if Bianca's out searching for Kendwa?'

'I'm a bit concerned that she is. I'm hoping he wouldn't respond.' She paused, staring up at the thatched ceiling. 'Rachel?'

'Yeah.'

'I think I love him. Not a little bit but like more than anything in this world.'

Rachel rolled over, watching her with an elbow on the bed, head resting on her palm. 'I knew this would happen. You find the right guy, and then BAM, you're a goner. What are you going to do about it?'

'Nothing. I'm leaving. I will keep away from him until I do.' *It hurt so much to say it.*

'But, why? Why can't you chase true love? Why do you have to run away from it?'

'It's my family duty to go back home.'

'What if he follows you?'

'I doubt he would, but he wouldn't want to take on the responsibilities I have back there even if he did. It wouldn't be fair on him. He's too much of a free spirit.'

'Wow, it's like you've known him forever.'

'It's so weird, but I feel like I have.'

'Then, find a way, girlfriend.'

The force of Kendwa's punch smashed the boxing bag against the wall. He'd gone to the gym at midnight to release his anger and frustration. Untying the gloves, he threw them at the wall. Sliding to the ground as he angrily unstrapped his wrists, his head dropped. Sweat dripped from his body onto the rubber matting. *Better to be punching a boxing bag than messing things up with Sharli.*

Knocking back Bianca's advances was a testament to how he felt about Sharli. Bianca arrived at the bar wearing a come-and-fuck-me kind of red dress showing every curvy inch of skin. It was more like a bikini than a dress.

The fact that she was panty-less, facing him and making sure he could see the view between her long legs didn't help. She'd uncrossed them so many times it had made him dizzy. *It's hard for a guy to look away when there's a vagina on display.*

It took every fibre of willpower not to take her somewhere in the dark, lift her dress, get his cock out and fuck her until he released the intensity of his desire for Sharli. Luckily, he'd had the good sense to run away to the gym before Bianca knew he had gone.

In the morning, when Kendwa tapped on Sharli's dormitory door, no one answered. Poking his head around the sanctuary areas nearby, he came up fruitless. He decided to try the kitchen to see if he could find the daily roster to figure out where she was.

Inside her room, Sharli heard the knock, ignoring it with hands clamped over her ears. Rachel had warned her he was on his way. Hiding was her only option because she physically couldn't see him. If she locked eyes with him, she wouldn't be able to control her growing emotions. *Why did love make you feel ill?*

The feelings he evoked were foreign to her. She'd never experienced such attraction and arousal. It was all she could do to control the urges. Then she'd feel a stone sink to the bottom of her stomach when she thought about never having a future with him. But of course, he didn't keep away. Kendwa said he'd come back, and he'd probably do it every day until she left.

In equal measures, she wanted to see him and dreaded it. Well, maybe that wasn't entirely true. She desperately wanted to be near him. It was like he was a magnet. In the end, the attraction won out.

She found him up a tree climbing with the orangutans. Umar stood on the grass, looking up. 'You've got them climbing better than the older orangutans. I've never seen anything like it,' he called to Kendwa.

The eleven-year-old female orangutan, Cinta, watched them from an adjoining tree. She munched on a left-over piece of watermelon as if she was sitting, eating popcorn at the movies.

Kendwa climbed higher. The bravest babies followed him. Cinta smacked her long, hairy hand on the branch beside her in delight, a wide toothy grin on her long dark face.

Sharli glanced from Cinta to Umar. 'It's good to see her back for a visit.'

'Maybe word has spread through the forest that there's a human up a fig tree,' Umar said, laughing.

Sharli shielded her eyes from the sun, calling up to Kendwa. 'Kendwa, surely that's high enough. It's getting dangerous.'

Shrugging his shoulders, he grinned. 'They're primates. They're meant to do this.' A baby climbed on his back, clinging to him like a koala. Kendwa looked at ease on the wide branch, with primates around him.

'I meant it's getting dangerous for you, not the primates.'

'I haven't fallen out of a tree since I was ten years old. Not a chance it will happen now, but I'll come down if it makes you happy.' He clambered down. Suddenly he slipped, his right foot dangled in the air.

Sharli gasped, placing hands over her face. She peeked through her fingers. Big hands held the above branch, righting himself, grinning down. She realised he'd been faking it. Jumping the last ten feet, he landed neatly in front of her, looking as cheeky as the monkeys he'd been climbing with.

Umar was in stitches, holding his stomach and losing his breath from laughter. 'Man, you need to stay here. That was amazing. You'd give old Cinta a run for her money.' Cinta jumped up and down, screeching happily as if the whole thing had amused her too.

'Umar, I can teach you how to do it safely. It's just practice,' Kendwa said, then to Sharli. 'Did you come looking for me?' A blue eye winked roguishly.

'No.' She looked away.

'Sure, you did. You can't meet my eyes. It's a tell-tale sign that you're lying.'

'I do not lie.'

'Fib?'

Smacking his arm softly, she conceded. 'Okay. Maybe I did.'

'Good. We need a chat.'

'No chatting about us. Let's just walk and talk about the forest.' To Umar, she called, 'See you later, Umar.'

They strolled along one of the muddy dirt tracks leading through the forest, talking about the weather, orangutans, his tours, anything but themselves.

The vegetation thickened. 'There are some nepenthes just in here,' she said.

'Pitcher carnivorous plants. Where?'

Hesitantly, she took his hand. 'Through here.' They stopped when they came to the amazing funnel-shaped plants. There were dozens of them clumped around the muddy ground. A plant of pinkish green with a lid at the top and what looked like lips.'

54

'They are amazing. The monkeys sometimes drink rainforest water from them.'

'I love how they lure insects in. Then they drown in the liquid inside them. Here we go.' He pointed to the biggest plant.

A bee had flown too close. Suddenly the plant snapped shut over the bee. They could hear the bee buzzing around, looking for an escape. It soon went quiet. Kendwa grinned. 'I love this kinda stuff,' he said as he bent to study the plants.

'I know you do.' Watching his expression as he contemplated the plant, she realised he was content in the wild.

Realising she was staring at him, he came to her, taking her in his arms. 'We're so perfect together. We have so much in common.'

Shushing him with a finger to his lips, she leant up, kissing him chastely. He pushed his lips to hers for more, but she stepped away. 'I have to get back to work. You know, I enjoyed our walk because we didn't talk about us. We just enjoyed each other's company.'

He scratched his head. 'Us? So, there is an 'us'? Maybe I want to talk about that.'

'Come on, I have to get back.' She ignored his question.

'Sharli?' He took her hand, pulling her around to him, but she squirmed away and began stomping up the path.

'I need to keep my distance from you. I'm leaving, remember.'

'Can't we? Sharli, I don't get it.' They'd had such a relaxed time together, talking. There were comfortable silences as they admired the beauty of where they were. They were building a foundation, at least that's what he thought.

'I'm sorry, Kendwa. It's the way it has to be.'

It stung him. He loved Sharli with everything he had, but it didn't seem to be enough. Wracking his brain for what he should do and how he should act, he was totally clueless.

What could he do next to convince her to love him back? *Or should he just give up altogether?*

Chapter 8
Borneo, Malaysia

'Sharli, I thought you'd be going out with Kendwa tonight,' said Rachel as she held a bottle of milk to one of the babies. Sharli was sitting across from her, feeding Mitto.

'No. I'm keeping away from him. I'm considering leaving early to avoid him.'

'I seriously do not get it, Sharli. I know you've got problems at home, but he seems like the sort of guy that would take it all on.'

'Oh Rachel, you should have seen him in the forest today. He's supposed to be in the wild, not back in Stone Town tending to my sick mother. It wouldn't be fair on him.'

'I don't see why you don't at least tell him and let him decide.'

Sharli gazed down at Mitto. It wasn't only Kendwa she would miss. She loathed the thought of leaving darling little Mitto and the other babies. Glancing at Rachel, she smiled. 'You've been a true friend, Rachel.'

'I'll miss you. I'm going to go and work the ski season at home, so I can save up and come visit you in Zanzibar. It sounds so exotic.'

'I'd really like tha,t Rachel.'

Over at the resort, Kendwa was having a drink with Umar. He was still in a foul mood over Sharli and probably drank more than was good for him, but he agreed to another beer anyway.

It was soon after ten. Umar stood to leave as Bianca took a seat at the table.

'Hi, Kendwa.' She said it with seduction in her husky tone.

Kendwa glared at her noticing the clingy dress that accentuated every curve of her model-like body. Blatantly, her cleavage was directly in his face as she sat. Shaking his head, he tried to clear it of the alcohol. There was an urge to rest his head on her boobs but he wanted them to be Sharli's.

Bianca ordered more drinks. He should have got up. Leaving was the intelligent thing to do.

Clouded by alcohol and thoughts of Sharli going back home to Zanzibar, he wavered. She rejected him. He didn't have an ego about it, even though he'd barely been denied in his life. Instead, he just felt sad, heartbroken even. *Another person he loved departing his life.*

'You look a little down tonight, Kendwa.' Bianca crawled her fingers on his seat, stroking his thigh, hidden from view by the table.

'It's Sharli. She's under my skin.' He lifted her hand, placing it away from him.

'Oh, you poor thing, and you can't do anything about it, can you?' She pretend-pouted.

'No. I don't know what to do. Sharli acts like she wants me, then she doesn't. It's so confusing.' He raked his hand through his hair.

'So, you're a little bit frustrated about it then?' Bianca's hand slipped back to his thigh, reaching between his legs.

He raised his eyes to hers, narrowing them to warn her off. The crotch rubbing gave him no doubt as to what she wanted. *Damn, it would be so easy to release the sexual tension with this, obviously, more-than-willing woman.* He took her hand away again. It was ironic she could brazenly touch him. Guys couldn't get away with the same thing reversed and the attention unwanted. With a rough push, he moved her hand aside again.

'I'll let you in on a little secret. I'm a qualified deep tissue masseuse.' She grinned. 'I could release all that tension for you. No sex. Just a massage to make you less stressed. I promise.' She crossed her heart. Her provocative boobs jiggled.

A tremor shook through his shoulders. He cracked his neck. *I do need a massage.* 'No. I'm fine. I probably need to go to bed.'

'Can I come?' Stroking his wide shoulder with one long-nailed finger, her eyes never leaving him showed depths of deep lust.

'No!' He practically shouted it. Other patrons turned around, startled.

Trying not to look at her, he rose, strolling to his room a little wobbly. Unlocking the door, he staggered inside. About to slam it shut, he faltered when she barged her way in.

'You shouldn't have followed me, Bianca.' He was about to push her back outside, but she'd already shut the door. The body-hugging dress was quickly down her hips as she stripped in front of him, grinning lasciviously. *God no, don't strip.*

'I had to follow you. You don't know what you really need, so I have to show you.' She played with her exposed rosy nipples.

Taking a step back, he raked at his hair, glancing at the ceiling, cursing. He was wonky on his feet. Wishing he hadn't drunk so much seemed irrelevant with a sexy naked woman shamelessly in front of him.

Kendwa wasn't a heavy drinker. Even though he was a big guy, it still went to his head quicker than he would have liked, especially when he was upset. Tripping over the coffee table to land upright over the side of his bed, he closed his eyes. *Go way, Bianca.*

'Oh, right where I want you.'

'Just put your clothes on and go. Please.' With eyes still shut, he waited for the door to open for her to leave. Blinking his eyes to see what she was doing, he realised she was on her knees in front of him.

'Let me do this for you.' With deft hands, she unzipped his fly, releasing his cock so quickly he didn't have time to react. Unfortunately, he was as hard as iron. Even when he didn't want to respond, his body betrayed him. He was about to push her head away. Hungry lips met the end of his tip, sending a shudder through his body. She sucked, gliding up and down his shaft. He was lost to it as she sucked hard and deep.

She gave him head for what seemed like ages until he was at the point of no return. His heart said, don't fuck her, but every nerve ending told him otherwise.

He shoved her on the bed. Checking with his fingers that she was moist so he wouldn't hurt her, he entered her. Her hands were all over him, scratching his back, pushing his buttocks, so he rammed into her harder. It turned him on in a primal way as he thrust into her. It was

59

plain fucking. There was no love in it, but he never hurt women, so he tried to slow it, trying not to be too rough, even though he was as angry as he was horny.

Then she yelled, 'Fuck me harder, Kendwa.' He couldn't help but comply. Sex was sex. It's all it was.

Twisting her neck, she kept trying to kiss his lips, but he refused her that. She'd got the sex she wanted, but he wasn't going to give her any affection. They rolled over. Brushing his chest with her boobs, she straddled on top of him, grinding her hips into him, yelling, 'That's so good. Oh, fuck that's good. Oooh, oooh.' Quivery uncontrollably, her head lolling, he watched as she climaxed. Shame washed over him.

He could feel his own ebbing climax because two thoughts entered his head. *Sharli. Condom.*

Pushing Bianca off, he swore, grabbing the sheets to cover his softening erection. 'Get out. Get dressed. Get out now. I'm sorry, but we shouldn't…fuck get out.'

Not even having the dignity to look upset, Bianca grinned. 'Thanks for that, Kendwa. I hope Sharli doesn't get too upset when I tell her about the love scratches on your back and how we made love.'

Quickly he strode towards her, sheet trailing, as she zipped up her dress. 'We did not make love. You took advantage of my state.'

She raised her eyebrows. 'Really, Kendwa. I took advantage of you. A big guy like you. I don't think anyone will believe that, least of all Sharli.'

As she opened the door, he stood with his fists clenched beside him. 'That was even better than I expected. Thanks, honey.' She blew him a kiss and left. He shut the door, slid down against it, putting his head in his hands. *What have I done?*

The following day, after no sleep whatsoever, he walked to the sanctuary. He needed to talk to Sharli before Bianca said anything. She had to hear it from him.

Taking a deep breath, he knocked on her door. She answered it quickly, yawning as she opened it. Wearing long pink pyjamas with a yellow puppy print, she looked adorable. He felt like a right shit.

'Oh, Kendwa. I wasn't expecting... What's happened? You look upset.' They moved away from the dormitory so as not to wake anyone because it was early.

Hands in his pockets, he didn't meet her eyes, instead looking down at the ground. He cleared his throat. 'Did you, um see Bianca last night?'

'Why? No. I was asleep when she came in.'

Regret and sadness were blatantly written on his face when he raised his eyes to her.

Sharli took a step backwards. She gasped then placed her hand to her mouth.

'I'm so sorry, Sharli. You have to let me explain.'

'You slept with her? You slept with Bianca?' She screamed. Tears fell like diamonds down her face.

Stepping closer, he put his arms around her, but she squirmed away. Pacing backwards and forwards, she stomped an angry path. Her mouth formed words, but nothing came out. Tears brimmed in her pretty golden eyes.

'Calm down. It's not what you think.' He had to try to make her understand.

'Calm down! Are you serious? It's disgusting.'

'It never would have happened if we'd got things clear about our relationship.'

'Wow, you're saying that you're blaming me for you having sex with Bianca?' She stood with her hands on her hips, bottom lip trembling.

Raking his hand through his hair, he blurted, 'No. No...actually, yes.'

'Yes? Are you for real?' she yelled.

'Yes. Sharli, you're doing my head in. You act like you like me. Then you don't. You're constantly turning me on then turning me away. You said you don't want a boyfriend, but you act like my girlfriend. You sit on my lap. We fit perfectly, and there's all the sexual tension between us. You say we can't make out, and your eyes and body say otherwise. You barely kiss me, then you lay one on me when I least expect it. I feel like a bloody yo-yo.' His voice rose.

61

'You can't make me be like the other girls. You can't force me to have sex with you.' She couldn't hold back the tears, wiping at them in anger.

Kendwa stepped near her reaching out his arms. 'I'd never force it, ever.' Again, she stepped backwards. 'Sharli, please don't cry. It kills me when you cry.' He paced, tearing at his hair. 'I didn't make Bianca sleep with me. She came to me. She… I can't even tell you how it happened. If I could take it back, I would. I want you and only you.'

'You do not. You're capable of hooking up with another woman. How many do you bed? I'd only be a conquest, another damn tick on your list.'

'That's not true. You know me better than that, Sharli. I'd marry you right this minute.'

Sharli's eyes widened, her bottom lip quivered. 'How dare you say such a thing to get sex?' Turning from him, she stormed back towards her room.

'It didn't come out right. Sharli, I mean it. I want to marry you.' *What a dumbarse proposal, mate!*

He thought about chasing her. Instead, he crouched down in the dirt, putting his head in his hands. *I've blown it.*

Sharli was his dream woman. The perfect girl. He'd let his cock lead him away from his heart. It would have been easy to cry if he wasn't so angry with himself.

Chapter 9
Borneo, Malaysia

The crocodile surfaced, its eyes peeking above the water line. Kendwa thought about slipping over the boat edge, landing in the water beside it to offer himself up as its lunch. It would be a fitting way to end it all. Of course, he couldn't do that to the tourists in the boat. Instead, he gunned the motor to head them back to the jetty, wondering what he could possibly do now. Maybe a run through the jungle would clear his mind.

Back at the sanctuary, Sharli packed her bags, flinging clothes in and squashing them to fit. Usually tidy when she packed, her anger had rendered her incapable of caring about neatly folded clothing. 'Rachel, stop trying to talk me out of it. How would you feel?'

'You know, just the same as you. Come on. You realise how pushy and brazen Bianca is. She even bragged to me about what she did. Kendwa didn't stand a chance, believe me.'

Sharli held her hands tightly over her ears. 'I do not want to know. It hurts enough to acknowledge that it happened, let alone hear the details. Besides, no matter what the circumstances, if he really loved me, he wouldn't have let it occur.'

'And you're seriously going to take off without hearing him out?'

'There's nothing more he can say.' Pushing clothes away from the zipper, she tried to shut the suitcase.

The door creaked open, allowing daylight to stream into the small shack. Bianca sauntered in with wet hair, a towel around her body and one over her shoulder.

Sharli hadn't seen her since Kendwa's confession. With moist eyes, she looked up at Bianca, trying not to cry in front of her. For once in her life, she wanted to scratch another woman's eyes out.

'I take it you heard about Kendwa and me hooking up?' Bianca said, sauntering towards her bed.

'You are such a bitch,' said Rachel with a snarl. 'You knew Sharli and Kendwa had something going.'

Bianca dried her hair with the spare towel. 'I had first dibs, remember. Anyhow it was a fuck, not a friggin date. If it makes you feel any better, Sharli, he does seem to have a thing for you.' She curled her fingers up in exclamation marks when she said 'thing'.

Sharli's bottom lip quivered, her eyes avoiding Bianca's. Rachel stood in front of Bianca with her hands on her hips, her eyes slits of anger. 'So why did you do it? You skank!'

'To fuck the sexiest guy ever. Too bad he wasn't into, damn it. I still got my rocks off.' Drying her damp hair some more, she smirked. Rachel stepped closer.

'You really are a piece of work.' Rachel turned to Sharli. 'See, he didn't want to. She made him.'

Sharli wiped at her eyes, grabbing the handle of her suitcase to haul it off the bed. 'It doesn't make a difference. Surely, he could have stopped it. I'll never see him again anyway. I've booked my flights. I have a taxi to get to Kota Kinabalu leaving shortly.' The suitcase on wheels trailed behind her as she strode to the door. She kept the wobble from her voice as she said, 'I have to say goodbye to the orangutans, Suellen and Umar.'

'I'll come with you,' said Rachel, taking the suitcase off Sharli. 'I can't stand to be in the same room as Bianca.'

'What, no goodbye?' Bianca smirked, dropping the towel around her.

Sharli and Rachel ignored her.

The jungle was dense and dim under a canopy of huge fig trees and ferns. Rays of light broke through, crisscrossing to create a magical effect on the lush landscape, so dark-green in places it almost looked black. Kendwa ran through the forest, leaping over roots and plants with no idea where he was running. Sweat poured down his body. The high

64

heart rate didn't bother him. It wasn't like it mattered. He didn't care if he collapsed. For the second time in a year, he wanted to die.

A wildcat, perhaps a clouded leopard or tiger snarled in the distance. Closer by the chatter of monkeys, bird calls, running water, breezes through the trees, chorused through the forest. The sports watch on his wrist would show him the direction he ran, but he didn't glance at it. A backpack over his shoulders held a water bottle, but he didn't stop, though his lips were dry with thirst.

Finally, he halted when he could run no further. Chest heaving, he sucked deep breaths. Slowly he collapsed on the ground, looking up at blue sky peeking through the canopy. 'Dad, Mom. Why aren't you here? I miss you both so much.' He'd been avoiding thinking about them. Being heartbroken about Sharli brought the grief back to the surface. 'How am I supposed to go on?'

There was a rustle of leaves behind him. Kendwa turned slowly, half expecting the wildcat he had heard. Instead, it was a huge snake, a banded krait. Kendwa's first thought was not fear but awe. The snake was about two metres long with black and white bands, practically a zebra looking snake. Rarely seen through the day, they were highly venomous but more prone to attack at night. He'd be alright—w*hat a fantastic animal.*

It slowly zig-zagged towards him. He tapped the ground behind him, hoping the vibration would startle it back the other way. Otherwise, he kept very still. The snake's venom could kill a human in 30 minutes. *Move on, snake.* Mesmerised by it, he somehow didn't even care if it bit him.

The snake slithered closer, hissing, raising its head. *Shit, I'm in trouble here.* He realised he didn't want to die after all.

Kendwa kept still, but he was taking ragged breaths from his run. As he watched the snake move towards his feet, his adrenaline spiked. Shifting his finger slightly, he readied to grab its head. It struck him suddenly. There was no intense pain, but he knew it would come soon.

Swiftly he grabbed the snakes head before it raised itself to strike again. He flung it about fifteen metres into the vegetation, hearing it thunk in the bush. Hopefully, it was frighten too and would slither the other way. Deep bite marks on his thigh showed pinpricks of blood. The survival instinct kicked in. *I don't want to die, Sharli.*

Mobilize the wound, get to the road, flag for help, save yourself. Most of all, see Sharli again.

Kendwa shrugged the backpack off his shoulders, pulling out a bandage. It was common sense for him to prepare when running alone. Stretching his arm, he reached for a long twig. Snapping it in half, he placed it against his calf. Using the bandage, he wrapped his leg from thigh to ankle, took a sip from the water bottle, put the backpack back on and stood. Fallen branches littered the ground. He needed a long, thick one. Limping over to a branch about half his height, he picked it up. It was moist, but it was sturdy enough to hold his weight.

Using it as a crutch, he shifted his weight to his other foot, trying to keep the injured leg as still as possible. The more he moved, the quicker the poison would travel through his body. Firming his jaw, he gritted his teeth, grimacing, feeling dizzy as the poison gradually seeped through his veins. It was imperative he got to the road quickly before being paralysed. *Hang in there. Just think of Sharli's face.*

A huge fig root blocked his way. Somehow, he managed to clamber over it. He glanced at his watch to make sure he was heading in the right direction. Eyes blurred, making him fall. He pushed himself up again.

Vomit rose to his throat. He buckled over to throw up. Wiping his stinky mouth, he forced himself to continue. Stopping to vomit wasted precious moments. Throbbing pain pounded in his head. The poison was spreading fast. Soon his nerves wouldn't cooperate. *Keep moving.*

In front of him, a woman appeared. *Saved.*

The lady turned. What? *How could that be?* He blinked. His mother hovered toward him, floating and ethereal. 'Keep going, my son. Not far, only over there. She'll find you. I know she will.' She faded out.

'Who, Mom? Who?'

The image of his mother drifted back. 'You'll live. You must go looking for Noah. You have to find the elephant cave.' Her image disappeared.

'Noah? Cave? I don't understand. Come back. Don't leave me again.' Through the fog of the poison, he kept staggering forwards. Engines of cars travelling the nearby road broke through the forest noises. He scrambled, slipping on the muddy ground. The track widened until it joined the asphalt road. The first car he tried to flag down didn't stop. *I'm going to die*—despite what his mother had said.

66

The taxi slowed down. From the back seat, Sharli tapped the driver on the shoulder. 'Please speed up a little. I may miss my plane.'

'There's something…up ahead.' The taxi stopped when the driver slammed his foot on the brake.

Glancing up the road, she raised her eyebrows. A man was lying on the asphalt, face up. His wavy hair was matted. The body shape so familiar. Reaching for her door handle, she screamed. 'It's Kendwa.'

'Who?'

Opening the door to sprint to his side, her eyes wide with terror, she called to him. 'Kendwa.' He was motionless. With her palm, she tapped his cheek. Eyes fluttered but remained shut. Tilting her head to his chest to check his heartbeat, she raised panicked eyes to the driver who neared. Fingers to his pulse didn't ease her concern.

'Is he alive?' the driver asked with doubt in his voice.

'Ring an ambulance. Ragged breath, weak pulse.' The strapping on his leg seeped with two drops of blood. 'Oh, my gosh. Snakebite.'

Kendwa mumbled, opening his eyes groggily.

'Kendwa. Stay with me. Please, Kendwa.'

'Banded krait. Tell them it was a bbb..banded krait,' he mumbled, his voice husky.

'A what?' Did he know what he was talking about? He seemed delerious.

Tuah, the driver, said, 'Banded krait. Very poisonous. We need to drive now. He doesn't have time for an ambulance.'

'How quick would a snake like that take to kill?' Sharli gulped back her fear. Goose bumps run down her shoulders and arms.

'Thirty minutes, maybe more for a big man like him.'

'Okay, let's get him in the back seat. Will they have anti-venom and a respirator in an ambulance here?' To Kendwa, she said, 'How long ago were you bitten?'

'F, f…' Slowly he lifted his hand, showing five fingers, then five more, dropped it. He tried to lift it again.

'He only has another fifteen, maybe.' Trying to still the dread in her heart, she gulped back her fear.

'Can you drive, Sharli? I'll make calls. They'll understand me better.' Tuah nodded, moving to the other side of Kendwa.

They put their arms under Kendwa, trying to lift him. It took them two goes to start budging him. A small woman and a thin Malaysian somehow found the strength to move the 202 pounds, six-foot-two man and place him in the back seat. They sat him up against one door, so his leg remained straight.

Sharli drove off at speed while Tuah rang the ambulance again, speaking in Malay, relaying to Sharli as he talked. They were heading in their direction. Yes, they had anti-venom and a respirator. They should meet in under ten minutes.

Sharli glanced over her shoulder at Kendwa, slumped against the door with his eyes shut and an insipid complexion, his chest strained with each breath. 'Kendwa. Stay with us,' she yelled. They could hear the siren coming towards them.

Pulling up when they saw the flashing lights, the ambulance drove up in front of them. Sharli ran for the taxi's back seat, putting her hands on each side of Kendwa's face. 'Please fight this, Kendwa. I love you. Please. Please. I love you so much.' She cried, holding his handsome face, feeling how cold his skin felt.

Squeezing her hand, he blinked. The corner of his mouth turned up a little. The paramedics arrived, so she moved out of their way while telling them his statistics, as taught at university.

Kendwa was her first patient outside her practical training. Remaining calm was difficult. Inside she crumbled because he wasn't any ordinary patient. He was the man she loved.

They trolleyed him towards the back of the ambulance. Tuah asked if she wanted to catch her plane. She'd already climbed in the ambulance and was by Kendwa's side. 'No. I'm sorry. I have to go with him.'

'What about your luggage?'

'I'll pay you to drop it at the hospital. Phone me when you get there. You have my number from the booking? Thank you, Tuah.'

The paramedic closed the back doors. With sirens blaring, the ambulance sped towards the hospital.

'His vitals are improving.' The female paramedic said, smiling at Sharli. 'Are you a nurse?'

Sharli held Kendwa's big hand in both of hers. 'Recently finished my studies in Sydney. He's my first...emergency.'

'Someone special to you too. That's always difficult. You did a great job. Your assessment was spot on. You've probably saved his life.'

'And my driver, Tuah, because he knew the banded krait snake is venomous.'

Kendwa's eyes fluttered open. He groaned. On seeing Sharli, he gave a half-smile. 'Sharli. Am I dreaming?' Looking around warily, blinking, he must have realised he was in an ambulance.

The paramedic adjusted the drip's fluid.

'No. I'm here for real.' Leaning down, she softly kissed his lips, looking deep into his glazed eyes. Her own were moist, but she smiled through the tears of gratitude. 'You gave me a fright.'

Laughing, he coughed, taking a long ragged breath. 'I gave me a fright.'

Resting her head gently on his chest, she let the tears release. Moisture pooled in his own eyes as he stroked her silky dark hair. *What had he done to deserve her devotion after hurting her so much?*

What if she still left him after he recovered from the snake bite? He shut his eyes again, trying to still the terror wrapped around his heart.

Chapter 10
Borneo, Malaysia

Machines beeped, the ventilator whooshed in and out, all a reassuring sound considering what Kendwa had endured fighting the venom. Heart monitors covered his bare chest. In his left arm, a drip pumped antibiotics from a half-filled bag. An oxygen mask covered his handsome face, and the normal latte skin held a tinge of grey.

Sharli paced as she watched his chest rise and fall. Her hands clutched around her upper arms. At that moment, though she was a nurse, she hated the hospital smells of antiseptic and linoleum. The rage about Bianca had evaporated the moment she knew she could lose Kendwa forever.

Only hours before, she'd thought she could forgive him. The strong man she'd come to know looked defenceless in the hospital bed recovering from the snake bite. That vulnerability cemented what she'd probably known all along. She was madly, deeply, totally, uncontrollably in love with him.

Shoes tapped on the hard floor, coming their way. Sharli dragged her eyes from Kendwa.

'Oh my God, Sharli. I got here as soon as I could,' Rachel said as she entered the private room. Hugging Sharli, she looked over her shoulder at Kendwa. 'Is he going to pull through?'

Sharli broke their embrace, strolling towards the bed. Stroking his arm from shoulder to fingertips, lingering there, she sighed. 'Yes, he's through the worst of it. He was close to respiratory failure. His lungs were at the point of paralysis, but the anti-venom kicked in just in time. He's on the ventilator to give his lungs time to recover and his breathing to return to normal.' She sat down, taking his big hand as Rachel took a seat facing her.

'He looks so pale, for him. What happens now?'

'They said he'll stay overnight. They're amazed he survived it at all, but he's recovering well. There's no neurological damage. He'll probably be out by morning.'

'What about you? Are you going to stay now?'

Sharli paused, squeezed Kendwa's hand, glancing at Rachel with moist eyes. 'Rachel, I was so close to losing him. I can't lose him again, though I must be honest with him about my situation at home. Ultimately, he'll have to decide what he wants to do. I have to go home.'

From the bed, Kendwa mumbled. He tugged the oxygen mask and tore it from his face. Then he fidgeted with the heart monitors on his chest. Sharli stood gently, grabbing his hands. 'Kendwa, stop it. Keep still. It's okay.'

Bewildered, he looked around, then back at her. Slowly a lopsided smile broke out on his handsome face. 'I still thought I was dreaming that you were here.'

'I'm no dream, Kendwa.' Bringing her hands to his cheeks, she kissed his lips.

He glanced over her shoulder at Rachel. 'Geeze, I must have been near a goner if I have visitors.'

Rachel nodded at him. 'I'm glad you're okay, Kendwa. I'll leave you both for a sec and get some coffees.' She winked at Sharli on her way out.

'Come here,' he said, pulling her hand, urging her onto the bed in the small space beside him. Lifting his right arm, she slipped into his embrace, curling up. Her hand rested on his chest. 'I don't know what to say, Sharli.' Still hooked up to so many things, he squeezed her to him as best he could.

'Let's just never talk about the B-word again. I love you, Kendwa. That's all that matters.'

Frowning, he raised his eyebrows. 'The B-word, huh?'

Placing a gentle finger to his lips, she silenced him. 'Don't say it.' He kissed her finger then turned until his lips met hers. They kissed tenderly, then deeply. She was hungry to taste him to know he was alive.

'Sharli, I've never loved a woman the way I love you. You are my world. I'll do everything in my power to keep proving it to you every single day of our lives.'

'I thought I'd lost you…It made me realise I couldn't live without you.' Tears trickled down her face. 'I have to ask, though. What were you doing out there in the forest by yourself?'

'Running off some steam. Literally, I ran until I was out of energy. That's when the snake got me. I didn't expect it to attack, but I should heed my own advice, and that is, every wild animal has the potential to attack. Luckily I take survival supplies wherever I go. But I guess it was touch and go.'

'You had your leg strapped expertly. How did you manage to get to the road? It seems a bit superhuman.' Kissing him on the cheek, her hand stroked his chest.

'I had a guardian angel showing me the way.' Staring at the ceiling, his eyes held a faraway look, and a frown turned his lips.

Sharli cupped his face turning him back to her. 'What do you mean?'

'I know it was probably the poison messing with my head, but my mom was there. She told me, 'she will find you'. She meant you. She mentioned some other stuff too that I'm still working out.'

'Ahem!' A male nurse cleared his throat, tapping the clipboard he held with a pen.

Sharli got off the bed, looking sheepish but smiling at Kendwa, who winked.

'Why is the mask off?' the nurse asked sternly in a thick Malay accent. He checked the monitors, writing notes on the clipboard, his eyes raised in bemusement. 'Mmmm, it can come off anyway. I've never seen a recovery from a banded krait like it. You are one very strong and lucky young man.'

Sharli stepped out of the room, gratefully taking a coffee from Rachel. 'How's he doing?'

'Fantastic.' Eyes glowing, she grinned over the top of her coffee.

Rachel laughed. 'There's the look of love if I ever saw it. Did you tell him about your mom?'

'Not yet. The nurse came in. He talked about his mom and called her his angel.'

'Is she dead?'

73

'I'm assuming she is.'

'Oh, that's sad. Does Kendwa have anyone else?'

'I don't think so. I tried to bring up the family when we went out to dinner that time. He avoided talking about it, only saying something now because the poison made him hallucinate. His mom was telling him I would save him.'

'Well, you did. Maybe the ghost of his dearly departed mother actually was there. That's a bit eerie.' She shook her shoulders as if warding off the chills.

'Sure is, but it gives me so many questions. I don't know very much about him really, do I?'

'What's there to know? Gorgeous, sexy guy, who is super sweet.'

'Despite the B-thing,' Sharli interrupted.

'Yes, despite the B-thing. He is a nice guy. God, he's strong enough to recover from probably the deadliest snake in Borneo, which is kinda sexy in itself. Top it off with the fact he has a massive crush on you. You don't need to know any more than that, do you?'

'Probably not.' She smiled. 'Thanks, Rachel.'

'Sooooo, you're going to stay here?'

'I've booked a motel for two nights. Hopefully, Kendwa and I can sort something out before I fly out on Tuesday. I have to go home.'

The nurse left, shaking his head as if he'd never seen a patient like Kendwa. Rachel poked her head in the room. Kendwa waved them back in. 'Looks like he wants company. Too bad it's not my company he desires.' Rachel sighed. 'I wonder if he has a brother. When I visit you in Zanzibar, if he has a brother, we can double date.' She gave Sharli a long hug then stepped nearer the bed, kissing Kendwa's cheek. 'Look after Sharli, or I'll come after you,' she joked mock-sternly.

'I will, Rachel. I promise you I will. A soon as I get out of this god-damn hospital.'

'Rest up and do what you're told.' She wagged a finger and left.

Sharli stepped towards the bed, putting her coffee on a table. 'Visiting time's almost up. Do you want me to come and get you in the morning? I want to talk to you about a few things.'

'I'd like nothing better than you to pick me up. I've got some things I want to talk about too.'

74

She leaned in to kiss his cheek, but he turned his face, so their lips met. They kissed before she pulled away. He grinned, and she felt herself melting with the heady rush of love. 'I'll get you some fresh clothes. I can smell yours from here.' They glanced at his backpack on the floor beside the bed. 'I'll see you tomorrow.' She left before she did something stupid like climb on the bed.

When she returned in the morning, she found his bed empty. Heart skipping in fear, she clutched it, glancing around. *Had something happened through the night?*

Steam escaped the ensuite bathroom as the door opened. Kendwa limped from the bathroom with a bandage around his calf, a towel around his hips. Though he wasn't one-hundred percent well, he looked fabulous to her. His naked torso, still dripping with water, was a sight to behold.

He grinned on seeing her. Trailing her eyes from his pecs down his sinewy six-pack stomach, navel and the trail of hair below it, she threw the bag of clothes at him to distract herself.

'Good morning. You look a lot better this morning,' she managed to say. *U-N-D-E-R-S-T-A-T-E-M-E-N-T He was freshly-showered, barely-dressed, all-kinds-of sexy.*

'Thanks,' he said, taking the bag, tipping the clothes on the bed. He slipped the white t-shirt over his head. 'Perfect fit.' Lifting cream drawstring shorts, he held them in front of the towel.

'I hope those fit. I wasn't sure...'

He dropped the towel to put them on.

Holding her hand to her mouth, she looked away. 'Kendwa!'

'Oh, sorry. I wasn't thinking. That's how comfortable I am with you. I didn't think twice about it.' He turned his back to her.

She peeked through her fingers, her heart thudding. He pulled the shorts up over a firm sexy bum. *Nice!* The image of his full-frontal was still in her head. An overwhelming urge flared through her body. She was a nurse. *A penis was a penis. Wasn't it? Why then had his, rather massive one just made her womb twist?*

Finally dressed, he turned to her, placing his arms around her, kissing her forehead. 'Let's get out of here.'

His warm skin wafted with fresh soap and deodorant. It only intensified the overwhelming urge to love him intimately. Hugging him back, she hoped he couldn't sense her flaming desire. After all, they'd been through, they needed to take it slow. But there was probably no way to douse the fire in her. By the smoulder in his aqua eyes, the same applied to him.

At the small motel room, she insisted he lay on the bed to rest. 'I heard what the doctors said. Nothing strenuous for a week or two.' Switching the television on, she then paced, bitting her nails, before going to the sink to pour a glass of water. Keeping her distance was a good idea. Being in a room with a man was against her values.

Placing the water beside him, she walked to the small sofa, curling her feet under her bottom. *Distance.*

He observed her with an amused grin. 'Stop fussing, Sharli. I'm not an invalid.'

'I'm totally aware of that. I like fussing over you.' She laughed. 'You did almost die.'

'I can get used to this.' He put his hands behind his head. Neither of them paid attention to the television. It was only white noise. They couldn't take their eyes off each other. Her breath quickened, and she trailed her tongue along her bottom lip. He looks so adorable it hurt deep in her heart. *And womb.*

After a while, he said, 'You're not going to stay there, are you?'

'I'm trying to keep away from you. I'm finding it difficult to do, especially with your arms up like that.' Waving her hand at him, she pointed.

Glancing each side to his biceps, he shrugged his shoulders, which only made them dance for her. With a wicked-come-to-bed-with-me smile, he revealed his dimples. One tilt to his head and a slightly raised eyebrow undid her resolve.

Slowly she stood, strolling on wobbly legs towards the end of the bed facing him.

Patting the space beside him, he crooked a finger at her.

'You're supposed to rest up, remember.' Her hands rested on her hips, but her smile showed anything but anger. For the first time in her life, she enjoyed the anticipation of the game of love.

'I want to hold you, Sharli. We don't have to do anything you don't want to. Please come here.'

Crawling up the bed over the top of him until they were face to face, she giggled. Her hair fell like a silk curtain around them. 'I don't want you only to hold me, Kendwa. I want you to make love to me.' *Oh, my,* she'd said it.

Groaning, he grinned, kissing her, parting her mouth until their tongues danced. Breasts pressed against his chest, crushing into him until her nipples were on fire. Legs straddled his waist, pushing her pubic bone over his erection. Thick matted hair tangled through her fingers as she drew his face closer still. His hands blazed across her body, every nerve ending tingly at his touch.

Untangling herself to sit up, Sharli undid the buttons on her blouse while he held his faltering breath. He watched, mesmerised when she slipped it off her shoulders, winking.

Reaching behind her back, he unhooked her bra. A gasp escaped his lips when her breasts tumbled out. 'That there is perfection,' he said, kissing one nipple to suck it. Pausing to kiss her lips, they found the other breast. Cupping them up, he feasted on both hungrily, then resumed kissing her lips.

The kisses trailed her neck and behind her ears. He whispered, 'Are you sure about this? I told you I could wait for you.'

Breathlessly she answered, 'Please, Kendwa, yes, yes. God yes!'

Rolling over, he gently placed her beside him to shrug his shirt off as she squirmed out of her skirt. Quickly he flicked his shorts.

Locking eyes, he savoured the few seconds of being naked side-by-side. Putting a hand on each side of Sharli's shoulders, he paused before kissing down her neck, over her breasts, down her stomach, as his hands followed, slowly down to her open her legs.

Holding his hair and massaging his head, she nodded at him eagerly as he glanced up to check her approval. His fingers trailed her thatch of dark hair to outside folds of silky soft skin. His tongue darted in and out, creating exquisite moisture. Fingers rubbed her clitoris until it budded like a flower while his tongue licked and sucked, enjoying the way she thrust herself closer.

Bucking her hips, she shuddered and shook as the orgasm took hold of her. Savouring her pleasure, he didn't stop until she was sated and still. He crawled over her smiling down while she caught her breath, hair dishevelled over the pillow like waves of silk.

He reached for the side table draw where he'd stashed condoms and sheathed himself.

When her breathing slowed, he prodded her with his erection. Smiling, she nodded, groping to take a firm grip forcing him into the overwhelming desire to make Sharli his. He entered her slowly while she clung tightly to his shoulders. 'Kendwa, that was so…ah, oh.'

Cupping her bottom, he kissed her, grinding into her heavenly core. 'You are so beautifully perfect,' he said. His breathing intensified. 'Jesus, Sharli.' Feeling out of control as the pleasure rose to heights he'd never known, he reached a climax, shuddering into her and collapsing above her. Rolling off her quickly, he brought her with him, so their bodies still melded. He hugged her tightly, letting out a long breath.

Marvelling at his hammering heart and what they did, she sighed. 'You were supposed to be taking it easy and relaxing.' She stroked his chest, watching it rise and fall.

'I'd say that was about the most relaxing thing I've ever done.' He said lazily, kissing her nose, sighing contentedly.

'There are no words for what just happened. I've never felt like that.'

'I haven't either, Sharli. That was not just sex. It was making love. I adore you, sweet Sharli.'

'I love you too, Kendwa.'

They kissed deeply. *I want to marry this beautiful woman.* It wasn't the right moment to ask straight after probably the best sex of his life, tempted as he was. The last time he had done that, it blew up in his face. And he supposed asking while in bed wasn't ideal. Something romantic would work better. Something faultless for the perfect woman.

Reaching for the sheet, he pulled it over them, cuddling her closer. 'I'll follow you to Zanzibar as soon as I can finish here.'

'You don't know what my life is like back there. It's not all carefree.'

'It doesn't matter as long as we're together.'

'That's the thing, though. We wouldn't just be together. There will always be my mother.'

'I can deal with your mother. I'm sure she's a special lady, having raised a beautiful girl like you.'

Stroking his handsome stubbled cheek, she frowned. 'She was.'

'What aren't you telling me?' He rested his head on his palm as he gazed at her with concern clouding his aqua eyes.

'She needs me, Kendwa. I don't think that would be fair on you.'

'Let me be the judge of that.'

'That's what Rachel said.'

'Well, Rachel is a smart woman then. Come on, what's wrong with your mom?'

'She needs constant care. She has MS and will be wheelchair bound eventually. Her body barely functions now. My sister has cared for her while I'm away, but it will be my duty when I get back. I shouldn't say duty because I do it gladly. She's my mother. I love her dearly.'

'I don't see how that affects us.' He scratched his head.

'I have to live with her, Kendwa. I wouldn't have enough time for you to have a fair relationship.'

His strong arms tightened around her. 'We'll make it work. I have a business to build on the mainland. I won't cramp your style and be underfoot all the time.'

'You would never cramp my style.' She giggled. 'I want you to know that it's not easy looking after my ma.'

'I don't care if it's nearly impossible because we will find a way to make it work. Believe me, Sharli.'

'I believe you, Kendwa.' Cupping her bottom with his hands, he pushed his erection towards her. They made love again, this time with less haste.

Afterwards, he felt like the luckiest guy in the world. He wasn't concerned about Sharli's home situation. He'd help her care for her mother. The role would suit him because he was still raw from losing his mom. Though he didn't want to talk about his family yet, he'd be able to tell Sharli, eventually, when the time was right.

Though he knew he would never discuss Noah. *So why was Noah in his head, and why had his mom told him to find Noah?*

79

Chapter 11
Borneo, Malaysia

The screeching chatter of monkeys fighting in the forest nearby woke Sharli from a blissful sleep. The motel was empty. *Where was Kendwa?* Patting the indent where he had slept, she rolled into his spot, placing her nose on the sheet to smell him. Stretching her arms and legs languidly, she smiled.

The door opened slowly. A huge bunch of flowers preceded Kendwa into the room. Pink and white orchids. 'Hey there, beautiful,' he said with a smile.

Pulling the sheet demurely over her bare chest, she sat up. 'You should be resting up. Where have you been?'

The flower perfume hung in the hair as he brought them over to her. 'For you. I know not a practical gift when you're leaving, but they made me think of you. And I thought you'd be a little hungry.' He revealed a small brown bag. 'Sweet banana pastries.'

'I'm starving. Thank you. I was wondering if you'd done a runner.'

Looking sheepish, he rose his eyes. 'Of course not. I had some stuff to take care of.'

'You were on the phone with someone too.'

'I spoke to my boss, explaining what happened and that I'd be back in a couple of days. Then I rang my mate, Toby. He took the piss out of me for getting bitten.'

'He what?' She fake-frowned, raising her eyebrows.

'He's Australian. It's something he says, you know, like mocking someone for doing something stupid.'

'Oh.' Stroking a velvet orchid, she bit into one of the pastries. 'They are so pretty. I'd better put them in water.'

'Let me.' He took them from her, ransacking the small kitchen for a vase.

She slipped out of bed. 'I'll shower.' Naked, she strolled to the bathroom and into the shower, sliding the shower screen across. Within minutes he slipped in beside her, grabbing the soap to leisurely rub it over her body. Then he dropped it, crushing her smooth, soapy body to his, kissing her.

'I was going to let you shower alone, but I couldn't help myself when I saw you get out of bed.' He shook his head. 'Sharli, what you do to me.' Nibbling her ear, he then kissed her neck. He neatly picked her up, sitting her over his erection. Bracing his feet each side of the shower, he slowly entered her as she enthusiastically ground her hips into him, meeting his urgent thrusts.

'I don't think I'll ever want to shower alone again,' she whispered breathlessly in his ear.

He silenced her with a kiss. Muscles bulged in his arms where he held her. Panting, with her head back in ecstasy, she clung to his neck. They melded together, he deep inside her. The water and slippery soap didn't deter them, though he had to stand firm so they didn't slide. Her body quivered to a climax again and again as he simultaneously joined her. Slowly he put her down, hugging her to him, water cascading over their heads and down their slick bodies.

'Phew! That was amazing.' He kissed her wet lips. They were silent in their rapture.

'Thank you for sharing my shower.' She giggled.

'Anytime.' He grinned. 'Hey, can you please wear a pretty dress today? Not that you wouldn't look amazing in a brown bag. I have somewhere special to take you. Let's make our last day extraordinary.'

'You already have by being alive and in my life today. Are you feeling up to it, though? You're...'

'Supposed to be taking it easy. I know. What can I say? I heal quickly. I feel fine. In fact, when I'm with you, I feel like a million dollars.'

They strolled through the bustling Sandakan's markets, where he bought her a silver and turquoise bangle and a pretty yellow scarf with pink hibiscus flowers. She purchased him a canvas first aid kit. 'Just to keep you safe next time you go running in the wild,' she said, making sure there was a bandage to replace the one he'd used to splint his leg after the snake bite.

The market's exotic herbs and spices wafted through the humid air. There were large paintings of tropical Borneo scenes, carvings and jewellery. Colourful sarongs and beach clothes hung around the small stalls, flapping in the breeze.

'We'll catch a taxi soon. We've got time if you want to try the seafood first? I thought we could go to Trigg Hill Restaurant. I hear the seafood is fresh and delicious.'

They took a table, ordering a large plate of king prawns with a delicious seafood sauce with a hint of chilli. He liked the fact Sharli peeled hers expertly. Head, then tail, legs and mid-section with one flick, dipped the prawn in the sauce and popped it in her mouth, chewing with relish. Leaning over the table, he kissed her salty lips.

'Gotta love a woman who can peel a prawn like that.' He did the same to his. They chatted about Borneo and how beautiful it would be except for the palm oil plantations. They agreed on most things, particularly the wildlife.

Later, they arrived at the Sanctuary. 'Why are we here?' she asked.

'I thought you'd want to say goodbye to your friends since I delayed your flight. I also have a little surprise.'

They strolled hand in hand along the rope bridge leading to one of the clearings the orphans often congregated. When they were almost across it, Kendwa pulled the hibiscus scarf from his pocket.

She lifted her eyes in question.

'Trust me,' he said as he tied it around her head to blindfold her.

'What are you doing?' She laughed.

'Come on.' Taking her hand, they strolled for a while, her listening to the forest because she couldn't see it. Anticipation and fear raced around his heart.

Sharli heard the orangutans. Smiling, she raised the corner of the scarf. 'Kendwa, what's going on?'

'Okay. We're here.' Gently he untied the scarf.

Six orangutans surrounded Umar. Rachel stood next to Suellen, who gave little Mitto a shove towards them. In his long fingers, he held a small pillow. Sharli glanced at Kendwa, wondering what was going on. He dropped to one knee. Mitto waddled to him with the pillow but got distracted by Sharli, trying to climb her. She picked him up with a broad smile. 'Mitto, I've missed you already.' She hugged him while Kendwa attempted to pull the pillow off him. Sharli got it in hand, passing it to Kendwa, not noticing the ring tied to it.

'Sharli?'

Glancing at Kendwa on one knee, she put Mitto down. Slowly it seemed to be dawning on her what was going on.

Kendwa took her hand, showing her the solitaire diamond ring tied to the pillow. 'Sharli, will...' Untying the ribbon, he held the ring up to her.

'Yes, yes, yes!' Trying not to cry tears of happiness, she pressed her palms to her cheeks.

'Hey, let me finish,' he said seriously. Realising she'd said yes, his heart was about to burst. 'Sharli, will you do me the honour of marrying me? I promise to love, respect and protect you. I will forever be your best friend,' he winked, 'with benefits,' he whispered out of earshot of the others.

Giggling, she nodded as he slid the ring on her finger, clutched her hands and stood up. As they kissed, everyone clapped, particularly the orangutans.

'Yes, Kendwa. I will marry you and be your wife and best friend.' She tried to say it seriously, but you couldn't wipe the grin from her radiant face.

They kissed for a long time before pulling apart to stare in wonder at each other. Sharli did a happy dance with her ring finger in the air, running over to embrace her friends. They congratulated them with applause and shrieks of delight. Umar slapped Kendwa's back before shaking his hand. Sharli played with the orphans for a while and then said final goodbyes.

'Where's B?' Sharli whispered to Rachel.

'Kendwa warned her off coming anywhere near you or him.'

Kendwa and Sharli sat together at the motel on the small sofa with Kendwa's arm over her shoulder. They recapped their wonderful day and how much they loved each other. He planned to be in Zanzibar within the month. There was further research he needed to complete to start his eco-friendly resorts in Africa.

'Where do you think you'll build the first one?' she asked, amazed at how much knowledge he possessed. Kendwa wasn't just brawn. He was intelligent too.

'Probably Kenya. Dad owns...' He paused. His cheek twitched. 'I own some land there, on the edge of the Tsavo.'

'I'd like to go there with you at some stage. If I could get a carer for Ma for a small amount of time.'

'I'd like to show you the wildlife. You'd love it so much.'

She gazed deep into his gorgeous turquoise eyes, the same colour as the stone in her bangle. 'Kendwa, did your parents pass away?' she asked tentatively.

Reluctant about talking of his family, her look reassured him to try. His cheek twitched again. Pulling her closer, he gulped. 'Only Toby knows what happened to my parents.'

Gently her fingers trailed his freshly shaved cheekbones. 'It's alright. Just tell me when you're ready.' Taking her fingers, he curled them into his hand.

'They...it's only recent. It's still raw.'

She waited silently, squeezing his fingers.

'Mom...Mom had terminal cancer, but before that, we had the happiest family life, mostly,' he paused, looking up at the ceiling as if asking for the strength from someone above. 'Dad and Mom met in England. They said it was love at first sight, a bit like us.' He smiled down at her. 'He was born in Africa but went back to the USA, where most of his family lived. Dad wanted to stay in England for Mom, but he hated the cold, and eventually, they moved to Florida. Dad wrangled alligators and taught me how. We went back to Africa nearly every holiday. Dad was at his happiest saving wildlife as a ranger or taking photographs of them. Mom was real dainty. Africa didn't suit her as much, so eventually, Miami became home to them.

'When I turned eighteen, I travelled to Australia to sharpen my wrangling skills. That's where I met my mate, Toby.'

'I was wondering where he fit in.'

'Anyhow, Toby and I went to Miami a couple of years ago to work together. I returned because Mom was diagnosed. Toby because he was a bit of a nomad, and we liked hanging out together. He's kind of like a brother to me—my best mate.' He paused, rolling his tongue in his mouth, tring to find the words.

'Mom was so brave dealing with her illness. She never complained or said, 'why me'. She handled it with grace and dignity. Dad didn't deal with it. He couldn't stand that he wasn't able to save her and protect her. He raged about it. It changed him.' Kendwa stood, pacing the room, head down.

'You don't have to tell me anymore. It's upsetting you. We can talk about it another time.' Her heart broke for him.

'No. I need to get it out.' Tearing at his hair, he continued, 'Three months ago, I called in after work to check on Mom because she was on morphine by then.'

'They were alleviating her pain.' Close to dying, thought Sharli, sadly. That would have been terrible for Kendwa to watch.

'It did little. She still looked to be in agony, so frail, thin and that horrible grey colour. It was awful to see.' Wiping his eyes, he paused. 'I was so proud of how selfless she was. She always said she loved me and that she'd eternally be around. She believed in the afterlife. I guess it was the one beam of hope in an otherwise black time.

'Anyway,' he paused, blinking the tears from his eyes. 'I got to here house and knew something was wrong. I tried my key, but the door was unlocked. They always locked their doors out of habit from their London days.

'I found them on their bed.' He sat back down heavily.

'Them?'

'Mom curled up next to dad...' His eyes shifted to the ceiling. 'Dad was cuddling her. He'd sh...shot her first and then himself. There was blood, so much blood, but it was the way they were that really got to me. He couldn't live without her, but how he'd got the strength, after seeing her go, to do that to himself and still be able to wrap his arms around her after dropping the gun. It was gut-wrenchingly tragic but beautiful at the same time.'

'I understand what you mean. Their love was so strong he knew they needed to go together, and she was in so much pain.' Kissing Kendwa's tear-stained face, her tears mingled with his. 'Oh, Kendwa. No wonder you looked so angry and sad when I first met you. You were still grieving.'

Slowly he smiled, stroking her face. 'Still am. It felt good…hard but a relief to tell you about them. I wasn't angry when I first met you. You created light from that darkness. I was smitten. Seriously, I didn't know how to handle a girl like you without wrecking it.'

'You've done alright after a few hiccups along the way.' Kissing him, she smiled.

'And I even got you to say yes.' He shook his head. 'I still can't believe it.'

'How could I say no when Mitto was involved in the proposal?'

'I knew he'd be my trump card.' He smiled weakly, kissing her damp cheek.

'Played well, Mr Ely.' They high-fived. 'Wow, I'll be Mrs Ely one day.'

'Speaking of one day. Let's set a date.'

'As soon as possible, while my ma is well enough to enjoy it.'

They agreed on two months. It coincided with the Christmas holidays. It would be small— family and a couple of friends.

'I'll have to ring Toby. I'm sure he'll be my best man. Didn't think I'd be beating him to the aisle, though.' Grinning, he reached for his phone.

Kendwa rang Toby. 'I've never been happier, mate. Now I understand the power of what happened with you and Katie. Yeah, of course, we'll come to Australia for yours.'

Sharli watched the happiness on Kendwa's face as he told his best friend the news. She couldn't wait to tell Metra, her childhood friend, but she wanted to do it face-to-face. It could wait until she got home.

Happiness bubbled inside her, though she had an odd feeling about going back to Zanzibar. It was as if something terrible was going to happen. She pushed it aside, smiling at her handsome fiancé. *Big, brave, strong Kendwa is my fiancé. Why am I so scared?*

Chapter 12
Zanzibar, Tanzania

Usually, Sharli took the ferry from Tanzania's capital, Dar es Salaam to her island home, Zanzibar, but she yearned for home. The ferry, though a beautiful ride, took two hours. Instead, she boarded a ZanAir flight that would only take twenty minutes. She missed Kendwa and couldn't wait for him to return too.

From the tiny plane, below dhows and cruisers crisscrossed the Indian Ocean, coming and going from Unguja, the main island, and the smaller island Pemba and other little islands. As usual, the water was dark turquoise. It glistened as small waves whipped in the tropical breeze. Sharli smiled, feeling deep contentment to be back home.

Soon the colour of Stone Town came into view. There were minarets beside palm trees, old townhouses, shady giant fig trees, whitewashed buildings and narrow streets. It always felt magical. A mostly Swahili inspired town that still had an old-world feel.

The shoreline's rock walls dipped past the waterline, concealing the tragic ancient slavery past's tiny prison cells. A long time ago, the traders imprisoned men and women stolen from tribes on the mainland. Those still alive were shipped overseas, far away from their homeland. A statue pit depicting slavery still gave Sharli chills.

The large white House of Wonders and the timber jetty came into view as the plane banked overhead. It rounded the southern tip of the island and came down to land at Kisauni Airstrip, bumping along until it halted. The propellers slowed to a stop.

'Home,' Sharli smiled. It felt bittersweet without Kendwa, but at least he would be joining her soon. Until he did, she would make up time with her mother and catch up with her friends. Though she would have dearly loved to call into Stone Town and wander the bazaar, instead, she caught a taxi to the northeast of the island and the beachside town of Kiwengwa.

Colobus monkeys climbed trees looking for fruit as they drove through the Pongwe Forest. It smelt different to Borneo because it wasn't as humid with less rainfall. The forests weren't thick and dense like the Malay ones. The island was more sand than mud—all the smells of home. Kiwengwa's sheltered waters were the colour of Kendwa's eyes and the sand white and pristine.

When she pulled up at the modest banda hut in the little village behind Kiwengwa's beach resorts, her sister, Aashi, greeted her. They hugged warmly. 'How is Ma going?'

'She's had another bout about a week ago. They tried a new drug. Her vision isn't great. I'll show you her schedule later. First, let's have some zam zam and talk about your adventures. Ma's sleeping.'

They entered the simple whitewashed concrete home with its thatched roof and small rooms. Sharli put her suitcase away. Before returning to the kitchen, she peeked in on her sleeping mother, kissing her cheek. Scraping a chair, she sat down at the dining table across from her sister.

Sharli picked up her mug of zam zam, a spiced Zanzibari tea and smiled at Aashi. 'The taste of home.'

Aashi smiled back, raising an eyebrow. 'You look different. Happier, healthier. Studying overseas has been good for you. I'm so proud of what you've done.' Her sister was older by two years but had already been married for five with two adorable daughters a result of their young marriage.

'Where are Bela and Keshi?'

'They're at the markets with Metra. She's been a fabulous help to Ma and me. She's let me get back home to the mainland most weekends to see Achal. Or he comes here after leaving the mines.'

'I'm sorry it's been so hard on you, Aashi.' Sharli sniffed the spiced tea. Taking a sip, she looked over the cup.

'We all had to make our sacrifices. I knew it would only be for two years. It's the only way we can help Ma cope with the MS.'

90

'I know, but it's a shame I couldn't get the last two years of my scholarship closer to home. I did love Sydney, though. Australian's are so friendly. It's a beautiful trendy, happening place. I enjoyed university.' She paused, 'I learnt a lot in Borneo too.'

Aashi pulled a face. 'What? What is that look?'

Sharli smiled.

'You've met a man?'

'Perhaps.'

Aashi laughed. 'Your face always shows everything. He'd better be Hindu.'

'No, I don't think so, but he is from Zanzibar.'

'Really, how could you meet a guy from Zanzibar in Australia?'

Sharli shrugged her shoulders. 'Actually, we met in Borneo. He showed me a clouded leopard and pygmy elephants.'

'An animal lover like you. Now you have to tell me everything about him.'

'I will later, but when Ma's awake. Let's talk about how much the girls have grown in the last two years.'

They talked about the girls, laughing at their cute antics. Sharli couldn't wait to see her little nieces. Soon the chug-chug sound alerted them to Metra's car loudly spluttering outside. It was a battered-up Volkswagen combi Metra used it to transport the orphaned children in her care. There was no denying the noisy chug-chug engine.

Sharli ran out the front. Two cute-as-buttons-little girls ran to her arms. 'Aunty Sharli,' they screamed in unison.

'I've missed you two. Wow, you've grown.'

Four-year-old Bela would barely remember her, but Keshi at seven told Sharli that she'd lost two teeth while she was away and she'd done some drawings just for her.

Metra stepped from the kombi with two hessian bags of groceries, filled to overflowing. Aashi took them so the best friends could hug. Metra, as always, was dressed in long pants and a flowing shirt. A pretty hijab covered her hair and wrapped loosely around her neck. It didn't matter that she was Muslim and Sharli Hindu. They'd been best friends since they were toddlers.

'I've missed you, Meet. Can you get any prettier?'

'Look at you. You're glowing.'

91

'Ask her why?' said Aashi, winking and smiling as she ushered her daughters inside.

Metra held Sharli's hands, looking deep into her eyes. 'You're in love.'

Sharli nodded, smiling. 'Metra, he's the perfect man. He's gorgeous, loves animal, the environment He's thoughtful. He's strong, and he's even from Zanzibar.'

'Do I know him?' They strolled inside arm-in-arm.

'I don't think so. He's older than us and left Zanzibar for the mainland mostly.'

Once inside, they noticed Sharli's mother sitting on the long sofa that sometimes doubled as a bed. A blanket rested over her lap. She appeared pale and thinner than Sharli remembered.

'Salamu, Ma.' Hugging her gently, she kissed her cheek before sitting next to her. 'I love you so much.'

'I'm proud of you, Sharli. I'm doing okay. We might change the medication again, but I can't complain.'

'You never do, Ma.'

'Your sister said you may have something to tell me.' Her mother patted Sharli's hand with curled fingers.

Aashi passed her daughters a piece of bread smothered in mango jam. Shrugging her shoulders, she grinned at Sharli, licking her fingers of the sticky mango jam.

Sharli glanced at them all. They stared at her expectantly, Aashi winking. 'Well, I met someone…someone really special. His name is Kendwa Ely, and…,' she pulled a small pouch from her pocket, tipped it to her palm, presenting the ring. Sliding the ring on her finger, she lifted it. Light reflected off the sparkling diamond. Smiling proudly, she displayed it around the room, 'we're getting married.'

Aashi and Metra jumped towards each other, dancing around the room. The little girls giggled into their hands. Sharli's mother hugged her. 'I have lots of questions about your Kendwa, but I can tell he makes you happy. That's good enough for me.' She coughed. Her eyes clouded with unspent tears. 'I'm very happy for you, my sweet girl.'

'Okay. You must tell us everything. How you met? All of it.' Aashi could barely contain her excitement, holding her hands to her mouth.

Sharli raised her eyes. 'I'll start at the beginning. I was about to get in a tour boat to see wildlife up a Borneo river that meanders through the rainforest. I was thinking about animals, not men at all. When I looked up at the handsome guide it was that instant something; connection, thumping heart, the works. His bright blue eyes, handsome dark face, thick wavy hair and his...' She held her hand to her mouth. 'Sorry, Mom but he has the hottest body, big, powerful, muscular.'

'Sexy?' Metra assumed.

'Yes. So much so.'

Aashi was in fits of giggles. Metra smiled. 'Go on.'

'It's not just that. We connected on a deeper level. There's substance to Kendwa. He cares about wildlife, ecosystems and people. Seriously, can you believe he proposed with a bunch of orangutans as his helpers? I think that's got to be about the most romantic thing that's ever happened to me.'

Aashi held her stomach. 'Surely, it can't be love at first sight, and all be so perfect. You are such a dreamer, Sharli.'

'Well, we did have a small fight. A misunderstanding, really. Then a snake bit him. It was highly venomous. He could have died. The medical staff couldn't believe he didn't as if it was like superhuman. It was then that I realised I couldn't live without him.'

'Huh?' Metra asked, furrowing her brow.

'Now I'm thinking you're making the whole thing up,' Aashi said, finally composing herself.

'No, I'm not. He's truly amazing. He can climb trees as high as the orangutans too.'

'He's a monkey man,' said Bela innocently, with mango on her cute chubby cheeks.

'Well, he's very strong and fit, like a monkey.' Sharli smiled at her niece.

'Oh boy. I can't wait to meet this guy, Sharli.' Aashi cleared her children's plates, wiping their mouths with a wet cloth.

'When is the wedding?' Sharli's Mom asked, lifting Sharli's hand to admire the engagement ring.

'Two months. It will be here, of course.'

'That soon,' said Metra. They sadly glanced at her Mom, knowing why Sharli wanted the wedding as soon as possible.

Excited by thoughts of a wedding, they began planning the details of where to hold it and who to invite. Sharli said Kendwa had no family but a few old friends still on the island and a couple from Australia. They wanted to keep it small and intimate.

Now that Sharli was home, Aashi packed up her belongings and readied her children to return to the mainland and her patient husband.

'Now you can get back to normal life.' Sharli smiled.

'I know, but it's been okay. Ma and I have gotten close again. It's been good for the girls to spend time with their Nani.' They said their goodbyes.

Sharli strolled towards the beach. Though she was meeting Metra later to have a catch up while her mother slept, her home beach was drawing her to it. Salty smells of the ocean beckoned her to the beloved beach. Wading in the shallow waters would calm her mind.

The sun warmed her skin as she strolled the sandy streets, mindful of falling coconuts from the tall palms. Barely a cloud dotted the cyan sky. The sheltered water was pearl white, showing the pristine sand in the shallows, turning turquoise further out until it hit the reef where it was a darker azure blue.

A full-piece swimsuit clung to her graceful body under the kanga she wore. She slipped the fabric wrap off, relishing the feel of the East African sun on her skin. Wading into the water, she giggled at the delightful, refreshing feel of it. It was about twenty-six degrees and perfect for a swim. She dived under, surfacing to lay on her back, floating, staring at the sky.

Imagine how fun it would be playing around in the water with Kendwa. She missed him so much already—the kisses and the hugs particularly. Oh, and yes, if she was perfectly honest, she missed the sex too.

In her twenty-four years, she'd only had sex with two men before Kendwa. To her first crush Damien, a French chef who had worked at The Kiwengwa Beach Resort. They'd dated for two years before she allowed it to happen. Though he was French, he wasn't skilled. She'd never really enjoyed it. To him, it was a quick race to a finishing line she didn't know was in sight.

The second was while at university in Sydney. Bob had been a nice guy. He'd befriended her, helping her study often late into the night. It had been obvious he liked her. On one of her lonelier nights, with a bit of wine for courage, she'd had sex with him. Again, it hadn't been as nice as she'd anticipated.

Things were different with Kendwa. It was the first time she anticipated and looked forward to having sex. With him, it was making love in every aspect. She enjoyed each part of it; the lead-up, the looks of lust, the hand holding, kisses, stripping, touching and then the mind-blowing all-consuming lovemaking. It was as if they blended as one. The powerful orgasms he gave her were like a drug. Once she'd had it, she couldn't get enough of it.

Hopefully, Kendwa would get things done quicker in Borneo than expected. Clutching her heart, she missed him so much it hurt.

This was love.

Finally, she'd found it; real, true, perfect love. So why was there a niggle of fear running down her spine now and then? It was as if someone ran a bony finger along her back. Never ignore hunches, but she had no idea what was to come, just a feeling of dread. It should have been the happiest time of her life, planning to marry Kendwa.

Why then did she feel such trepidation?

Chapter 13
Lake Turkana, Kenya

The birds spooked, skirting across the lake, fleeing into the sky, narrowly avoiding the jaws of the two enormous Nile crocodiles. Water lapped the stony ground. Birds squawked overhead, long grasses at the lake edges crackled in the gusting wind.

The 7,000-km desert lake, also known as the Jade Sea, was a breeding ground for the Nile crocodiles. Kendwa often wondered why so many turtles also called the place home. Perhaps the abundant fish life kept the turtles safe from the crocs. Probably their robust shells put the crocs off them. The plentiful birds were easier meals, as were other wildlife that drank at the edges of the lake.

Kendwa watched the indigenous tribe, the Turkana, squatting in front of their mud huts on low stools, scooping turtle meat from a large shell. As usual, even where people had little technology, they still became more dangerous to animals than other apex predators.

Kendwa lifted a flat stone, skipping it across the water, swearing as he did. There was no way anyone, let alone a three-year-old boy, would survive in the Turkana waters. It was hot, windy, dangerous.

It would have been preferable to go straight to Zanzibar and into the arms of his beautiful fiance. Still, the dreams of his mother came back night after night. Perhaps the snake bite had messed with some of the neurons in his brain to think it was a good idea to revisit the lake.

Sulphur smoke broke through the blue sky, rising from one of the active volcanos of the Chalbi Desert and the crater lake islands. Kendwa pinched his nose. The smell was awful, though the place was beautiful in a weird way, especially for him. Thinking about why he had come jumbled his thoughts like twisters across the desert. If he didn't find any answers, he would give up the quest for good. *Maybe not.*

It was ironic that his whole life, he'd been protecting wildlife like crocodiles, even despite what probably happened to Noah. His father's words came back to him, 'We all share Earth, son. We can't blame animals when things happen because it's usually man's fault, to begin with. Just always tread mindfully in this world.' Most importantly, 'Be a carer, not a killer.'

Maybe his dad said those words to convince himself. Proving it with the life he led, fighting for the environment physically and with campaigns. Usually, he put his money where his mouth was, funding so many good causes that Kendwa lost count.

Kendwa promised himself that he would never speak Noah's name again if he found nothing in Kenya. Being one of the few left on the planet who knew should have made it an easy thing. The crocs surely got his baby brother. It was his fault. Glaring at the sky, he searched for Noah's face. He'd never seen it after that day. That cute cherub face he had loved more than himself.

Noting the nearby Turkana, he wondered if any were watching back when Noah disappeared. Maybe Noah had walked away from the water, but that way, the desert held the danger: wild animals, thirst and death. *Could someone have saved him out there and his family have not known?*

The tribe were closest to the area where Noah vanished. Kendwa would ask questions he wasn't sure he wanted answers to anymore. If it weren't for the dreams, he would never have come back. Waving to the tribe, he checked the ties to the hired runabout boat before striding towards them.

The Turkana were used to passing tourists. Very few ventured towards them. They were startled and unfriendly as he approached. The men wore animal hides over their shoulders and waists, elaborate, colourful beading wrapped high around their necks. Women wore wraps of woven materials. Most of the children were covered around the waist. Some played in the dirt naked.

Kendwa spoke to them in Turkana. The men looked at each other bewildered. It wasn't often a khaki dressed not-quite-white-not-quite-black man, knew their language.

An elder, the chief, smiled a wide toothless grin, his plaited, beaded hair rattling around his narrow head. Kendwa smiled back. A smile was universal.

They spoke for a bit. The older man slowly shook his head. The tribe watched him with wide eyes. One of the ancient women looked downright hostile. She glared at him with narrow eyes as she scrubbed an earthen pot, shaking her head, speaking in barely audible spitting whispers. Kendwa thanked them, strolling back to the boat, thinking maybe he'd breached some tribal protocol. He couldn't put his finger on it.

There was a campground on another side of the lake. He guided the boat there to sleep the night. It was on high ground and had a barrier fence and rangers patrolling the outskirts for crocodiles, lions or cheetahs. He usually set up his own fire and campsite, but he wasn't taking any chances when he had Sharli waiting for his return.

Once on his bunk, he gazed up at the cerulean night sky, hoping sleep would come. Picking out the constellations, he watched shooting stars hoping they were a good sign. You could barely see black night from the infinite shining stars in a place so far from civilisation.

Sharli would like those stars. He pictured her beside him holding his hand. A smile lingered on his stubbled face, but the smile faded when the old tribal woman invaded his thoughts. There was something about her bugging him. The Nilotic words seemed a warning, something about a strange woman.

Enough of the melancholy. In the morning, he would leave Kenya for Tanzania and Zanzibar. He didn't have a home to return to because his family never stayed there long enough. Without a doubt, he would make one with Sharli.

A monkey skidded in the sandy soil beside Sharli's feet when she returned to the little banda house. A bigger monkey followed, trying to retrieve the banana it carried. Sharli passed fruit to the other one. 'Here you go. Stop fighting. You can just climb up that banana tree and get your own. Silly monkeys.'

'Silly monkeys? Only you would say that,' Kendwa said, striding towards her with his arms out.

99

Dropping the basket of bananas, she ran into his arms. Lifting her off the ground, she wrapped her legs around his waist as they hugged. Laughing happily, they kissed. She cupped his handsome face squealing, 'I can't believe you're actually in Zanzibar.'

'All I've thought about is getting here and holding you. God, Sharli, I've missed you.' He put her down. 'I'd better get my stuff.'

Retrieving his suitcase and backpack out of the taxi, he paid the driver and turned to Sharli, grinning. Collecting the bananas, she kept smiling up at him.

He shifted from foot to foot. 'We haven't discussed it, but for your mother's sake, I'm going to book into one of the resorts. At least until we're married.'

Holding the banana basket on one hip, she flicked long hair out of her face. 'I was thinking the same thing. It wouldn't look good, you staying here. Ma is a liberal Hindu lady, but it wouldn't be right.'

'I respect that. It's okay, Sharli. It's the right thing to do. Besides you can come to visit me. I'll make sure I find somewhere close by.'

'I have the perfect spot. I'll just put these bananas inside and check Ma is still sleeping. She's had a relapse and is feeling fatigued.'

Returning quickly, she skipped beside him as he carried his bags. 'You're skipping. That's sort of cute.'

'I'm happy.'

'I am too. How long does your ma usually sleep?'

'At the moment, at least an hour or more.'

'We probably won't need that long. Though we could make it last if you wanted.' Smiling slowly, he winked.

A tingle went through her core, settling on her womb. 'I want it to last forever.' She blinked up at him.

'So do I, Babe, so do I. Where too?' They faced the beach. With his free hand, he shielded his eyes from the sun reflecting off the azure water.

'Up here. Zanbluu has an infinity pool dug into the sand. The rooms are cozy but with ocean views. I've done some housemaid work here and know the owners, so you'll get a good deal.'

'I don't care about the price. You had me won at the infinity pool and then cozy did something else to me.' Winking, he kissed her cheek with a wide grin.

Once he was booked in, they made their way to the room with hurried steps. There was no time to admire the perfect view because it was each other that they wanted to take in.

'Let's go slowly,' said Kendwa huskily. Untying her kanga, he leisurely unwrapped it from her body, not touching her. Keeping at arm's length, he slid the shoulders of her swimsuit down her arms, edged it away from her body, pausing to rake his eyes over her breasts, pulled it down her hips and to the floor. While he was down there, he glanced up between her legs smiling. Languorously she stroked his hair as he tore his eyes away to stand in front of her.

Dimples dug as he looked down to unbutton his shirt. Sharli watched, mesmerised as he slowly revealed his solid chest, then six-pack, navel and hair trail. He shrugged the shirt off to show his bare muscular arms. Cheekily he grinned again. Sighing, she stepped closer. They could feel each other's quickening breath and body heat.

Unbuttoning the top button of his trousers, he slowly unzipped the zipper, sliding the trousers to the ground. His underwear bulged, outlining everything. Sharli gasped. She stepped closer again, slipping her hands to his hips to glide the underwear to the floor. Her lips went ever so close to the tip of his penis. Then she stood facing him, a sexy pout on her face.

Leaning forward, he touched his lips briefly to hers before trailing to her earlobes, then her neck. Over her shoulders, his hands massaged up her neck to cup her head. Cuddling him to her, her own hands found his firm buttocks, squeezing. 'Jesus, Sharli.'

'I know,' she said as their lips crushed together. Their eager bodies collided.

'I wanted to go slow, kiss and touch you everywhere and…'

'We've missed each other too much. We can do that later. I want you inside me, Kendwa. Now. Quickly.'

'Ahhh. I'm so glad you said that.' Picking her up by the bottom as she clung to him, they kissed madly with tongues entwined, deep and needy. Placing her on the mattress, he braced his arms on each side of her.

Eyeing her thatch of dark hair where her swollen clitoris showed him how ready she was for him was his undoing. Then she opened her legs wide, guiding his penis to her. Pausing, he rubbed it against her clitoris.

Edging him on with little thrusts, he entered her bit by bit. Slowly then faster, she met his every push, consumed with the need for him inside her. He grabbed at every inch of her, trailing his hands through her luxurious hair as they came to a simultaneous, earth-shattering orgasm.

He rolled off her, keeping her in his arms. They both panted, grinning. Stroking his wavy hair away from his sweaty face, she kissed his lips. 'Wow.'

'Can it get any better?' he asked. 'You are heaven, Sharli.'

'Yes, because now we have time to do it slowly.'

'Oh babe, I want to kiss every inch of your exquisite body.'

'Ah, Kendwa.'

They explored each other's bodies from top to toe, making slow, beautiful love.

When they had showered and dressed, they strolled towards her mother's house. They tried to stay apart on the sandy track with difficulty, knowing what the locals thought of non-marital affection. It was important to remain discreet, though problematic, because they were so in love.

'Only a week, and it won't matter what anyone thinks.' Sharli looked down at the fingers that she kept away from his.

'I'll be able to take your hand any time I like once we're married. I can't wait. Will it be wrong to hold your hand in front of your Ma?'

'No. She knows how I feel about you. Of course, she doesn't realise that we've consummated that love.'

'Jeez, I hope not. I wouldn't want her to get the wrong idea about me. I love you for everything you are, Sharli. It's much more than how we make love.'

'I know. Anyway, here we are, and Ma's ventured to the porch. She must be feeling a bit better.'

Kendwa's Adam's apple bobbed.

Sharli looked up at him smiling. 'Are you nervous?'

'A bit.'

'She's my little ma. She won't bite.'

'Her approval is important to me.'

'Come on.' She crooked a finger at him. 'Ma, this is Kendwa.'

'I thought he must be. Hello, Kendwa.'

'Kendwa, this is my mother, Vedi.'

Kendwa stood awkwardly stepping from foot to foot, not knowing if he was supposed to cuddle, kiss Vedi's cheek or do nothing.

Vedi stood, reaching her thin arms around him. 'My, you are a big, strong young man, aren't you?'

Sharli giggled. 'Don't embarrass him, Ma. He's trying so hard to impress you.'

Kendwa glanced at Sharli, smiling. 'Hopefully, my strength can protect Sharli. I will do everything in my power to love, respect and protect your daughter, Mrs Ahu. I promise you that.'

A wide smile broke out on Sharli's ma's face. Despite her illness, she was still a beautiful woman. Kendwa could see where Sharli inherited her exquisiteness. They had the same long, dark, luxurious hair, though Vedi's had grey streaks. Though fifty-three, she looked no older than forty with few deep wrinkles and unblemished olive skin.

'That's enough for me, Kendwa, and the fact that Sharli has never smiled so bright. And call me Vedi. Welcome to the family.'

They walked inside the house. Sharli brewed some fragrant zam zam. She placed it on the table, passing him and her mother a cup. They sat down to talk about the wedding. With little time left, they had to get the details right.

Kendwa felt welcomed and content, but it was bittersweet. Watching Sharli's mother opened the hole in his heart. The one that only a mom could fill.

If Vedi succumbed to her illness, would that leave them both orphans? He didn't want to see Sharli endure the grief of losing her mother. Somehow, he needed to help her find a way to save her. They both couldn't be motherless. How could he ensure that? He didn't understand anything about multiple sclerosis, but he was going to find out.

103

Chapter 14
Zanzibar, Tanzania

A Zanzibar taarab band melodically played on the beach. The drums beat a steady rhythm with maracas and claves. Beside them a guitarist strummed a tune to a poetic Hindu love song.

Timber poles formed an altar, draped in white organza, flowing in the breeze, adorned in pink frangipanis, red hibiscus and orange flying plates plants with flowers like tiny bells. Thirty guests were seated in folding chairs facing the beach. In front of them was a small fire pit burned brightly, though it was still daylight.

Kendwa wore an African print shirt in shades of blue and loose white trousers with bare feet. A silk turban adorned his head. Beside him, Toby wore the same except without a turban. His crisp shirt, a lighter blue.

Toby glanced at Kendwa, raising an eyebrow. 'Can't believe you're wearing a turban, mate. And standing under an altar ready to get married.' He grinned.

'The turban is for Sharli, the Hindu part of the ceremony. The altar is called a mandap. So many religions have been part of my life it seems normal to me.'

Toby nodded. 'Katie has settled for a church wedding. I love this being at the beach. It's perfect for Zanzibar, Sharli and you.'

'It doesn't bother me what we do as long as Sharli and her family are happy with it. Again, thanks for coming, Toby. It's important to me.'

Toby slapped his back, pointing at the aisle between the chairs. At that moment Vedi stepped forward, pressing a coloured tilak dot to

Kendwa's head. He bowed. Rice, a lamp and a garland sat to the right of the mandap.

The music intensified. Aashi danced towards them in a pale pink sari adorned with colourful jewellery, clicking her fingers. She smiled at her excited daughters, who were throwing rice and flower petals in the air.

Sharli followed.

Kendwa took a breath, trying to still his hammering heart. He smiled with his face almost bursting as she strolled towards him, slightly swaying her hips in time with the music. The bright pink and red sari accentuated her trim waist. A split on one side revealed lovely slender legs and bare toes with pink nail polish. Henna tattoos wrapped her arms along with jewellery. Beads and jewelled necklaces hung from her neck, trailing over her breasts, including some Maasai beads.

A flowing pink veil with a gold Hindu headdress over her forehead adorned her luxurious long dark hair—*a princess out of a magical fairy tale.*

Kendwa reached for her hands when she drew close to him. Their eyes locked, drowning in each other's souls.

The Hindu priest directed them to the bridal bench under the mandap. Aashi came forward (as there were no brother's in the family). First, she lifted Sharli's feet and then Kendwa's, placing them in the little trough in front, washing their feet with water and milk.

Once that tradition was complete, they stood to face each other with their hands up and palms touching. Aashi lifted the pitcher of water and milk beside the trough and waited for Vedi. Slowly she walked to them her hands out as she felt the air in front of her because her sight was failing.

Touching Sharli's shoulder, she placed her palms facing the sky, above theirs. Aashi poured the liquid over their hands, blessing the union of Kendwa and Sharli.

Aashi waited for the priest to speak, moving to Sharli's right.

'We now signify Kendwa Ely's and Sharli Ahu's unbreakable bond by tying their hands together.' With a piece of cotton thread, the priest tied Sharli's right hand to Kendwa's right hand while the couple continued to smile at each other as if no one else were on the beach.

106

They sat again on the bench, facing the fire. The priest recited holy scriptures. Kendwa whispered in Shali's ear. 'You are the most beautiful bride I've ever seen. I can hardly believe you chose me.'

She whispered back, 'Believe it. We chose each other.'

Though dying to kiss her, he waited for the ceremony to unfold, knowing the importance to Sharli and her family. They were liberal about the traditions, but some Hindu beliefs were necessary.

'Please rise and walk around the fire four times reciting your vows,' announced the priest.

Still tied together, they promenaded around the fire, side by side with arms crossed and hips together. Kendwa began speaking first. 'I, Kendwa Ely, promise to love, honour, shelter, cherish, nurture, adore, treasure, appreciate and protect you, Sharli Ahu. I also promise to laugh with you, share my soul, nourish and sustain you while being your best friend and lover forever into eternity.'

Sharli smiled at the wedding guests. 'How can I match that?'

They laughed.

'I, Sharli Ahu, promise all the same things to you, Kendwa Ely. Total love encompasses everything I feel for you. I promise we will be that way for eternity too. I also promise to be the mother of your children, if we are lucky enough to have that, and shower them with as much love as we give each other. I declare my undying love to you.'

Before the priest could say anything, they kissed. The guests clapped, whistling and cheering.

Toby stepped forward with both rings. 'As your best man, with no role other than these rings.' He whispered. 'Since you didn't give me time to have a buck's party for you, I thought I'd better quickly give them to you before you take off on your honeymoon already.'

Kendwa laughed. 'Thanks, Toby.' Slipping the tiny ring on Sharli's finger beside the engagement ring, he let out a big breath.

Toby passed the bigger ring to Sharli.

Looking at it in wonder, she slid it on Kendwa's ring finger. They clutched each other's hands, gazing at the rings, hardly believing that they were truly married. The priest recited a few more things and finally declared them married. They kissed again, untying the cotton to wrap their arms around each other.

The guests dropped offerings into the fire, which crackled and hissed. The flames rose in the humid air, smelling of cloves, flowers and paper.

Metra offered to photograph the wedding. She ordered the wedding party to stand under the mandap with the beautiful ocean behind them. After the photos, people moved up the beach, where a long table was set up adorned in white fabric, multi-coloured flowers and gold candles. The candles flamed even though the sun was yet to set. Colourful lanterns hung on ropes crisscrossing over the top of the table.

Metra hugged Sharli. 'That was a magical wedding. I'm so proud to be a part of it with you.'

'You are unofficially my bridesmaid. Just because we only had one each, and it had to be my sister, you know how important you are.'

'It's okay. Mixing Hindu, Muslim, Catholic, Maasai, and Atheist would have been a bit much for Vedi to handle. It was all perfect the way it was. Now let's celebrate with the divine food the waiters are placing on the table.'

The girls strolled arm in arm towards Kendwa, hugging an old African man much smaller than him. Kendwa was laughing as he turned towards them.

'Ah, here is my beautiful bride. Jambi, this is my wife, Sharli.' His voice was filled with pride as he smiled at the older man, who took Sharli's right hand, grinning a wobbly grin. Rheumy eyes danced in his wizened dark face.

'It's wonderful to meet you, Sharli. I can see you've made Kendwa a happy man.' Like a blessing, he kissed each of her cheeks.

'Thank you, Jambi. It's so nice to meet one of Kendwa's friends.'

Kendwa said, 'Jambi has known me my whole life. He was my father's best friend. The finest fisherman around. That's the only thing he and dad ever disagreed about. Dad loved land and bush. Jambi's greatest love was the ocean.'

'The ocean still is,' said Jambi, smiling wide, glancing out to sea. 'I miss your father.' His look was far away, as if searching for the USA.

Kendwa patted his thin shoulder. 'Me too, Jambi.'

Metra softly spoke to Jambi, who supplied most of the fish to the women's shelter where she volunteered.

Kendwa took Sharli's hand. Leaving footprints in the sand, they made their way along the beach, out of earshot.

'He seems sweet,' said Sharli, glancing back at Jambi. It was sad that Kendwa only had Jambi and Toby at the wedding. Toby hadn't even brought Katie because she discovered she was pregnant and didn't want to risk coming to Africa, believing it to be full of disease and danger.

'He's a great old guy. But I want to talk about you, my wife. How are you feeling?'

'Wonderful,' she leaned up, kissing his lips. 'Blessed and the happiest I've ever been.'

He kissed her hungrily. 'Me too. I have so many plans for us. We are going to have a beautiful life together. Once the eco-resorts are into profits, you'll be able to live like the princess you are today.'

'Oh, Kendwa, I don't need to be treated like a princess. I wouldn't care if we were poor as long as we are together.' They kissed again. People called their names.

Turning to see more food placed on the table and guests sitting down to eat, Kendwa said, 'We'd better join them.' Giving her another kiss on the cheek, they returned with arms comfortably around each other's waists.

'To the bride and groom,' announced Toby raising a glass of wine. Alcohol was only allowed on the beach for approved weddings and functions. Adhering to the Muslim customs of the island was an essential part of Zanzibar life.

Kendwa and Sharli sat mid-table with the beach to their backs, allowing the photos to include the beach. Toby was to Kendwa's left, Metra to Sharli's right. Aashi had joined her family and mother on the other side of the table.

'Ma looks so happy, Metra.' Sharli smiled across at her mother, who looked ethereal as she spoke to the friend beside her.

'Yes, I think this wedding has been good for her. She seems to have so much more movement in the last few weeks.'

'I hope that can continue, and she stays in remission.'

Kendwa's large hand absently stroked her thigh. Placing her own on top of his, she squeezed it. He smiled. 'Are you enjoying yourself?'

'Of course. It's perfed as I imagined. Everything is impeccable. I was thinking, though, since Toby has come so far to see you, you should both go out before he leaves.'

Toby leant in front of Kendwa, raising his glass to Sharli. 'I was just trying to convince him of the same thing.'

Kendwa shook his head. 'I can't do that to you, Sharli. We just got married.'

'I didn't mean tonight because tonight is our honeymoon, but the next night is fine. Perhaps Metra and I will come out with you for a while and go home early to leave you boys to discuss whatever it is you do.'

Toby bumped Kendwa's shoulder with his. 'Come on, mate. Sounds like a plan to me. Listen to your wife.'

Kendwa raised his eyes at Sharli for reassurance. Smiling and nodding, she squeezed his hand tight.

Kendwa glanced at Toby, who had his eyes wide and hopeful. 'Okay, only because my wife is the most awesome wife in the world.' The boys high-fived.

The women rolled their eyes.

Once everyone was full, the guests mingled and danced to the band. The music transitioned to a mix of rap and rock. The lanterns glowed in the night, illuminating the beach.

Sharli, head resting on Kendwa's chest, snuggled closer to him as they danced slowly. 'Let's say goodnight to everyone and start our honeymoon,' she suggested.

'I was about to say the same thing myself. As soon as Aashi took your mom home, I've been thinking about it.'

She giggled. 'Me too, and lots more than once or twice.'

Through the thin fabric of her dress, he pinched her bum. He followed her around to say goodbye to people he hardly knew. They'd all been accepting of him, kind and gracious like his bride. Slapping each other backs, he and Toby hugged and said goodbye.

Once at the resort, the newlyweds wasted no time. 'I know we should be savouring this but watching you look so sexy and gorgeous all day has been doing something crazy to me, babe.'

Kissing with bodies pressed against each other, she managed to say, 'When I first saw you, with the backdrop of the water. You wearing those loose pants, where I could see the outline.' She stroked his penis. 'And your shirt unbuttoned to show your chest, with the sleeves too tight on your amazing arms. Your hair covered by a turban. Your handsome face and eyes watching me with that special smile you give only me.'

Their hands explored.

'Mmmmm.'

'Well, seeing you made me feel like I could barely breathe. I pinch myself that it finally happened.' Running her hand through his cropped hair, she continued, 'I can't believe you got a haircut either. I like the feel of it shorter. It's like carpet.' She massaged his head.

He hushed her with another kiss.

'Can you undress me now, husband?'

Grinning at the way she said, 'husband', he quickly helped her out of the sari as he managed to disrobe as hastily as he could. They eagerly, though slowly, made the sweetest of love for the first time as husband and wife. Making sure of showing her his affection, he showered her body with kisses, touching all the places he already knew she loved. To his pleasant surprise, he found a few more.

She explored him too. When her lips hugged his penis for the first time, his ecstasy at the intimate moment broke something in him. It was nothing like the seduction of Bianca. It was tentative and sweet like she'd never done it before but wanted to love and pleasure him. Stroking her hair, he gazed down at her. 'Honey, you don't…'

'I want to. Kendwa, you've adored me everywhere. I want to do the same for you.'

With her mouth hungering around him, he couldn't argue with that. The exquisite love motions made him ready to burst. Before he did, he gently rolled over so that she could straddle him. There was intoxicating wetness to her as he lifted her delightful bottom, placing her onto him. He entered her bit by bit, controlling his need for her, so she was as ready as him.

As he felt her body blending in the exquisite bliss of their lovemaking, his thoughts became clear. *I am finally home.*

Chapter 15
Zanzibar, Tanzania

The booming ocean tide, hitting the outside reef, lulled Kendwa as he yawned, turning his head to his sleeping wife. The thought struck him, twisting his heart, as his chest expanded like a balloon. Gazing at Sharli, he felt soft and fragile. Though he had promised her he'd be strong, something about her made him feel pathetic and weak. She didn't need feebleness. He had to be tough. Admiring her long eyelashes and beautiful face, he sighed, feeling the most vulnerable he'd ever felt. Swallowing the lump in his throat was difficult.

The helplessness wasn't for himself, of course. It was the responsibility of protecting Sharli, having failed at that duty before. Though he tried to get the monkey off his back, it climbed back on at the thought of failing her. Trying with all his might to ignore those fears, he knew the alternative was untenable. *What if one day he did fail her?*

Eyelashes fluttering, she let out a sweet little sigh, waking up to look at him. Immediately her face broke into a heavenly smile.

'Hey there, my adorable wife,' he said, kissing the tip of her nose.

Squishing her small body into his, so her nipples and breasts teased his chest, she said, 'Good morning, my husband. It feels perfect waking up in your arms. It's like a dream.'

'I know how you feel. I've been watching you while you sleep, wondering how I got so lucky.'

They kissed for a while until the boisterous tourists arguing outside their door distracted them. Kendwa stretched his arms. 'Today starts the rest of our lives. I thought we should make some plans. First, I need a better look at your mother's house. I want to build some ramps for the

113

days she needs the wheelchair. Because of her eventual blindness, we need a place for everything so she can get around without bumping into things.'

Sharli rested her head on her hand, gazing at him. 'You would do all that for my ma? You are amazing.'

'Nothing amazing about it. She's my mother-in-law. I need to make her life and yours easier. I figure you must have studied nursing to be able to look after her. I think *that* is amazing.'

'I did it for that reason but also because I like helping people. I wanted to work in Zanzibar at the hospital or medical centre. I asked about work when I got back. There's nothing casual yet. I couldn't work full time the way Ma is getting.'

'You don't have to work. I'll worry about that. You do what you need to for your mom. I'll have to head back to the mainland in a few weeks. I need to start on your mom's place straightaway. If I build an extension, we can live with her separately enough to feel like husband and wife. The sooner I begin, the better.'

'Not today. It's our honeymoon. I want you to myself. Besides, Aashi is staying for a couple of days. This afternoon we'll meet up with Metra and Toby and sort out somewhere nice for dinner. Then I want you and Toby to stay out before he goes home. I'm sure you have a lot to catch up on.'

Kissing her deeply, his hands roamed her bottom, moved to her hips and then between her legs. 'You are the perfect wife. Have I told you that?'

'Just show me, Kendwa. Just show me.'

And he did.

Late afternoon they were sitting at the Bravo Club under its high thatched roof, facing the unbelievably blue view of the pool and further out to the reef. The boys had a bottle each of Kilimanjaro Lager, Sharli, a glass of Zanzibar Cellars white and Metra nursed a glass of water.

Toby was in a cheerful mood, telling funny stories about the wrangling of crocodiles and alligators. The girls hung off every word, as Toby expected.

'I can't believe you did all those things,' said Metra.

'I can,' said Sharli. 'Kendwa climbed a tree with the orangutans in Borneo. I couldn't believe a man could get that high up.'

'We used to swing from vines and flip into waterholes in north Queensland.' Toby laughed. 'Of course, we always made sure they were safe from crocs.'

'So, has the move back to Australia with Katie settled you down any?' Kendwa grinned over the top of his beer at his best friend.

'Not straight away. I wanted to head north and wrangle again, but when Katie found out she was pregnant, we decided against it. We're at my parents at Currumbin until my placement comes in at Taronga Zoo with the reptiles. They're looking for a specialist advisor for the African enclosures too. That would be a terrific job for you, Kendwa. It's only temporary.'

Sharli looked up at Kendwa, a frown on her face. Shaking his head, she smiled at her reassuringly. 'I couldn't do that, Toby. I've got a lot to do here. This is our home now.'

'Yeah, I know, but think about it. The project doesn't start for six months, and that's when you'll be over for my wedding after the baby is born. You could take the three-month contract. It's exceptional money, and you're about the only one I know who could do it right.'

'I'm tired from our early start yesterday,' said Metra. 'I think I'll call it a night.' Holding her fist to her mouth, she yawned.

'Yes, and I want to call in on Ma and Aashi. I need to check on Ma's meds and sort out her schedule for next week. Plus, it's time you boys had your own time together.' Sharli stood. 'I'll see you in the morning to say goodbye before you fly back to Australia, Toby.'

Kendwa stood too. 'I'll walk you both.' Sharli affectionately brushed his shoulder with her hand

'No. Metra and I will be fine. We'll go back together. You two stay.' She leant up, kissing Kendwa's lips.

'If you're sure.'

'Yes. I'll see you later tonight.'

The girls left. Toby proceeded to the bar for more beers. They clinked bottles when he returned. 'To our women and us,' said Toby. 'Man, I can't believe it happened so quickly. Girlfriends, wives and a soon-to-be baby.'

'How do you feel about the baby?'

115

Toby smiled, holding his heart. 'It gets me right here. I can't wait to meet the little person I'll call my son or daughter. The moment Katie saw the blue line, she was in shock, but I was like, yes and fist-pumping. I was so happy I picked her up and swung her around the room. Then I realised she was crying. I'm like, honey, this is great. I'm pleased. I'm overjoyed. She says, did you even think for a moment that I'm not ready for this. She stormed out of the bathroom and didn't talk to me all night.'

'I'm sorry, Toby. That must have been hard.'

'It was. I needed to scream it to everyone. Katie didn't even want to acknowledge she was pregnant. Anyhow a week later, she was back to normal, being my gorgeous, cute Katie girl. She told me she was just shocked it happened so quickly with us and that she wanted to be married first.'

'Do you think that's all it was?'

'I hope so. I don't want to think otherwise. Katie's a complicated girl at times. My mum hasn't warmed to her, you know. Which annoys me.' Sipping his beer, Toby lowered his head.

'Crystal? Serious? She loves everyone.'

'Mum loves you, Kendwa. She doesn't love everyone she meets. That clairvoyant thing she thinks she has, gets in the way. When she has a certain vibe, she goes with it. She acknowledged she probably had a bad day when she met Katie and apologised. Of course, to appease me, she said she'd try harder, but it irks me.'

'That's tough, but I know how your mum feels. I get on edge with people I can sense have some deeper agenda than they're revealing. Of course, Katie is fine, and your mum is overprotective. My creepy instincts are usually about poachers.'

'Ha! I thought your good instincts were women and wildlife.'

Kendwa grinned. 'The womanising is over. Finding Sharli has made me realise that there's only one woman for me.'

'Yeah, I feel the same about Katie, even with her complications. That's just a challenge for me. I've never been happier.'

'Me either. Cheers to that.' They clinked drinks again as two well-dressed women, who'd been eying them off from the bar, sauntered towards their table.

116

Before they even got there, though Kendwa had his back to them, he put his hand up, showing his wedding ring, frowning at Toby. 'They're still coming, aren't they?'

'Yep.' Toby rolled his eyes, nodding.

One sat beside Kendwa. The other sidled over near Toby. Kendwa said through grit teeth, 'Ladies, we'd prefer our own company.'

The tall, pale English woman beside Kendwa said, 'Oh, that's a shame. We're tourists looking for English speaking men to share a table and light conversation.'

Abruptly Kendwa said, 'Try over there.' He pointed to a rowdy table full of twenty-something-year-old men.

'You look much more interesting,' she said. 'Wow, your eyes are the most amazing eyes I've ever seen.' Stroking his shoulder, she stared at his hostile face. 'My, you are well built too. What a package.'

Kendwa moved his chair out of her reach. Her bottom lip dropped. She eyed Toby.

The other woman, a cute redhead with freckles, had hold of Toby's hand. 'No wedding ring on your finger. That's a good sign.'

Toby pulled his hand away. 'I'm engaged. Have you ever seen a man wear an engagement ring? Please, ladies, you'll have more fun company with some other blokes. We're catching up and would prefer our own company.'

The woman on Kendwa's side put her chin on her hand, facing Toby. 'You have the sexiest Aussie accent. It's a shame you don't want to talk to us. I'd love to keep listening to it.'

Kendwa's jaw twitched. When he noted Toby smiling at the woman, he rolled his eyes. Toby had always been more of a pushover than Kendwa.

The woman then turned to Kendwa, wriggling close enough for him to smell her wine breath. 'I'm as horny as a hare on heat and looking at you two sexy guys. It would seem such a waste not to at least try to seduce you. We could even have a foursome.'

Kendwa stood, knocking back his chair. It clattered to the floor. 'Sorry ladies, but I'm happily married and un-seducible by any woman other than my wife.'

Toby stood too. 'The same goes for my fiancé and me.' He glanced at Kendwa. Quickly they left the bar. 'Man, you saved me then. The

117

redhead had her hand close to my crotch. Back in the day, I would have jumped at that opportunity.'

'Those days are over for us, and we're damn lucky to have found the women we have. All I can think about is Sharli. I hope very soon we'll be able to announce a baby too. Wouldn't it be something if our wives both had little ones around the same age?'

Toby patted Kendwa's back. 'That sure would be something. Let's find a quieter bar.'

'I'd be ready to head home,' Kendwa said.

'Nah, come on. I came all the way to Zanzibar for your wedding.'

'So you keep reminding me. Okay, one more.'

At least another four more, and the boys drunkenly staggered back to the motel. Kendwa dropped Toby at his room, showing a bit of man love when they stayed hugging at his door. Kendwa pushed him off. 'Tobes, were you starting to snore?'

Toby scratched his head. 'Maybe. Night, Kendwa.'

Kendwa tried tiptoeing into his room, but the light switched on. He shielded his eyes from the brightness, blinded by the light.

'It's after midnight,' Sharli said. 'I was getting worried.'

Grinning lopsidedly, he tried to shrug his trousers off, losing his balance, wobbling and grabbing the wall. 'It's Toby's fault. You shouldn't worry, babe. I'll always come home to you.'

'You're a bit drunk.'

He put his hand up. 'Again, let's blame it on Toby.'

'You're a grown-up, Kendwa.'

The smile froze on his face before turning to a frown. 'I'm sorry, babe. It was our last guy thing. I wanted to come home half a dozen drinks ago.'

She got off the bed. Unashamedly he admired her nakedness. 'Do you need help?' she asked.

'Man, it's so good to come home to this. You are so beautiful.'

She lifted her arms, her boobs jiggling as she slipped his t-shirt over his head, kissing his chest. 'Come to bed.' Reaching for her, he nearly fell over as she moved out of reach.

Slipping back under the covers, she tapped the bed. Crawling in beside her, he spooned his body to hers. His big hand cupped one of her breasts.

118

In moments he was snoring on her neck. Sighing, she pulled the covers over them both.

It felt so good to have him home safe and warm beside her, but something niggled her. She hoped it was indeed the last time he would come home drunk to her. It reminded her of his excuses about Bianca and being too drunk to stop her.

Where had he been all this time? Had he been faithful? She crushed her hands to her ears to try to stop such thoughts. Annoyingly, her eyes filled with tears. Kendwa was her husband, and she trusted him. Feeling the rise and fall of his chest rise against her back did not quell her concerns as tears slipped down her cheeks.

Chapter 16
Maasai Mara, Kenya

The lion opened its jaw wide, exposing sharp yellow teeth. It roared as if appreciating its meal, with blood matted over its chin and through its long mane. The lionesses fed on the disembowelled impala, soon followed by the eager cubs. The male lion rose slowly, shaking his huge head with mane swaying. He ambled away from the pride, satisfied with the feed.

'You see. It's much better when lions have enough food and don't go near our cattle,' said the Maasai herdsman.

Kendwa dropped the binoculars, smiling. 'The biodiversity here is improving?'

'It's all about education. Some of the older tribes don't understand what we're trying to do to sustain land, water, livestock and wildlife. There's a fine balance.'

'Yes, there is. Thank you for showing me what you've been doing out here. I'm sure it will help me find that equilibrium with eco-safaris and self-sustainable accommodation.'

'I'm sure you will, Kendwa. You'll probably receive an eco-warrior award as well. It's a shame our government won't listen to what we have to say often enough.'

'They would learn so much. Hopefully, one day soon, you'll receive the same rights as other indigenous people around the world.' They shook right hands. Kendwa climbed into his open jeep, driving towards the east.

At the Maji Moto Eco Camp, he was enthused by what he saw. It was a true Maasai village, made by the locals. A tall Maasai greeted him in red robe. Striking beaded jewellery adorned his traditionally tattooed chest and arms, and earlobe drooped from heavy bone earrings.

'No trees were felled during construction of the camp,' he told Kendwa. 'And you'll see here,' he tapped on a solid wall, 'it's composed of dung, sticks, stalks, stone and grass. It provides good insulation, so we don't need heating.'

Kendwa observed the building as he stood on the natural flat-rock paved deck. The thatched wide pergola roof structure was supported by tree trunks and branches, giving a naturally bent but sturdy structure. At one end was a bar made up of reeds that looked like cane. The same materials had crafted furniture and seats. Plain timber trestle tables were surrounded by khaki director's chairs, looking out to the broad escarpment view toward the savannah and further to the Maasai Mara.

San, the host, smiled wide. 'You like our camp.' It wasn't a question.

Kendwa smiled back at him. 'Wow. I love it.' Leaning on one of the narrow tree-trunk support beams, he tested its strength. 'Very strong. All-natural.' Rubbing the wood, he gazed at it in wonder. 'You've done a fine job.'

'Thank you. We don't often have guests this time of year. You're the only one today. I'll share a sundowner with you unless you prefer your own company.'

'I'll shower and join you. I love how you use the nearby hot springs for your water. Everything is self-sustainable. I'm in awe.'

'That's where we got the name from, Maji Moto, hot springs.'

Kendwa strolled to the double tent with a front deck facing the view. A worn knapsack sat on one of the low beds. Being dog tired, he glanced longingly at the other. Rummaging for fresh clothes, he pulled out long trousers and a jumper. He then strolled down to the bathroom. It was an open shower, surrounded by rocks and blocked off with an orange shower curtain. The vanity basin sits in the rock surrounded by bamboo.

'Nice,' said Kendwa as he let the warm fresh spring water wash over his body. He wished again that Sharli could have taken the trip with him. It was hard being away from her for three weeks, but he had to start investing his inheritance in something of substance. Without research, he couldn't proceed with it properly. He was enjoying the exploration side but feeling lonely nonetheless.

122

Looking down at his penis, he spoke to it, 'You're missing her too aren't you, buddy?' He could jerk off but felt it wasn't right. Sharli was all he needed. It would be some homecoming with all his pent-up sexual desire for her. A woman had never distracted him more than his wife. He groaned, letting the water dilute his thoughts.

San was waiting for him with a couple of Tusker Lagers. Passing an open one to Kendwa, they clinked bottles. Raising them to their lips, they drank in the cold beer and the spectacular golden sunset over the savannah. 'Got to love a sundowner in the middle of Africa,' said Kendwa.

'There's not much better in life.' San crossed his long legs at the ankles, leaning back in his chair. 'You've been around here before as a young boy?'

Kendwa narrowed his gaze at San. 'I thought we'd met before. Yes, my family used to come past here. My dad was part of the Kenyan Wildlife Service. He would oversee the rangers and keep projects on track.'

'Mmm, I remember him. Great man. He spoke Maa well. He did a lot of good. His name was Jamal, wasn't it? I was in my twenties; you would have been about fourteen the last time you were here. Is that correct?'

'Yeah, that was my dad. You have a good memory.' He looked closer at San. 'I know, you helped him that time that elephant calf got stuck in that ditch. I remember you falling in next to it, with so much mud on you we couldn't see you.' He raised his beer with a laugh.

San hooted, slapping his thigh. 'No wonder the poor little fella was stuck, then I got stuck too.'

'It was pretty funny with the calf's mum and aunties getting irritated at our lack of progress and you needing to be pulled out as well.'

'You were a strong young boy, grabbing hold of the rope with your dad and the rangers to get us out.'

They went silent, watching the orange orb of the sun sinking in the west until darkness descended over the vast savannah. San had already lit a fire. It seemed bigger and brighter against the starry black sky.

'I've got some mutton with bush spices wrapped underneath the coals. Should be ready soon.'

123

Kendwa put his empty bottle down. 'I'll shout us one more.' San nodded towards the bar. When Kendwa sat back down, passing San a drink, he asked San, 'Do you believe in spirits visiting us? I know there's your god Ngai. It's just I keep having these visions.'

'Of course. Spirits guide us in some way. What are these visions? And what are they telling you?'

'It's usually my mom. She's asking me to look for Noah, which is annoying and stupid because he's dead. Then she tells me to find the elephant cave. It doesn't make sense to me.'

'I'm no expert. Maybe you'd be better talking to our clan's Laiboni.'

Kendwa put his beer down, stretching his arms high, clinking his neck, relieving the stiffness from driving. 'Mmm, a witch doctor. Maybe.'

'The elephant cave could be Mt Elgon, Kitum Cave. The elephants go into the caves there and scrape the walls with their tusks. It's rich in sodium salts that they break off to eat.'

'That's something I'd forgotten that elephants did. Funny how they know the salt is there. It's to add salt to their diet. They are amazing animals, aren't they?'

'That they are. Do you want to meet our Laiboni?'

'Yeah, I should. It may give me some answers. Then maybe I'll know whether I need to explore those caves or not.'

'You'd better get the Laiboni to protect you from the Marburg virus if you are going to the caves.'

'From the bats?'

'They're not sure but probably.'

They enjoyed their delicious meal in silence, savouring every mouthful. 'Thanks, San. That was just what I needed.'

Saying their goodnights, Kendwa ambled to his tent. Staring at the canvas ceiling, thinking about his wife, he lay on his bunk. Glancing at his watch, he realised it wasn't too late. Fishing his mobile phone out of his bag, he swore at the no bar signal. He tilted his head, achieving one bar, hopefully, enough to get through to her. Hoping, he dialled.

'Hey, gorgeous,' he said, feeling his heart lurch.

'Funny, I was about to ring you. I miss you.'

'I miss you too, babe.'

'How's it going?'

124

'I've sorted the first site and talking to builders but trying to get the biodiversity side in sync is more problematic than I'd imagined. There's a lot to consider.'

'I'm sure you'll do it, my clever husband.'

'I'm staying at an eco-lodge near the Maasai Mara. Everything is made from local sources, twigs, grass, cow dung, stones, branches. Their hot water comes from a natural spring. You would have loved the sunset.'

'Describe it to me.' He did so with a smile. They talked for a further twenty minutes before saying goodbye, though the reception wavered at times. She sounded a little stressed, which bothered him, but she said she was fine.

The next day he found himself sitting in front of a Maasai shaman, wondering why he was bothering. The Laiboni shook bundled grass over Kendwa's head, blessing him, then went into a trance, speaking in tongues.

The shaman, an old woman with a saggy shaven head, was dressed in lion pelts. Her dark skin shone with the animal fat rubbed over her body. A bone necklace with lion and leopard teeth wrapped around her craggy neck. A scary sight to most westerners, but that didn't faze Kendwa. He only wished she'd get to the point.

Rheumy eyes lifted and cleared. Eerie words were spoken in Maa. Kendwa understood enough of it. 'I see a man, younger than you but like you. He has a guitar. He sings of a forsaken family.'

Kendwa stared at her. What younger man? Maybe Toby. They were often mistaken for brothers, though Toby was fairer than Kendwa. He did play the guitar. What did it have to do with anything?

Putting an arthritic hand up, she paused, closed her eyes, then snapped them open again. 'Your mother tells me. You must find him. The elephant cave may give you answers.'

Kendwa felt a chill run down his spine. How could she know what his mother had told him in his dreams? *Too creepy.*

She began to sway. 'Woman. White. Alone. Sick. Wanted a child.'

'Who? What woman? What child?'

'Go to the elephant caves.'

Kendwa raked his hand through his hair. 'But what do I do when I get there?'

125

Saying nothing, she stared at him with bloodshot eyes until he couldn't hold her gaze any longer. Goosebumps pricked his arms. Shaking the bundle of grass over his head, she stood, leaving without a further glance.

Kendwa rose slowly, shook his head and kicked the stones at his booted feet. If he drove to the caves on the Kenyan, Ugandan border, it would put him behind schedule to return to Sharli. Perhaps he could do it another time, but the shaman had stirred something in him. There may be answers at the caves. Unfortunately, the Laiboni gave him more questions than answers.

After thanking San for his hospitality, he began the drive north to Mt Elgon National Park. Driving through the park entrance, he paid the 300 shillings' entrance fee. A herd of red duiker chewing on the low grass barely lifted their heads as he passed.

The road opened to the campsite where he parked. Retrieving his backpack, he checked his supplies, particularly bandages, water, DEET insect spray, and a torch. Leaving the jeep behind, he started up a dirt track. Soon he traversed the rocky hills, passed bubbling streams, lush forests and long grasses. Baboons watched him from the trees, and bird calls sounded like an out-of-tune orchestra.

The ground steepened as he came close to a vast caves' entrance. A herd of elephants wandered outside a cavern. Somehow, he knew this was the one he needed to enter.

A large entrance narrowed around the rock as Kendwa slowly walked inside. He wondered how the elephants squeezed through a space a lot smaller than the largest of the pachyderms. As he strode inside, chills ran down his spine. Feeling the salty dampness, he ran his hands along the creviced walls of the cave. Elephant tusks etched telltale scratch marks in the rocky outcrops. Putting a finger to his lips, he tasted the salt. The elephants would go 60 metres further inside to the softer rock. Switching on his torch to light the way, he checked the compass on his watch before proceeding further.

Salty, smelly damp air assailed his nostrils—elephant droppings scattered along the ground where a herd had passed. With keen eyes, he examined the newly scraped part of the rock wall. It felt wet, crumbling under his fingers. There were smaller marks down very low where the tiniest of calves would have been learning to feed. Two metres or more above him were scratches from the older elephants.

'What an amazing place.' The underground springs flowed and dripped somewhere further along the tunnel. Moving towards them, he shone the torch until it reflected off the water. He scooped some in his hands. It was cool but clear. A bat swooped overhead, its wide wings sounding louder in the echoic space. Ducking, he thought of the disease they carried. 'Other than seeing another inspiring place, I haven't found a thing. You dumb shaman,' he yelled, his voice echoing off the walls.

As he started back, something on one of the rock ledges caught his eye as it deflected off his torchlight. Climbing a lower ledge for a better look, he hoped the crumbling shelf would hold his weight. On it was an oil lantern. Under it sat a small leather-bound journal. He lifted the lantern, picking up the book. It felt damp. *Probably ruined.* He pocketed it anyway. Maybe he could dry it and see who owned the journal. Making his way towards the entrance, he faced an elephant trying to enter the cave, blocking his way out.

Flattening himself against the wall, he moved off to the side near the spring, pushing himself into a crevice to give the elephants room to pass him. He watched, mesmerised as they strolled past him. They glanced at him with intelligent eyes framed in long thin eyelashes as if they wondered what a man was doing there, but they were unconcerned by him. The ground rattled under their weight. Parts of the cave walls crumbled when they squeezed their bulky bodies around walls.

The second last of the seven elephants was a calf. Probably only about twelve months old. It still had tufts of hair and paler patchy skin. It looked at Kendwa, lifting its small trunk. Startled, it bumped into the legs of the elephant in front. A larger elephant followed it, moving the baby along with its thick trunk, with long tusks trailing near the ground.

Kendwa chuckled. *The things you see in Africa.* He couldn't wait to tell Sharli about the wildlife encounter. Once the elephants moved on, he strolled out into the sunshine, feeling euphoric as he always did in the wild.

The journal dampened his jeans. Patting the pocket to feel its bulk, he wondered who owned it. *What words were within its pages? Could any of it be relevant to his search for what happened to Noah?*

Chapter 17
Zanzibar, Tanzania

'Babe, you're doing great. Keep climbing. Don't look down.' Kendwa yelled to Sharli, who was halfway up a coconut tree. Slipping a little, she clung to the tree tightly. 'Okay, come down now. I'm here.'

Kendwa stood at the bottom with his arms out, ready to catch her if she fell. As she wriggled her way lower, he eyed her delicious bum and smooth brown legs. Slowly she climbed down towards the ground. 'I got further up than I thought I would,' she said breathlessly. About a metre from the ground, she let go of the tree. Kendwa caught her neatly.

'That was the best beginners climb I've ever seen. You're a natural.' Kissing her forehead, he put her down. Shielding her eyes from the sun, she grinned up at the tree.

'That was fun, but there's still a coconut up there that I want. I'd try again, but it's exhausting.' Raising her eyebrows, she grinned at him.

Without hesitation, he leapt onto the tree, wrapping his arms and legs around the trunk. Agile as a monkey, he climbed it. Taking the knife from his belt, he slashed a coconut free. 'Is one enough?'

Stepping back away from the falling coconut, she called, 'No, please get the other two. I want some fresh coconut water to rehydrate. I've been feeling the heat, and you will when you're working in the sun today.'

Slashing two more, he made sure they landed away from her, then climbed down the tree. Leaping off at the end, he landed neatly, grinning. Lifting the other two coconuts, he cradled them in his arms.

'There's a gorgeous waterfall on the mainland that I'll take you to one day. It's got some seriously huge vines. I can teach you to swing into the water.'

She shifted the heavy coconut in her hands. 'I'd like that.' They strolled back to her mother's house. Vedi was sitting on the bench seat out the front with a colourful kanga over her lap. 'Hi, Ma, how are you feeling now?'

'I couldn't hold the kettle to pour zam zam earlier. Just now, I couldn't see you two until you were right in front of me, but other than that, I'm fine.'

Sharli kissed her cheek, sitting down beside her.

'I'll leave you ladies to it. I've got more construction to do out the back.' He passed Sharli the coconuts, strolling away.

'Ma, aren't those meds working?'

'I don't feel that they are, Sharli. Maybe I need to go back and ask Daktari Cloutier if we need to look at something else.'

'I'll take you to Stone Town tomorrow. I want to ask him again if he has any casual positions.'

'I thought Kendwa didn't want you to work.'

'He doesn't, but I want to help out. He toils so hard. All his money is invested in the safari resort on the mainland. Until it's built and taking on guests, financially, we'll be struggling. Plus, I didn't go all the way to Sydney to study nursing and then not be able to use my skills.'

Her mother patted her hand. 'My sweet daughter. You are using your skills brilliantly with me. They are not going to waste.'

'I know, Ma. That's the most rewarding thing for me, but we need money for your medication too. Me working as a nurse will at least pay for that.'

'You can ask the doctor, but if I were you, I'd talk to Kendwa too. He's your husband. Don't let him think he's not providing enough for you. Men can be touchy about such things.'

'I'll talk to him. In fact, I'll do it now. Are you okay if I leave for a while?'

'If I just sit here, yes.'

130

Sharli walked around the back where Kendwa was stacking bricks at the base of the extension. Lifting an arm, he wiped the sweat from his brow. Matted, damp hair plastered around his face. It had already started growing out from the shortcut he'd worn at the wedding. His back was bare, sweat glistened down his shoulders, accentuating every muscle. *Wow, just build for me anytime, husband.*

'Do you have water? You look thirsty.' Her thirst was only for him. 'I'll go and milk one of the coconuts and come back.'

Turning around, he flashed her a dimpled smile. 'I reckon I'll have the walls up by later today. We could even sleep in here tonight.'

'And christen it?'

'Definitely.' He winked.

'I'll get you that water.' Seeing him sweaty and shirtless made her womb shift. He was just so damn effortlessly sexy. Mostly she was sure that he had no idea of the impact he made.

Returning with a canvas water bottle filled with delicious and refreshing coconut water, she called to him. 'Here you go. Did you notice ma has deteriorated?' She passed it to him. 'I'll have to get her to the doctor tomorrow and perhaps try some new meds.'

'A bit. Sure. I'll drive you both. I have some business to do in town anyway.' Bringing the water bottle to his lips, he took a deep drink, wiping his mouth with his forearm. There was further progress with the wall he'd been building.

'Are they the bricks you made from goat dung, straw and stuff?'

'Yep. Pick one up. They're light but sturdy. Should be great for insulation. Maybe I'll make more and redo the wall in your ma's bedroom, so she sleeps better at night.'

She kissed his sweaty, coconut flavoured lips. 'You are so kind to her.'

'She's kind to me. She's your mom, Sharli. I want you both to be happy.'

Cuddling, she did not care that he was sweaty. 'I love you.'

'I love you too.' He patted her bum. 'Now, scoot. I need to get this done. Go and read more of the novel your mom's been enjoying. You read to her so beautifully.'

'I will. And you better get this finished because I intend christening that room with you, complete or not.' She winked.

'God, woman. How can I even keep my mind on the job now?'

'You will if you know what's good for you.' She giggled.

'There's no doubting I know what's good for me. Now leave,' he said, shaking his head, grinning.

Later that afternoon, Kendwa showered and went in search of his wife. Both her and Vedi were inside the extension, marvelling at what he had done. The separate room had a small deck that would fit two chairs and a café table. Inside, the natural brick walls appeared straight and sturdy. The thatched roof was high to give the small room a feeling of spaciousness. There was a wide window on the east-facing wall. Double doors opened wide to the deck to allow the ocean breeze to flow through.

The women turned as he entered. 'This is wonderful, Kendwa. Thank you so much for doing this for us,' said Vedi.

'I am once again amazed by you. It's perfect.' Sharli ran her hand along the brick wall.

'It will be when we get a large bed in here.' He winked. Vedi giggled behind her hand.

'Yes, I was wondering about that,' said Sharli. They heard a car engine outside. 'Someone's here.'

'Those someone's would be Jambi and Ralf.' Kendwa strode outside to greet the men who had large timber pieces, boxes and a mattress in the back of the old ute. 'I'll help you guys.' They moved the bits of bed inside.

Sharli stood with her hands on her hips. 'You've bought a bed already?'

'Yup. Not just any bed either. You and your mom go outside while we put it together. Oh, we will need some linen, though. My man brain didn't go that far with this plan.'

Sharli laughed, kissing him. 'How long till we come back?'

'Fifteen to twenty,' said Jambi, already putting pieces together.

When Sharli returned carrying a bundle of linen, the men were gone. Kendwa stood aside proudly as she came into the room. The bed was creamy timber, obviously made from recycled driftwood and naturally felled timber. It had a shiny varnish to the beautiful timber, that curled towards the ceiling as a four-poster. With mouth open, she stared at it. 'Kendwa, it's magical. I can make some drapes for over the top to form a canopy, so we have mosquito netting. It looks very Swahili. I love it.' Dropping the linen on the high mattress, she bounced on it with her bottom.

'I'm glad you like it.' Coming to her, he brushed hair behind her ear, cupping her face kissing her deeply. His tongue entwined with hers, exploring and connecting. 'I've been dreaming about what we could do on this bed all day.'

She sighed as he nibbled her neck. 'So have I, and I didn't even know we had a bed.' She laughed.

Trailing kisses from her neck to her shoulders, he slipped the top she wore down to expose her breasts. Standing with him, nipples eagerly erect, welcomed his mouth as he kissed each in turn. Her dress found its way to the ground. The panties quickly joined it. Scooping her into his arms, he tenderly placed her on the bed.

'This is our marital bed, Sharli. It is like home to me, but I promise you this, I will build our very own house, a little banda on the island just for you.'

'This is a beautiful start, my husband.' Her eyes trailed him as he undressed and stepped to her. Wanting him inside her so bad she ached a delicious pain, reaching for his erection. Stroking down her flat stomach, he explored the entrance to her vagina before inserting his fingers and teasing for her responsive wetness. His cock magnetised towards her.

On entering her, the tightness hugged him perfectly. It was amazing how good she felt. Their body blended as one with the rhythm of their lovemaking getting faster, needier, slower, then quicker again until they could no longer control it. They both exploded with orgasms that left them sated, breathless and smiling.

The sheets were still in a pile at their feet. Reaching down the bed, he grabbed one, flapping it out so it covered them both, pulling her close.

'I can make the bed,' she said, having trouble moving at all.

'Nah, let's enjoy the moment of pure bliss.' Lifting his arm, he let her nuzzle into him.

His rapid heartbeat reassured her through his rising chest, where she rested her head, smiling.

'Thank you, Kendwa. You are the perfect husband.'

'Don't say that, Sharli. I'm far from perfect, but I'm doing my best for you.'

'You're faultless to me.'

Softly he kissed her and then said, 'I'm serious, Sharli. Don't put me on a pedestal. I'm a man trying my best to be a good husband.'

'Okay then. I think you're doing a wonderful job at being a husband so far.'

'I'll settle for that. And you are doing a flawless job of being my wife. I must confess I felt bad being away for those three weeks, so soon after we married. I felt I'd failed you then.'

'No, you didn't. You're building the business. It's something you must do. I believe in your dream too. I'm supporting it every step of the way.'

'Why are you going to ask for a job with Daktari Cloutier then?'

'Ma told you?' Sharli was apprehensive about his tone.

'She's worried about us.'

'She doesn't need to stick her nose in.' Sharli frowned.

'It doesn't matter. You don't need to take it. I have enough left from the initial down payment to support us fine. Please don't feel like you need to work.' Kendwa could tell Sharli was annoyed. He changed tack. 'But if it's what you want to do for you, I'm all for it.'

'You are?' She raised her eyebrows.

'Of course. One of the things I loved most about you when we first met was your independence. The other thing was that you knew Borneo's top five.'

'Huh! That was our first day.'

'Maybe it was love at first sight.'

'It was for me.'

They kissed then snuggled to sleep. But Kendwa didn't fall asleep. He stared at his new ceiling, wondering why he hadn't told his wife about the journal he'd found. He reasoned that he wasn't game to look at it yet. Though not much scared him, for some reason, he was

134

terrified of what he would discover inside the leather cover of the journal. *What secrets did the damn book hold?*

Chapter 18
Zanzibar, Tanzania

Jambi's battered truck rattled along the road to Stone Town with Kendwa at the wheel. Sharli sat beside him, chatting brightly. Vedi was on the passenger side, staring out the window, deep in thought.

Kendwa leaned over his wife, speaking to his mother-in-law. 'Vedi, are you okay? You look a little pale.'

Trying to smile, she turned to him, then coughed. 'I'm fine, Kendwa. Just feeling a little motion sick is all.'

'Do you want me to pull over?'

'No, no. Keep driving. The sooner we get to see the doctor and sort out what's going on with me, the better.'

Kendwa slowed the truck to avoid potholes from recent rain, patting his wife's leg with his free hand. She lifted her eyes to him gratefully. The beautiful golden in them reflected the worry about her mother's health.

They arrived at the clinic situated in front of the hospital. The women got out as Kendwa called, 'I'll come back in an hour or so.'

'We'll stroll the bazaar or sit at the gardens until you get back. I know you have things you need to do, and we're not in any rush. Take your time.'

'I'll be back as soon as I can,' he said before waving. Frowning as he drove, he was concerned about what they would find out about Sharli's mom. Turning his concentration to his own tasks, he knew there was nothing he could do about what the doctor would confirm.

Sharli held her mother's elbow as she led her into the doctor's office. Doctor Cloutier was a handsome Canadian who had been on the island a few years. Most of the locals had seen him at least once or twice. The doctor greeted the women with a warm smile, lingering a little too long on Sharli's cleavage. On numerous occasions, he had asked Sharli on dates. Since he was in his late forties, she considered him far too old for her, though he was quite a dashing man.

'Hello to you both. Mrs Ahu, let's see what's going on with you.' Consulting notes, he left a folder open on his desk. Flicking the stethoscope around his neck, he turned his stool to face them. 'Sharli, you can sit there.'

Sharli sat and said, 'She may have a urinary tract infection, as she's in a bit of pain and struggling with incontinence. Her fever's a little high with a shallow breath, low vision and spasticity comes and goes.'

'Thank you.' He spoke to Vedi. 'Any fatigue?'

'Yes, a little.'

'Forgetfulness? Disrupted sleep? Deep breath in, please.'

'No. My mind is as good as ever. My sleep is disrupted most nights.' Coughing raggedly, she took as deep a breath as she could. The doctor checked her chest with the cold stethoscope.

Silently he listened, turning to Sharli when he'd finished. 'Are you still after some casual work?'

'Yes.' Sharli smiled.

'Not here, I'm afraid. I had to fill a quota from the medical school on the mainland. I'm trying to find you a position, but it wouldn't be for some months. Housemaid jobs are going at the new resort when completed in a few weeks. They'd like someone who knows first aid.'

'Oh.' Sharli couldn't hide her disappointment. 'I doubt if my husband would approve of me working there since they cleared the natural habitat of the monkeys and other wildlife.'

'Mmmm.' To Vedi, he said, 'I heard your new son-in-law has extended your house and added a ramp. That's good because I think we may organise a wheelchair. You're fatiguing too much, and I'm concerned that you'll have a fall. Sharli is only a small woman to be picking you up. Do you want that yet, or do you want to manage longer without it?'

138

'I think it's nearly time.' She paused taking a deep breath. 'Perhaps we'll see if what you prescribe me makes an improvement.' Tears pooled in her eyes when she said it. They broke Sharli's heart. 'What else, Daktari?'

'I'm concerned about your chest, and, yes, you do have a urinary tract infection. I can treat the infection with antibiotics, but I also want to x-ray your chest.'

'Pneumonia?' Sharli asked, frowning.

'Possibly, but we'll organise the x-ray and get some bloods done. I'm going to change your medication to prednisone. Since you have a nurse living with you, we'll also have some intravenous Zinbryta to help your antibodies. And of course, once the bloods are back, I'll prescribe further. I can have the wheelchair ordered whenever you need it.'

Vedi shifted in her seat as he tested her blood pressure and made more notes. Lifting sad eyes to Sharli, they were moist from unspent tears. Sharli mouthed, *it will be okay,* looking away, her own eyes filling.

Sharli strode out the front angrily, pacing for a bit while the doctor e-rayed Vedi. Her mother had deteriorated. If she did have pneumonia, it was serious and would need to be closely monitored. Perhaps her ma needed hospital admittance if that was the case. Sharli wished she could do more.

Sharli wiped the sweat pooling on her forehead, staring up the narrow lane near the hospital, biting her lip. The vibrant colour of the kanga stores, local artist's paintings, wildlife carvings and glass lanterns filled the bustling cobbled streets of Zanzibar's capital Stone Town. Spicy herbs, particularly cloves, were thick in the humid air, the smells so familiar they were normally like a caress, but not today with her mother so sick.

Two turban-headed boys played soccer against the old walls, giggling and pushing each other as they tried to steal the ball and kick it. They bumped a massive intricately carved door and heard someone inside shout at them. Giggling behind their hands, they moved further up the alley. She half-smiled at them.

Twisting her wedding ring, she pondered Kendwa being a dad. The smile broadened. It would make her ma happy if she had a baby.

139

Without a doubt, Kendwa would be a wonderful father. They'd only been married over two months, but every day with him was blissful. He constantly surprised her with his skills; building things, climbing trees, saving animals. The kindness he showed seemed second nature, but he was sensitive and funny too. Little quips made her laugh. It astonished her how much she liked that. Kendwa brought her joy. Other relationships had lacked that spark.

If it weren't for her concern for her mother's well-being, she'd be ready to have children with Kendwa. It didn't seem the right time until her mother was in remission and coping better with her health. Ma had to be her priority.

Though Sharli and Kendwa had stopped using condoms, she'd been taking the pill since she realised she was sexually keen on him. It would have been nice to stop taking it and start their little family, but how could she look after a child when she had to look after her mother? Shaking her head, with no answer forthcoming, she strolled inside the clinic to find out more about her mother's condition. There was no use getting worked up over things until she knew her mother's ailments.

Doctor Cloutier stood outside his examining room. He moved closer when Sharli passed, fingers brushing her bottom as he ushered her in. She shot him a warning glare. Out of the doctor's lecherous reach, she took hold of her mother's hand and quickly sat beside her. Clearing his throat, the doctor pointed to the chest x-ray in the lightbox.

Sharli was already examining it. Her tense shoulders relaxed slightly. 'A little bit of cloudiness here.' The doctor showed a small area in Vedi's lungs.

'Yes, but it's manageable,' said Sharli, squeezing her ma's hand.

'You came to see me promptly, so that's worked in favour of a good outcome. I'll write out the scripts. Mrs Ahu, as long as you listen to your nurse daughter, I think you'll be breathing fine by the end of next week.'

'That's such a relief. I was feeling like a burden on both Sharli and Kendwa, particularly since they've only been married for a short time.' Getting up from the seat slowly, she hugged Sharli.

'Ma, you're never a burden, and Kendwa likes looking after us both.'

Doctor Cloutier looked up from his notes. 'I heard about Kendwa Ely through some friends. He'd been away from here a long time

140

travelling. They reckon he's like some sort of Tarzan. Surely he can't wrangle crocodiles, survive venomous snake bites, climb trees and stuff like that? They say the snake was a banded krait, really?'

Sharli laughed. 'Yes, he can, and more. I'm sure you'll meet him soon enough. It was a banded krait. The doctors were stunned he survived that. He's bound to get bitten by a snake or something and need your help, sooner or later.' She clamped her mouth with her hands, then crossed her fingers. 'I shouldn't say that and jinx him, should I?'

'I may meet him down at one of the bars and share a shisha pipe with him. I'd prefer that to having him as a patient. I'm sure you would too.'

'True, doctor. That's for sure. Thank you.' Sharli collected her ma's prescriptions from him. The women strolled outside towards a chemist. When they'd collected the medication, they travelled up the narrow lanes with Sharli supporting her ma's weight with her elbow.

The busy Darajani Bazaar was filled with stall owners and eager haggling tourists. A hot wind blew dust and flies. Awful smells passed with the breeze from the hanging slabs of meat strung at one of the stalls. Neither could look at the grotesque dead animals. They passed the stall quickly.

The air cleared to waft with pleasant smells of fruit and spices. The fruit stalls piled high with mangos, bananas, dragonfly fruit and coconuts. They bought a huge mango then moved to the herbs where the scent of cloves, nutmeg and ginger was strong. Vedi sniffed the spices as she inspected them.

'We need some turmeric for the curry,' Vedi said before turning to sit on a bench. 'Just need to catch my breath.' Wheezing, she clutched her chest.

'Ma. Just stay there. I'll buy some. Then I'll find the seafood Kendwa likes and be back. When you're ready, we'll go and sit under a shady tree near the clinic while we wait for him.'

By the time she returned, her mother's eyes were shut. Her lashes rested on pale cheeks. Sharli gently tapped her shoulder. 'Ma?'

Vedi blinked her eyes open. 'Just resting. I'm fine. Let's find your young husband and go home.'

Kendwa was pacing out the front of the hospital. 'Oh, there you are. I was getting worried.' Raking his hand through his hair, he strode to the other side of Sharli's mom, urging her to lean on him. 'Let's get you home. You look exhausted.'

Glancing up at him, she coughed weakly. 'You're the best son-in-law I could ask for, Kendwa.'

He grinned back at her. 'Thank you. I think you're a very special mother-in-law too.'

Sharli carried the groceries, placing them in the back of the truck. The rusty door creaked as she tugged it. It finally opened with a screech. Climbing in, she moved to the middle to make room. Kendwa helped her mother in, gently closing the door. He shot a concerned look across at Sharli, giving a half-smile, which she returned.

Running around to the driver's side, he slid in, turning the key. Driving slowly, he glanced at his precious cargo of wife and mother-in-law.

Sharli explained what the doctor had said.

'So, putting it simply. You have to go easy, rest and recover?' He summarised.

Vedi sighed. 'Yes, but I've been doing that anyway. I'm sick of rest. I'd do anything to have a bit more energy.'

'It will come, Ma. Once we've got both infections under control, you'll feel so much better.'

Later, Sharli told Kendwa to sit out on the deck and not peek in the kitchen. Sharli and Vedi lovingly cooked a delicious prawn-chicken curry with mango to thank him for his hard work on the home.

Once the meal was ready, Kendwa was practically salivating.

'You know I could smell both the prawns and the curry,' Kendwa said after chewing a mouthful of food. 'My mouth was watering before I even tried it. This is seriously amazing. Yum.'

'We're glad you like it. It's an old family recipe.' Sharli smiled at Vedi, then back at Kendwa.

'Let's have more of those recipes if they're all going to taste this good. Do you mind if I have seconds?'

Vedi nodded with a laugh, moving the ceramic dish towards him until the ladle was around his side. Scooping another full serving into his bowl, he ate with relish.

'You can eat a lot, Kendwa. I don't know where you put it.' Sharli giggled.

'I burn it all off, just doing stuff. Building, running, climbing and swimming. Did I tell you I saw those dolphins again this morning? They came right up and swam around me.' Using his fork, he circled his head.

'I knew I should have got up with you instead of sleeping in,' said Sharli. Vedi yawned. 'Ma, how 'bout I get your medication sorted, and you can have an early night. I've got to set the intravenous again too.'

Vedi stood up shakily. 'Thanks, sweetie. I am tired.'

After Sharli had settled her mother, she found Kendwa onto their deck. 'Thanks for doing the dishes.'

Grabbing her waist, he pulled her to sit on his lap with her back to him. Kissing her hair, he sighed. 'You don't have to thank me. We all do chores. There's no man-does-this-woman-does-that bullshit in this family.'

'I'm glad you think like that. Does that mean you'll be cleaning the toilet too?'

Squeezing her waist with his big hands, he kissed her shoulder. 'Come on! A new-age guy can only go so far. Besides, I dry-retch near the toilet. You know that.'

'So, it's a medical condition?' Turning to face him, she stifled a laugh.

'Must be. Would you like to diagnose me, Nurse Ely?'

Placing her small hand on his forehead, she shook her head. 'You are hot. You may have a temperature.' Kiss. 'Or perhaps you are hot because you're so boiling-over sexy. Purely my medical opinion only.' Giggling, she turned all the way around, so her legs straddled his hips. They were pressed groin to groin, the way they liked it.

'I have a medical opinion of my own about how sexy you are, sweetheart.' He kissed her lips hungrily. Hers parted to let his tongue enter and play. Picking her up as they still kissed, he carried her to their bed. 'Okay, nurse, you need to make me better.'

'You know I will,' she teased, biting his bottom lip softly.

They made love frantically as if the role-playing instigated further heat to their already erotic lovemaking.

Later, curled in each other's arms, she asked, 'What did you do today in Stone Town?'

143

'I went to the museum to see if the curator could help me with something.'

'The museum? Why?' Wide eyes stared at him.

Turning to his side, he reached his arm towards the side table, producing the leather journal. Wordlessly he passed it to Sharli.

'What's this?'

'It's a long story. I found it in Kenya, remember I told you about the elephant caves. I wanted to see if we could open it to find out who owned it. It was moist from the caves. Most of the pages were stuck together. Be careful. It's fragile.'

Stroking the leather cover, she slowly opened the book. 'Some are still stuck.'

'Yeah. At the museum, they said the salt in the caves would have prevented fungi. It could be salvageable. I need to dry it out totally before trying to open more pages. Some of the ink has faded. I haven't deciphered much. It's written in English, so it might be a traveller or NGO or someone. There is mention of Australia a few times.' Watching her study the journal, he scratched his head.

Sitting up, she glanced at him, frowning. 'Why do you look so pensive? What is this book about?' The sheet slipped low, exposing her breasts. He grinned, reaching to touch, but she slapped his hand. 'Don't try and distract me, Kendwa.'

'But your boobs look bigger, fuller, touchable, kissable.'

Changing the subject from her changing body, she asked, 'Why is this book important to you?'

'I don't know if it is. You remember after the snake bite, I told you my spirit mom said some things, and I didn't understand them. I've still been having dreams, nightmares about them. One of the things was going to the elephant caves, so I did. I found this.' Taking the book from her, he held it up. 'It could mean something or nothing. I don't know.' He placed it on the side table, frowning.

Slipping back under the sheets, she cuddled into him. 'It's a long way to go exploring because of a dream.'

'I know it's stupid.' He kissed the tip of her nose.

'When you have those bad dreams, why do you call the name Noah? Who is Noah?'

Kendwa stiffened.

144

'Kendwa?'

Chapter 19
Zanzibar, Tanzania

'That's wonderful news. I'm so happy for you both. Hold on a second, Toby,' Kendwa held the phone to speak to Sharli. 'They've had the baby.'

'Congratulate them for me.' Motioning for him to keep talking to Toby, she smiled.

'A little girl. Wow, you must be chuffed about that. Is there something wrong?' Kendwa listened intently, occasionally nodding as Sharli wondered what they were saying. 'Stay strong, mate. Yep, see you next month. I'll think about it. Yeah, you too.'

Shoving his mobile phone back in his pocket, he paced the deck. Sharli came to him, wrapping her arms around him. 'What's wrong? Is the baby okay and Katie?'

'Yep. Katie's fine. It was a long labour. The baby was bigger than normal, so she was exhausted. They're doing tests on their baby girl. It's nothing major but something. Toby doesn't care what's wrong. He just wants to protect them both, but Katie is having trouble…bonding.'

'Oh, that's sad. She may have post-natal depression. They'll figure it out. It may take time, but she'll be okay.'

'I hope so. Toby sounds excited to be a dad, though. God, I hope it all works out for them. I can't believe he has a baby now.'

'The wedding is still on next month?'

'Toby says it is. Have you organised your sister to come over and look after your mum?'

'Yes, for a fortnight.'

147

Kissing her forehead, he half smiled. 'A fortnight is all we'll need. I won't take the job at Taronga Zoo.'

'I realise you want to, and it will help fund things until the resort is complete.' Raising her eyes to him, she smiled.

Lifting his eyebrows, he asked, 'You don't mind if I take it? Really?'

'Didn't Toby say it's only a three-month contract? I can deal with that if I must. Plus, if you start the week we get there, I'll be with you for the first two weeks, so it will go fast. Plus,' she paused, 'we'll need extra money when there's another mouth to feed.' Her golden eyes softened as she glanced down at her stomach.

It slowly dawned on him. His gaze shifted to her larger breasts, then back to the angelic smile on her beautiful face. 'You're, we're…pregnant?' Placing his hand tenderly over her stomach, she grinned down at it, putting her hand on top of his.

'Yes, Kendwa. I'm only sixteen days since my last period, but I'm sure I'm pregnant.'

Still staring at her stomach, a huge grin split his face. 'The pill didn't work? I'm glad. I wanted a baby anyway. You did a test?'

'Yes. It's positive. We'll have a baby by November.'

Finally realising he would be a dad, he lifted his hand. Punching the air, he whooped, then danced around the deck, coming back to her, lifting her, kissing her delicious lips. 'You have made me the happiest damn man in the world. A child of our own, wow! And on the day Toby's baby arrived. It's like it was meant to be this day.' Putting her down gently, he frowned a little. 'You'll have to stop climbing coconut trees and take it easy from now on. I'll carry everything and…'

With a gentle finger, she silenced him. 'I'm pregnant and pregnant women are not fragile. I can do everything I'm already doing. Okay, I'll give the coconut climbs a miss, but everything else is fine.'

'But!'

'No buts, Kendwa. I am fit and healthy. You do not have to wrap me up in cotton wool.'

Laughing, he put his hands up in surrender. 'I should have known my feisty little wife would say that. You will be fine to travel, won't you?'

'Yes, the trip to Australia is fine. We'll be okay for the christening one as well. I can't miss you becoming a godfather.'

148

'Good. Have you told your mom yet?'

'No. You, my husband, had to be first. Shall we go tell her now?'

'Sure. I want to tell the whole world.'

'Let's just start with Ma.'

'I'll ring Toby back after that.'

'And I'll phone Metra, my sister and cousins.'

They strolled hand-in-hand to the front of the house, knocking before going inside. Spicy ginger filled the air. Vedi stood in the kitchen stirring a large pot with a wooden spoon. It seemed one of her better days. Smiling down at whatever she was cooking, she sang in a croaky sweet voice. Glancing up at them, she raised her eyebrows.

'Why do you two look like the monkeys that got the bananas?'

Clutching hands united, they stepped closer. Their smiles beamed at her. Sharli nodded at Kendwa.

'Ma. We have news...' Before he could finish, Sharli butted in excitedly.

'We're having a baby.'

Vedi came to them. 'I thought so. You glow already, my dear girl and Kendwa, there's no denying the smile of a man who's about to be a father.' She hugged them. Looking up with tears in her eyes, she said, 'Congratulations, you've made this old girl very happy.'

Sharli said to her ma, 'It won't prevent me looking after you, Ma. We hadn't planned it to happen this quickly.'

'Don't be silly. I couldn't be happier. I think the new medication has put me back in remission. I may have more energy for a grandchild. It will give me a new lease on life.'

'Once I get back from Australia, I can get things sorted out on the mainland, then I can help more too,' said Kendwa, smiling adoringly at his wife.

'You're going to the wedding in Australia? It will be nice for you to catch up with your friend Toby,' said Vedi, as she walked back to stir the pot on the stove.

'We'll both go over for that, but I'll stay a couple more months. There's a consultancy job at Taronga Zoo. It's to expand the African Wildlife enclosures, and the pays worth me taking it for my little family.'

149

'I'd assume it's also something you'd love to do.' Vedi smiled knowingly.

'Yes, but I wouldn't go if Sharli wasn't happy about it.' His jaw twitched.

'I'm sure you wouldn't. Anyhow Sharli and I will cope just fine. Though we love your help, we did survive without a man around.'

'Speaking of having a man around, Ma. I noticed that dad's old friend Chand has been calling in to see you often,' Sharli said. Vedi looked down. A blush filled her cheeks. 'Ma? Do you like him?'

'Well, yes. Chand is nice, but you know I couldn't possibly date again. It's too long since your father.'

'Why not Ma? Everyone needs to have love in their life.' She turned to smile at Kendwa, who watched the exchange with amusement.

Vedi was a beautiful woman. Though Kendwa knew she didn't see herself that way. He hoped Chand would treat her right because Kendwa would protect the two women with his life if he didn't. Though he liked the idea that someone would love Vedi. Without a doubt, he'd still be loving Sharli long after she'd become older than her mother was. They would grow old together.

The Zanzibar sun was warm on his skin as he strolled outside, letting the women talk. Fishing his phone out of his pocket when he reached their deck, he rang Toby with a smile on his face.

It would have been nice to have more family to share his news. There was his aunty in England, but he'd lost touch with her long ago. He thought about reaching out and finding her again to keep his tenuous link with his mother's family. There were reasons it was difficult to see her. He still felt too raw about losing both his parents. He didn't know why he thought that linking with his aunt was important. After all, he had Toby, who was as close to family as a real family could get.

'Toby, I have some news for you. We're having a baby too. How cool is that? Yeah.' He paused, listening to Toby's congratulations but hearing some underlying worry. 'Tobes, what's going on over there?'

Sharli came around the corner as he hung up the phone. Running his hand through his hair, he paced before he said goodbye to Toby and hung up.

'I'm going over to Metra's to give her the news. Chand has turned up to be with Ma. Do you want to come?' Sharli hugged him.

'Nah, I'll leave you with the girlfriend stuff.' Hugging her back, he kissed her forehead.

Taking a better look at him, the smile from the happiness of her pregnancy died. 'You're upset. Don't you want the baby?'

Squeezed her tightly to him, he said, 'I want our baby more than anything in the world, babe. I'm deliriously happy about us. I'm just worried about Toby.'

'Oh, I'm sorry. Is there something going on with their baby daughter? Is she okay?'

Scratching his chin, he said, 'Not sure.' Spinning her around to face the way to Metra's, he patted her bottom. 'But you're not to worry about that. Go and see Metra. I know you're dying to. Off you go.'

Blowing him a kiss, she grinned, skipping towards Metra's house. 'I love you, Kendwa,' she yelled from the corner.

'I love you too, babe,' he whispered as his thoughts turned to Toby. He'd do anything for his younger friend. They were literally brothers. The problem was he couldn't help Toby at all. There was nothing he could do to alleviate Toby's pain, not that Toby seemed perturbed. Toby wanted to take it on, which was typical of him. Always the upbeat one in their relationship, he never gave up on anything.

Deciding to put his worries into something constructive, Kendwa strode to the beach. There he collected driftwood and branches. He wanted to surprise Sharli. It was only the start of the things he would create for his beautiful wife. Glancing at his sports watch, he considered she would be gone an hour or more. Her mom was being looked after by her beau. Kendwa smiled, knowing he had time to finish his project and temporarily banish his worries about Toby.

Sharli arrived home as the sun was setting. Sitting on the deck with a beer, he raised it to her, smiling wide.

'What are you looking so chuffed about?' she asked. 'At least you don't seem so worried about Toby. Hey, is Chand still with Ma?'

'Yep. They are having dinner; by candlelight, I suspect.' He winked.

She playfully slapped his shoulder. 'Don't.'

151

Putting his beer down, he stood next to her. Smelling the sweet coconut shampoo in her hair, he hugged her to him. 'I have something to show you.' Grabbing her hand in his, he led her inside.

'Surely you can't be horny. We had a marathon this morning...' She paused when her eyes saw the cot beside their bed. It was rustic, curled and twisted with differently sized woods. It had four posts bending over the top to form a canopy. It looked like something out of *George of the Jungle*, but it was beautiful. It matched their big bed perfectly. Tears welled in her eyes, her hand over her open mouth.

'Do you like it?'

Stepping towards it, she stroked the timber, not taking her eyes off it.

'Sharli? I still have to add a couple of coats of varnish or oil, whichever you prefer.'

'It's perfect. I didn't expect...how did you do this so quickly?'

'It's been in my head for a while.'

'We only just found out.'

'That doesn't mean I haven't been hoping.'

On tip-toes, she kissed his lips, holding her hand under his chin. 'I love it, and I love you even more.'

Kissing her back, they melted together. 'You've made me so happy. I wanted to thank you with this.' He pointed to the cot.

'There's no need to thank me. As I recollect we made this baby,' she patted her still flat stomach, 'together.'

'Yep, I recollect a few things we did to make that baby.' He winked.

His hand roamed her body before resting on her stomach.

Placing her small hands over his, she smiled up at him. 'It's a little miracle, isn't it?'

'Our little miracle. It feels amazing to be sharing this with you, Sharli. Who would have thought that only last year we didn't know each other?'

'And that we were in Borneo at the same time to meet.'

'It was all meant to be. I've never felt this alive. I'll try to be the best husband and father I can be for you and our baby.'

'You're already the best husband. I can't wait to see you with our child.'

With his heart near bursting, he kissed her. She moved to the bed. He followed her. Gently he placed his head on her stomach, stroking it with his index finger. 'I want to watch the baby grow and the changes in your beautiful body.' Reaching up, he touched her breasts, cupping their weight. 'These are going to get bigger.'

'They already are.'

'I know. I like that. Wow, I didn't think I could love you more. It's so intense, Sharli.'

She shushed him with a gentle finger on his lips. 'I feel the same way, honey. Make love to me.'

'Are you sure? You know the baby is definitely, like safe?'

Giggling, she shifted, spreading her legs in answer. 'The baby is definitely safe, and I am verrrry horny. Maybe it's the pregnancy, or maybe I can't get enough of my sexy husband.'

No need for further encouragement, so began the tenderness of lovemaking with a baby in mind. He was cautious and caring. She was needy but gave in to his slow path to ecstasy.

Later, sated in each other's arms, Sharli softly snored on his shoulder. Watching her, he smiled, thinking how serene and beautiful she was. He tore his eyes from her to stare at the ceiling. His thoughts drifted to his family.

Moments like pregnancy announcements intensified his grief for his mom and dad. Dearly, he wished he had them to share the pregnancy news. It made him sad and angry at the same time. *Why couldn't they be here for this?*

Then his thoughts turned to Toby. It was probably wise to warn Sharli about the baby, but he didn't want her worrying unnecessarily because it could affect her pregnancy. When they arrived in Australia, she would learn the truth soon enough. He hoped that Katie was made of tougher stuff for Toby's sake than he presumed she was. Toby and Katie would need their combined love to help their dear little girl. The battles life had thrown her would take strength.

Selfishly Kendwa hoped that Sharli and he would not have a concern like that. *Poor Toby. Tough and resilient as he was, how would he cope?*

153

Chapter 20
Sydney, Australia

To Kendwa and Sharli, the flight from Tanzania to Australia passed quickly. They recounted their previous visits to the big island continent. Sharli laughed at Kendwa's escapades with Toby in the country's north. Kendwa listened intently when she talked about university life in Sydney and how much she enjoyed her studies.

'It will be nice to be back,' she said, watching out the window as the Harbour Bridge came into view over deep blue water with its busy waterways around the city.

'It will. I can't wait to see Toby and meet his baby daughter.'

'I'm looking forward to cuddles. I was clucky enough. Now that I am pregnant, babies seem magnetic.'

'I know what you mean. I bet she's super pretty, like Katie.'

Sharli shoved his shoulder. 'You never told me you thought Katie was pretty.'

'Of course, she is. Toby wouldn't have it any other way. She's got nothing on you, babe.'

After clearing customs, they headed to their hotel. Soon Toby was at their door.

'Hey, Tobes.' Kendwa and Toby hugged at the door. Toby strode in with a wide grin, wrapping Sharli in his arms. 'How's it going, Sharli?'

'Good, Toby. You look happy.'

'I'm about to marry the girl of my dreams, and I have an adorable daughter.'

'Where are they?' asked Kendwa.

Toby laughed, but it seemed a fake laugh. 'She's banished me. Something about bad luck to see the bride in the days leading up.'

'But what about the baby? We want to meet them both.' Sharli pouted.

Toby paced over to their balcony, looking out onto the dark blue water of Botany Bay. 'Maybe tomorrow.' He paused, taking in the view. 'Are we crackin' a beer or what, Kendwa?'

Kendwa looked at his watch, raising his eyebrows. 'Two pm?'

'Beer o'clock, mate.'

'If you say so. I'll run down to the bottle shop at the corner and get a six-pack.'

'Make it a carton.'

Kendwa shrugged his shoulders, kissing Sharli's cheek. They strolled to the door as Toby made himself comfortable on a seat out on the balcony.

'What's going on?' Sharli whispered to Kendwa.

'Don't know yet, but one thing I know with Toby is if he has a few beers, he usually lets out whatever's bothering him.'

'I'll keep him company until you get back.'

'Just don't ask more about Katie. Talk about food, reception, venue, flowers, anything but the baby and Katie, till I get back.' He kissed her lips before shutting the door.

She stood near the doorway for a few moments digesting what he'd said. *What wasn't he telling her about Toby's baby?*

Walking to the balcony, she sat in the chair next to Toby. 'I'm so happy for you, Toby.' Noting the view instead of meeting Toby's eyes seemed a better way to start a conversation.

There was silence for a few moments. 'Thanks, Sharli. Congrats on your baby news. I wonder what you guys will have.' He faltered as if a million thoughts were going through his head. 'I love my daughter so much.'

'It will be a nice surprise. I'm glad you had a little girl. And you've got a wedding to look forward to. Wow, there's lots going on. Is it all organised?'

'I suppose. That's all Katie's thing. I just show up.'

'I'm surprised she didn't want to go back to the States for the wedding.'

'Her family are filthy rich. They didn't need much of an excuse for a holiday in Australia. They're happy to have it here. They can show off about it when they get home. It suited my parents better. They couldn't have afforded a trip to Florida. They can barely pay their mortgage. I couldn't get married without them.'

'Well, it's all worked out well then.'

'Yep.'

Kendwa returned, shoving the carton of beer in the fridge. Grabbing two cans, he strode to the balcony. 'Here you go, mate.' He passed Toby one. Toby cracked it open with a hiss and couldn't get it to his mouth quick enough.

Sharli rose, kissing Kendwa's cheek as he sat down. 'I'm going out exploring. I need some fresh air after our flight. I'll bring back something for dinner. Enjoy your catch-up, boys.'

Once she'd left, Kendwa let Toby finish a couple of beers as they talked about nothing in particular. When he passed him the third beer, he didn't hold back. 'Now Toby, what is going on with you? Is the wedding still on?'

Toby turned, his eyes moist. Gulping down a few mouthfuls of beer, he faced the view and said, 'It's been a bit emotional, these last few days. Our daughter's problems aren't as bad as first thought, which is great, of course. I already love her to bits. It's hard because Katie is refusing to name her.'

'Have you given her some suggestions?'

'Yeah. I like Hope.'

'Katie?'

'Dunno. She won't talk about it. Said she wants to concentrate on the wedding first. It's her time to shine—apparently. Our baby is three weeks old. She needs a name soon.'

'Are you bringing her to the wedding?'

'No.' He frowned. 'Katie's great-aunt has offered to babysit back at her hotel. Katie said she doesn't want her there and instead wants to concentrate on marrying me.'

'Is she expressing milk or something?'

'Bubs is already on formula. I do most of the feeds.'

Kendwa raised his eyebrows.

157

'Don't look at me like that Kendwa. I love feeding her. Those big, beautiful eyes looking up at me with such adoration. It, like, expands your heart so far that it's sure to burst.' He smiled.

'So, you have no problems, but Katie's taking time to adjust. Sharli said it could be post-natal depression. Is it?'

'It's more complicated than that. Katie's been pampered her whole life. Now she must…like, I dunno, give more than she gets. It's my fault too. I treated her like a princess. Ah, I still do.' He smacked his forehead with his palm.

'I understand.' Kendwa swigged his beer, not really understanding but not knowing what to tell his best mate. Katie was a spoiled brat who should be putting her daughter first, not herself. For that matter, she should have been considering how it was affecting Toby. Toby had a heart of gold. Kendwa knew he would do anything for those he loved. It made him wonder if Toby had made the right choice with Katie. It was a bit late now. They had a baby and were getting married in two days.

Deciding to change the subject, he asked, 'When do they want me at Taronga.'

'You have four days to enjoy Sydney with Sharli. I told them you'd be hungover after my wedding. They gave you some leeway.'

'Nice impression that would make.'

'Nah, they know it's a one-off. They recognise your record and realise how lucky they are that you could fit the project into your schedule.'

'Really?'

Toby chuckled. 'That's how I sold it to them. I'm glad you decided to take it on. Sharli sure seems an understanding wife.'

Kendwa grinned at his friend. 'Man, in so many ways. I can't believe I got so lucky.'

Toby raised his beer to Kendwa's. 'Yeah, me too.'

Kendwa could read Toby's face better than anyone. They'd spent many years working side-by-side where silence and a nod spoke volumes. Get one signal wrong in the wild, and you could end up being crocodile food.

The sun started to sink, the sky taking on a pink-orange glow reflecting on the harbour water. Lights blinked on in the city. Kendwa glanced at his watch. 'Sharli should be back by now.'

'Don't worry. She's probably enjoying some shopping.'

'She's not the shopping type.'

'Seriously? Aren't all women?'

'Nope.'

Toby shook his head. 'She can't be perfect.'

'She is...' Kendwa paused, realising that he was probably hitting a touchy subject. Usually, they were honest with each other, but Toby seemed more fragile than Kendwa had ever seen him. There was always something off-subject with men but usually not with them. 'Okay, not perfect, but she tries. Like I'm trying for her.'

'Yeah, there's lots of compromise in relationships. Hey, I haven't told you about the buck's night yet. I still don't know why you didn't want to be here for it.'

'You know why. You held it up in your hometown, Currumbin?'

'Yep. That's where my old school buddies are. So typical. Most of them haven't grown up one bit. A few of the Territorians came down too. It was a blast. Well, at least until they tied me naked to a light pole outside the RSL. Lucky a security guy came by and undid me and called a cab. Nice cabbie, too, to ignore my nakedness until I got out to my folk's place. Dad paid the cab, trying not to laugh. Mum ran out with a towel to cover me, mortified.'

Kendwa slapped his thigh. 'Man, I wish I had been there. I like your mates' sense of humour. I can picture your parents.'

'Yeah, the old man and mum are unchanged. You'll see them at the wedding, of course.'

'Looking forward to it. I guess Dobbo was at the bucks. Did you say g'day to him from me?'

'Sure did. He said the territory has never been the same without you up there.'

'He still goes back for work?'

'No. Now he only returns to fish barramundi.'

'He loved fishing.'

The door opened. Sharli smiled a greeting. The room filled with the smell of oriental spices. Holding two large paper bags, she placed them on the kitchen counter. 'Hello, you two. You look happy. Recounting more croc stories?'

'Kind of,' said Toby, smiling.

'Do you want to stay for dinner, Toby?'

He got up a little unsteadily. 'Something smells delicious, but no thanks. I've got to look after bubs tonight. Katie has a bridesmaids' meeting.' Shrugging his shoulders, he continued, 'Which is pretty much a gossip fest. I'll be keeping bubs with me. What are you two up to tomorrow?'

'We thought we'd come visit and meet the baby,' Sharli said, looking hopefully up from the sink, where she was filling a glass of water.

Kendwa shot her a don't-talk-about-the-baby look. 'We'll do a bit of sightseeing. I haven't seen much of Sydney.'

'You'll need to call into the address I sent you and make sure your suit fits. We could catch up for lunch. After that, we have all the wedding stuff to do. You'll have to be at the rehearsal.' Toby waved to Sharli.

Kendwa opened the door, leaning on the jamb with his arms folded. 'Lunch would be great. Text us where to meet. We'll be there.' He slapped Toby's shoulder before he left, then shut the door, turning to his wife, exaggeratedly wiping his brow.

Coming to him, she wrapped her arms around his waist. 'That bad, huh?'

'No, it was great to catch up. Love the guy. There's just something that's bugging him. Maybe it's the jitters, but he usually has nerves of steel. I've never seen him this way.'

'Perhaps, it's just handling being a first-time dad and a wedding. It's got to be emotional.'

'Yeah, you're right. Now, what delicious concoction have you sorted for dinner?'

Taking his hand, she led him to the kitchen. 'Chinese takeaway. I couldn't be bothered cooking. I'm feeling a little jet-lagged.'

'Yummo. That'll do me. We'll have an early night, go exploring in the morning, have another early night, and then we'll be fresh for the wedding.' He rummaged through the dinner bags, placing the food containers on the counter. 'What? No dessert?'

'I have a different kind of dessert in mind.' She grinned.

Scooping fried rice into his mouth with a spoon, he grinned with a mouthful. When he swallowed, he said, 'That's my kind of dessert.'

Hopefully, Toby was still getting dessert too. Something was really bugging him about the way Toby was acting. It wasn't just about Katie, as Kendwa had seen through her girl-next-door act and didn't have the heart to tell Toby that. It bothered Kendwa more about the baby.

Chapter 21
Sydney, Australia

A green tree frog stared at them from a low branch. Its shiny green body was casually hanging with one long gold foot with big sucker toes dangling. Kendwa studied it up close.

'It's a fair size. Nice to see healthy frogs. It's good for the environment,' Kendwa said. The frog ribbitted as if in agreement.

'It's gorgeous. Look at the flowers below. They're camellias of some sort. It's so beautiful here.'

They were strolling hand-in-hand through the Royal Botanical Gardens along the Farm Cove walk towards the Sydney Opera House. The deep blue water sparkled in the harbour, dotted by boats and the blue, yellow and white Manly Ferry that chugged by pushing up wakes of water.

'Yeah, I couldn't live here permanently, but it's a gorgeous place in lots of ways.'

'You will be living here for the next three months.'

'Are you still okay with that, Sharli?'

Squeezing his hand, she glanced up at him. 'I'm fine with it. Of course, I'll miss you, but if we want to have a wonderful marriage, we must sacrifice a few things. I know this will help us. And I have a feeling you're looking forward to the challenge.'

'I am, actually. I want to ensure that the enclosures are as close to their natural habitat as possible. Zoos are important parts of educating people, but the animals suffer if the enclosures aren't planned correctly. I can't stand that. Luckily, Taronga Zoo has a superb record, so I know they'll work with me to ensure my vision.'

163

'I love the way your eyes light up when you talk about this stuff.' She gazed at him with adoration. He leaned down, kissing her lips.

'Thank you for understanding me. It's not such an easy thing.'

'I think it is. You're a very uncomplicated man.'

They neared the opera house. 'It's the weirdest building. Isn't it?'

'It's more like art than a building. It's like boat ends poking up or something.' She tilted her head.

Kendwa consulted his watch. 'Viking ships, so I've heard. We don't have time to explore it now. We'll have to head to that café to meet Toby.'

'I'll come down this afternoon while you're at the rehearsal for the wedding. You'll have months here to check it out. I missed it last time I was here.'

Toby was already at the café with a pram beside him. Sharli smiled at Kendwa. 'We're going to meet the baby.' Kendwa frowned before he smiled.

Toby pushed the pram backwards and forwards. Baby cries like a mewing kitten came from the pram. Toby smiled wide. 'Hey, you two.'

'Hi, Toby. We're so glad you brought the baby,' said Sharli.

The boys patted each other's shoulders. All three of them glanced inside the pram. The baby girl had a beautiful round face, slightly-slanted wide-set eyes and the healthy chubbiness of a happy baby. Cooing softly, she smiled up at them.

Toby was still smiling as he lifted his eyes. There were a thousand questions in them.

Sharli was first to speak. 'Oh, Toby. She's adorable. Can I pick her up? Please.'

'Sure,' said Toby. 'I've named her Hope. She needs a name, and Katie doesn't mind.'

Or doesn't care.

'Hello, little Hope. I'm your...' Sharli gently picked the baby up with a hand behind her newborn head.

'Aunty Sharli,' said Toby grinning even wider, if that was at all possible.

'She's a pretty little girl, Toby,' said Kendwa, touching the baby's chubby cheek in Sharli's gently rocking arms.

'Let's sit,' said Toby, motioning to the table, moving the pram to the side. 'Did you tell her, Kendwa?'

'Nope. I didn't think it was important. I just wanted Sharli to meet her first.'

'You mean to tell me about the down syndrome? She's an adorable child. She'll have as much opportunity and happiness as any little girl. You may not have thought so at first, Toby, but you're blessed.'

'Thank you, Sharli. I loved her at first sight. Yeah, I was stunned when the midwives acted all weird at the birth, but she's my daughter. We'll deal with her obstacles. When they said she has Trisomy 21. I was, like, what? Tell me if she's going to live. That's all I wanted. Apparently, she's about a 1 in 1100 chance. I think it makes her very special.'

'She is,' said Sharli.

'I think so. But apparently, it's common and happens randomly. Try and convince my bride of that.'

Kendwa hadn't taken his eyes off Sharli holding the baby. 'She's a gem, Toby. And she's lucky to have you as her dad.'

'I'm glad I have your support at least.' He rubbed his chin. It was obvious he was thinking about Katie.

Kendwa reached for the baby with a weak smile. Sharli handed her over. 'How do I hold her? I'm new to this baby stuff.' Awkwardly he shifted the baby in his big arms. Sharli moved the baby's head to sit securely in the crook of his arm.

'Make sure her head is supported. She's too young to hold it up herself yet.'

Toby laughed. 'Yeah, babies are more difficult to hold at first than a baby gator.'

'Wow isn't she somethin',' Kendwa said, smiling down at the child with a dopey look on his handsome face.

'Well, look at you. Who would have thought I'd see you looking clucky? Just coincidental that you two have a bun in the oven too.' Toby laughed, picking up a menu. 'Better order so we can make it to the rehearsal in time. Don't see why we need one, but Katie and her mum insisted.'

'I guess they want everything to be perfect,' said Sharli, admiring the way her big strong husband looked with a tiny baby in his arms.

The waitress did a double-take when she noticed the good-looking men. They ordered sparkling water, considering Sharli was pregnant and the boys would have enough alcohol at the wedding. Toby passed the waitress the menus when they'd ordered their meals.

Sharli wondered about what sort of woman Katie was. She could understand her shock at having a child with down syndrome, but it wasn't an obstacle they couldn't overcome. They still had a happy, healthy baby. Hope cooed in Kendwa's arms as if to confirm how content she was.

'She's yawning and looking red in the face like she's gonna cry,' Kendwa said, shifting uncomfortably. 'Oh boy. I think she's done a stinker.' Screwing up his nose, he held the baby away but still supported her head.

Toby and Sharli laughed. 'That's normal, Kendwa,' said Sharli. Toby took the baby, reached under the pram and slung the baby bag over his broad shoulder, like a daddy pro.

'I'll go and change her. You look like you're about to dry retch, Kendwa. You've smelt worse things out in the bush.'

'Don't I know it.' His eyes watered. 'There's just something about baby shit that gets to me.'

'You will learn to change our baby's nappy but, won't you?' Sharli rolled her eyes.

'Sure. It might take me a bit to get used to it.' He patted her hand. 'I will definitely try.'

Once Toby returned, he nursed Hope with a bottle to her hungry little lips. Their lunches arrived with two waitresses wide-eyed at each other as they placed the men's meals in front of them. Kendwa had ordered Sydney Rock Oysters and a sirloin beef steak. Toby had the same. Sharli excused herself to the bathroom at the sight of the oysters and the smell of the steak.

'Oops, looks like morning sickness just hit your wife.' Toby settled Hope in the pram. Slowly her eyes shut. Her little-pursed mouth was half-open from feeding on the bottle.

'Sharli seemed okay with the Chinese meal last night. Perhaps I shouldn't have ordered oysters.' Kendwa tucked into his meal with gusto anyway.

166

'She looks healthy and happy. Pregnancy seems to suit her. Unlike Katie, who complained throughout and kept asking if she looked fat.' Toby shovelled a piece of steak in his mouth. 'Cooked perfectly, rare.' He nodded his approval. 'Yeah, so I'd say to her, no honey, you're pregnant. You're beautiful.'

'Oysters are so fresh.' Kendwa tried to change the subject. His wife had not complained one bit about being pregnant. Last night, after making love, they both watched her only slightly rounded stomach for any baby movement. She'd said she couldn't wait to feel a tiny hand or foot under her skin. 'So, Toby, are you going to stay on at Taronga Zoo in the reptile area or are you moving the family back to the Gold Coast?'

'My parents would love that. I've enquired at Currumbin Wildlife Sanctuary and Dreamworld but haven't heard yet of any openings. I don't know which will make Katie happier, the bright lights of Sydney or the calmness and beauty of the southern Gold Coast.'

'Why don't you ask her?'

'I will after the wedding is over and we're on our honeymoon. The one night, of course, because I don't want to leave Hope for any longer than that. Katie wanted to take a week away in Tahiti.'

Kendwa fought the impulse to roll his eyes. Sharli returned, looking a little pale. Sitting down, she lifted her fork, stabbing at the salad, taking tentative bites.

'Babe, are you okay?' Kendwa asked, kissing her cool cheek and stroking her thigh.

'A typical pregnant wave of nausea. It's to be expected.' She smiled.

'Are you sure you're fine?' He loved that she never complained.

'Yes, Kendwa. Now that both your steaks are eaten, the table doesn't smell as bad. Plus, I want to eat this because it's good for the baby.' Taking another mouthful, she patted her stomach with the other hand.

The boys talked about the environmental programs at Taronga Zoo. Sharli gazed at the water view, caught up in her thoughts. Glancing at Hope, she wondered what it would be like to have a baby like her. Toby and Katie would have to reassess what they'd expected of being parents, particularly Katie, by the sounds of things. Toby seemed to be rolling with the punches and thriving. Obviously, he loved being a dad.

Sharli wondered if Kendwa would warm to it that quickly, especially if there happened to be something wrong with their baby. *Don't be silly.*

167

Our baby will be fine. She refused to allow negative thoughts to enter her head, but being pregnant intensified all her emotions.

'Hey, Sharli. You're lost in thought,' Toby said. 'We were just saying we'd better get a move on.'

'Do you want me to walk you back to the Opera House before we go to the rehearsal?' Kendwa asked, rising and stretching his arms.

'No. I'd like to enjoy the Sydney sunshine. I'll head back to the unit and have a lie down after that. I'm feeling exhausted.'

Toby organised the baby stuff in the pram, stroking his sleeping daughter's pink cheek before taking the handles. 'My car's this way, Kendwa.'

Sharli kissed Kendwa before walking towards the Sydney Opera House. The men strode to the car, with the pram and sleeping baby out front. Toby glanced at his watch. 'She'll kill me if we're late. I've got to get Hope to the aunty first because Katie doesn't want her distracting everyone by crying.'

Away from Toby's view, Kendwa rolled his eyes out the window. He said, 'Hope's barely made a whimper. She's a great baby.'

'I know, but you know the saying, happy wife, happy life?'

'Mmmm.'

At the beautiful old dark-brick catholic church with colourful stained-glass windows, they ran towards the timber entrance. Kendwa glanced up at the high steeple towering into a clear blue sky, just making out a bell towards the top.

They were greeted on the doorstep by Katie's father 'Toby, just in time. You can imagine Katie's about to lose it.'

Toby was fond of Katie's dad. He seemed to understand the women in his life and their eccentricities. 'Hi, Joe. This is my best man Kendwa. Anyhow, we're on time.' He glanced at his watch again.

Joe and Kendwa shook hands. Joe led them into the church. 'Early would be better when there's a stressed bride and teary mother of the bride.'

Toby rubbed his chin, stretching his neck. Kendwa tried not to be annoyed by Katie, but he felt for Toby and what he was going through. If Katie was stressed, it was no concern to him. Why couldn't she think about Toby and Hope for one second?

Toby went straight to Katie, who glared past him directly at Kendwa, as he kissed her cheek. Great, she could blame him as long as she didn't blame Toby. He shrugged his shoulders.

They rehearsed the ceremony. When it finished, Katie sauntered over to Kendwa, hugging him. 'Thanks for coming for Toby's sake.'

'Of course, I would. He's like my brother.'

'But he's not. I'll be his family now,' she paused, glancing at Toby, 'I love him so much, Kendwa. I can't wait to marry him and be all the family he will need.'

Kendwa's jaw twitched, but she turned away from him to speak to someone else. Striding away from her, he went in search of Toby but stopped when he heard Katie talking to her friend.

'I'm so lucky, Siena. Toby is the sexiest guy in the world.'

Kendwa smiled, but Katie continued in an undertone.

'It seriously sucks that the most handsome guy couldn't give me a perfect baby. At least he loves her, so I won't have to. I'll still be able to do all the things I planned. He'll have to parent her instead of me.'

Kendwa's blood ran cold. Clenching his fists, he strode off because he couldn't bear to hear any more. Telling Toby was out of the question. How could he say to his best mate that his bride had said such a callous thing? Talking it over with Sharli first would be the better option before saying anything that could ruin his friendship with Toby. Sharli would know how he should handle it. He couldn't get back to her quick enough.

When he arrived at the unit, he let himself in. Noting Sharli wasn't in the lounge area, he dropped his keys on the kitchen counter. Finding her sound asleep on the bed, he tiptoed around her, trying not to wake her. Carefully, he sat on the bed, taking his shoes off. One beautiful golden eye open and she smiled.

'You're back. I was missing you,' she said in a sleepy voice.

Laying down next to her, he put his arm under her head. 'Missed you more. Did you like the opera house?'

'It's amazing. Though only one auditorium was open to the public.' She yawned. 'How'd the rehearsal go?'

He rolled his eyes.

'Katie?'

'Yep. She's a pain in the ass.'

169

Sharli laughed. 'It's not like you to say that about anyone. What did she do?'

'It's more what she said,' Kendwa told Sharli what he had heard.

'Do you think Toby would even listen to you? He loves Katie and wants to marry her, despite how she feels about Hope. You'd just be wrecking your friendship for nothing.'

'Okay. My wise wife. I won't say anything. Monkey see no evil, hear no evil and speak no evil.' He pecked her lips.

'Exactly.' Though she was tired, she responded immediately when his hands explored her bottom. Their kisses deepened, their tongues tangling delightfully.

'I am so lucky to have you in my life, Sharli Ely.'

Trying to banish his worry for Toby, he concentrated on making love to his beautiful, understanding and compassionate wife. He wished Toby's wife-to-be was the same. In his soul, he knew that his best mate would only find heartache with Katie, but there wasn't a damn thing he could do to warn him. They already shared a child. The wedding would go ahead.

Chapter 22
Sydney, Australia

Kendwa loosened his tie, cracking his neck. The suit was uncomfortable. It didn't help that Deana was one of the bridesmaids. Winking at Kendwa, she sashayed down the aisle in time with Bruno Mars, *Marry You.* He looked away, catching Sharli's beautiful face watching him. Mouthing the words 'hot' to explain his fidgeting, he half-smiled back at her, hoping she hadn't noticed the way Deana had winked at him.

What was the point in telling Sharli about Deana? It was a one-night stand on the day his parents had died. The encounter meant nothing to him, and he'd been sure it wasn't anything to her either. *Perhaps he was wrong about that.*

Deana sat close to Kendwa at the rehearsal dinner, taking her role as maid of honour a little too serious. Practically acting like they were a couple, she stood too close, grabbing his hand, smiling into his eyes. She didn't seem the least dissuaded when he rebuked her or by the fact he was happily married and expecting a child.

'Looks like you're more nervous than me,' Toby said to Kendwa.

'Nope. But I am a bit hot. Not used to wearing a stupid tie.'

Toby looked at his black suit and red tie to match the bridesmaid's dresses. 'Me neither. Can't wait to get out of it, in fact.' He winked.

Kendwa chuckled. 'Well, here comes your lovely bride…' he paused, '…last chance to run.' Trying to make it sound like he was joking, he secretly hoped Toby would sprint out of the church.

'I can't wait for her to be my wife. Look at how gorgeous she is. Like wow.' Toby's eyes were moist, his smile wide.

171

Kendwa decided it was best not saying anything. Perhaps he'd heard Katie's words out of context. They certainly looked in love when she sauntered towards Toby with her hand on Joe's arm. On reaching the altar, Katie fluttered her long lashes under her veil. Joe shook Toby's hand and sat on the bride's side of the church. Katie turned to Toby with a beatific smile. They held hands as the preacher went through the motions.

Deana grinned at Kendwa, raising her fake eyelashes demurely before winking. Trying to concentrate on the back of Toby's head, he willed the preacher to get on with it. It would have been preferable to be a guest so that he didn't have to leave Sharli alone. Though his wife understood that he had to be Toby's best man, it didn't ease his disliking of her fending for herself in a room full of people she didn't know, especially at the reception. There'd be hours of bridal party photos before he could even join Sharli for a moment. Glancing over his left shoulder, he shot her a smile that said, *I wish this were over.*

Sharli smiled back at him. Kendwa looked uncomfortable in the dark grey suit that was too tight on his muscular arms. The tie was annoying him. He shifted from foot to foot and kept clicking his wide neck. The maid of honour seemed to be making eyes at him. Sharli saw him averting his gaze, trying to ignore the irritating woman. Smiling, she knew how handsome he was and the effect he had on other women. She was proud of him.

Toby also looked extremely good-looking in his suit. Only slightly shorter and leaner than Kendwa, they could easily be mistaken for brothers. Kendwa's skin and hair were darker, but they both had the chiselled jaw and brilliant eyes. Toby's greener/blue than the aqua of Kendwa's.

Katie was a lucky girl. Toby had already proved to be a good father and was sure to be a doting husband too. Sharli just hoped that Katie would be a better wife than she'd been a fiancé and mother so far. Maybe the marriage was what Katie needed to get her priorities right.

Finally, the happy couple kissed long and deeply. The bridal party moved in behind them to lead the congregation outside. Deana giggled, turning beetroot when Kendwa bent his elbow, as they'd practised, so she could link arms with him. Kendwa rolled his eyes to smile and wink at Sharli as they passed by.

It was emotional seeing him arm-in-arm with another woman, even if it was only for his friend's wedding. Kendwa didn't concern her. She didn't doubt his love, but the woman looked a bit too territorial for her liking. *Keep your hands off my husband.*

Once most guests had left the church, Sharli followed them out into the sunshine. A lady in a bright, colourful swirling dress came up to her, smiling warmly. 'You must be Sharli.' Embracing her, she then placed her hands on Sharli's shoulders, giving her the once over. 'Kendwa said you were gorgeous. He was right.'

'Thank you. Yes, I'm Sharli. You must be Toby's mother.'

'I'm Crystal, and my husband Derick is over there having a cigarette. I know; a nasty habit, but at least he goes away from everybody. He'd never dare smoke near me or inside either.'

Sharli watched him put out the butt by squishing it against a brick. Some of the younger men were already drinking bottled beer. Picking up one of their empties, he inserted the cigarette butt, placing it on the garden edge, probably for later cigarettes. Hands in his pockets, he strolled towards them. A weathered, handsome face and sparkling grey eyes showed he was probably in his late fifties. Pulling his hand out of his trousers, he reached a sun-spotted hand to Sharli. She took it, feeling the callouses on his fingers. Someone who worked hard his whole life.

Crystal said, 'Derick, this is Kendwa's Sharli.'

'He's done even better than our son, I think. Oops, should I say that? Hello, Sharli. Welcome to the family. Kendwa is like a son to us. Those boys have been good mates for years. The things those two got up to together would make you blush.'

Sharli laughed. 'Don't worry I've heard a lot of their escapades already. They'll have to go a little easier on things now there's babies as well as wives.'

'Oh, that's right, you're expecting. Congratulations, honey,' said Crystal, embracing her again. 'Now, you probably don't know anyone, so you just hang out with us. I'll introduce you to Toby's friends who've come down from the Goldie. They're a lovely bunch and closer to your age. Come along. We'll head to the reception and wait for the bridal party to come back.'

The reception was in a lavish hotel in Balmain overlooking Goat Island and the sparkling blue waters of the harbour. The ceiling, draped in red and white organza, was decorated with red and peach roses and orchids. The tables were red and white fabric with fine gold cages, huge candles inside, and gold cutlery.

Derick whistled when he moseyed in. 'This would have cost a pretty penny.'

'They've gone over the top. Look at the cake. It's five-tiered.' Crystal lifted a few place cards looking for their names. 'Oh, we're here. Where are you, Sharli?'

Sharli checked the next table. 'Here. Next to someone called Dobbo, and the other side of me is Sid.' Shrugging her shoulders, she smiled at the friendly couple.

'All Toby's mates,' Derick said, sitting down still looking around at the lavish surroundings. 'Jeez, I'm glad we're not forking out for this, Crystal.'

'Well, Katie's family wanted it like this, so they can pay for it. Oh, don't mind us, Sharli. We're happy they have their wealth if that's their thing, but we live more modestly.'

'I do too. In Zanzibar, we live minimally. I prefer it that way. Material things don't matter as much as love.'

'I like your way of thinking,' said Crystal. 'I do hope Toby's friends don't get too rowdy for you. After all, you won't be drinking.'

'I'll be fine. I'm sure if they're Toby's friends, I'll like them. He's the sweetest guy I've met, other than Kendwa.' She sat down, thinking how lovely Toby's parents were. It made her wonder about Kendwa's parents and what they would have been like. Even though her dad had been gone so long, she still grieved him. She was sure Kendwa still held grief too.

People arrived. A big bald bloke with a beer gut and tattooed arms showing through his rolled-up sleeves sat down. 'Hi, I'm Dobbo. You're Sharli. Everyone knows that you're Kendwa's wife. We've all been asking who the stunning brunette is. Kendwa was always the lucky one with the pretty girls.'

A guy took a chair on the other side of her. 'You kiddin' Dobbo. Any girls. Kendwa only had to snap his fingers. Toby too. Hey, I'm Sid.' He reached to shake her hand with long skinny fingers.

174

More people sat and were introduced to Sharli. It was difficult to keep up with all their names, but the place cards helped.

Finally, an MC announced the bridal party. The bride and groom came in, followed by Kendwa and Deana. Kendwa's eyes searched the room for his wife. There she was in-between two of the biggest yobbos Toby could have put her with. *Seriously?*

Kendwa sat to Toby's right, whispering in his ear. 'What's with Sharli sitting between them? They'll be swearing and getting drunk in two seconds flat.'

Toby shook his head. 'Sorry, mate. I suggested she sit with my mum and dad, but Katie said the young people had to be with young people and put her there. I had nothing to do with table seating. I had nothing to do with any of this wedding except turning up.'

Kendwa glared across the table at Katie, who had her back to him. It wasn't the first time she'd annoyed him that day. He could see she was conniving to get him close to Deana all day. It wouldn't be wise to show Sharli the wedding photos. Deana had been all over him. He was glad that the men were on one side of the table and the women, the other as traditional with weddings. The further he could distance himself from Deana and Katie, the better.

Excusing himself, he stood. 'Just gotta go to the toilet before this all starts.' He didn't go to the men's room but over to Sharli's table. Dobbo was telling a joke. Everyone around the table and one nearby laughed, including Sharli. Wiping her eyes, she glanced up at Kendwa. Her smile widened. Before she could get up, Dobbo did.

'Kendwa, maaaaate! How ya been?' Dobbo shook his hand. 'You can sure pick a bride. Sharli's amazing.'

Kendwa's jaw twitched. He just wanted to hug and kiss his wife and check that she was okay, but Dobbo blocked him. 'Yes, she is, thanks, Dobbo. I'd like to see her, actually.' Dobbo stepped aside. Kendwa waved to the rest of the table, grabbing Sharli's hand pulling her up to him, taking her to a quiet corner.

Kissing her lips, he pulled her close. 'Babe, how are you going? I wish I could be sitting with you.'

'I'm fine. Everyone has made me feel very welcome. Toby's mum and dad are lovely too. Don't worry about me. You're Toby's best man. You've got to do your thing.'

'I know. I just miss you. I want to spend every second with you before you go back home.'

'Me too. Just get through the speeches and come find me for a slow dance,' she said, winking, stroking his arms. 'You look very sexy, though a little uncomfortable in that suit.' She giggled.

The tinkle of a spoon-tapped glass made them turn. The master of ceremonies called out, 'The best man and bridesmaids are needed at the bridal table.'

'Damn, that's my cue,' swore Kendwa. 'Babe, those blokes will probably be fun until they're drunk. Go sit with Toby's folks if they get rowdy.' He turned to the table as he led her back to her seat. Pointing to his eyes and then the table, he said to Dobbo and Sid. 'I'm watching you all. Look after my wife.'

Sid gulped, glancing around at anyone but Kendwa. Dobbo shook Kendwa's hand again. 'You can count on it, mate.'

Kendwa didn't believe him. Dobbo was a nice enough bloke but could get a bit stupid after the dozen beers or more. He was bound to consume even more than that at a wedding. Kendwa leaned down, kissing Sharli's lips. 'I look forward to the slowest dance.'

Kendwa returned to the bridal table. With hardly a falter, he made a brilliant speech about his friendship with Toby. It had everyone laughing and Toby's mother crying. Sharli clapped with pride. Then he said the bridesmaids were beautiful and made a toast to them. Sharli watched Deana's notable preen. Kendwa sat quickly, avoiding Deana's eyes. *What was going on with that?*

The bride and groom slow waltzed their first dance to Jack Johnson's *Better Together*. After the first verse, Kendwa led Deana onto the dance floor. The other paired groomsmen and bridesmaids followed.

Deana pushed her breasts against Kendwa's chest. Kendwa shifted his body backwards so that they weren't touching. Looking around for Sharli, he noticed her dancing with Dobbo. Maneuvering the oblivious Deana towards them, she got the wrong impression, pushing her body close to his again.

Kendwa let go of her hands, abruptly stomping towards Sharli and Dobbo. 'Dobbo, can I cut in, mate?'

Dobbo hurried away. 'Sure, Kendwa.'

Kendwa took Sharli in his arms, drawing her close to feel her heat. 'At last.' Sighing, he kissed her forehead.

'Are you sure you don't want to keep dancing with the maid of honour?' Sharli pouted.

'Of course not. I couldn't wait to get away from her to dance with my beautiful wife.'

Sharli glared at Deana, who was now dancing with Dobbo but watching them with narrow eyes. 'What is it with her?'

'What do you mean?' *It was heaven to be holding Sharli again.*

'The looks she's been giving you. She's like, possessive of you. She's not an old girlfriend or something?'

Kendwa paused.

Sharli's eyes widened. 'Kendwa? Why wouldn't you tell me.'

'It's not important. She's not important and wasn't a girlfriend at all.'

Sharli pushed his chest. 'I need to go to the bathroom.' She stormed off. Kendwa scratched his head, retreating to the bridal table. He skolled a beer as he watched the door to the ladies'. Soon he saw Deana stride towards it. Sharli was still in there. *Oh no, that's not good.*

Kendwa got up, striding quickly towards them. On entering the hall leading to the ladies, he could hear Deana's high-pitched voice.

'I had him first. We've got history.'

Sharli fists balled at her sides, but her bottom lip trembled. Kendwa's anger surfaced like a slow crocodile.

'He's my husband. Please leave him alone. You're making a fool of yourself.'

'Why should I? He was the best fuck I've ever had.'

Kendwa rounded the corner. 'I don't even remember it. And if I did, I definitely wouldn't go there again. Come here, Sharli, baby.'

Sharli wiped at her eyes. 'But she said that you…'

Kendwa brushed Deana aside, putting his arms around Sharli, who cried on his chest. 'It's all bullshit. There never was anything with her and me.'

'But.'

Deana slunk away.

He lifted Sharli's wobbling chin. 'Babe. Trust me. There's only you. What did she tell you?'

'That you rekindled your love last night. That you never got over her in America.'

Kendwa laughed sarcastically. 'Wow. She is delusional. I came home as soon as I could last night. Toby will verify that. I couldn't wait to have you in my arms.' Jaw twitching, he ran his hand through his hair, clearly frustrated by the turn of events.

Lifting sad eyes to him, she admitted, 'I'm sorry. I'm so hormonal and sensitive.'

Stroking her hair behind her ear, he said softly, 'I know, babe. This has made me so angry. How dare she try to put a wedge between us!'

'Kendwa, but it's obvious that you were both together at some stage. She still carries a torch for you. Be honest with me about that.'

Leaning against the wall as if exhausted, he brought her with him, so her beautiful body was pressed against him. Stroking her satin hair, he glanced up at the ceiling and back to her expectant face. 'To be honest. I never want to ever think about that day.' He paused. 'That morning, I found my parents...dead. That night I needed a release. Katie brought her around. I'd never met her. She was there, you know? That was all it was...a release from the pain of that day. She knew it too. I told her that.' Tears welled in his eyes. As if to block out the memory, he shut them.

On tip-toes, she stretched up, kissing him softly, lifting a hand to wipe the tears from his cheeks. 'Thank you for your honesty, even though I know you didn't want to bring that up.' She kissed him until he looked at her. 'I do love you and trust you. I wish other women would leave you alone.' Squirming out of his arms, she pulled away, tugging his hand. 'Come on. Here's our slow song. I want to dance with my husband. I need to leave those bridesmaids with no doubt that you love me.' Smiling back at him, she was happy to see his dimples emerge.

'I can definitively prove that.' They strolled to the dance floor and blended as one, with their hips pressed together. Her arms wrapped around his waist, his hands on her curvy bottom. 'I am madly deeply in love with you, Sharli.'

And crazy mad at anyone who would try to put anything between us. Something kicked inside him like a wild brumby pummeling his heart. He would do everything in his power to make his wife feel loved and secure—no matter what obstacles they faced.

Chapter 23
Zanzibar, Tanzania

Stone Town was its usual noisy, colourful, aromatic self. Chickens scurried down the narrow-cobbled alleyways, squawking and pecking, followed by turban-headed boys. Bicycle riders dodged and weaved between them, balancing produce and fruit piled high. Paper lanterns and kangas blew in the salty breeze.

Sharli listened to the sound of her home, smiling as she waited for Metra to return from a store nearby. Metra had been a godsend while Kendwa was away. She didn't know how she would have coped without their friendship to distract her.

It had been a lovely day strolling the bazaar, reminiscing about their childhood. Chand was with Sharli's mother. It was nice that they seemed to have gotten closer. Metra ran towards Sharli, almost tripping over a stray chicken, slow to be rounded up by the young boys.

'Look, I found them. Aren't they cute?' Metra said, holding up a pair of azure blue silk baby booties.

Sharli laughed. 'They are adorable but blue?' Raising her eyebrows, she took the baby shoes, smiling. Imagining her child wearing them on its tiny feet, she stroked the soft fabric.

'Yes, but only because they are such a pretty colour. I have no idea whether you're having a boy or a girl.'

Sharli rubbed her slightly rounded tummy. 'I think it's a boy. Kendwa said the same thing on the phone last night.' Looking wistful, she chewed her bottom lip as she slipped the booties into the bag over her shoulder. 'Thank you. They are beautiful'.

'You miss him a lot, don't you?'

181

'So much. I've never had this need for someone in my life like him. It's so intense it scares me sometimes. I know I told him to take the job, and I thought I was independent enough to handle it. I never realised three months would feel like forever.'

'He's home in a couple of days. Hang in there. I'm so happy for you that you've found someone like Kendwa. He loves you just as much as you love him.'

'I know. I feel very blessed.'

They walked past a stallholder with old journals and antique metallic lamps. The old woman waved an arthritic hand at them, smiling a nearly toothless smirk.

The girls waved back but hurried past. Sharli shook her shoulders. 'I just felt a chill. I can't believe she still scares me.'

Metra giggled. 'I know. I think we were about nine years old when she stroked your hair that time. She told you your hair was your beauty, but it would also be your undoing. Then she slid her finger along her throat, and she said you must chop it all off.'

'Yes, that was the first time I got that weird tingle down my spine. I still get it every time I see her. As an adult, I keep telling myself she's a harmless old lady, not someone to be scared of.'

'Maybe she is, maybe she isn't. I still reckon she's a witch who can cast magic spells. Remember that lamp I bought from her?'

'Yes. It was a beautiful antique one, not like the fake ones in other stalls.'

'I made a wish on it. I know that's odd, but I thought it couldn't do any harm. Allah hadn't answered my prayers lately, so I thought I'd give it a try. I was just being silly, but I think it worked.'

'Really? How?'

Shifting one foot in a circular motion, she grinned. 'I've been offered the scholarship in London.'

Sharli opened her mouth in shock and then smiled wide and hugged her friend. 'Business management studies?

'Yes.'

'Wow. That's fabulous. Congrats. You deserve it so much. I'd love to see London.'

'Maybe one-day Kendwa will take you there. I have a feeling all his plans will make you both rich, eventually. I think he is right in saying eco-sustainability is the way of the future.'

'I know. I'm so proud of what he's done so far. Even without investment bankers, he's moving forward with it. It will be a struggle for a while, but we'll get there if we support each other. Now, I just want him home in Zanzibar.'

'I know you do. Should we head home?'

'Yes. Hey, when do you leave for London?'

'In a month. How exciting is that?'

Sharli frowned.

Metra danced around in front of her. 'Don't worry, Sharli. I won't miss your baby's birth. I'll find a way to get back for that.'

'Oh, sorry, I was thinking about myself, but yes, I really want my best friend around for that.'

'I know. You can count on me.'

Sharli strolled towards her house, having waved Metra off at her own. Vedi and Chand were sitting on the front bench, holding hands, smiling as they chatted.

Vedi looked up at Sharli's footsteps. 'Hi, sweetie. Did you have a nice time with Metra?'

'Yes. Lots of reminiscing and laughing as usual. You look bright and healthy lately, Ma. I think the doctor can cancel that wheelchair for a bit longer.'

Chand smiled and said, 'Let's hope so. We have a few nice plans in store before that happens.'

Vedi beamed. 'Sharli. I think I'm glowing because I'm in love.'

Chand nodded, squeezing Vedi's hand, looking hopefully at Sharli.

Sharli gasped. 'I knew it. You both look so joyful.'

'Like you and Kendwa do when you are together. You haven't looked so peachy while he's away,' said Vedi, rising and giving her daughter a warm hug. 'I bet you can't wait for him to get home.'

'Oh, Ma. I've missed him so much my heart aches.'

'At least it's only a couple more sleeps, and he'll be home.'

The next day Jambi's old ute pulled up at the house. Kendwa stepped from the passenger's side. Leaning into the tray, he grabbed his travel bag. Hefting it over his shoulder, he then tapped the truck. Jambi reversed back as they waved each other off.

No one was home. It was how Kendwa had planned it. Surprising his wife for being understanding and patient was his priority. Even though he was dying to see her, he knew his surprise would be worth it. She deserved it and so much more.

At their extension, he placed his bag beside their bed. His wife's shampoo still lingered on the linen, making him smile. Picking up her pillow, he put it to his face before placing it exactly where she had arranged it again. Glancing at the cot his smile widened.

Stroking the timber he'd so lovingly crafted, a cute pastel mobile hung above it with elephants and giraffes. The cot held a matching blanket and a stuffed grey elephant, with a cute pair of blue booties beside it. He wondered if they were having a boy. Picturing the special little person who would soon be in their lives, filling it with more love and joy, made him smile. Overwhelmed by his emotions, somehow, his parents surfaced in his thoughts. That was the bittersweet part of it; them not being able to share their grandchild.

Putting those thoughts aside, he strode to the back shed to grab a shovel. He strode up the sandy track towards the beach, the heavy shovel over his shoulder. Singing Ed Sheeran's *One* romantic ballad as he walked while thinking about his gorgeous wife.

Sharli arrived home to find Kendwa's bag by the bed. Looking around, she grinned, expecting to see him jump out and surprise her.

Running to her mother's side of the house, she yelled, 'Ma. Kendwa's home.' Breathlessly she asked, 'Ma? Have you seen him?'

'No.' Vedi smiled a knowing smile.

'Ma, did you know he was coming home early?'

Vedi chopped carrots, not looking up from her kitchen bench. 'Maybe.'

'So, where is he?' Sharli jumped up and down.

Vedi shrugged her shoulders, dropping the knife, stepping around the bench. She opened her arms to her daughter.

'I'm so excited I'm nervous.'

'I expect he probably feels the same way.' Vedi looked over her daughter's shoulder towards the doorway. She smiled as Kendwa entered, looking relieved that they were there. Vedi took her daughters shoulders, turning her around.

Sharli's hand went to her mouth. *How could he get even more handsome than she remembered?*

Kendwa stepped forward. She fell into his open arms, clutching at his tight t-shirt, standing on tip-toes. Her lips met his with hunger and yearning. Matching her intensity, he then broke their embrace, taking her hand. 'I've missed you so much, sweet wife. I want to show you how much. I have a surprise for you. Hi Vedi.' Vedi waved them off.

'Oh, Kendwa, I've missed you more than you'll ever know. Especially at night.'

'I know, baby. The nights were the worst. I felt sick from missing you.'

Following him outside, feeling the cool sand on her bare feet, they took the path to the beach. They stopped to kiss. Consumed by it, their hands roamed. 'Stop distracting me with kisses. We need to get to the beach,' he said firmly but with a smile. He patted her bum forward, grabbing her hand again. 'Come on.'

'We're heading to the beach? It's getting dark.'

Coconut trees loomed overhead, casting shadows in front of them. Lamps illuminated beach was up ahead. Sharli gawked, glancing at Kendwa. The light reflected on his beautiful sparkling eyes. 'You did this, Kendwa? Wow, it's so romantic.'

Lit candles spread across the sand leading to four burning lanterns at the corners of seats dug into the sand with a sand-table between them. Over the table, a bright purple kanga was draped, topped with hibiscus flowers and a big candle in a crystal holder that reflected and flickered the light from the other candles and lanterns.

Kendwa led Sharli to her seat, helping her down. Jumping down, he sat across from her. Putting two fingers in his mouth, he whistled loudly. A waiter materialised with two wine glasses and a bottle in an ice bucket.

Placing her hand over her glass, she shook her head. Kendwa laughed. 'I have not forgotten my wife is pregnant.' The waiter showed Sharli the bottle.

'Non-alcoholic wine. What does it taste like?'

'I don't know. Probably like monkey pee, but I'd like to toast to us with something.'

While the waiter poured them each a glass, she giggled at his joke. Lifting her glass, she took a tentative sip. 'It's actually not bad.' She smiled at Kendwa, leaning across the table, so their lips could meet. The surf crashing onto the reef kept a rhythm in the background. Bird tunes and monkey cries broke into the lulling sound.

'Here's to our child and us. May we always be in love the way we are today.' They clinked glasses. 'Also, I have another surprise.'

'Kendwa, you arriving home early was the best surprise I could have, let alone this or anything more.' Her excited eyes took it all in, and her arms spread wide, turning to view all of it.

'There's this extra thing that I think you will like.' He passed her a document that he had hidden beside their table.

Sharli's golden eyes grew wide reading it then filled with tears.

He frowned. 'It's the deed to some land over there. Behind the beachfront about 600 metres back.' He pointed to the west. 'Why are you crying?'

'Kendwa, it's a dream come true, but what about Ma?'

Kendwa reached his hands across the table, grabbing hers squeezing. Letting go of one, he wiped tears from her cheeks. 'I've run this by your mother. Her and Chand are making plans. We'll be in their way if we stay there. It will take me a couple of months to build a small banda for us on the property. Also, I'll add more ramps to your mother's home in case she'll need a wheelchair later, but at this point, she's in remission and feeling fantastic.'

'We can finally live together alone?' Her voice rose a little as she kept reading the document.

'Yes. We'll be close enough for you to check on your ma regularly. It's going to be wonderful for all of us. Are you happy, Sharli?'

'It's something I didn't expect. Yes, I'm happy. Can you see this smile?' She pointed to her upturned mouth.

The waiter returned with a large seafood platter that he placed between them. It smelled salty delicious. 'I thought you'd like this. All healthy seafood for your pregnancy.'

'If you had put that in front of me a month ago I would have run off into the bush to throw up. At least I have my appetite back. Mmmm.'

Picking up a juicy prawn, she peeled it, popping it into her mouth, chewing happily. 'Yum.'

Joining her once he was satisfied she was happy, he ate with gusto. Swallowing a mouthful of crab, he gazed into Sharli's eyes. 'Babe, I really want to build a special home for us. Working in Australia gave us that. I want to thank you for being so patient and understanding while I was away. Please say you're truly pleased with the property.'

'I am. Thank you. It's a lovely gesture. I'm just worried about us overextending with you pouring all your inheritance into the business and now a parcel of land as well. Maybe we wait a while before you begin building the house on the land.'

'Okay. I will wait to build but get the plans ready. I don't want you stressing about anything.'

'Once again, you always surprise me, Kendwa. I never know what to expect.'

'I like keeping you on your toes.' He laughed.

'I feel like I'm too far away from you over here.'

'I know the dugout beach seating isn't as romantic as I'd pictured it.'

'It's romantic. I've just missed being close to you, is all.'

'Me too. Have you finished? Let's go for a stroll along the beach.'

Dipping hands in bowls of water and drying them with napkins, he climbed out, walking around to her side. Raising her hands to him, he pulled her up from the sandy seat. They didn't stroll for long because he picked her up, so her legs wrapped around his waist.

Kissing deeply, his hands trailed through her long hair, cupping her head. 'God, I've missed the feel of you and the smell. There's nothing like your hair.'

Strangely a chill climbed her spine, like bony fingers. Ignoring it, she squished her body against his, feeling his strong warmth. Breathlessly she broke from the kiss. 'Let's forget the beach. Let's go home to bed. I've missed you so much.' His erection pushed against her thigh, making her wet and aroused.

'That's the best idea. I've missed you too.'

He whistled to let the waiter know that they had finished. They strolled back towards the house with their arms around each other's waist.

Though he was happy, he wondered about his wife's words and if he was getting in too deep financially. Wanting to do everything he could for her wasn't a crime. Building a home for his wife and baby felt like the only way for him to provide them security. Should he tell her about the problems the business had on the mainland. No, it was not something his wife needed to know. He just hoped she would never find out, though he knew she would wonder why he would have to leave her again so soon after he'd returned.

Chapter 24
Tsavo National Park, Kenya

The elephant herd grazed at the edge of the waterhole. The cows kept a close watch on the babies getting too close to the muddy edge where crocodiles lurked.

Kendwa and his guide sat quietly in the open jeep as the tourists in the back higher up took photos of the herd. Kendwa had interviewed the guide before he left for Australia and was happy with his knowledge and passing it onto their early guests. 'See that big one. He's the patriarch, but he only joins them sometimes. It's usually the females, the matriarch keeping the heard together,' said the Maasai guide, Mingati.

The small group of tourists consisted of a Hungarian couple in their sixties and two younger couples from the USA. They asked Kendwa why he sounded slightly American. He explained about his time in both Africa and the USA.

An American woman asked, 'I've heard most of the Maasai being called Moran. How did you get the name Mingati?'

Kendwa grinned at Mingati, letting him answer. 'I was Moran until I killed a lion, then I became Mingati or the fast one. I don't believe in doing that anymore because I have learnt about conservation, and I want to protect our wildlife.'

'That's nice to know, but you would kill one if it came too close to the camp?' one of the men, skinny and pale, asked.

'We would rather use tranquilisers. We rarely shoot to kill because Lions need to be protected. They don't like fire. We keep the campfires burning all night around the perimeter and in the middle. Just make sure

189

you all abide by the camp rules. There's a large lion pride to the north. We don't want anyone going outside the campsite, particularly during the night without a guard. The amenities are close, but we keep them far enough away, so you can't smell them. Eventually, the resort will have ensuite villas. You're getting a raw experience, as requested.'

One of the American's asked, 'How do you get hot water here? I didn't notice any solar panels?'

'The natural spring underneath provides hot water,' said the Maasai guide, smiling at Kendwa. 'We will be adding solar panels to add to the generator and electricity in the coming months.'

Kendwa added, 'Yes, that's right. Just checking that everyone is clear on the rules, though? They are essential.'

They nodded. There were yups and yeses in agreement, but Kendwa wanted to make sure they understood. He looked pointedly at the Hungarians. 'Do you understand?' he asked slowly.

'Uh, hu.' In faltering English, the man from Hungary said, 'Understand.'

They drove away from the waterhole, passing zebra and lesser kudu. Kendwa soon spotted some lion paw prints and scat as the open jeep drove the dusty track. He pointed them out to Mingati, who nodded. They watched the bush with interest. Soon Mingati pointed to the pride, lazing on a rocky outcrop.

Slowing the jeep to a stop, Mingati told the tourists to stay within the jeep, pointing to the lazing pride.

'Oh. They are beautiful,' gushed one of the women.

'I think we're a bit too close,' said the skinny man, moving to the middle of the jeep.

'You'll have to take quick photos here. We'll need to head back to camp,' said Kendwa, trying not to laugh at skinny man's jitters.

They soon drove away from the pride who had barely raised their ears or eyes to the jeep. They looked full and content, but they had cubs playfully bounding around them. The pride would protect the cubs but didn't need to eat. Kendwa hoped they would stay where they were and not venture too close to the nearby resort.

The small resort had started trading four months before. The first guide had not been suitable, and they were yet to find a manager. The main reception extension had not been completed, but the footings were down. In keeping with the eco-tourism Kendwa only wanted to source natural materials for the extension. It would allow the guests to assemble at dusk for sunset drinks and to view the wildlife below the large deck.

It was great that they could trade, but he wanted the swimming pool dug out and small villas around it for the guests to enjoy the beautiful environment and have ensuite facilities, so there was no need to venture outside to go to the toilet. Those things would take another couple of months. Sourcing the perfect business partner to help him oversee the progress and advise him had been the most challenging task. He was reluctant to leave Sharli any more than he had to and not in the last stages of her pregnancy.

Watching the tourists go to their tents, he chewed on a piece of straw, feeling proud of what he'd accomplished so far. Each tent was a vast, thick canvas over wide decks that stretched out to the view. Kendwa's staff decorated them with beautiful handmade furniture. Plush beds, clean white linen, colourful Maasai woven blankets and hanging space in the tents. A sitting lounge on the deck fenced off to the wildlife below.

The Hungarians gave him an uneasy feeling. Their English was limited. He doubted they had understood everything he and Mingati had told them about safety at the camp.

The tourists began to congregate back in the dining area in the middle of the camp. A big round fire pit was the focal point, and beyond it was the savannah view. The fire was already rising, crackling and flickering ash into the air. Staff placed meat and vegetables under the fire to cook for their evening meal.

Kendwa went to his tent. Grabbing his mobile phone, he hoped he had enough signal to phone Sharli. 'Hey, babe.' When she picked up, he listened to her happy sweet voice. 'Progress is good. I must find the bushman Chiumbo to consult on a few things. They said he'd gone bush again. Apparently, he's the best there is. I need him in charge. Even my dad knew about him. He'll be the best choice to oversee the safaris and the eco-side of the business.' They talked for about twenty minutes before reluctantly saying their goodbyes. 'I love you, babe. See you next week.'

Sweet kisses into the phone made him miss her even more. *How did he end up with the most beautiful, kind-hearted wife in the world?*

The dinner fire glowed as he joined the others around it, animatedly chatting about their adventurous day. His mind was spinning a million miles an hour with everything he had to do to complete the resort. Soon he'd be able to draw a good income to provide for his growing family. There was pressure in so much responsibility, but he figured all husbands and fathers felt that.

A couple of hours after the sunset, they started making their way to their tents, with the guard and Mingati lighting their way and ensuring everyone was secure. Mingati told them to make sure they waved their lamp in front of their tent if they needed to go to the bathroom in the middle of the night. Once the resort was complete, they'd have a closed walkway to the amenities, just to be safe, but many resorts worked the way theirs was.

Kendwa was in his tent on his bed, just nodding off to sleep, when he heard a noise he would never forget. A horrific scream, a loud growl and the crunch of bones. He was up as quick as Usain Bolt, grabbing his tranquilliser gun, shoving a torch hat on his head, and running towards the sound, yelling as he ran, 'Stay in your tents. Close them and stay in your tents. Mingati?'

'It's too late, Kendwa. Did you hear its bite?' Mingati's rifle was over his shoulder aimed at the bush. 'She's gone quiet. Not a good sign. Why would she do that?'

Kendwa, still running, only nodded as his eyes scanned the bush. 'Come on, maybe it's only got her leg, and we can save her. Quick.' Kendwa's adrenaline was high as a passenger plane. He glanced at Mingati, who bravely followed him closely. 'Which woman was it?' Kendwa already knew the answer to that.

'The one I can't understand.'

'She mustn't have understood us either. Shit.'

'Oh, God.' Mingati pressed his finger on the trigger.

Kendwa heard the click as he raised his tranquilliser gun to his eye. 'Let me tranquillise…' Mingati's gun went off, the bang echoing in the still night. The bullet struck the lion on its right shoulder. The force pushed it backwards, so it slumped to the ground. Golden eyes clouded in pain watched them, blood dripping from its jaw. 'She was protecting her cubs. She was leaving too.' Kendwa's torch lit over the ground near the still bloodied woman and the cub prints beside the bigger ones of its mother.

Mingati lowered his gun with moist eyes. 'I had no choice, Kendwa.' He prodded the lion making sure it was dead.

Kendwa nodded, slowly stepping towards the horrific scene. 'Keep an eye out for the rest of the pride. No one deserves to go like that. I'd say it was quick. Shit, shit, shit.' Kendwa rubbed his forehead and looked up at the starry sky before glancing back at the woman.

The lion had gripped the back of her head and neck, tearing her spinal cord from her body and leaving a gaping wound. It would have been instant. She had no chance. Though she had that moment when she'd screamed, knowing she was going to die. The thought made Kendwa feel sick, horrified and temporarily incapable of moving.

Mingati sighed. 'What now?' It snapped Kendwa to his senses.

'I'll call the guard to bring a tarp to wrap her in. Her husband is going to lose it.'

'He heard the scream. He would know.'

'Yep, but seeing and possibly blaming is another thing. Did you see the lantern wave?'

'No. I watched all the tents. Definitely not.'

Kendwa pulled his phone from his jeans to speak to the guard, explaining what had happened. Then he called the police, asking if it was okay that he wanted to cover her, so the husband didn't see. They also needed to move her back to camp in case the pride came back. Taking a couple of photos of the ghastly scene, he messaged them to the police.

The guard came towards them. His torch bounced its light towards them. He ran, breathless with the tarp under his arm. As soon as he saw the lion and woman, he looked away, dry retching. Kendwa took the tarp, pulling gloves out of the box he had asked the guard to bring. Slipping them on, Mingati did the same.

Trying not to look at the woman, Kendwa laid the tarp beside her. Mingati joined him as they tried to roll her into it, pushing her spinal cord and bones, trying to keep her intact. Kendwa was a tough man of the bush, but it had to be one of the most awful things he'd had to do.

193

Raising his eyes to Mingati with silent agreement of their morbid task, they rolled the tarp around her.

'Grab the end. We'll have to drag her towards camp,' Kendwa finally said.

They moved her a couple of hundred feet and could see the resort, but the guests couldn't see them through the trees.

Kendwa spoke to the guard. 'Please go back. Ask the other four to pack. Take them over to the Voi Lodge in the main jeep. I'll cover it. I'll call the lodge now and let them know they are coming. Tell the guests an ambulance is on its way, and she'll probably be okay. Do not tell them she is dead. It will scare the living shit out of them.'

The guard nodded, trotting back to the camp as the sun was rising in the east. It cast an eerie pink glow over the scene. A lion roared in the distance.

Mingati said, 'The lions probably rounded up the cubs and took off after the gunshot. They may come back tonight to see what happened to the lioness.'

'You're probably right. I'll talk to the local rangers.' Kendwa relaxed his tense shoulders. 'Once the guests are gone, we'll go around the amenities side, so the husband won't see her. The police can handle that part. But I think we'll have to tell him. I think he understands English better than she did.'

They observed the dust cloud follow the jeep as it left for Voi Lodge. Dragging her to a hiding spot, they glanced nervously for the husband to appear. Once placing her in a concealed area, they disposed of their gloves, cleaning the blood off their arms. There was some on Kendwa's t-shirt, so he took it off. Better no shirt than letting the husband see his wife's blood. As they rounded the corner towards the tents, the husband rushed towards them.

Blotchy-faced, red circles surrounded his moist eyes like he'd already shed all his tears. 'Tell me. Guard won't talk. Need to…to know.'

Mingati glanced at Kendwa with sad black eyes.

Kendwa said, 'It's okay, Mingati. I'll handle it.' Taking the man by the shoulder, he led him to sit on a bench. 'It was extremely quick. She wouldn't have felt anything.'

The man blubbered. 'But…I..I heard her scream. The scream…it…'

'I promise you it was the instant after she saw the lion. It was fast.' Kendwa rubbed at his forehead, running his hand back through his hair. There was nothing he could say to this man to ease his pain. 'We are so sorry for your loss.'

The man shook his head, rubbing his wet eyes. 'She...I...She said she heard a cub...wanted to see it. I was half asleep. I didn't think she'd...' He put his head in his hands and wept. Kendwa patted his shoulder, knowing there was nothing further he could say.

A siren blared closer. The gravel crunched as the police pulled up in a dirt-soiled police car. Kendwa knew they wouldn't lay any charges. It was a clear-cut case, but he felt guilty for her death nonetheless. Ensuring the tourist's safety was paramount. Though he thought he had everything in place, the tragedy had reinforced how unpredictable human nature was.

What would the tragedy do to their reputation and livelihood?

That poor woman, but she was gone. There was nothing that could hurt her now. Everyone who had heard her or seen her after the event would be haunted by it forever. The police strolled towards them. Kendwa spoke to them succinctly, pointing to where they had laid her body.

The husband was in a world of pain. Kendwa watched the police take him to view the body, shaking his head. The poor man's body slumped like he'd folded in on himself. One of the policemen propped him up by the elbow. The guttural howl as he saw his dead wife was the third sound in those few hours since the attack that Kendwa would never forget.

Chapter 25
Zanzibar, Tanzania

Kendwa crawled into bed beside Sharli, trying not to wake her. She stirred, turning towards him, snuggling into him. The delicious nakedness of her body greeted him. Not being able to stop himself, he planted kisses down her shoulder. She opened one golden eye and then the other as a smile broke out on her sweet lips. He kissed her gently, then deeply.

'You're home early. I'm so glad,' she said, curling her tiny hands around his neck.

'You don't know what it does to me to come home to you naked in bed.' Tenderly he stroked inside her thigh as she jutted her hips towards him. A firm erection was like a homing device towards her. Though he was bursting with pent-up desire, mindful of the baby, he entered her slowly.

Kissing his ear, she whispered, 'Do to me what you do best. I'm so ready for you.' Words like that could tip him over the edge of desire, let alone her body. They met each other thrust for thrust.

The pregnancy seemed to intensify her hormones, meeting his needs with her own. His desire for her assuaged the guilt of what had happened on the mainland.

Later, entwined, sweaty and sated, he bit back the words to tell her. Letting her know of its horror because he wanted to talk about it wasn't fair on her. Also, he didn't want to relive it in the telling. Each night since it happened, he'd been reliving it anyway.

In the morning, he awoke with a start. Wiping his forehead, he shook the nightmare of the lion attack from his waking mind. Luckily, Sharli

197

was already up. He wouldn't have to explain his panic. Flicking the sheets off, he got up to stroll around naked, trying to find his clothes.

Carrying a basket full of washing, she strolled in. 'Nice butt,' she said cheekily. 'Are you looking for these?' She placed the basket on the bed.

'Yeah, thanks.' He fished through the basket, grabbing underwear, shorts and a t-shirt. Lifting the shirt over his head, he put it on.

Smiling, she watched his pecs dance. Then frowned, picking up another t-shirt, holding it to her chest. 'Why was there blood on this shirt?'

'Umm.' The t-shirt he'd worn on the night the lady was mauled. He ran his hand through his hair, avoiding her eyes, stepping into the shorts.

Placing her hands on her hips, watching him dress, she waited for an answer. 'Kendwa. Why was blood on that shirt? Were you dealing with poachers again?'

Putting his arms out, he stepped towards her. 'It's okay, sweetheart. I'm fine.'

'You know how worried I am about you chasing after poachers. How many rangers have been murdered this year alone? You have a wife and baby now. You can't be so reckless.'

Placing both hands on her shoulders, he spoke softly. 'It was nothing, just, umm, blood from the goat I helped slaughter one night for food. I'd forgotten about the shirt.' Wrapping his arms around her, he glanced at the ceiling, asking his mom and dad's forgiveness for lying to his wife. Especially while she was pregnant with their child, he didn't want her worrying any more than she already did.

Kendwa held her tight, suddenly realising her belly had grown. There was movement from her protruding stomach.

Sharli giggled, breaking the sombre mood in an instant. 'Did you feel that?'

Grinning, he sunk to his knees, placing his hand on her belly. He looked up at her with wide eyes. 'Was that a foot or something?'

'Yes. He...or she has been moving a lot. I feel a foot imprint and sometimes a tiny hand.'

'Oh, wow, Sharli. This is the most amazing thing.' Gently his hand swept her stomach.

'You can press harder. Sometimes it makes the baby push back.' She placed her small hand on top of his, pressing it firmly.

A joyful smile spread across his face. 'I can feel a foot. Must be a boy. He wants to play soccer.' He moved his hand to find the foot again.

'Or a girl who also wants to play soccer better than the boys.'

Sharli watched Kendwa's handsome face smiling at the miracle of their child. Though delighted, he looked vulnerable somehow. She wondered what had really happened on the mainland. Watching him drag his hand through his hair always rang alarm bells. He always did that when he was worrying or thinking. As if he were considering what he should say, he had hesitated before answering her. She didn't want to be annoyed with him, but he seemed cagey every time he returned home.

Not wanting to break the spell of his wonder about the baby, she held her tongue, choosing a better time to ask him what was going on. It would have to be soon. She needed to know what was happening with the business and whether he was in danger. Being his wife gave her the right to know. She just wasn't sure how she would ask him without sounding like she was accusing him of lying. *Was he lying, and if so, why would he lie to her?*

Kendwa surveyed the land he had bought for their family banda. The acreage had plenty of banana trees and taller canopies of trees that monkeys would love along the boundary edges, where the forest was thicker.

Clearing only where he planned to start a pad for the future house, he ensured the rest was as environmentally sound as it had been before he started. It didn't need to be big. He desired a homey little banda that had everything they needed. It needed to be warm and welcoming. Tipping a bag of spray cans, measuring tape, rope and tent pegs, he began working. Shaking a can of bright red paint to hear the bead rattle inside to mix it, he paced the area, checking his measurements were correct with the tape.

Pressing the spray nozzle, he marked rooms of the house on the sandy ground where he'd already measured and roped straight lines with pegs. Cheerfully he imagined the special place he would build for Sharli and their child. *Yeah, I did tell her I'd delay the build, so what!*

The problem was, he couldn't keep delaying it. A home needed to be built sooner rather than later, ready for the time the baby would be born. The land that stretched further than his eyes could see was theirs. A real home had eluded him for a long while, but not now he could build one for his very own little family.

Mom and Dad would have been proud of what he'd accomplished in Zanzibar, perhaps not so proud of the safari company yet. Yet, he had to repeat that word; yet. It was going to become financially viable, just not 'yet'.

A notification about the inquest into the Hungarian woman's death had arrived that morning. Lucky, he had retrieved the mail that day instead of Sharli. It would have been difficult to explain an official court envelope. He and his company had been cleared of any wrongdoing but were given a safety warning. They also had to pay a fine to the police. It was more like a bribe, but that was just the way it sometimes worked in Africa. He'd write out a cheque at the end of the week and mail it off, trying to forget the incident that still haunted his sleep.

There had also been a letter from his aunt in England. The envelope had her handwriting, with its curling letters with her name and address on the back. He'd tucked it in his pocket earlier. Remembering it was there, he pulled it out of his jeans, unfolding it, then tore at the top. He slid the sheet of paper out, taking a deep breath.

Sitting down on his haunches, he read:

Dear Kendwa,

Thank you for letting me know about my dear sister and Jamal. I am terribly saddened and have a hole in my heart. Don't worry, I am fine about the fact that you sent the letter through the lawyer. He said you were too upset to do so personally. I understand that. I was terribly shocked by what happened, but I believe they are at peace and eternally together. They had a great love. Take solace in that.

I am so sorry you had to go through that without Uncle Rufus, Noah, Joanie and I. We are your family and send our love to you, dear Kendwa.

It took me some time to find out where you had gone. You've done some travelling, America, Australia, Borneo and back to Africa. I think

200

both your mum and dad would be happy that you had returned to Zanzibar. Let alone the fact you are now married to a lovely Hindu girl.

I do hope I meet her one day. Perhaps you can visit and stay with us sometime. You're always welcome. I have a few of your mother's things I'd like to give to you too. Perhaps we can celebrate your wedding again so she can have your family a part of it too.

Please stay in touch. We do care about you and love you a lot. Keep strong as you always do, but don't be strong alone.

Lots of love, Aunty Marge, Uncle Rufus, Noah and Joanie. Xxxx

Tears dripped down Kendwa's face, landing on the sandy soil. Folding the letter, he shoved it back in his pocket as he rose, glancing at the sky, angrily wiping his tears.

'Some days, the hole through my heart seems bigger. Today's one of those days.' Adam's apple bobbing, he was about to yell out in anger.

Footsteps behind him made him turn to see Sharli coming towards him. Making sure the tears were gone, he turned, a smile planted on his face.

'Hey, what are you doing here?' she asked, taking his hand, squeezing it.

'I could ask you the same thing.'

Shielding her eyes from the mid-day sun, she smiled. 'I was curious as to whether you'd started yet.'

'You told me not to.'

'I know, but I didn't think you'd be able to help yourself.'

'You know me too well.' Cuddling her to him, he sighed.

'Are we standing in our lounge room?'

'We are.' He turned her to face east. 'We'll get the sea breeze here in summer.' Wrapping his arms around her, he kissed the top of her pretty head. It would be perfect. He pictured them on a patio sharing their end-of-the-day news.

'It will be lovely.' Turning around to face him, she kissed him. 'I want to ask you something.'

He silenced her with a deeper kiss, and a thought popped into his head. 'How would you like to go to London and visit Metra at her university?'

'What? Really? When?'

'We have to travel to Australia for the Christening. I thought we could divert our trip to Dubai and go to London for a few days, then back to Dubai and Australia.'

'Are you serious?' She jumped up and down, holding her stomach.

'You're not too pregnant for the flights, are you?'

'No, no. I told you I had the all-clear for the trip to Australia. I never imagined we'd be heading to London first. I've not seen London. It's just, soooo exciting.' Doing a little twirl while holding onto his hand, she danced around.

'So, you're happy about it?' He laughed.

'I sure am. Metra will be beside herself. I'll have to phone her.' She hugged him tightly. 'You are the best husband in the whole wide world.'

'Just so you're prepared for meeting my family.' He pulled the letter out of his jeans, handing it to her. He looked away as she scanned the pages.

'Oh, Kendwa. I thought you looked sad when I first got here.' Kissing his cheek, she wrapped her arms around him, then handed him back the letter.

'I guess I got a little emotional reading it. Aunt Marge is mom's only sister. She looks exactly like her. It will be hard to see her, but I'd really like you to meet them.'

'I'd be honoured to meet them. We could have a wedding dinner or something with them, so they feel involved in our marriage. Celebrate your birthday there too, well if you want to.'

'That would be nice. Wouldn't it? Not the birthday, though.' He hated the idea of celebrating his birthday. To him, it was his parent's death day.

'Yes, but we won't do the Hindu wedding thing.'

'How about we just dress up? Do a small traditional ceremony and then dinner? Just us, them and Metra, if she wants to.'

'Perfect. I couldn't wear my sari, even if I wanted to. Smiling, she patted her engorged stomach. 'Hey, stop kicking, little one.' She laughed.

Kendwa placed his hand where he could see a protruding foot. 'Be kind to your mom, baby. Hey, what were you going to ask me?'

'It doesn't matter.'

He kissed his wife before picking up the spray can. Marking more areas of their home, he explained what he was planning as she looked on smiling with her beautiful golden eyes.

England may hold the key to his dead mother's message. It was another reason to go. Though did he really want to see his mom's sister and miss his mother all over again? Could his mother's words be about his cousin Noah, not his brother?

Wondering why he needed to go to England, he realised he'd better write to his Aunty and let her know they would be coming. She'd left no email or phone number on the letter, so it would have to go snail mail. He wanted to warn her not to mention his brother Noah. It would be hard enough seeing the aunty, who was his mother's identical twin, let alone his wife, learning about what had happened to Noah. *Some things had to remain secrets.*

Chapter 26
London, England

Big Ben, the clock, chimed loudly. The London street was a drab grey.

A white coat dwarfed Sharli's tiny body, even with her pregnancy clearly showing. A double-decker red bus swerved past, splashing water over Sharli's booted feet. Kendwa pulled her closer. It wasn't raining, just drizzling enough to be annoying. There was a possibility of snow.

'It's so cold here. I think we'll be doing a lot of cuddling to keep warm.' Sharli rubbed her gloved hands together. 'These are the best things I've bought so far. I don't know how Metra survives here.'

'My dad didn't like the cold either. Mum, though she felt the cold, never complained about it. I guess being born in London, she couldn't grumble.' Kendwa grabbed Sharli's gloved hand, leading her past a squawking flock of pigeons, rising and falling like snowflakes, as people passed them. 'Enough sight-seeing. Let's get that hire car and head to Dover.'

'I can't wait to meet your family. How are you feeling about seeing them?' Bracing their faces against the chilly air, they stepped forward. Mist escaped their lips like puffs of smoke.

'I'm fine. It could get emotional. It will make me think of Mom and Dad and...' He stopped himself from saying Noah's name. Instead, he spoke about his cousin Noah. 'I get on with them all, except Noah. He's a pompous little Pommy shit.'

Sharli giggled, squeezing his hand. 'I've never heard of you talking about anyone like that, except Katie. He can't be that bad.'

205

'Ah, you just wait until you meet him. He thinks he's the king of England. He went to the best schools. Now, of all things, he's a politician.'

'Oh, no! Not one of those.' She rolled her eyes.

'Don't tease me. You'll see.' They found Hertz Rental, hired a car and then drove it to the motel. It wasn't anything swank because they'd only had enough time to stay in the city one night.

'How long will it take to get there?' Sharli asked, looking at her watch.

'By the time we pick Metra up at Faversham, the trip will be about two hours. We should be there by lunchtime.'

Water drizzled down as they began the drive. Sharli watched out the window. 'It's so green, isn't it? So different to home. Look, there's a castle. I know we have the sultan's ruins at home, but these are so old and kind of gloomy.'

'I guess the owners would have been protected from the cold inside those thick brick walls.'

'The windows are so tiny. No sunlight could get in. I can't believe we'll be getting married again, at an actual castle. It's lovely that your aunty organised that.' Closing her fist in front of her mouth, she yawned.

'Are you tired, sweetheart? Put the seat back a little and sleep until we get to Metra.' The pregnancy was sapping her energy. Angling the seat down, she closed her eyes, clutching her belly protectively. It made him smile. *Sharli would be a wonderful mother to their child.*

Driving carefully on the wet roads, he hoped that the weather would clear by the time they got to coastal Dover. He thought about the reunion with his English family. Marge was a beautiful warm lady, so like his mother. Rufus seemed abrupt but had a soft heart, though he was very old school. Joanie was a pretty spirited teenager. Then there was surly twenty-five-year-old Noah, who was born the same day as his brother Noah. It was an odd quirk of twin fate that the sisters had given birth on the same day and unknowingly named their son's Noah. *It ended up being cruelly ironic.*

Cousin Noah was a constant reminder of what his own family had lost. Maybe that's why Kendwa never liked him. Perhaps he should make more effort, especially for Aunt Marge and because he didn't want Sharli to endure any family tension. He'd rather she had a wonderful time.

Kendwa drove onto Canterbury Road, looking out for Metra, who had agreed to meet them on the main road. He spotted her in front of a modern unit block. Slowing down, he tooted the horn. Sharli stirred, sitting sat up to gaze out the window.

'There's Metra. I'll pull over here.'

'I can't wait to show her how much I've grown. Well, the baby anyway.' As soon as he'd stopped the car, she slowly got out to greet her friend. They hugged at the side of the road, looking each other up and down, talking non-stop.

Kendwa shook his head. *Women!* 'Hey, you two. Let's get moving.'

Sharli held her lower back with one hand as she shuffled to the car. Metra opened the back door, throwing her overnight bag on the seat. 'Hi, Kendwa. Thanks for picking me up.' Adjusting the bright pink scarf over her dark hair, she pushed the sleeves of her pale pink knitted jumper up her arms. Rubbing her white trousers, she said, 'Glad you have the heat on. It's cold out there today.' She longer resembled the Metra who lived on Zanzibar in flowing clothes and hijabs.

'Hey, Metra. Thanks for being a part of our wedding – again,' Kendwa smiled through the rear-vision mirror.

Sharli unhurriedly got in the car, holding her pregnant stomach. There was sallowness to her face.

'Are you okay, honey?'

'Baby's just giving me a bit of hell.' She smiled. 'Going to be a rebel, I bet.'

'That would serve Kendwa, right.' Metra laughed.

Kendwa cautiously pulled out into the traffic, driving towards Dover. Glancing in the rear-vision mirror at Metra, he said, 'Leave me out of it. The rebel in the baby would definitely come from its mother.'

Sharli playfully punched his arm. 'I'm not the one who catches crocodiles and poachers or the one who climbs high trees.'

'You climb trees. At least you did before bubs came along. I miss watching your sexy bum up those trees.'

Metra rolled her eyes. 'Nothing's changed with how loved up you two are. Sharli, the pregnancy is showing so much now. Do you know what you're having yet?'

Sharli squirmed to face Metra in the back. 'No. We want it to be a surprise.'

'I thought you'd be more curious, Kendwa?'

'Nope.'

'I'd want to know. I can't wait to meet your baby. I'll try and fly home after the birth. The semester will be on break then.' The girls kept talking, catching up on everything, while Kendwa drove.

Memories came flooding back when they pulled up in front of the old red brick house. Though he'd lived there for a short time since he had visited the home his uncle and aunt had owned for over thirty years, only a handful of times. It held the ghost of his parents.

He pictured his mother commenting on her sister's blooming roses, leaning down to sniff their fragrance. Sharli tapped his shoulder. 'Kendwa, I asked you if this is their house. Are you okay?'

Speechless, he nodded because his Aunty came out the front door towards them. Tears welled in his eyes, but he refused them by blinking hard. It was like looking at his mother. He gulped.

Sharli frowned, kissing his cheek. 'Come on. You'll be okay.'

Crankily he wiped his eyes. Sharli got out first. Marge held her arms wide. They hugged warmly, both smiling in greeting. Marge, looked over Sharli's shoulder as Kendwa blinked back his brimming eyes, glancing away. Metra came up shyly. Sharli introduced her before they stepped aside, waiting for Kendwa.

Kendwa took a deep breath, slowly getting out of the car. Striding towards his aunty, he stopped in front of her but out of reach. Smiling through her tears, she stepped closer, placing her cool hand on his face.

'Kendwa. You don't know how much it means to me to see you again.' He put his arms around his diminutive aunty, hugging her, trying his best not to cry, but tears dripped on her shoulder nonetheless.

The girls returned to the car to retrieve their luggage, leaving them for a few private moments. Kendwa wiped his cheeks, glancing up at the sky then back at his aunty. 'I'm sorry, Aunty Marge. I didn't mean to...'

'My dear boy. Do not apologise. I know how much I look like my sister. I worried that it would be difficult for you. It's still such a short time. We'll both be grieving for a very long time to come. Let's get out of the cold. The family are inside by the fire. We're used to the chill, of course, but we were sure that you'd all be feeling it after leaving the heat of Africa.' She bumped his shoulder, smiling. 'And, by the way. Sharli is an adorable young woman. I'm very happy that you have her in your life,' she paused, 'and a child on the way. There's lots to be grateful for.'

The girls followed Marge inside. Kendwa gave himself a few moments to regain his composure before bringing the luggage inside. When he stood in the doorway to the large sitting room, with a wood fire burning brightly, the curtains drawn back to allow the muted sunlight in, everyone turned to look at him.

Joanie jumped from the lounge, running gleefully into his arms. 'OMG. You are as handsome as ever. Sharli is such a lucky girl.'

Kendwa kissed his young cousin's cheek, winking at her. 'No, Joanie. I'm the lucky one. How old are you now? You've grown up.'

'Turning seventeen in a month. I can't wait.' Her face flushed, but she was still smiling.

'Wow, you must be driving already.'

'Gosh, yes. I'll take you for a spin in Dad's car sightseeing, later if you like.'

Noah grimaced. 'If you want to put your life in her hands,' he said dryly.

Uncle Rufus shuffled towards Kendwa with arm outstretched. They shook hands with a solid hold. Rufus's eyes showed their concern. 'Kendwa. We're glad you could come. It's good to see you, young man. Don't worry, Joanie is a good safe driver.'

Lastly, Noah stood, flicking his straight blonde hair from his eyes. 'Hi, cousin. We haven't seen you in so many years.' They shook hands briefly. Kendwa thought it was a weak man's handshake. 'At least you've finally settled down and stopped acting like Tarzan.'

Kendwa's jaw twitched. Noah always had to add a jibe. Kendwa ignored it. 'Ah, thanks, Noah.' To the rest of the room, 'Thanks for having us. It's good to be around family again.'

'I'll get some tea and cake. We can talk about the wedding plans and catch up on what you've all been up to. Joanie, can you show Metra to the spare room and Sharli to the suite we've set up for her and Kendwa? Thanks, sweetie.'

Joanie smiled at Metra and Sharli, beckoning them to follow her up the long hall. Marge retreated to the kitchen. The men were left to talk. Rubbing his cold hands together, Kendwa moved closer to the fire.

'How's the safari business going?' Rufus asked. 'Take a seat, Kendwa.'

Kendwa sat on one of the green velvet sofas. It sunk with his weight. It was old and needed more stuffing. Kendwa raked his hand through his hair, noticing Noah smirking. 'It's still early days, but it's progressing. We've opened the one near Maasai Mara for camping and setting up the resort side as we speak. The pool will be getting filled next week. I'm proud of the self-sustainability and eco-solutions, but there have been a few hurdles.' Explaining in more depth, it was good to get feedback from his uncle, the manager of a chain of hotels in the UK. They weren't self-sustainable, but there were things Kendwa could learn.

'What are you doing these days, Noah?' Kendwa asked, trying to turn the attention away from himself.

'I just got elected to Kent County. Youngest ever. I'll be prime minister by the time I'm forty.' He glanced towards his father, pushing out his skinny chest.

'Yes, Noah is really going places. Politics does seem to be his forte.' Rufus patted his son's shoulder.

Noah looked towards the door smiling. Kendwa turned to see Sharli and Metra return, not before noticing the way Noah's eyes lit up. *His attention better be on Metra and not his wife.*

Marge returned, carrying a huge silver tray she could barely hold. It was topped with cakes and teacups. Kendwa took it from her, placing it on the coffee table. Gratefully, she smiled at him. His heart ached. His mom's smile, at least before cancer had wasted her face away. It was how he wanted to remember his mom, looking vibrant and beautiful, like his aunt, though she was thinner than he remembered.

Sharli placed her hand on his knee, whispering in his ear. 'Don't be sad. Enjoy your time with her.'

Glaring at his cousin who was flirting with Metra, he nodded, whispering to his wife, 'Did you warn her about him?'

'Shhhush!' She patted his leg.

Marge asked, 'You must be excited about the baby?'

Kendwa placed his hand on Sharli's stomach smiling proudly. 'Just a bit.' He winked at his wife.

Joanie giggled. 'Just imagine how gorgeous the little mite will be. Golly, I reckon the baby will be just perfect.'

Sharli smiled at her, placing her hand on top of Kendwa's. 'We're already in love with the baby. Do you want to feel it, Joanie? It's kicking me now.'

Joanie jumped up to sit beside Sharli. They moved their hands. Joanie tenderly placed her hand on Sharli's engorged stomach.

'Press harder. It's okay. You'll make the baby move. Oh, there you go. Feel that.'

Joanie's eyes were wide. 'Oh, gosh. I feel it. It's a whole foot. I can feel toes. Mother, you have to feel this.'

'Can I, please?' asked Marge, standing.

'Of course.' Sharli smiled, waving her over.

Marge placed her hand feeling around for the baby. A look of wonder spread across her beautiful face. Kendwa watched her, imagining it was his mom instead. Willing her ghost to be in the room sharing the moment, he glanced at the ceiling. Briefly, her image and his father's drifted across the ceiling. They were there, but Noah, his little brother, wasn't. It bothered him that he could see their spirit but not his brother. It sometimes made him wonder if Noah was still alive. He shook his head. That just wasn't possible.

Marge suggested they visit the castle where they were going to hold the small ceremony. Marge, Kendwa, Sharli and Metra got in Marge's car for the short drive to Dover Castle. It wasn't huge by castle standards, but it wrapped up and down the green hilly headland. It majestically stood with the unsurpassed view over Dover Strait.

On a clearer day, they could have seen France. The raw handmade bricks formed high square interlocking areas of bridges, ramps and stairs. It had narrow medieval arched windows typical of the period.

'Let's go down. I'll show you a piece of our history,' said Marge. They'd explored the labyrinths of mazes tunnelled under the castle, which protected the castle's vulnerable side back in time. It had been military headquarters, notably during a siege way back in 1216. The old cannons and the tunnels eerily took them back in time.

211

After that, they'd visited the colourful interior of the Great Tower, where the décor replicated the medieval past. The blue, reds and golds of the furnishings showed how lavishly some of the occupants had lived.

Metra and Sharli were enthralled. They had plenty of history on Zanzibar, particularly Stone Town, but the castle was intriguing. The medieval was vastly different to the Omani influences of their home country.

Kendwa barely noticed anything. He couldn't keep his mind off his own family, particularly Noah. *If his Noah wasn't dead, where was he?*

Chapter 27
London, England

Dover Castle was washed in subtle sunlight as the sun broke through the cloudy sky. At least it hadn't rained yet.

Sharli glanced at Kendwa in one of his uncle's black suits. It was far too snug on him, particularly around his chest and arms. He fidgeted with the tie. With a clean-shaven face, he was even more good-looking to her. It brought out the blue in his eyes. To look smart for his Aunty, he'd cropped his hair short again. She liked his hair longer. It was like she was drifting through a dream. *He's my tall, dark, handsome hero.*

Facing the stunning view, they stood outside with the castle behind them. Kendwa held Sharli's hands, smiling down at her. It felt odd to dress in a long lacey white dress over her engorged stomach and a flower-topped veil over her long dark hair, but she was glad they were doing a traditional service for his English family.

'You look stunning,' Kendwa whispered, winking.

'You've said that already.' She squeezed his hands.

'I'll keep saying it too.'

'Uh, mmm.' Clearly, Rufus wanted to get on with the proceedings. 'Better finish things before the drizzle starts up again. Now with the power vested in me. I now pronounce you man and wife.' Rufus looked down at the bible in his hands, not that he'd read anything from it because they didn't want a religious ceremony, just a declaration of love.

Kendwa and Sharli kissed before he said anything further. It was a long, intense kiss with their eyes locked as long as their lips. The family clapped and cheered.

Noah yelled. 'Gawd, that's enough.'

Pulling apart reluctantly, they smiled at their wedding guests. Metra handed Sharli her bouquet of white roses, all freshly picked from Marge's garden that morning. 'Congratulations, again. I preferred your beach wedding, but this was unique and beautiful too.'

'It feels surreal,' Sharli confessed. 'I feel like I'm in a historical romance novel.'

Kendwa held her hand high. The family threw confetti over the top of them. They strolled towards the top of the headland for photos, with the castle in the background and then later, the dark water of Dover Harbour was behind them. Metra took photos knowing that the wind blowing through Sharli's long hair would make for wonderful images.

'Don't know why they'd bother doing it twice,' Noah said to Metra, flicking his blonde hair from his face. He was a handsome man, but he didn't smile enough for his face to show any warmth. Though his eyes were a similar blue to Kendwa's, they were nowhere near as mesmerising. His complexion was paler and his body thin, though not firm with anything resembling muscles. Obviously, he didn't exercise more than it took him to walk up the stairs to the county council building.

'It was magical. They did it for your parents. I think it's a lovely thing for them to share with family who was so far away from their Zanzibar wedding,' Metra said before lifting the camera from around her neck to take more photos.

'Well, they didn't even get invited to that.' Noah sulked.

'That's not fair. You know Kendwa wasn't particularly keen on getting in contact with the family back then.'

'And why is that?' Noah asked, moving into Metra's personal space.

The mint on his breath was strong. Stepping to the side, she took another photo of the bride and groom, ignoring him. He hadn't got the hint. 'If you don't mind, I have wedding photos to take. Ask your cousin. It's none of my business.'

Noah stalked off, shaking his head.

When Metra finished the photos, Metra showed Marge through the camera preview. Marge's eyes filled with tears for about the tenth time that day. Sharli watched her, realising how much Kendwa's aunty loved him. It made her heart warm that he did indeed have family who cared, other than his friend Toby.

Kissing Kendwa's cheek first, she strolled towards the women. 'Marge, thank you so much for organising this. It's been beautiful.'

Marge smiled at Sharli. 'You are so welcome, dear girl. Have you seen these photos? Metra's done a jolly good job. I'd love a copy of every one of them. You two are so photogenic.'

'They are, aren't they? Not one bad shot.' Metra laughed. 'Sharli, look at this one with your hair flowing wildly behind you. Kendwa's love-face is priceless.' She turned the camera back to Sharli. Sharli smiled, rubbing her pregnant belly, feeling the baby move.

Marge put her arm around Sharli's waist. 'Come on. I think it's time for wine and some lovely food. You and Metra head off. My nephew and I have something we must do.'

Kendwa took his aunt's hand and Sharli's bouquet. Sharli nodded, turning towards the marquee, not wanting to watch his pain. She had figured it out, but he didn't know that yet. Kendwa and Marge strolled to the cliff edge.

'I didn't know if the best day for you to get married again would be today.' Marge wiped the tears rolling down her flush cheeks.

'It's the perfect day, Aunty. My birthday would have been hell otherwise.'

'Did you tell Sharli that your birthday was the day they died?'

'I've been a bit vague about it.'

'You should have told her.'

'I wish they were here.' Changing the subject off telling Sharli, his jaw twitched.

'Me too. Ready?'

Together they flung the bouquet over the cliff edge.

'Rest in peace, my dear sister.'

'And my wonderful dad.'

They stood for a while, both in their own thoughts, staring out at the turbulent sea, wind blowing through Marge's upswept hair. Kendwa thought of the child that would soon enter the world and never know his grandparents. It crushed him, making him clutch his aching heart. Out into the universe, he sent a wish that somehow, they would witness

215

their special child growing up. Smiling weakly at each other, eyes red and moist, Kendwa and Marge returned to the others.

They strolled towards a white marquee set with ten seats, big heaters glowing above them. Sharli sat at in the middle with Metra on Sharli's right, waiting for Kendwa on her left. Noah was in the next seat. Marge at the head of one end, fixing her messy hair. Rufus was at the other, with Joanie and her boyfriend George, facing the bride and groom. Marge had invited her best friend Renae and her husband, Tony.

Rufus asked everyone to raise a glass. 'To Kendwa and Sharli. May their marriage be long and filled with love, laughter and prosperity. Oh, and the pitter-patter of lots of little feet.' They raised and clinked wine glasses with cheering.

Kendwa and Sharli wrapped elbows. She sipped a glass of water while he drank champagne. 'To us,' he said. She smiled into his beautiful eyes.

'Thank you for bringing me here. It feels somehow like we are more married after the blessing of your family.'

'It's weird that way, but it kind of does. Not that I didn't already feel like your husband.' He winked. 'In more ways than one.'

'Shhhush!' she rolled her eyes.

Waiters dressed in old-fashioned traditional clothes of ballooning white pants, ruffled shirts and long red coats placed plates of food on the table. Steam rose from the silver platters piled high with colourful roasted vegetables. Delicious smelling poached chicken piled high on another. Tall silver jugs held thick aromatic gravy.

Kendwa, always hungry, tucked in. 'Yum, Aunty Marge. Good choices for cold weather.' Conversations flowed as they enjoyed the banquet.

Noah elbowed Kendwa, swallowing a mouthful of food. He put his cutlery down, wiping his face on the white napkin. 'How long are you going to keep this up?'

Kendwa glared at him, trying to savour the food. His cousin could be more than annoying.

'Don't ignore me, Kendwa.'

Kendwa raised his eyebrow. 'What are you on about, Noah?'

216

'You know this married stuff. It's not you. You travel the world being wild. Now you've been married. Not just once, but twice, to the same girl. She's lovely, by the way. I just don't get it with you.'

'We're not all black and white, Noah.'

Noah had the gall to laugh at that.

Kendwa continued, 'I'm twenty-nine today. It was just time I found the right girl and settled down. Besides, I still have an adventurous life through my work.' Smiling to himself, he knew that his cousin was jealous of the lifestyle he led. Though of course, he'd never say it.

'How does your gorgeous little wife feel about you going back to Africa so often?'

Kendwa's jaw twitched. He took another mouthful of food and glanced at his Aunt, hoping she'd keep talking to Sharli. It gave him time to think before he answered instead of acting impulsively. 'Sharli is the perfect wife. She supports everything I'm doing to build the safari business.' Sharli was deep in discussion with Metra, Renea and Marge.

'Ah, so you haven't told her about your past. I suspect you let her think I'm the only Noah.' Noah smirked.

Kendwa dropped his cutlery, glaring thinly at his cousin. Through gritted teeth, in a whisper, he said, 'You are. Shut up. Never ever mention...'

Joanie cut into their exchange. 'So Kendwa. You head to Australia tomorrow. You must be proud of what you did at Taronga and the Western Plains Zoo.' Her boyfriend, George, looked at Kendwa with wide eyes. Joanie turned to kiss his cheek. They were very loved up. 'I've been tellin' George about some of the stuff you do.'

Kendwa laughed. Happy to not have to talk to Noah, he turned his attention to them. 'Yep. I'm proud. It was a fun project.' He patted Sharli's thigh. 'I'm just a lucky guy to have a wife who approves of me taking these rewarding jobs. She's one in a million.'

Sharli smiled at him. 'George, there are so many stories they'd take a lifetime to tell. My favourites are the crocodile stories in northern Australia. Tell him about those, Kendwa. That one about the guy who had his hand bitten off.'

Kendwa told that story and a few more. He explained about crocodile wrangling. It had them all listening avidly, which seemed to make Noah seethe. Noah got up, excusing himself, shooting Kendwa an angry

217

glare. Kendwa shrugged his shoulders. Rufus and Marge exchanged glances.

The main meal platters emptied. A chocolate mousse dessert soon followed them. Sharli took a small spoonful, savouring the flavour but feeling too uncomfortable and full to eat it.

Rufus swapped seats with Noah. Kendwa's tense shoulders relaxed. Sharli wondered what Noah had been saying to upset Kendwa. She turned to Metra. 'I'm glad they changed seats,' she whispered, 'Kendwa doesn't get on with him at all.'

'I've noticed, but now he's next to me and intruding my personal space. He's ridiculously good-looking, but he creeps me out for some reason. Sleazy could be the word.' Metra glanced at Noah to make sure he hadn't heard them.

'I can't put my finger on it. I think there's more to those two.'

'It's probably a long story. Just a clash of personalities. Kendwa's a free spirit. Noah is…well, he's uptight.' Metra laughed. 'You and Kendwa will be married forever. You have plenty of time to find out. Just enjoy this lovely time with the rest of his family. There's always a black sheep.'

'I suppose.' Rubbing her engorged stomach, she winced. 'I'm feeling so full. The baby is tight in there. It's hardly moving since I've eaten. I can barely stand, but I have to get up and go to the toilet again.' Wrapping a shawl around her shoulders to ward off the cold wind, she rose gingerly. Holding the back of her spine, a spasm of pain shot through her lower back. Trying not to grimace or ruin the afternoon by anyone noticing, she saw Kendwa glance at her. Giving him a weak smile, she said, 'Just off to the toilet again. Baby must be pushing on my bladder.'

'Are you okay, babe?'

'Yes. I'm fine.'

Kendwa noticed her cheeks were pale. Her beautiful face scrunched in pain, and she bit her bottom lip. She pushed her hand over her lower back. Obviously, she was keeping her pain from him, but he'd do anything to protect her and their child. Turning to the guests, he suggested they all have their last drinks and head back to the house. The

218

chilly wind had picked up. Sleet rain began to fall dripping at the edges of the marquee. Though it had heaters above them, the cold was becoming unbearable, at least for the Africans.

Kendwa found Sharli leaning against a wall. 'Babe, you look pale. Are you okay, really?' Placing a hand on her forehead, he frowned then kissed her there. 'You're not hot, but I'm concerned about you.'

'I just overate. There's not much room for my stomach and an ever-growing baby. It's just all part of pregnancy. Don't worry.' Stroking his face didn't reassure him. 'Just prop me up to the car. My waddle is getting duck-like, isn't it?'

'Cutest duck I ever saw.' Leaning on him, she placed her arm through his bent elbow. Smelling the sweet rose perfume of the flowers on her veil, he kissed her forehead. 'Once again, you were the most exquisite bride. I am the luckiest guy on earth. This time though, being pregnant has taken it out of you. I'm going to tuck you in bed for an early night before our flights tomorrow.' He lifted her chin to him. 'You would tell me if there was something wrong, wouldn't you?'

'Yes, Kendwa.' She took a breath. 'There's nothing wrong. Just all normal pregnancy stuff. Stop worrying.'

He wasn't convinced. When they arrived back at his aunt's, he tucked the blankets around her. She placed a pillow between her legs and curled one leg over it, shifting her stomach until she was comfortable. Emotions washed over him as he traced the curve of her belly with his hand. Did she realise just how important she was to him? Something was going on. It made him anxious. *What secret was she keeping?*

'I'm glad you had a happy birthday. I wish you would have let me buy you something.'

'You being my bride is all I need.'

'I've done the maths. I do know there's a much bigger reason you don't want to celebrate the day as your birthday. I'm even surprised you agreed to the wedding today.'

'I wasn't keeping it from you.' He sighed. 'Yes, it's the anniversary of my parent's death. I just can't talk about it and spoil your day. Maybe one year I'll be into birthdays again. It's just too soon.'

'I guess so, but you could have shared it. I love you.' Yawning, her eyes fluttered shut.

219

In the lounge room, Marge and Rufus sat side by side with cups of steaming tea. 'Are you sure you don't want a cuppa, Kendwa?'

'No thanks, Aunty Marge. Just like Sharli, I'm too full to even fit a cup of tea in.' Dressed in a more comfortable long-sleeved t-shirt, he patted his washboard stomach. 'Where are the others?' He sat facing them, the old journal twisting in his hands.

A small timber box sat on the table. It had a tiny padlock. Kendwa glanced at it, wondering why it was there.

'Joanie went to Georges. Noah is around here somewhere. Has Sharli settled?' Rufus asked.

'Yep. Out like a light. You'd think she was in her last month of pregnancy because the baby is exhausting her. I'm keeping an eye on her.' His jaw twitched. 'We thank you both for today. It was so different to our first wedding but just as perfect. Very English.' He laughed.

'We're so glad it all went off so well, especially today.' Marge wiped her eyes with a large linen lace handkerchief. 'Love, I have something of your mother's.' Glancing at the box, she reached forward, pushing it Kendwa's way. 'And what do you have there?'

Wordlessly, he passed her the journal, studying the box but not touching it.

'Someone's diary?' Marge carefully flipped the fragile pages.

'Probably nothing. It's a journal I found in the elephant caves. I...' Picking up the tiny key to the padlock, he held his breath as he unlocked it. 'When did Mom leave this with you?'

Marge glanced at Rufus, frowning. 'It was about twenty years ago.'

Kendwa's hands were clammy. Slowly, he flicked the padlock opening the box, closing his eyes, bracing himself for what he would find. What happened twenty-two years ago had been on his mind ever since his snake bite.

Marge and Rufus watched him. Marge held a fist to her mouth; her eyes were moist. In her other hand, she clutched the lacey handkerchief tightly.

Kendwa lifted a blue velvet jewellery box. Opening it, he found a dainty filigree heart locket necklace inside. Glancing at his aunt, who nodded, he attempted to open the locket. His short nails couldn't get the catch. Wordlessly he passed it to his aunt. Deftly she opened it, gasped and passed it back to him.

A black and white photo was inside the locket. It was of Kendwa as a seven-year-old, his arm over his baby brother Noah's little pudgy shoulders. His father took it the year Noah went missing or died, or whatever happened when Kendwa was too young to know.

Closing the locket, tears brimming, he kissed it before placing it back in the velvet box, snapping it shut. Marge jumped. Running his hand through his hair, Kendwa's jaw twitched. Slowly he lifted a letter from the box.

Rufus interrupted Kendwa's dark thoughts. 'Would you like us to give you some space, son?'

Kendwa shook his head, eyes downcast as he unfolded the paper. It had yellowed with time. He recognised his mother's cursive handwriting and took a deep breath. Slowly, he read as his aching heart hammered. Gulping, he imagined his mother's voice as he read it aloud in a quiet voice.

Dear Darling Kendwa,

If you are reading this, I am now a spirit. I'm with you and around you always. Remember that. I may just be a wisp of wind, or a soft touch of sunlight, a bright rainbow after a storm, stars in an ink black sky, the full moon guiding you; whatever it is you'll know that I never really leave you or Noah.

Kendwa paused, wiping the tears pooling in his eyes. *Real men do cry, don't they?* He glanced at his aunt, who was blowing her nose into the hankie. He continued reading.

I am sorry that I have had to keep something from you. You were too young to know at the time, but you'll be old enough now. There was no point telling you on the day it happened. Perhaps I could have told you since, but that would mean your father has passed away. I promised him I wouldn't tell you while he was alive.

Perhaps this isn't making sense but it's all still so raw as I write this, I'm a bit of a mess. You know that I love both you and baby Noah with my heart and soul. You are the shining lights in my life. You make my world complete.

Noah was taken from us so cruelly. It left a hole in me so large I wanted to dive into it and never surface. I know I haven't been the best mother this year. Sorry, I'm writing and forget that you may not read

221

this for a long while. The whole year after Noah was gone, I didn't love you enough or look after you properly. I am so sorry, dear son.

You probably thought I didn't love you. I loved you too much. I didn't want to lose you also. You and Noah, though four years apart, were two peas in a pod. He looked exactly like you as a baby. He would have grown to look like your twin, I'm sure. He wanted to be you, his hero brother, I know that much.

Kendwa noticed a stain, a dot of smudged ink where his mother must have cried on the page. One of his tears dropped right on that stain.

I had to write this letter in case we never tell you while we are alive. You are not to blame. I hope I've told you that over and over through the years. Kendwa, you are not to blame.

This is what happened, not what we made you believe. You and Noah were playing at the edge of the lake. Dad and I were only metres away. We were arguing about where we were going to live. I wanted to stop coming to Africa, at least while you were little boys. I wanted you to go to good schools in England. We were trying to compromise because we loved each other. Your dad talked about America if we could not stay in Africa. I didn't want to go anywhere but England. We were distracted as we debated it.

Your father blames himself. He wanted you boys to be strong and brave. He thought Africa could give you that.

It's so hard to tell you what really happened. We told you Noah drowned. You were just a baby yourself. I grabbed you. Your dad just ran and ran towards the kidnapper. You didn't see the lady take Noah because you were digging him a hole, away from the water. You were keeping him safe. You had your eyes to the hole. I don't know when she came, but by the time we looked up, she had run a couple of football fields away. You looked around you and began calling for Noah. You were looking at the water. Your little body was shaking with tears. I'll never forget how you yelled for him.

I grabbed you and cuddled you to me. I don't know how I picked you up. You were such a big boy.

Dad kept running. She had her hand on Noah's mouth. That's why we never heard him. She had a camel waiting. There was a man also. They galloped away. They stole my baby. They stole Noah.

Noah didn't drown. Crocs didn't get him. He didn't wander off into the desert. The thing is, and I believe it, Noah is probably alive.

We searched and searched for him. We spent a whole year searching for him. That's when you were sent back here to live with Aunty Marge before we moved to Florida. We probably should have told you the truth when we couldn't find him. The authorities told us that we probably never would. We decided to let you believe he had drowned.

We knew what a determined young man you were. If you'd known that he was alive, you would have spent your whole life looking for him. We didn't want your life ruined as well. We wanted you to at least have a normal life. We are sorry, but we know it was the best thing to do for you.

Now that you are older, it is up to you if you want to find your brother. The rest of the contents of the box will be what we found out. We'll never stop looking. As I'm writing this, my sister, your aunty, has agreed to receive any information we find over the years. I'm hoping this letter is irrelevant. Perhaps we have already found Noah and we've all been reunited. If not, dear Kendwa, this will all be a shocking surprise. A secret that perhaps we shouldn't have kept.

Remember I'm all around you, guiding you through the rest of your life with eternal love.

Love forever,

Mommy and Daddy.

Kendwa brushed his tears and threw the letter down.

'Damn it. I always knew Noah was alive.' He grabbed his heart. 'I knew it in here.' Smacking his chest, he stormed out of the room outside to the freezing English air.

Sharli stood in the doorway, holding her hand to her mouth. To ease her back pain, she had been waddling up and down the hall. Noah, for some reason, paced the hall too. With a sly grin, he told her she should hear what they are talking about in the sitting room. Her ears pricked at 'finding your brother, Noah'. Now Kendwa's nightmares where he screamed Noah made some sense.

Rufus called it a night. Leaning down to kiss his wife's head, he frowned, patting her thin, pale hand. She merely nodded.

223

Kendwa returned and went to stand near Rufus. Rufus pushed his shoulder. 'Sit, son. Your aunt has more to tell you now you've cooled off. I think it's best if it were just both of you.'

Kendwa watched his aunty shifting in her seat. 'What more can you say today, Aunty Marge?'

'Has Sharli got family?' Her voice was a hoarse whisper.

'Yes, a mum, sister, cousins. Why?'

'I. Umm. Sorry. It's awful to have to do this to you. You lead a dangerous life at times, especially when you are in Kenya. Make a will early to provide for your family. In case, God forbid, anything happened to…' She wiped further tears. 'You never know what will occur in your life. I'm so glad you came for this visit.' Taking his hand, she squeezed it weakly.

'You're looking far too serious, Aunty. What is it?'

'I have, unfortunately, the same cancer as your mum.'

'No.' Squeezing her hand back, he frowned. 'That…that can't happen.'

'I'm sorry, but I do have it. I'm not surprised. We were genetically so close I was prepared to have the disease as well.'

'You're not scared of dying?' Eyes misting, he shook his head, refusing to believe it.

'No. I'll join my sister. She's there, wherever we go, so I shouldn't be afraid.' She gave him a reassuring smile, squeezing his hand. 'When you write, your will don't include me. I'll be long gone. Just keep everything in order. Your business and your family. It may be the last advice I give you. If you find Noah, and I hope you do, make sure he is in a position to care for your family if you are gone.'

'Aunty, I don't want to hear this stuff.'

'I know.' She coughed. He noticed her pallor realising she'd been concealing her disease until she was ready to tell him.

'This is so unfair.'

'My dear boy, that is life and death. Unfair perhaps, but that is what it is.'

He went to her, hugging her tight, showing her how much he cared. She cried on his shoulder, but he was cold as stone, angry at the world.

Chapter 28
Sydney, Australia

The boom of the engines and the force of the aircraft taking off had Sharli clutching the armrests. Kendwa grabbed her hand, giving her a reassuring squeeze and smile.

Her hand lingered on her stomach as the plane rose and levelled out. The seatbelt signs went off with a bing. Through the hum of engines, seatbelts unclicked and the murmur of travellers getting set for a long journey drifted.

Kendwa undid his belt then helped her with hers. Stretching his long legs as much as he could, he shut his eyes. 'It's been a big few days. We should get some sleep while we fly.'

Avoiding confiding in him about feeling off didn't sit well with her. After everything he'd learned in Dover, she had no choice. Clutching her stomach, she reassured their baby it would be okay. Hopefully, the flight would not make her any worse. The trip to Australia was important to Kendwa. She hoped it would take his mind off the revelations in England about his family. Even though she still had plenty of questions she wanted to ask him, she would do anything to support him.

The silence since he opened his mother's box had both worried her and annoyed her. If only he would stop bottling things up and talk to her.

He opened one gorgeous blue eye, smiling at her sleepily. 'You're watching me?'

'Sprung.' She laughed. 'I was thinking how peaceful you look. Especially after everything that happened in the UK.'

Opening his other eye, he sighed. Sitting straighter, he gently placed his fingers on her left hand, glancing at her engagement and wedding rings. 'I know you heard some of our conversations, and I know you have questions.'

'I have plenty. Like what did your aunty think about the journal you found in the Elephant Caves? What has it got to do with your family?'

'Nothing. Maybe the Sharman I saw, you know, the crazy Maasai Laiboni I told you about, meant me to go to the Elephant Caves to find it and be reminded of my aunt. I needed to see her considering her diagnosis.'

'Maybe, but there's too much coincidence. What else did the journal mean?'

'Look, Aunty just flipped through it and told me to put it in the box with the other stuff and to sort it out later. When my mind had digested the facts.'

'Why would they have lied to you about him? It doesn't seem fair to you. It makes me so sad for you, Kendwa.' She kissed his shoulder.

'Babe, you are so sweet. Please, Sharli, let me get my head around things first. I promise we will talk about it.'

'Okay.'

'Just okay? You're not going to grill me further?'

'When do I grill you?'

'Lately, you seem to be questioning everything I do.'

'I just want to be involved. I'm your wife. I don't like you keeping me in the dark.'

'You're not. I tell you everything.' Cracking his neck, he patted her hand, sliding down into his seat. 'The family stuff is something I have to sort out first.'

'Do you think Noah is still alive? The brother Noah, not the cousin.' She frowned.

Letting go of her hand, he stared out the window. Taking a while before he finally spoke, in a low voice, he said, 'Sharli, please let's just drop it for now. I think you need a good sleep. So do I. Not only do we have the christening, we also have the opening at the zoo. I don't want you worn out. You're looking like you're in pain and tired lately.'

Tapping his shoulder, she smiled weakly when he turned to face her. 'Kendwa, I'm...' Placing a finger on her lips, he silenced her.

226

'Babe. I know you well enough. There's something about the pregnancy you're not telling me. So, don't. You keep that secret, and I'll keep mine until we are ready.' With that, he shut his eyes, ending the discussion.

Tears sprung to her eyes. She closed them tight. It was like she was a million miles away from him, as he dealt with his hurt and anger that his brother may have been alive all along. She understood that. What she didn't understand was why he was shutting her out.

They slept until Dubai. Sharli, in fits of broken sleep. Kendwa, seemingly contentedly snoring. They were in better moods when the plane took off again. 'I'm sorry, honey,' Kendwa said, kissing Sharli's cheek.

'Me too.' Their lips met. He tasted so familiar and delicious. 'I'm a bit emotional with the pregnancy. My hormones are all over the place.'

'Maybe we shouldn't have included London in our travels. You don't look so well.' Love shined in his eyes as she rubbed her tummy.

'I told you I'm fine. Just the pregnancy. Millions of women deal with it. Anyway, I so loved seeing Metra.' She had a faraway look on her face. 'We had the most romantic wedding too.'

'Except for freezing our butts off.' He grinned.

'God, it was so cold. I'd be happy never to go back again. Give me Zanzibar any day. Even Australia. At least it will be summery there.'

They laughed and talked about the horrible English weather and the things they'd seen and done in their short time there. There was no further mention of Kendwa's brother or her health. Trying to remain upbeat, but both were not their usual selves, each caught up in their own worries. There had been a shift. They were holding back. *Could their secrets ruin the love they shared?*

The air was humid and warm as they disembarked the aircraft at Mascot Airport. Kendwa was about to hail a cab when he noticed Toby waving madly from a white Holden. 'I've come to pick you up. I was near here anyway. Get in quick before the security guys move me on. I'm supposed to be a taxi if I'm driving through here.'

Kendwa quickly loaded their luggage in the boot as Sharli climbed in the back. Kendwa had just slammed his door when a security guy came running over, yelling at Toby. Toby flicked him the bird and drove off.

227

Kendwa laughed. 'You're still such a larrikin.'

'Mate, how are you? Didn't lose any of your tan in good old freezin' London.'

Kendwa slapped his shoulder. 'Yeah, fuuuunnnny! Good to see you haven't lost your sense of humour.' A baby cried. Kendwa turned to see Sharli staring into the baby capsule, with her hand resting on the side. The baby had curled her fingers around hers. 'You have Hope with you?'

'Sure. She's my baby. Where else would she be?'

Kendwa and Sharli exchanged glances.

'Hi Toby, thanks for picking us up,' Sharli said. 'Hope's grown so much. Listen to the little sounds she's making. So sweet.'

Toby flashed her a wide smile through the rear-vision mirror. 'She's seven months old. She gets cuter every second.'

Kendwa leaned in the back. 'Hello, Hope. Do you remember your Uncle Kendwa and Aunty Sharli?'

Hope cooed in reply, clinging tightly to Sharli's finger.

Toby glanced at Sharli. 'Sharli, are you sure you don't have twins in there?'

'No. The scan just shows one little baby. Or should I correct that with the big baby?' She patted her tummy.

'No idea of the sex?'

'We want a surprise,' Kendwa said. 'Where are we heading, Toby?'

'Didn't you say you were staying at the same motel?'

'Yep, but you're driving west, aren't you?'

'Just for a sec. I've got to pick up the christening dress from a shop a few blocks away.'

'No worries. I thought Katie would have been running around doing the christening stuff.'

Toby shot Kendwa a don't-ask-mate look. Sharli doubted that Katie had improved at all with her mothering skills.

Toby parked the car leaving the engine running, so the cool air-conditioning remained on. He came back quickly carrying a wrapped parcel that he threw in the back. Returning to the wheel, he pulled out into unrelenting peak-hour Sydney traffic. A truck cut them off. Toby swore as he swerved to avoid him, honking the horn.

'What's the plan for the Christening?' Sharli asked Toby, placing his parcel on the seat. She would have loved to open it and peek at the dress but wasn't game to ask.

'The address is on your invite. Probably allow twenty minutes for your trip, so hail a cab or Uber with plenty of time.'

'What's the process? I've never been to a Christening,' asked Kendwa.

Toby glanced at him. 'Me neither, mate. Mum's taken over. We were doing it in Currumbin, but Katie said she wouldn't even come if we went up there. She has a group of girlfriends in Sydney. They have to be a part of everything.'

'Not the American friends?' Sharli asked too quickly. No way did she want little-miss-trying-to-steal-my-husband anywhere near Kendwa.

'No, they all went back. They're chicks she's met doing yoga. Apparently, they get her in the zen.' He used his fingers for exclamation marks, quickly placing them back on the steering wheel.

Toby made light of it, but Kendwa could tell his mate wasn't happy with his wife.

'Do they have husbands? Do you socialise as a group?'

'I've never asked. She brings them over too often. They all giggle, get drunk on expensive wine and flirt with me. They're not my type of people. I've got plenty of friends at the zoo, other keepers, zoologists, my tribe.' He turned to Kendwa. 'We got a massive old crocodile called Norm. You should see him. He's my best mate down here.'

Kendwa laughed. 'That's kinda tragic, Tobes.' But he understood Toby's love of the reptiles because he held them, dear, himself.

Toby pulled up at their motel as a valet strolled over. Toby waved him away. 'There you go, guys. See you at 11 am tomorrow.'

Sharli kissed Hope's cheek. The baby was sound asleep, smiling with her chubby cheeks rosy pink. 'See you on your special day, little Hope.' Kendwa opened Sharli's door, helping her out, noticing her sluggishness as she held her lower back. *My wife is in pain, and I feel useless.*

When they signed into their room, he was gruff with her. After dragging the luggage in, he went to the bathroom. Trying to shift his

229

anger, he splashed water on his face. Why wasn't she talking to him about her pain? He wasn't just annoyed and frustrated by his wife, he was also worried about Toby. He was livid Katie was the most useless wife. She didn't deserve a top guy like Toby.

The perfume of fresh-cut flowers filled the room. Kendwa stiffened when he found Sharli with her hands on the kitchen bench rotating her hips. 'What the hell is going on, Sharli? The baby isn't due for eight weeks. Shit, you look like you're in labour.'

Fear was evident in her golden eyes when she glanced at him. She recovered quickly. 'No, no. It's called Braxton Hicks. It's false labour pain that happens for weeks leading up to birth. Apparently, it gets the body ready for it all. Nothing to worry about. Could you just rub my lower back for a sec? I do have a bit of pain there.'

'Sure, babe.' He wasn't convinced. Placing his hands on her lower back, he rubbed, feeling her warm, soft skin. Just touching her made him horny. God, his wife, was a beautiful woman, particularly while she was pregnant. A mix of worry about her and the news that had blown him away in England combined to make him irrational. He had to rein it in and be kinder to her. She was the most precious thing in the world to him.

'That feels good. The baby keeps tightening my skin. Here, you feel my tummy is like a drum.'

Spinning her around, he placed his hand on her stomach, feeling the firmness. 'Is that part of the Braxton Hicks too?' he asked doubtfully.

'In fact, it's the main part.'

'Okay, whatever you say, babe. One thing you need to promise me.' He lifted her chin, kissing her sweet lips. Not concealing the worry in her eyes, she blinked at him. 'You will tell me if our baby is coming early. Eight weeks is too soon, but if it happens, we'd need to be prepared.'

'Yes, of course. But it's just Braxton Hicks. Stop wrapping me in cotton wool.'

Yep, sure it is, and I'm the sultan of Zanzibar.

Chapter 29
Sydney, Australia

Christenings, as far as they go, are either long drawn out religious affairs, or like this one, a quick, no-nonsense baby naming, without religious fanfare and bible bashing.

Sharli was glad of this as she clutched her stomach, trying not to reveal her womb pain to Kendwa. Toby's mother kept giving her knowing glances that unnerved her. Though she was a kind woman, Sharli didn't want her to notice. The last thing she needed was to take the focus off beautiful little Hope and her special day.

It was bad enough that Katie was barely involved in the proceedings. Yawning, glancing everywhere but the ceremony, she looked bored like she wanted to be anywhere but at her daughter's christening. Katie never smiled at Hope, avoiding eye contact with her daughter, instead focusing on their guests.

With Toby, on the other hand, Katie still seemed smitten. Her hands always found him. She was very touchy-feely, smiling deeply into his eyes. Toby, noticeably, paid more attention to the baby than his wife. Perhaps, that was the tug-of-war. Katie wanted Toby all to herself. Toby was Hope's prime parent and doted on his daughter.

It was as if Katie resented their baby. Hope's Down Syndrome may have been a factor, but watching them now Sharli, firmly believed that Katie was obsessed with Toby. Any daughter would have ruffled her feathers in the same way. Perhaps she would have been a different mother if they had a son.

Hope was a perfect baby. She didn't even cry when the priest poured water over her head to purify her. Katie reluctantly held her for that, while Toby spoke softly to his daughter to let her know what they were doing would not hurt her. Katie handed Hope back to Toby as soon after the family photos. Retreating quickly to her huddle of yoga girlfriends, they spoke in whispers behind their hands, eyeing off Toby and Kendwa.

Once Kendwa had signed the paperwork, as the godfather, he found Sharli talking to Crystal. 'You should at least sit,' said Crystal with concern in her tender voice, patting the seat beside her.

Kendwa bristled. 'Sharli?'

Looking up, she smiled. 'Just a bit of heartburn and more Braxton Hicks, honey. Congrats on officially becoming a godfather.' She sat rubbing her stomach. Crystal shot him a do-something glance.

'Are you sure that's all it is?' Sitting next to her, he watched her down-turned golden eyes. Eyelashes so lush and long, framing her eyes like thousands of caterpillar legs. Fluttering them up at him, he gulped. 'Do you think you're in labour?'

She paused, sighing. 'Maybe, but it's too soon. It's just a false alarm. Let me sit for a bit. Our baby will settle back down.'

Crystal stood smiling at them. 'It's hard to tell with first babies. You look healthy enough, though. At least one of the couples is still loved up caring for each other.' She shook her head towards Katie, who ignored Toby as he rocked Hope in her pram. It only took moments for him to give up to Hope's cries, picking her up, placing her gently on his shoulder. They could see his lips cooing a lullaby in her ear.

Crystal stood. Arms outstretched, she strode over to her son. 'Toby, let me have her for a while.'

'Sorry, Mum. She was fine before. Now she's unhappy. Maybe the Christening was too much for her.'

'Perhaps, she needs a mother who gives a shit.' Pointedly she glared at Katie, but she was too engrossed in her girlfriends to hear.

'Muuum!'

'Just saying it how it is, son. Here comes your dad. I'm sure he'll share my opinion.' Gradually Hope settled to some hiccup, slurpy cries and then silence while her grandmother rocked her gently.

Derick slapped Toby playfully on the shoulder. 'Great work, mate. That was a sweet ceremony. Hope was such a good girl for you.'

232

'Thanks, Dad. I'm glad she's having a nap now so I can share a beer with Kendwa.'

Kendwa glanced from Sharli to Toby. 'Not sure about that, Tobes. Sharli's a bit under the weather.'

'Rubbish. Go have a drink. You can only have a couple because you have to open the Zoo enclosures later,' Sharli said, patting his thigh.

'Sharli can stay with me. We'll take Hope back to the motel. They can both have a rest until you come back.' Crystal placed Hope in her pram, tucking a soft pink blanket over her. 'Come on, Sharli. I'll make you a nice camomile tea. That should help.'

Sharli stood slowly. Kendwa pulled her gently to her feet. 'Is that what you want to do, Sharli? I don't mind staying.'

'Don't be silly. As I keep telling you, I'm just pregnant. It's all normal.'

Kissing her cheek, as usual, he felt grateful that his wife was so understanding. 'We'll only be an hour, and then we'll head out to the zoo, so I can cut that ribbon and show you the work I've done. Are you going to be up for that?'

'As soon as I have a mother-to-be nap, I'll be fine.'

He whispered in Crystal's ear. 'If she needs me for anything at all, call Toby's mobile. Thanks, Crystal. Derick, do you want to join us?'

'Nah. Think I'll take a kip myself. I drove straight through from the Goldie to get here for this shindig.'

Once the boys took a seat at Coogee Bay Hotel, overlooking the beach, Kendwa turned to his friend. 'Spit it out, Toby. You're not yourself.'

Toby's sad blue eyes watched the perfect sets of waves crashing and rolling towards the sandy shore. A full beer middy sat untouched in front of him. With a finger, he drew lines in the condensation on the cold glass. 'I think I've made a huge mistake, Kendwa.'

'Katie or Hope?'

Toby lifted the beer, sipped and then turned his eyes to Kendwa's. 'Definitely, not Hope. I'd die for Hope.' *Simple as that.*

Kendwa nodded. He already knew the answer. It was obvious to him that the glow of Katie had worn off for Toby. Where she may have been gold before, she was more like rusty copper.

'Anyway, I want to hear what happened in England. You seemed down about it,' Toby changed the subject.

'I wouldn't know where to start.' He took a long look at Toby. Everyone always mistook Toby for his brother. *What if Noah had been under his nose all the time?* No, they were two years apart, not three nearly four. Plus, his mom and dad had both met Toby. Toby looked a mix of Crystal and Derik. Derick has the same pale blue-green eyes that have greyed with time. Plus, he was Australian. *Jesus, where was he getting these way-out theories from?*

'Try me. I'll tell you about my shit after you tell me yours.' Toby broke his thoughts.

'We don't have much time but, in a nutshell. Noah, my brother, not cousin, may be still alive.'

'Shit, wow.' Toby rubbed his head. 'That is big. Must've been a shock.'

'It was, but it wasn't. I'd been considering it after the stupid vision of my mum. You know how I found the journal at the elephant caves. I still thought to find Noah meant going to London. I guess it did. I was assuming it meant my cousin, not my brother.'

'How is that pompous ass?'

Kendwa grinned. 'Same old self-important fuckwit.'

They laughed for a bit.

'Are you going to look for him, your brother, I mean? I can help somehow if you need.'

'I'll worry about it after the baby is born. Sharli and the baby are my priorities right now. Aunt Marg gave me a box of stuff to go through. I haven't had a chance yet. Mom never stopped looking for Noah, which is sad. I understand why they kept it from me, in lots of ways, but it makes me angry too.'

They sipped their beers for a while, taking in the sparkling water and the hundreds of surfers vying for waves in the congested surf. It was a warm day, around 30 degrees Celsius, which meant towels, buckets and spades, body boards, umbrellas and people of all sorts scattered over the sand.

Kendwa watched Toby with his eyes on a family a few metres away. The young couple were cuddling and kissing a baby between them. The baby held sand in her hands, watching it dribble out of her fingers.

234

To Kendwa's dismay, Toby's eyes filled with tears. Toby took a deep breath. 'I can't stay with her. I love her. I'm still hot for her…' He took another deep breath. 'I don't respect her.'

Kendwa rested his chin on his hand. 'Can it be that simple in a marriage?'

'When there's the welfare of our daughter at stake, yes.' Toby sipped his beer again. His tears were drying quickly, a grimace contorting his face.

'What do you plan to do?'

'Go back up to Mum and Dad's with Hope. Katie will be shocked. She may cause problems. She thinks she can still have a relationship with me and ignore Hope. She'd rather believe our beautiful daughter doesn't exist. It won't work like that. Only this morning, Katie stripped, and I still get my rocks off because, hey, she is beautiful. We have mind-blowing sex. Then, I hear Hope crying. You know what Katie said to me?' Toby slammed his empty beer on the timber bar with so much force it was surprising it didn't smash into pieces.

'No, I don't, Toby. What did she say?' Kendwa could barely imagine it and didn't want to hear about their sex life but listened anyway.

'She said, let's put her in an institution and go back to how we were. We're perfect but not with her. Can you imagine how much that hurt, hearing the mother of my adorable child say that so callously?'

Kendwa shook his head. His heart ached for Toby, fists clenched for Katie. 'You have no choice, then do you?'

'I don't, Kendwa.' He shrugged his shoulders. 'I can handle being a single dad.'

'You probably don't need me to point it out, but you practically are already.'

'I know. Everyone thinks so. Mum and Dad have talked to me about Katie. Mum even tried the old Crystal charm on her, but nothing will change the spoiled, selfish brat. I should have taken more of your advice on women.'

'What advice was that?'

Toby laughed. It was good to hear.

'When I first met you. I was nearly sixteen. You were eighteen. I was shagging lots of girls but not having a clue. It was innocent fun.' He laughed. 'I remember you telling me that it's even better when you

235

find a connection. You said there are plenty of charismatic girls who aren't classically beautiful and that I needed to look a little deeper.'

'Jeez! Did I say that? I was a very philosophical young man.'

'You always have been. I've usually taken your advice. This time?'

'I didn't give you advice on Katie.'

'You told me to run at the wedding. I know you were trying to make it sound like a joke, but you weren't kidding. Guess the gag is on me now.' Frowning, he shook his head.

'We all make mistakes, Toby.' Kendwa patted his shoulder. 'It will work out okay. You are fantastic with Hope. You'll get over Katie, and she'll eventually get over you.'

'It's just so hard. I'm disappointed that it's failed.' Looking down, Toby glanced at his watch. 'We'd better get going.'

They strode as far as the door when Toby's phone rang. Fishing it out of his pocket, he listened, frowning. 'Okay, Mum. He's here.' He handed Kendwa the phone.

Kendwa took it with a racing heart. Listening to Crystal's panicked voice, his worst fears rose, making him ill. Composing himself, he handed the phone back to Toby. *He'd be no help to Sharli if he lost his shit now.*

'St Margaret's Hospital?' He didn't have to say more. Toby already held his car keys. They ran to the car.

On the way there, Kendwa stared out the window. It was a blur of speed. His frantic thoughts ran through his head just as hazy. Sharli was on her way to the hospital by emergency ambulance. He couldn't bear the thought of losing them both. Clutching his shaking hands together, he willed himself to be strong for his wife and child.

Chapter 30
Sydney, Australia

It seemed like there were people everywhere as an intern led Kendwa into the labour ward. Doctors, nurses, midwives and anaesthetists rushed about with surgical instruments, unsettling his rising panic.

The hospital gown over his clothes was too tight, and he fidgeted with the mask on his face, trying to breathe. He gulped the fear in his throat, lodged and immovable, with his heart near exploding.

A sheet draped Sharlie lower body, legs up and bent wide, with doctors and midwives between her thighs. He felt useless. They were speaking in urgent-foreign-medical tongue. *What was going on?*

The midwife next to him said kindly, 'Hold her hand. She has one or two more pushes, and the baby will be here.'

Already. Shit!

With wide eyes, he nodded, doing as he was told. Avoiding looking at the blood and fluid pooled at Sharli's feet or how pale her skin looked, he tried to give her a reassuring look. Soaked in sweat, her long hair plastered around her face, she seemed delirious. 'Kendwa,' she said in a high-pitch raspy voice. 'I'm s…sorry.' Tears slipped from her eyes. A guttural scream tore from her throat.

Grabbing her hands, he kissed her tears. She held him so tightly he could feel her nails digging into him. *Give me your pain, honey.*

The midwife urged. 'Breathe, Sharli. We're nearly done. Just making sure you don't tear. We don't want to have to give you stitches. You can push very soon.'

'Breathe, honey. I'm here. We'll get through this together.' Kendwa copied the deep breaths.

Sitting more upright she glared at him. 'I'm the one fucking giving birth, Kendwa. Not WE!' She gritted her teeth, puffing raggedly, turning her eyes away from him to concentrate on what she had to do.

Kendwa had never heard her swear. Birthing stuff was more than he'd ever expected. *Holy hell, she must be in pain.* He felt about as useless as a fish on land. Stroking her hair out of her face, he let her squeeze his other hand until it was almost bleeding.

The doctor glanced at them between her legs. His eyes smiled over the mask, but there was concern in the doctor's eyes. 'Sharli, you need to push now.'

Kendwa heard the guttural cry that came from his wife's throat as she pressed down with her hips, barely believing the sounds were coming from her. When the contraction stopped, she punched him in the arm, letting out a last deep breath.

'One more,' the doctor urged. A midwife hovered closer with a small trolley.

Sharli moaned, then suddenly stopped, relaxing her hand in Kendwa's. A half-smile on her lips, she leaned forward. The doctor lifted a squirming slippery white child in the air, still attached to the umbilical cord. Rubbing the baby's back, he mumbled. The sound of newborn cries echoed around the room, soon after followed by cheers of the medical staff.

Kendwa gazed at Sharli. An angelic smile planted on her face as she reached for the baby.

'Congratulations. You have a son. Sorry, luv. We need to check him first. Being premature, we will assess his lungs and vitals.' He looked at Kendwa. 'You can cut the cord, but you'll have to get around here quick. We can't waste time.'

Kendwa let go of Sharli's hand, giving her an I'm-sorry-but-I-have-to-do-this look. The doctor passed him a sterile pair of scissor-looking surgical equipment. Sweat lined his forehead when he clipped at the point the doctor indicated. The baby separated from the cord. Kendwa looked on dumbfounded. There was no mistaking that they had a boy.

The doctor placed the baby on the trolley. Midwives huddled around him, moving him to an adjoining room.

238

Sharli cried. 'Is he okay?' She looked too exhausted even to wipe her tears. Kendwa strode towards her, plucking tissues from the box beside the bed.

A midwife smiled kindly. 'For a premi, he's doing fine. It's just procedure. Please don't worry about him. Now you have more work to do. We must get the placenta out and check that you're all clear. You've lost a fair bit of blood, so we're setting up a transfusion.'

'Is that why she looks so pale?' Kendwa asked, gently wiping the tears from Sharli's eyes. He felt a mixture of awe and pride. His wife gave birth to their son, but there was anxiety about what was going on. He hoped with all his heart they were both safe. The midwife must have noticed his baffled looks.

'Yes, that's why she's pale. We need to monitor her for a while. The baby will probably need an incubator for at least a couple of days. His lungs won't be fully formed yet. We must give him every chance. Our neonatal unit is first class, so you're lucky it happened here.'

A second doctor, Kendwa hadn't noticed before, came into the room. 'You have a healthy son. His Apgar score was 8, but that's not bad for premature birth. He's 2.2 kg or about five pounds, which is impressive too. We have him on a ventilator, but we think his lungs are doing a good job. We're going to monitor him, but it's looking excellent.'

Kendwa shook the doctors still gloved hands, smiling widely. 'Thank you.' To Sharli, he said, 'Wow, babe. You were friggin' amazing.' Kissing her cheek, he wanted to jump around the room.

The midwife checked between Sharli's legs. Glancing at Kendwa, she said, 'Go and see your son. We need to look after your wife for now.' She nodded at the door. 'Okay, Sharli, let's get that placenta out. Push.'

Kendwa followed the doctor, taking a last look at Sharli, hearing her painful cry. A swell of pride rolled from his toes to his head. It was a tidal wave of emotions.

The neonatal ICU had two tiny babies in glass incubators. They were attached to so many tubes he could barely make out the blanket wrapped babies. He wasn't shown to either of these. Letting out a steadying breath of relief, he saw his son in a less severe condition.

'Here he is,' said the doctor. 'You can touch him. Wash your hands over there. Nurse Rolf will show you.'

239

Kendwa did as told, watching the nurse wrap his son tightly in a pale-blue cotton blanket. 'Touch his face gently and talk to him. They like to hear the voices they've heard in utero. We'll be able to take him off the respirator soon. His stats are good. They said they'll let us know when you can go back to your wife. Perhaps you'll be able to surprise her by taking him. Have you got a name for him yet?'

Kendwa stared at his tiny son, barely hearing her. He was too captivated. Tearing his eyes from the baby, he smiled. 'We had settled on Jai for a boy. Jai Jamal Noah Ely.' Kendwa gently touched Jai's face with his index finger. 'He's so soft. Tiny. How will I know how to hold him? Can I harm him if I do it wrong?'

The nurse smiled knowingly. 'You won't hurt him. I'll show you how to hold him. I'm sure with your big strong arms, the last thing you'll do is drop him.' She adjusted the baby in his arms, keeping the breathing tubes attached. Blushing, she walked to a huddle of nurses, whispering in the ear of one of them. They fanned themselves. Kendwa didn't notice the exchange. He dreamily stared at his son.

His thoughts turned to Sharli, his heart hammering with relief, pride and concern. *Why hadn't they come to tell him he could see her yet?*

It seemed ages before the doctor returned. 'Mr Ely. Your wife is very tired but wants to see you before she sleeps. Her blood count has come up, though her blood pressure is still low. It was a traumatic birth, so it's to be expected. Don't keep her too long.'

Kendwa stood. 'Can I take our son?'

The doctor glanced at the nurse, who hurried over as the doctor looked over Jai's chart. He unwrapped Jai's blanket, checking his chest with the stethoscope, making notes on the chart. To Kendwa's relief, he turned off the respirator. The nurse unhooked Jai from the tubes, dabbing cream of some sort on him. After what seemed like an eternity to Kendwa, the doctor said, 'Yes. Take your son. He'll have to sleep in the nursery until your wife can feed him. He's remarkable for a premature baby.'

The nurse showed Kendwa how to wrap the baby again. 'Can I try?' he asked. Jai moved his hands and feet, his eyes still closed. Kendwa wrapped the blanket to the left. Jai moved his curled-up legs out of it as soon as Kendwa tried to tighten it. Kendwa glanced at the nurse. 'Looked easier than it is.' He shrugged his shoulders.

240

She laughed kindly. 'You'll get the hang of it. I'll do it this time. You, go see your wife.' Neatly she wrapped Jai, placing him in the crook of Kendwa's arm. 'Keep his head supported.' The memory of holding Hope for the first time, and Sharli's words, popped into his head.

Vulnerability plagued him as he gingerly stepped towards Sharli's cubicle. Making sure he still looked comfortable in his arms. He kept glancing at Jai. He'd never held a more valuable parcel.

Sharli lifted her eyes to the sound of footfalls on the linoleum floor. The sight of Kendwa carrying their son burned into her memory for all time. It was the most precious of remembrances. His big strong arms held the tiny bundle with a softness contradicting their strength. The look on his face was pure awe. He smiled when he saw her watching them, walking gingerly towards the bed.

Smiling in return, she took a deep breath. 'Oh, my.' It was all she could say. Words couldn't describe how happy she was.

'Hey, beautiful. I'd like you to meet our son, Jai Jamal Noah Ely. He is perfect in every way. Sharli, he's so light it barely feels like I'm carrying him.' Gently he placed their baby into her waiting arms.

Volumes of tears streamed from her eyes. She was speechless.

Kendwa kissed her salty wet cheek. 'I don't think I've ever seen anything as amazing as you today. And look at him. Early as eight weeks and perfect, like you.'

Making room for Kendwa, she shoved over in the bed, never taking her eyes off Jai. Kendwa looked over her shoulder. For moments they silently stared at the miracle that was their son.

After a while, Jai foggily opened his eyes one by one to stare up at his parents. Sharli stroked his still vernix-wet hair. 'Hello, baby boy.'

Kendwa chuckled. 'Welcome to the world, Jai. You were loved from the moment you were a seed, but wow, man, now...so much love.' He pressed his hand to his heart. 'Your daddy is going to always protect you and your mommy. I promise you.'

Sharli smiled at Kendwa lovingly. 'I love you both so much.'

'I know, babe. I love you more.' He kissed the top of her head. 'Can you believe he has blonde hair?'

'Curls too. Look at his gorgeous skin. He's so much more you than me, already.'

'Let's let him grow a bit. I reckon he'll soon pick up some of your bad habits.' He laughed. 'Hey, what's with his mouth. It looks like he's sucking for air.' Kendwa looked panicked for a moment.

Sharli gently shifted Jai in front of her left breast. 'Kendwa, can you slip my top buttons undone and open my shirt? The milk won't have come through yet, but they say the colostrum is good for the baby too.'

Jai's mouth got more intense as his lips got closer to his source of food and comfort.

Kendwa fumbled with her buttons. She giggled. 'Come on. You never usually have trouble undressing me.' Finally, her engorged breast popped out. She gently touched Jai's lips with her finger, guiding them over her swollen raspberry nipple as the midwives had explained. Jai dropped off at first, looking frustrated. His little face scrunching up and red.

Again, she tried until she felt him connect. The feeling of the soft, avid suckling was overpowering. A maternal love flowed from her breast to her son, with nothing sexy in it. The feeling was unlike when Kendwa touched her breasts. It was the best nurturing sensation. She hadn't realised she would enjoy it so much. It was empowering, too, that she, as a woman, could do this wondrous thing.

Kendwa observed Sharli feeding Jai as if it was second nature to her. He'd never doubted that she would be the perfect mother. Watching her letting Jai suckle on her breast stirred something primitive in him. Though he felt strong and protective, at the same time, he was vulnerable and small, his heart aching equally with joy and fear—*joy of the miracle; fear of losing it.*

Chapter 31
Zanzibar, Tanzania

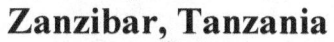

A monkey screeched outside. Sharli could hear it jumping on their thatched roof. Running outside, she threw her arms around. 'Shoo off, monkey. Jai is sleeping.'

It skittered off the roof, landing at her feet. A tiny baby red colobus monkey stared up at her with pleading, big round eyes. Its long thin tail swished on the sandy ground. Reaching a hand, it tentatively touched her leg before trying to climb up it.

Sharli looked to the roof then down at the small mite. Unwrapping its tiny limbs from her leg, she lifted the fly-weight, nursing it in the crook of her arm like she would her own baby. 'Where's your mother, little one?' The monkey suckled her thumb. 'Still feeding too. Your ma can't be too far away.'

Kendwa stormed around the corner, his face ablaze with anger. It evaporated the moment he saw Sharli nursing the baby monkey. 'At least it's baby is okay.'

'What are you talking about?'

Clenching his fists at his side, he stomped across their deck. 'The Papa Resort just cleared more forest. I found a dead colobus. Her teats were full. I figured the baby would die too. It just makes me so mad.'

Sharli shushed him because Jai was asleep, lifting the monkey towards him. 'What do we do with the baby then? Won't it die without its mother?'

'Not in our care.' He rubbed his hand through his hair, quietening his voice. 'For now, just wrap it up in one of Jai's fleecy blankets. I'll make a makeshift sling cot when I get back if we need to. Can you just watch it while I go looking for a surrogate mother out in the forest?'

243

She smiled at him. 'It's not like I haven't looked after monkeys before. Besides, what're two babies in the house compared to one?'

Stroking the snuggled monkey's fine fur, he kissed her cheek. 'You're amazing. Have I ever told you that?'

'Keep telling me.'

He kissed her again, this time on the lips. 'Hopefully, I won't be long. Don't let the monkey near Jai, though. It may carry disease. We want our son safe.'

She saluted. Kendwa laughed as he strode off towards the forest. Ambling back inside, she checked on Jai, the monkey curled in her arms. Jai was still sleeping. His cute mouth was half-open, long lashes resting on his sweet cheeks.

He'd grown a lot in the four months since he'd been born. Where he'd looked thin, after his early arrival, now there were rolls of healthy baby fat. Thick ringlets of blonde hair curled over his forehead. His face had filled out to chubby, rosy cheeks, pert full lips, and his skin had darkened to a toffee brown.

It always made her heart rise at the sight of her perfect child. She felt her breasts harden. Jai wasn't due for a feed, but the milk had come on early because the monkey was nuzzling her chest. 'I hope we find you a new mumma soon,' she cooed, stroking the monkey's fur. It looked up at her with solemn confused eyes.

Kendwa had better return quick. She didn't want Jai stirring while the monkey was still in her arms. The pram was in the corner of the room. It had been gifted to them by her mother. Placing the monkey in it, she wrapped a blue blanket over the top of it. It settled quickly as if exhausted. It soon fell asleep.

Patting at the wet patches where her breasts were leaking, she thought of her mother.

Vedi hadn't been surprised that Sharli gave birth early. She had a feeling they would be returning from Australia with a newborn to surprise her. The arrival of her grandchild had temporarily halted her disease, giving her a new lease on life. Often, she took Jai for pram-walks with Chand, especially when Sharli was tired or emotional.

Kendwa constantly seemed on the phone to the mainland about the resorts or to people on the island trying to get rid of snakes. It was a new job he'd picked up. Word spread quickly of the fearless snake catcher. He loved finding, as he called them, beautiful pythons and speckled green snakes. He explained to people that they helped keep vermin away and were, in fact, the best animal to cohabit with.

Sharli was unsure of how many he convinced. It didn't dampen his enthusiasm. Though she was proud of him for doing what he loved, it annoyed her how often he was away from them. It would have been okay if he charged for all the call outs. Too many were favours. Sometimes he was paid with an exchange of food, crafts and other items. Though it would have been preferable to have her husband to herself more often, or at least have remuneration for his efforts.

Sharli walked away from the monkey in the pram, worrying that it had been without milk for too long. Her breasts ached. She pressed both hands on them, trying to still the milk flow. They ached and were rock hard.

A whimper escaped Jai's sweet lips, his tongue curling out, seeking her. Watching him with a smile, she wanted to pick him up to ease her breast pain. Instead, she gave him time to at least call her to him, trying to set good habits for them both. Face scrunched, his cheeks blazed red as he began to cry in earnest. Tiny tears lined his cheeks.

Gently she picked him up, cuddling him close. Pillows were already propped on the bed, ready for comfortable feeding. Leaning back into them, she lifted aside her kanga. Jai attached, suckling quickly, milk dribbled out his mouth and over the bed sheets. As the pressure eased on at least one of her breasts, she sighed in relief. After only moments she switched sides. Jai suckled, looking up at her with big blue eyes. *The eyes of his father.*

Kendwa proved to be a good dad, going out of his way to provide for them. She smiled, thinking about how he loved watching her feeding Jai. The only thing he didn't like about it was the fact that she could no longer stand him sexually touching her breasts.

'But they look so great. So big, full, touchable,' Kendwa would say.

She told him it was only while she fed Jai. The feelings would return after they'd done their nurturing maternal job.

Unfortunately, Kendwa seemed to take it personally. She'd had to show him that they could still make love without her boobs being a part of it. There were plenty of places she still loved to be touched.

Settling a sleeping, contently full Jai back in his cot, she checked on the monkey. Its chest was still rising and falling as it also slept. Tiptoeing out of the room, she sat on the patio seat, waiting for Kendwa. It was tempting to sleep because she was so tired. It took all her effort to keep her eyes open because of the monkey in the room. It was a harmless baby, but her human baby was in that room with it.

When Kendwa returned, he found Sharli with her eyes closed and head lolling. Sitting beside her, he took her weight on his shoulder. 'Hey, beautiful. You're so tired, aren't you?'

Stretching her arms, yawning, she smiled at him weakly. 'I guess it's to be expected. Jai's still very dependent and hasn't found a perfect sleep pattern yet. It won't last forever.'

'Should I stop doing the snakes?' He pulled her closer to him.

'No…maybe just a bit less. I'd like to see you more.'

'Okay. How's the monkey?'

'Asleep in the pram. I've moved it to the other end of the room away from Jai.'

'How's he been today?'

'Feeding, sleeping, pooping. The usual.'

Kendwa laughed. 'That kid shits more than an elephant.'

'It feels that way some days. Hey, what about the surrogate monkey?'

Feeling foolish, he pondered how to ask her. Gazing into her gorgeous golden eyes, he got up the courage to ask, 'Do you need to express more milk? You said when you get full, it makes you feel better.'

'I did earlier. I was so engorged from holding the monkey, and then when Jai woke up, he was half asleep and relieved them minutely. I have two full bottles in the fridge.'

'I know it's a weird request, but would you mind if we used one to feed the monkey?'

She stood, pacing in front of him. 'Would my milk be too strong, or weak, or wrong somehow for the monkey?'

'It's been used before. I've seen it happen with Chimpanzee, and there was even a miniature golden lion tamarin that survived after being fed human milk. That was at a zoo in Brazil. I heard the primate keepers

246

at Taronga discussing it, to try it on one of their orangutans if the surrogate didn't work.'

'Did they try it at Taronga?'

'They didn't need to because the surrogate accepted the baby.'

'So, we…'

Shushing her with a finger, he stood, taking her in his arms. Solemnly. He held her by the shoulders. 'It's your milk, Jai's milk. You make the call.'

'The monkey needs it?'

'The monkey will die without milk.'

'Of course, we'll use my milk. I wouldn't even hesitate. I just didn't want the poor little mite getting sicker. Let's try it.'

'Thank you, honey. The sooner, the better. Poor little fella's probably gone without it for a couple of days.' Kendwa frowned, following her inside, playfully patting her luscious bum on the way. That turned his frown into a smile.

'We'll have to mark the bottles and teats so they don't get mixed up with Jai's. I haven't used any bottles for him yet, but I may need to if Ma has him overnight later.' She bent over at the fridge, retrieving a bottle.

Kendwa smiled, appreciating the extra curves she'd gained through the pregnancy. He loved them. She didn't.

Turning around to find him ogling, she slyly winked at him. 'Some things never change, Mr Ely.'

'Can I help it if my wife gets more gorgeous every day?'

She laughed, loving the way her husband made her feel. 'Okay, what now?'

'I'll gently wake the monkey.' Ever so softly, peeling back the blanket, he placed his big hands on the tiny monkey. The monkey blinked up at him with huge eyes. It shifted a little in fright but didn't protest when Kendwa picked it up. 'Hey, little guy. You must be starving.'

It made a chitter-type cry. Sharli passed Kendwa the bottle as he sat down on the bed. The tiny cream-furred monkey was barely visible in his big arms, except for its tiny head straining towards the bottle. Kendwa pushed the teat towards its mouth. It moved its head sideways, its funny hooked nose getting in the way of the teat.

'Try tapping it gently at the corner of his mouth. Keep the bottle up, so the milk flows,' Sharli suggested as she wrung her hands together, pacing in front of them.

Kendwa attempted to feed the baby again. This time it latched on, suckling avidly from the bottle, wrapping its little hands around the bottle bringing it closer to its face. Kendwa looked up at Sharli with moist eyes. 'He's got the hang of it.'

Sharli sat beside him. 'It's amazing, isn't it, that they are so close to human?'

'Sometimes, I think they are more human than a lot of people.'

'Like poachers?' She placed her hand on his thigh.

Kendwa nodded, a frown hovering. A smile replaced it on seeing the happy monkey gazing back into his eyes. Jai cried. They turned to the sound. So did the monkey. Jai only cried for moments before cooing and making slurp noises.

Sharli stood. Jai cooed up at her, his face lighting with a smile on seeing her. 'Hello, my darling boy. You look happy. Come and meet your new roomy.' She picked him up, carrying him towards Kendwa, planting a kiss on Jai's cheek. Holding him upright so he could focus, she moved him towards the monkey. His blue eyes widened in surprise then a cheeky smile broke out on his face.

Kendwa chuckled. 'I thought he was smiling at Daddy, but look at that. They've locked eyes on each other.'

'I think it may be lucky that Jai is too young to crawl yet.'

'What if they grew up being friends?'

Sharli moved Jai a little closer. The monkey reached out, touching his hand. 'Kendwa, you told me once that wild animals need to remain wild. They aren't pets. I know that look on your face.'

'True. As soon as this little guy is healthy, we'll integrate him back into the forest. He won't survive for a while yet.'

'You have to do that. Don't go soft on him.'

'Me soft? Never.'

'Kendwa, you may let everyone else believe you're big, brave and strong, but I've seen the soft side, and it's usually around animals and children.'

'Can we just call it compassionate, eh? Soft sounds so…well…soft.'

248

'Softy, softy,' she teased. Unperturbed by her mocking him, he grinned.

Glancing at the defenceless baby monkey, she hoped that the day would come that it could survive in the wild. In the meanwhile, they probably needed a name for it. 'Shall we call him Tumbili?'

'Sure, Tumbili means monkey, after all.'

Tumbili had hold of Jai's hand. Jai curled his fingers around it. Kendwa and Sharli exchanged glances. The monkey jabbered. Jai cooed. It was as if they were conversing in their very own language.

Chapter 32
Zanzibar, Tanzania

'Sharli, stop worrying about him. I have looked after children before,' Vedi said, taking three breast milk bottles from Sharli and placing them in her fridge.

'It's just overnight, Ma, I know. I've never been away from him before.' Sharli held Jai, rocking her body.

'I'm your mother, Sharli. The one person other than Kendwa who you can trust Jai with. Come on, hand him over.'

Sharli kissed her son's temple. 'Be a good boy for your Nānī.' She turned to Kendwa, who was standing in the doorway. 'Did you take the monkey to Jambi's?'

'Yep. All good. Jambi's taking Tumbili sailing. I hope he can keep him on the boat. I don't want to think about it, but I trust him. Hey, Vedi. Thanks for having Jai overnight.' Leaning in, he kissed his son's sleeping cheek just as Sharli handed him over to her mother.

Vedi beamed. 'He's such a gorgeous child. I hope I live a long time to watch him grow up.'

'You will, Ma. Thanks.' She hugged her mother without squashing Jai.

Jambi's truck rattled on the rough roads as they drove to Stone Town. After navigating the labyrinth of narrow lanes, specked with all sorts of wares, colourful materials, copper pots, medieval lamps, carvings, paintings and jewellery, they arrived at the jetty. They'd decided to enjoy the ferry ride rather than flying to the mainland.

Stepping on board the sleek modern vessel, they made their way to the front deck so they could watch the water for aquatic life. The dolphins usually played in the bow waves.

Holding hands, they sat closely with shoulders rubbing. The ferry was packed as usual, with various locals and tourists, plus livestock, one particularly smelly buck goat. 'It's nice to be alone for a little while,' Kendwa said, squeezing her hand. 'As alone as we can be on this packed ferry.' He laughed.

'I just hope Jai's okay without us.'

Kendwa sighed. 'Sharli, will you just relax?'

'I'm trying.' They were both quiet for a bit, letting the lull of the water and the hum of the engines fill the silence. 'So, I know we are going to Dar for a romantic night, but there's something else, isn't there?'

Kendwa clicked his neck. 'Yep. But I don't want to go into details until we are sitting at a candlelit table sharing a glass of champagne.'

'So, we are celebrating something.'

'Perhaps.' He grinned.

Playfully she punched his shoulder. 'I hate the suspense. Tell me.'

'Soon enough, sweetheart. Hey, there's your dolphins.' To distract her, he pointed them out. It was bad enough that he had barely registered the changes in his life. Toby's phone call had blown him away. Then he'd gone to the box that contained his mother's letter and paperwork. He'd discovered it was probably true. The results of his DNA test would prove it or disprove it.

At a plush restaurant in the capital of Tanzania, Dar es Salaam, Sharli sniffed her plate. 'I can smell the ginger. God, this looks delicious. Are we going to dig in?'

'Sure, go ahead.' Staring into space, Kendwa sipped a bottle of Kilimanjaro Lager, seemingly distracted. *Couldn't he just get to the point?* She knew him well enough to let him talk in his own time.

'Mmmmm, yum. Just enough spices and coconut cream. The chicken is tender. Are you going to eat your steak?'

Putting the beer down, he sliced into the thick steak, stabbing a large piece with his fork before popping it in his mouth. Annoyance bubbling, she watched him chew. What was supposed to be a romantic evening

252

was turning out to be a disappointment. He was so far away in his thoughts she may as well be sitting on her own.

'Steaks good. Maybe a bit overcooked but tasty.'

Could he talk about something other than their food?

When they'd finished their meals, Kendwa took her hands.

'Finally, you're going to tell me what's going on?' Sharli flicked her long hair over her shoulder, then re-held his hands.

'Okay. I'm glad you're sitting because you might fall over when I tell you this.'

'This must be big.'

'Bigger than an elephant. It's sort of like the elephant in the room, in fact. You know how Toby called the other week, and we talked for ages.'

'So? You call him all the time. Well, yes, you said it was about him and Hope settling in Currumbin and hoping Katie would calm down.'

'There was a hell of a lot more to that phone call.' Pulling folded paper out of the top pocket of his dress shirt, he unfolded them. Placing two official-looking letters side-by-side in front of Sharli, he waited for her reaction.

Picking one up, she scanned it. 'This is your DNA results. A match to who?' Lifting the other page to read it, her eyes widened. 'Really? You never knew?'

'Not for sure until today. I only got these from our postal box while you were getting ready.'

'But…wow. Are you happy about this, or shocked or…wow?'

With a half-smile, he said, 'I guess. It's confusing. Both Toby and I are still figuring it out. When Toby returned to Currumbin, he did some gene testing, for Hope's sake. He found out his parents aren't, in fact, his parents. Sharli, it's such a long, confusing story. How about I finish it curled up in bed?'

Scratching her head, she said, 'I can understand how confused you must be. I don't want dessert. Let's go. Then you can start at the beginning.'

Back at their hotel, they stripped off. Kendwa gently traced his fingers around her breasts. 'I know, they're Jai's now, but I can't help admiring them.' Hands roaming down her stomach to the moistness between her legs, he crushed his lips to hers. She was more receptive than she'd been since Jai's birth, pushing her pubic bone towards his probing fingers. It felt divine when her hand began stroking his cock. Then she guided him into her, wet and welcoming. From total arousal to bliss, their bodies danced in rhythm. They thrust together deep and hard, with longing.

Watching as wave after wave crashed over her, he held her eyes. She shuddered around his erection. His exquisite release followed soon after. Under his breath, he swore in satisfaction. Sometimes, he couldn't believe that his love for her could make him feel so sexually satisfied. No woman had ever made him feel so complete.

It wasn't only the sex. Every time Sharli looked at him, Kendwa's heart flipped. The way she moved turned him on. Every curve of her body was perfect, even more so with the extra weight since Jai's birth. Straight out of bed with tousled hair and no makeup, she was flawless. *It was time he told her everything.*

Snuggling into him, her arms around his muscular stomach, she waited for him to talk. Admiringly, she trailed a finger over a six-pack that was past the half dozen and more like a whole carton of beer.

'Let the story begin,' she said dramatically.

'Okay, but jeez, stop trailing your fingers over me. You're distracting me.' He laughed, peeling her fingers away, but she put them back with a smile.

'I'll keep them still, I promise. Come on, tell me. I want to hear how Toby could be your brother all along.'

'Toby probed into medical testing, mainly to ensure Hope would have the best quality of life. Knowing that Katie would no longer be a part of raising their child, Toby took all responsibility. As he was discovering about his DNA not matching his parents, their own story came out.

'His mother's sister worked in Kenya, particularly Mt Elgon, where the elephant caves are. She was a scientist trying to find cures for Marburg and similar diseases. She had become obsessed with having a child after suffering two miscarriages with her Kenyan husband.'

Sharli interrupted. 'Hang on. The journal? Is that coincidence?'

254

'No, but I'll get back to that. Toby's mom believed her sister was delusional when she found a child in Africa somewhere. She never explained much but said the child was gifted to her by a family who couldn't financially keep him. It was hard to tell if the child was Kenyan or not. He was olive but not dark, but his hair was blonde.'

Sharli held her fist to her mouth. 'Noah? She could have lied. Did she steal your baby brother?'

Kendwa frowned. 'It's surreal, isn't it? Anyway, when she was dying, she came home to Australia with the child. He was about three or four, but they had no way of knowing. She'd forged paperwork, said his birth certificate was burnt or something, and because she had Marburg disease. They were quarantined. For some reason, the child stayed with her.

'On her deathbed, she pleaded with Crystal to take the child, she called Toby, but of course, was in fact, Noah. It took them a few years to get through red tape and have Toby registered as an Australian citizen. There was nowhere or no one they could send him back to. He nearly became a ward of the state. Luckily Crystal was a resourceful woman. She wasn't letting welfare or the government take the child she'd grown to love.'

'I don't get it. Your parents knew Toby. How did they not figure out he was Noah?'

'It's weird when I look back on it now. Mom used to give him these long looks. I thought she was sussing my friend out. She used to ask him a lot of questions, like, where were you born? What do your parents look like? Stuff like that. Toby was so young he couldn't remember. When Mom and Dad met him, he was a grown man, so they couldn't be sure he was that person.'

'And?'

'Crystal had created a backstory, so Toby thought he'd been born at Tweed District Hospital. Dates differ from Noah's. Coincidentally his parents look like him a fair bit. They are light-haired and green-blue-eyed. Toby's are bluer, but you put them in a photo, and they look like family. I guess Mom had to take Toby's word for it. She probably dismissed it as just hope that he could be Noah.'

'I'm still confused. Toby finds out his parents aren't his parents, and he was stolen in Africa. How did he figure out that he was Noah?'

'It clicked with him. I'd talked about my baby brother to very few people in my life. Toby was one of them. The lady who brought him to Australia came from Kenya. I found pages in the diary to confirm the timeline of when Noah disappeared. Too much of it fit.

'It was uncanny how well Toby and I always got on. Just like we were brothers. People used to comment on it all the time. It did cross my mind—what if Toby were Noah? But I would brush it aside thinking I wished it was so because I liked him so much.'

'Wow, and now?'

'It's weird. We haven't spoken in a fortnight since that call. I guess we're both still figuring it out. The fact that I'd had those spirit visits from Mom, telling me to go to the elephant caves and find Noah. The Shaman directed me there, which is kind of creepy that she got a lot of it right.

'I was going to give up on looking for him for good until we went to England, and it all resurfaced. In Sydney, Toby and I spoke briefly about it. He was going to help me look for my brother. Ironic, eh? Then Jai surprised us, and I forgot about everything but you and Jai.

'Toby's phone call just blew my mind. I felt pleased that I'd found Noah, annoyed that he was under my nose all along and angry with all the adults involved, who had kept secrets from both Toby and me.'

'At least it's finally out.'

'Yes. It's a relief. The journal I found was owned by the lady who stole Toby, Noah. She wrote about the child, worrying that he would get sick too. She was desperate to find a cure for Marburg in case. I searched online for any news around the years Noah disappeared. There was a medical research station near the elephant caves. It must have been where she was working and how she got the disease from the bats. The journal must have accidentally been left behind, or maybe she put it there on purpose, so nobody would read it and know Noah wasn't her son.'

'Is much of it legible?'

'Enough for me to see Toby is in it. She never called him Noah. He could say his name. I'm sure he would have corrected her for a while.'

Sharli pressed her engorged breasts. 'Jai must be hungry.' She laughed. 'I'll have to get up and express some milk, or I'll end up with mastitis in the morning. 'Is there anything else?'

'No, babe. Go relieve yourself. There's nothing more to say. Maybe I should give Toby a call while you do it.'

'Toby, brother.' Kendwa was unsure what to say now that his best friend was his little brother.

'Kendwa. How are you coping with it?'

'Weirdly, I guess. I feel like I'm in a dream state. I've told Sharli.'

'Mum, Dad and I have been clearing the air. It got a little heated. I don't blame them because I would have been put into a home if they didn't intervene, plus they had no way of knowing that I was from your family. I needed to vent, though.'

'I know how you feel. I haven't exactly been mister-nice-and-normal to my wife.'

'It's sort of like we always knew at some level.'

'Yeah.' Kendwa ran his hand back through his hair and sighed. 'Where do we go from here?'

'I want to stay the same. You're still my best mate.'

'Yeah, me too. I'd come over for a visit, but I've promised Sharli more us time.'

'Stay there. Maybe I'll come when I get my shit together. Katie's not giving up on custody. She's pulling out the expensive lawyers, plus I'm still not over the breakup, being a single dad and all that, let alone this. I felt like I was having a breakdown for a while. It's all been so overwhelming.'

'I bet it has. I'm here for you, brother.'

'If I go away for a bit, I might be uncontactable but don't worry, I'm only protecting Hope from Katie's people. Enough on me. Hey, how is little Jai?'

'Great.' Kendwa smiled. 'Growing every second. Come to think of it, he looks like I remember you did.' And he did. Kendwa's mind went to the last time Toby was Noah, playing in the muddy sand beside him, looking up at him with blonde hair and cheeky smiling eyes.

'Really? You'd better email me some photos.'

Sharli strode out of the bathroom, still naked. Kendwa's jaw twitched. An erection rose. He winked at her. *Damn, she did it to him every time.*

'Will do. Sorry I hadn't phoned earlier.'

'We had to get it around our thick skulls, right?'

Kendwa laughed. 'Hey, Tobes?'

'Yep.'

'I'm glad you turned out to be Noah.' He wiped a thumb under his pooling eyes.

'Me too, big brother. Hey, and it's probably good they changed my name. I wouldn't have wanted to have the same name as your shithead cousin.'

'That's true. Sorry to wake you up.'

'I don't sleep much. I was awake. Talk soon, Kendwa.'

Kendwa hung up as Sharli slipped under the covers, reaching for him. He sighed. *It couldn't get better.*

Now that he had found Noah, the weight was off his shoulders. Beside him, turning him on, was the most beautiful girl in the world.

The secret was finally out. Little did Kendwa know that there was one more secret his wife was yet to learn.

Chapter 33
Zanzibar, Tanzania

The first flight back to Stone Town touched down before dawn. By the time Kendwa was driving the battered ute through the awakening streets of the old town, the prayer call had begun. The haunting Islamic call to prayer boomed from speakers over the tin roofs and minarets. A rooster crowed. Dogs barked.

Sharli sighed. 'That's the sound of home.' She laughed. They'd both been hearing the Muezzin call since childhood. It went for about two minutes, with men joining in loudly singing along with the call.

Men rushed towards their prayer mosques in long robes, wearing the Muslim headwear, the kofia. Kendwa and Sharli waved to a few they knew as they passed them down the cobbled streets.

'I've missed Jai,' said Kendwa as they left Stone Town behind and drove Jambi's battered ute towards the other side of the island.

Smiling at him, she patted his leg. 'I can't wait to hold him again. I think you're melancholy because of finding out Toby is your little brother. It probably makes you even more defensive of Jai.'

'I guess, but I was protective of Jai the moment you told me you were pregnant. It's just that I don't want to miss a moment of him growing up. After losing so much of Noah...Toby's life.'

Vedi was waiting out the front with Jai on her hip. In the day they were gone, he looked like he'd grown. Sharli was out of the car before Kendwa parked, running with her arms outstretched towards their son. 'Jai, baby. Mummy's here. Hi Ma, thanks.' She took him in her arms, showering him with kisses. He giggled the sweetest of baby-voice laughs, smelling of talcum powder and milk.

Kendwa wrapped his arms around them both. Tears filled Sharli's eyes. 'Babe, it was just a day,' he said.

'I know, but I missed him.'

Vedi led them inside. 'He's been a good baby. He kept looking around as if trying to find you, but as long as I fed him until he was full, he slept just fine.'

Kendwa tickled him under the chin. 'That's my boy.'

'Did you have a nice romantic time on the mainland?' Vedi asked.

'It was lovely, Ma.' Jai squirmed in her arms. She placed him on the matted floor. He pushed himself like a worm for a few minutes.

'Check him out,' said Kendwa. 'Vedi, thanks. It was nice to have some quality time together. Though, of course, we missed our little man.'

Jai pushed his knees up. He crawled two paces and then collapsed.

'Good boy. You've nearly got the hang of it. We got to have some long talks too.' Sharli glanced at Kendwa, who nodded. They sat around Vedi's small dining table. Sharli and Kendwa explained what he had found out about his family. Vedi stayed silent, only tut-tutting here and there. When they finished, she rose from the table.

'My my, that's a lot for a young man to deal with.'

'I have plenty of work to get my mind off it.' He kissed Sharli's cheek and then Jai's. 'I'll give Jambi the ute and pick up Tumbili.' He left in search of his friend and the baby monkey. The women chatted.

Sharli was sitting in Metra's mother's house, sharing a cup of zam zam. 'You wanted to talk to me?' Sharli asked.

'Metra posted me this paper clipping. I wasn't so sure, but anyway, she thought you should see it.' She handed it to Sharli, who read the tiny column of just one paragraph. It was from the Guardian in England.

The Hungarian woman died instantly. A ranger from the resort shot the lion dead. Owner of the resort, Kendwa Ely, did not comment...

'Why wouldn't he tell me this happened?' Sharli felt a pang of bitterness. He'd promised there would be no more secrets. 'When was it printed? Can I keep this?'

'Of course. Seven months ago.' Metra's mum patted her hand kindly. 'Sharli. From what I can see, Kendwa is a good man. Maybe, by not telling you, he thought he was protecting you.'

'He should have told me. Thank you.' *The lame excuses for blood on his t-shirt.*

Sharli thought back to the number of times Kendwa hadn't come clean. They were building in her head to a mountain out of a molehill, and she knew it, but she couldn't help it. She wanted honesty and trust in her marriage. It didn't matter how perfectly matched they were physically if they couldn't get on the same mental page. Stomping down the sandy path, she seethed.

Two rare Fischer's Turaco nestled on an overhead branch, though she didn't notice them as she usually would. The squat birds with blue wings, grey chest and pink crowns like a Mohawk eyed her curiously. She looked up when she heard their frog-sounding chirp. Even they didn't turn her lips into a smile.

Jai was with Kendwa. When she returned, the pram was missing. The monkey wasn't sleeping in the sling-bed Kendwa had rigged from the ceiling with hessian. She stamped her foot, fuming.

Vedi was hanging washing. 'Have you seen Kendwa?' Sharli asked.

'He said he was doing some work on the house. He took Jai and the monkey.'

'Huh. Mmmmm.'

'What's wrong, Sharli?'

'Nothing I can't handle, Ma.' She stormed off, thinking she was just about mad enough to throw something at Kendwa. *Perhaps I should pick up a coconut on the way.*

Kendwa turned to the sound of his wife's footfalls, then a yelling voice. Twisting the hammer in his wrist, he spat out the nails between his teeth.

'You're lying to me again.'

'Stop shouting. You'll wake Jai.' He pointed to the pram.

'Don't be stupid. You have a hammer in your hand. You've been banging.'

'I...' He dropped the hammer, striding to her with his arms outstretched. She stepped back. 'What are you on about, babe? Honey?'

'Don't call me babe, honey or anything sweet when I'm mad at you.' She shook her fists in the air.

Looking up at the sky, he raked his hand through his hair. When he glanced back at his wife, her eyes were blazing fire. *What the hell had he done?*

Wordlessly she passed him the newspaper piece.

Avoiding the look in her sad, angry eyes, he read it. 'I couldn't tell you about this. You were pregnant, vulnerable. You didn't need to know.'

Her tiny body shook with rage. 'I didn't need to know that our business could have gone belly up because of this? Worse still, that you watched a woman die, horrifically, and couldn't tell me. If I'd been through something like that, you would be the first person I'd tell.'

'You were pregnant.'

'Oh my god. Are you serious? Pregnancy doesn't make me frail and weak. In fact, it makes me stronger than I've ever been. You could have told me. How do you see a woman mauled by a lion and just come home to me and act normal? What sort of man are you?'

'Sorry.' He stepped closer. She moved away again.

Glancing towards the pram, he strode to it, peering in. Where was Jai? Futilely he moved his hands through the empty blanket. His heart shattered.

Parents arguing. Parents distracted. Baby missing.

Tears stung his eyes. He turned to her, speechless.

'Jai, Jai, Jai,' Sharli screamed, running past Kendwa, searching the area around their supposed dream home.

Frantic, they both called his name until their voices were hoarse. Without thinking, they came together clinging to each other. Sharli with tears streaming down her face, Kendwa with full eyes and a steely gaze. *Where was their son?*

Brushing her tears angrily, she pulled away first. 'I'll never forgive you if we don't find him. I'm going to get help. Keep looking.' Hugging her arms to her chest, her eyes shot daggers into his heart. She fled, calling Jai's name into the distance.

Kendwa sat on his haunches with his head in his hands. Without Sharli's panic around him, he cleared his mind. Jai was barely crawling. The monkey was missing too. Nobody was near them. He heard his wife's footfalls before her yelling voice. His hearing was acute. He would have heard a stranger on their property. A baby and a monkey couldn't get far—d*eep breath.*

Kendwa stood, his eyes scanning around for clues. The beach was too far away, which ruled out the possibility of Jai drowning. It was the wrong time of day for snakes to be out in a cleared area, plus he'd seen no signs of their trails.

Crouching near the pram, he surveyed the ground. Tiny paw prints, baby handprints, what looked like knee prints, led under a canopy of colourful lantana bush. Sharli had already run through the edge of it. In her blind panic, she didn't see properly.

There was an opening of broken branches where his wife had desperately searched. He noted blood on a snapped branch. She would be bleeding and probably hadn't even realised yet. He frowned. Lower, there was a smaller hole in the canopy. Kendwa peeled back some branches, moving his body into the gaps.

Monkey gibbering came from the bush. Then Kendwa heard the sweet bubbling sound of Jai's coos and giggles. Clearing lower branches near his feet, he smelt Jai's dirty diaper before he saw it.

'Phew, bubba. I could have found you just by following my nose.' Jai looked up at him with a filthy face smiling. It was normal for him to be in the bush with his best friend, the monkey.

'Tumbili,' Kendwa called. 'The monkey popped his furry face up on the other side of Jai. It leapt, climbing into Kendwa's arms. 'You've been leading my boy astray, haven't you?' Tumbili chittered an enthusiastic reply. The tiny monkey sat on his broad shoulder as he reached for his son. 'Come on, little man. You've given your mommy and me a big fat fright.'

Sighing in relief, he hugged his precious son. His heart was heavy with misery. The guilt of Jai disappearing under his watch broke something in him. Swallowing hard, he felt a wave of nausea, trying to steady his legs. *Would his wife hate him for a scare so close to the heart?*

Vedi, Chand and Jambi trailed Sharli as she ran back to the clearing. Placing her hand on her chest, she stopped when she saw Kendwa holding Jai.

263

'Jai. You're safe. Oh, my baby, Jai.' Trying not to make eye contact with Kendwa, she tore Jai from his arms. Though she'd noticed the fear etched there—the wounded look of a wild animal in pain.

'Sharli, look at me. Honey, he was safe. Just a few scratches. We just over-reacted because we were arguing.'

She turned on him, clutching Jai's head to her with her hand over his ears. 'Over-reacting? How am I over-reacting? Jai was missing. You weren't watching him. You don't deserve to be his dad.'

Kendwa's slumped. 'Sharli, don't say that.' His voice croaked.

Turning away from him, she ran. 'Don't come home.'

Jambi ambled over to Kendwa, placing a gnarled hand on his shoulder. The others followed Sharli. 'Son, she'll calm down. She's had a fright.'

Kendwa put his hands over his eyes, covering brimming tears. 'What if she doesn't?'

'It's up to you to make sure she does.'

'I've stuffed things up, Jambi. I don't know how I can make it up to her.'

Jambi looked around him. 'Show her your love. Finish the banda. Make it grand. I'll help you. Fish aren't running for the next couple of days anyway.'

Kendwa nodded, letting Jambi give him a brief hug. Picking up the hammer, he retrieved the nails. With gusto, he began hammering the frame he had been working on.

Jambi saw him glance at the pram. 'I'll take it to her and come back. You can tell this old bloke what you need to finish this. Eh?'

'Thanks, Jambi.' Kendwa kept his head down in case the tears came. He smashed a nail into the wood, his jaw set firmly. The act felt satisfying. He hammered another nail into the wood—*bang, bang, bang.*

It was as if his life had gone full circle since the day Noah was stolen. It wasn't a good arc. It was like he was reliving the same nightmare. He'd tried to be a protector, but he had failed. His mind tried to find the logical way out of the darkness, but it was blocked by his enormous heart.

264

How many men tried too hard to be strong that it made them weaker? Sometimes he felt that loving Sharli had turned him into a sook.

Sharli had been strong and powerful when she confronted him. He felt feeble. Had something shifted in their relationship that he could never restore? How could he rebuild his power as a man and regain his wife's trust? *More importantly, how did he reclaim her love and devotion?*

Chapter 34
Zanzibar, Tanzania

Kendwa woke in his swag, jolted by a noise in the bush. Was it a lion? He rubbed his ears, glancing around. *Not in Kenya.* Inside the shell of his banda on Zanzibar, alone, as he had been for a week. Another nightmare to add to his reality.

There was no longer any reaching for Sharli in the middle of the night. His pent-up desire was driving him crazy. Though he knew he'd give up a year of sex to prove to her, it was about love and commitment, not sex.

Sharli hadn't forgiven him, still refusing to see him. He hadn't seen baby Jai either. Imagining how much Jai could be growing, the milestones he could miss, hurt him deeply.

At least the banda was close to completion. Jambi and a few friends had helped him lift the thatched roof. There were walls to fill in with brick and mud, but the floors were down. A large patio faced the ocean. An electrician and plumber were coming in the afternoon.

Vedi arrived to tell him that Sharli and Jai were both fine and just to give her time. It was nice of her to do that.

'Kendwa, my daughter isn't a complicated person. Trust is a personal mantra. It's an important part of our family. She realises you have your reasons for some of your secrets, but as your wife, she's hurt that you kept them. She said something about feeling disconnected when you push her away.'

'I'm not pushing her away now, Vedi. I'd do anything for her.'

Vedi noticed Jambi carrying some wood. She waved to him. 'You know very well that, if it were just her, she would have already forgiven you. She loves you. Understand how much a mother loves her child. She feels responsible for Jai. Particularly while he is little, he needs her undivided nurturing.'

Pacing, he flicked up stones with his booted feet. 'But I cherish them. I do my best for an ordinary bloke. Am I to step back and let her be a sole parent? I don't want that. We're a family. I don't know what more I can do.' He picked up a piece of wood throwing it into the bush. It went a long way.

Vedi shook her head. 'It's about proving they'll always be safe.' Vedi sat down, fanning herself with a banana leaf. 'It's hot today.'

Kendwa looked closely at her. 'Vedi, are you ill?'

'No, fine. Just hot is all. Asanti. You are a caring man. I promise I'm doing everything to convince my daughter that you are.' Pulling a bottle of water from a small cooler, he passed it to her.

'What can I do?'

She sipped before saying, 'Asanti sana. As I said. Give her time. She's angry, but she's a smart girl. She'll figure out that you're the best thing that ever happened to her, other than Jai, of course, eventually. Just keep building this home. It looks like it will be beautiful.'

The house was the one thing that was making him proud. He smiled at it, picturing it finished with his family inside.

'And, may I suggest? No more snake catching or trips to the mainland for some time. Devote yourself to them…and if there are any more secrets, tell her. Trust is the most important thing in a marriage.' Patting his cheek, she rose, passing him the water bottle before leaving.

'Jai. Stop squirming. Tumbili quit pulling at his diaper.' Sharli was red-faced as she tried to change him. Parenting by herself was challenging without the strong calming influence of Kendwa. She hadn't realised how many diapers he changed or the number of times he'd placed Jai on his shoulder until he burped. Usually spewing milk all over him. Kendwa never cared because Jai no longer had a pain in his little belly.

The diaper unravelled again. Being mad was one thing, but the anger didn't make her love him any less. She ached for Kendwa. It was devastating without him near. The thing was, she'd dug her heels in. It was the principle of being truthful that made her not want to back down. That's what she told herself.

Kendwa came by two days before to get more of his clothes. Briefly, she let him hold their son. Jai was delighted to see his daddy, giving him the best of his baby babble. Watching Kendwa's face as he cuddled his son, speaking baby language back to him, made her heart twist.

When she had asked Kendwa if he'd regretted lying about the lion attack, straight-faced, he'd replied, 'For a start, I didn't lie. I just didn't tell you. No, I don't regret it.'

Before she could say anything back to him, he'd passed Jai back before storming out with his arms filled with clothes.

Each night she lay in their double bed, reaching for him across the sheets, hugging his pillow, crying. *Were they both just being stubborn?*

Suddenly, Sharli felt hot wet pee on her face. She pressed her hand over Jai, shielding her face with the other. When he'd finished urinating, she quickly wrapped him in a fresh diaper. Pulling an antiseptic wipe, she patted her face. 'Jai, I think you did that on purpose.'

Giggling, he kicked his tiny feet. Tumbili bounced on the bed. Footfalls neared outside. Turning, she saw Kendwa looming in the doorway, blocking the sunshine from outside.

'We need to talk.' He tilted his head sideways. His beautiful eyes held questions.

Swallowing the lump in her throat, she said, 'Here. Take Jai. I must clean up. He peed all over me.'

Kendwa chuckled, tickling his son on the chin. 'You do a lot of peeing, mate.'

'Don't laugh,' Sharli warned, dropping the wipes in the bin. Washing her hands in the small sink, she turned to see Kendwa holding Jai, so they were face-to-face. Jai's little hands were at the sides of Kendwa's thick neck. They looked at each other with wide smiles and enough love to fill the country, let alone the tiny room.

'Stay, Tumbili,' Kendwa ordered the monkey, pointing. The cute animal looked up solemnly but curled up on the bed as if it were sulking. 'We'll talk at the banda,' he said to Sharli.

'Why not here?'

'We'll talk at the banda,' he repeated, storming off with Jai in his arms. Jai's pudgy fist waved over his shoulder to his mom. She reluctantly followed. *Deep in her heart, she would follow them to the ends of the earth.*

As they walked, she tried to think of what she would say. How she would defend her reasons for not seeing Kendwa for two weeks. How could she not even discuss their marriage?

At the banda, they found Jambi on the patio with a broom. 'Oops, you're here.' He scuttled off around the back, out of sight.

Sharli raised her eyebrows. Kendwa took her hand. Enjoying the warmth of his touch, she let him, following him up a small step onto the patio. 'Look at the view,' he said, pride in his deep voice.

'It's okay.' It was glorious, but she wasn't prepared to melt in his presence and forgive just yet. They had far too much to discuss.

They entered the banda through a screened front door. 'This is a sunroom. I thought Jai could play here. We could watch him from the kitchen, lounge and bedroom.'

'There's all of that?' She took it all in; whitewashed rustic brick walls, polished timber floors, carpeted bedroom, sleek timber kitchen.

'Then there's Jai's room. I left it empty. I thought we'd like to decorate it together…or you could do it if you prefer.' The walls were painted a pale blue with white skirting.

'It's so big.'

Kendwa held his breath. Jai played with his nose, poking his little fingers up his nostrils.

Sharli stroked the walls with her fingers, strolling to the middle of the room. 'Together would be better.'

About to hug her with relief, a cry outside startled them. Placing Jai in her arms, he ran to the noise. 'That sounded like Jambi.'

Sharli curled Jai to her hip. He was getting heavy to hold. Jambi was sitting on the ground with his hand in the air. A nail impaled right through. Blood dropped in tiny round dots between his knees.

'We'll have to get you across the island to the Daktari,' Kendwa said. 'How did you do this?'

Jambi's dark face turned ashen. The electrician doing the final wiring to the mains strolled around the side of the house, stopping in his tracks. With long Rastafarian hair in beaded braids, he was a colourful sight. 'Man,' he said and took a step back.

Sharli laughed. 'Hi, Moyo. Jambi, are you okay?'

Jambi nodded, frowning. 'I was trying to eavesdrop and hammered my hand instead of the wall.'

Kendwa stifled a laugh. 'Keep your hand up…um' He looked around him. 'I have bandages. I'll get them.'

'Can you hold Jai, Moyo? Sharli passed Jai to him. He was a father of five adorable children. Sharli knew Jai would warm to him quickly, playing with his long hair.

Moyo said, 'Come on, little mate, we'll find some sand crabs. I don't like the sight of blood.'

Sharli knelt beside Jambi. 'I'm a nurse, remember. Let me have a look at you, Jambi.' Kendwa moved aside, striding inside the house to find the bandages. Gently Sharli took Jambi's injured hand, twisting it to see the top of the hand and then his palm. She pressed near the wound. 'It's not so bad.'

Jambi winced.

Kendwa returned with his backpack, pulling out a bandage. 'What else do you need?'

'Alcohol to clean the wound.' To Jambi, she said, 'Have you had a tetanus shot recently?'

He shrugged his shoulders. 'Oh. Is that the one that hurts like hell? I had one in my ass two years ago when I got a coral infection.'

'That would be it.' She turned to Kendwa. 'I don't think I can manage it, but do you think you could pull the nail out? It hasn't gone through any major arteries or nerves.'

'Yeah, sure.' Before Jambi could ready himself, Kendwa closed his fingers over the nail giving it a sharp pull.

'Bloody hell,' swore Jambi, watching the bloodstained nail drop to the ground.

Sharli quickly placed gauze over the wound stemming the flow of blood. 'The alcohol?'

Kendwa passed her a small bottle with some cotton wads. She lifted the gauze, neatly cleaning the wound. Kendwa passed her the bandage. She wrapped it firmly around Jambi's fingers, palm and around his wrist, clipping it tight.

Jambi nodded his approval.

'You okay, Jambi?' Kendwa placed his hand on his old friend's shoulder. 'You were pale for a bit.'

A large grin broke out on Jambi's dark face. 'Nah. Me, never pale.' He shook his head. 'Can't drive with this.' He lifted his bandaged left hand, and his bottom lip dropped. 'Drive me home, Kendwa?'

'Sure.' Kendwa glanced at Sharli. 'Will you be here?'

'I will. Jambi, take some paracetamol to ease the pain and keep your hand raised as much as possible. I'll get Kendwa to take me to you and recheck the wound tomorrow.'

Jambi nodded, staring at his bandaged hand.

Kendwa smiled, hesitated then kissed her cheek. 'I'll be back in about ten.'

While Kendwa was gone, she took Jai from Moyo, watching Moyo finish the electrical work. He asked her to test the light switches while he was out by the electrical box. Jai's sleepy head lolled on her shoulder as she went from room to room.

'They're all working except the kitchen.'

'Hang on. Give me five.'

She waited by the switch.

Moyo yelled. 'Try it now.'

The light flicked on, illuminating the pretty kitchen. Practically smelling the foods she would cook for her family, she imagined herself cooking there.

'Yay. All working.'

Moyo packed his tools, tickled Jai under the chin, then left.

Jai yawned, quickly falling asleep again on her shoulder. Sharli found Kendwa's swag and laid it out, curling up the ends and sides, to snuggly fit Jai. Placing his angelic sleeping body in it, she frowned as she looked around. It was sad that Kendwa had been sleeping in the swag alone for over two weeks. Guilt assailed her.

Aqua blue water twinkled in the distance. She walked to the sunroom deck to feel the soft ocean breeze blew as she enjoyed the view. She marvelled at what Kendwa had done, walking back inside, running her fingers along the straight walls. It was his way of showing his love, and she knew it. *How could she not forgive him?*

271

A pocket in the knapsack rang. Fishing out the phone, Toby's name flashed on the screen. She wondered for a moment if she should let it ring out.

'Hi, Toby. It's Sharli. Kendwa just ducked out.'

'You've made up? That's great. I knew you would.'

'No. Well, kind of. Kendwa told you?'

Toby paused. 'We're brothers and best mates.' She could picture him smiling. He was such a nice guy. 'He loves you more than anything, Sharli.'

'Why would he keep secrets from me then?'

'He only wants to protect you. The secret about me was something he'd buried until it all came out again. We're both still shocked, really. And the lion attack, you really wouldn't want the details of that. He didn't lie. He couldn't tell you is all. It was too horrific. He couldn't relive it with you. When he rang me, he burst into tears. How many times have you seen him do that?'

'I know that's not like him.' *Lately, a few.*

'Sharli, I don't mean to pry, but you kept your secret about your pregnancy. I heard him ask you if you thought you were in labour. You reassured him you weren't.'

'It's not the same.'

'Isn't it?'

They were silent for a bit as she chewed her bottom lip.

'What was the main reason you left Katie? Was it trust?'

Toby sighed. 'No. Respect. She didn't want to love Hope. She refused like her even. That made me lose all respect for Katie. I trusted her in our relationship, but she had no attachment at all to our beautiful daughter. It's not natural. It's callous.'

Sharli thought of Kendwa with Jai. They were the most adorable father and son. 'I'm sorry, Toby. Do you think trust is over-rated?'

He laughed. 'Sorry, Sharli. The way you see trust, yes. Trust in general, no. Let me tell you something. Until the day I die, I'll love Kendwa as a brother and a friend, but the most important part of our relationship is respect. Do you respect him, Sharli?'

It dawned on her. 'Yes, Toby. More importantly, I know he respects me.'

'He does respect you more than anyone in the world. Tell him I said hi. I wasn't calling for anything in particular.'

'Are you sure? You sounded a bit odd when I picked up.'

'No, it's all good. Katie's being a stalking pain in the ass, but I can deal with her.'

'Hey, on a brighter note, you're my brother-in-law.'

'I am.' He chuckled.

'Thank you, Toby.'

Hiding Kendwa's phone back where she found it, she thought up a plan. Using a stack of Kendwa's clothes, she made a bed for Jai to curl up in. Taking the swag, she laid it out in their empty bedroom.

The clunky motor of the ute alerted her to Kendwa's arrival. Smiling, she waited for her wonderful husband, her forgiveness complete.

Kendwa called out to her, his heart constricting. There was no dealing with it if she'd left.

'In here, Kendwa,' her sweet voice called.

Perfume filled the air. Stopping at the doorway, he took it all in— baby son sleeping peacefully in one corner of the room. Exquisite wife stark naked in the middle. She crooked a finger for him to come to her. Her breast jiggled as she did so, and a wicked glint filled her topaz eyes. Long silky hair cascaded down her shoulders like a satin coat. The thatch between her legs was neatly shaven and trimmed. Hips rounder. Lovely legs tanned and sexy.

Drinking every inch of her in before he slowly stepped closer, meeting the love in her eyes. He wanted to ask for forgiveness, but he guessed her nakedness answered that question. Reaching her, he placed one hand behind her head, bringing her lips to his. His tongue probed deep, entwining deliciously with hers.

'I've missed you, baby.'

Breathless, panting, reaching to stroke him, she sighed. 'I've missed you, my husband.' Haughtily, she placed her hands on her hips, pouting sexily. 'Now, would you please get undressed?'

Lying down on the swag, she spread her legs invitingly wide. Slipping trousers down, trying not to trip on them, he hastily joined her. His hands ran through her hair, down her shoulders, over her breasts, where this time she thrust them forward. Tentatively he touched the nipples, watching mesmerised as they came to life, so much bigger and rosier than before childbirth.

Grinning down at her, he was delighted when she smiled back with that look on her face he loved so much—their look of lust. Trying to hold back, he entered her slowly. As they were beginning the dance, a cry broke the air. They turned their heads to Jai. Red-faced, feet kicking and bottom squirming on Kendwa's clothes, obviously messing his diaper.

Sharli giggled. Kendwa's eyes were wide with disbelief. Screwing up his nose, he watched the runny poo dribbling out the side of Jai's diaper and onto the makeshift clothing bed.

Kendwa hung his head on her breasts. 'Why now?'

Sharli squirmed out from under him. 'We'll have plenty of time to continue this when we put him back to bed tonight.'

Still naked, she cleaned Jai, patting his cute little bare bum. 'Go to Daddy.' She passed him to Kendwa, who put Jai between them as she lay back on the swag. His big arms surrounded his wife and child.

Sharli felt the warmth of the embrace, raw and naked. It made her feel safe again. Not only because of the beautiful banda Kendwa had built them, but because Kendwa and Jai were her forever home.

Kissing Kendwa's lips, she said, 'Promise me something…'

'No more secrets.'

Bonus Chapter

**Spoiler: Do not read if you have not read
A Summer in Paradise yet
or insist on a happy ever after**

Eight months later, in Zanzibar

'I'll be okay. I'm only housekeeping. What could go wrong?' Sharli said, leaning to kiss sixteen-month-old Jai and rolling her eyes at Kendwa.

'You don't know that, Sharli. I have a bad feeling. And you were the one who had the nightmare, not me.' Kendwa's jaw twitched as he reminded her. His gut told him this was not a day for her to work at the Papa Resort. Their safety record was deplorable.

'I only have to do this job a couple more weeks until your business money comes through. It will be worth it for our future. You know that.'

'We can survive a couple of weeks waiting for it to clear. I'd rather you quit today. Please, do that for me, babe.' He took her hands.

Jai ran out the door after his monkey, Tumbili. Though he was still a toddler, he had the speed of a much older child, and they needed to keep an eye on their inquisitive son.

They followed him, keeping the best friends in eyesight. 'Don't go past the house,' Sharli called when he strayed too far following the monkey. 'Please, keep an eye on him, Kendwa.'

'You know I will. I'll even use the eyes in the back of my head.' He laughed.

She slapped his arm. 'You'd better.' She leaned up to kiss his lips. 'I'll see you around four.'

'No. I'll drop by the resort earlier and walk you home. Jai and I will go for a beach swim on our way.'

'It's a nice day for it. I've got to go. I'm running late. Love you' She kissed him again before walking over to their son, picking the toddler up.

'Love you too, babe.' Kendwa said with a smile.

Jai squirmed and giggled when she kissed his cheek before turning his cute puckered lips to her's. 'Bye, ma.'

'Be a good boy for Daddy, Jai. I love you to the moon and back.'

'Oon,' repeated Jai.

Sharli strolled away, waving. Kendwa watched the sway of her hips with a smile. Damn, his wife still turned him on like the first day. She was so beautiful today, almost perfectly so. He counted his blessing every single day.

He sighed. 'Come on, Jai.'

Sharli baulked when the resort manager strode inside the open door of the unit. The sheet she was about the throw over the bed dropped from her hands at the look on the man's face.

'I heard you were late again.' His chubby face glowed red.

'My young son…'

He cut her off. 'No excuses. I don't care that you have a child. It would be best if you turned up on time. Otherwise, you may not have a job to come to.'

She bit back her retort. For a start, she had only been five minutes late. Maybe Kendwa was right. Quitting today seemed like a good idea. There wasn't much more bullying she could take from the insufferable manager.

Later that day, Kendwa took Jai's tiny hand, and they strolled down to the white sands of Kiwengwa Beach. The turquoise water sparkled in the afternoon sun with dolphins frolicking in the outer shallows of the reef.

276

Kendwa picked up Jai before he ran into the water. 'Hang on, tiger. You don't go in without me.' He waded into the shallow water, dipping Jai down to his waist.

Jai giggled and kicked his feet.

'Use your arms, son.'

Jai's little arms swung up and down, scooping water.

'That's better. You'll be swimming like those dolphins in no time. Now, let's put your head under. Ready, one, two, three.'

Jai took a deep breath at two.

Kendwa pushed him under and up.

Jai shook his ringlet hair, and water sprayed over Kendwa. His little face held a delightful smile. 'More, dadda.'

'Okay. Ready?'

Jai nodded.

Kendwa marvelled at his son. Small things like teaching the precious child to swim filled his days with joy. Sharli being his wife was the absolute best thing that had ever happened to him. He'd never felt so much love. It was almost too perfect to be true.

'Are you kidding? Why should I get it out?' Sharli asked the manager. 'I don't work in the pool area.'

'The pool guy is on a break. It's only the spa, and I can't swim. Get in,' he commanded.

'You don't need to swim in water up to your waist. Admit it. You can't handle shit.' She glanced at the turd in the bottom of the spa.

The manager paled and held his mouth. 'That's true.'

'Where's the maintenance guy? Why isn't he doing it?'

'Because you were late today, and this is your punishment. Get that fuckin' shit out of there before our tourists see it. I don't want to have to drain the thing and start again.'

'Seriously. Is that ethical or safe? I wouldn't want my son in there until you either drained it or fixed the chemical balance.'

'Get in, you fuckin' bitch.'

Sharli took a deep breath and clenched her fists at her sides. 'No. I'm not getting in there because I don't get paid enough to do your rotten jobs. I quit.'

277

The manager considered it. 'You have a kid. Don't you clean up his shit all the time? And you clean toilets.'

'That's different.' She shook her head. 'I've given my notice.' She turned to leave, but he took her arm, squeezing his fingers into her flesh.

The man pushed her. 'Clean it, now,' he screamed, shoving her again until she tripped.

Sharli's head hit the side of the spa, and she fell into the water. With shaky fingers, she touched the lump on her head, glancing up at him with narrow eyes. The poo sat on the step beside her, beginning to dissolve in the water and float upwards. She scooped some, feeling the slime and flung it in the air towards his arrogant face. It splattered like thick brown paint.

His eyes bugged out. 'You fuckin' bitch.' He leant down, pushing her head underwater.

She had time to take a breath and hold it by instinct alone. *He would let go in a minute, surely. Don't panic.*

He did let go, sitting back on his haunches, wiping the faeces off by splashing water on his face.

The spa whirred to life, and water bubbled and churned to the surface. It exploded what was left of the turd and turned the water murky brown.

Sharli felt a tug on her long hair. She grabbed the nape of her neck, pressing her palm as the force pulled her under. Above the surface, she saw the manager's stricken face.

'Help,' her lips bubbled a cry.

The manager attempted to turn off the spa switch, but it must have jammed. He grabbed Sharli's hands, trying to tug her to the surface. 'Please, come up. Come on. You're joking. You can't be stuck.'

Her hair was so tight it felt like it was ripping from her scalp. *Panic.* She struggled with hair coming off in her hands. With her mouth gulping for air but not entirely making the surface, she tasted the disgusting faeces. Bile rose in her heaving throat.

Her hair didn't matter. She yanked some more. She didn't want to drown in a dirty spa. *Jai. Kendwa.* She squirmed, twisted, jerked—all to no avail.

The manager stood and ran, bringing back another hotel worker.

278

Putrid water filled her lungs. She glanced up to see Kendwa running towards her with Jai in his strong arms. *My loves.* A euphoric feeling filled her. *I'm water. I'm nature.* She was a liquid, fluid, free, flying. Above them, she watched, feeling detached. Part of her was missing. Heart? Body? Soul? She didn't know which.

Kendwa put Jai down and stepped into the spa, splashing water. He tried to pick her up and realised her hair was stuck. He pulled it from the spa drain, long pieces coming out in his hands. 'Fuck, no. No, babe. Noooo!'

Her eyes were wide open in death. *I'm dead. The old lady said I needed to cut my hair. I didn't listen. Now I'm dead.*

Jai stood with a thumb in his mouth, watching his father cry and swear at the sky.

Kendwa yelled at the resort staff. 'Do something. Turn this damn spa off.'

Jai's big eyes turned to the sky and stared at the moon.

Do you see me, baby boy?

Jai nodded.

I'll watch out for you, Jai. Look after your daddy. He'll be sad for a while.

Kendwa kept tugging his dead wife from the spa. A technician worked on the mechanisms, and it finally stopped. Kendwa was able to pull her hair free and lift her from the water, with clumps of hair missing from her scalp.

A lady in a housekeeping uniform stood comforting Jai, who cried on her shoulder.

Kendwa placed Sharli away from his son and did mouth to mouth. Her usual malleable lips were cold as ice. He pressed his hands over her chest, pushing hard until a rib cracked. 'Sorry, babe. Please, please wake up.'

No breath escaped her sweet lips. Her beautiful breasts were still. She was dead, but it didn't register—couldn't compute in his mind. Only that morning, they'd made love.

He tried to keep his anguish in to protect his son, but something primal came over him. He wailed to the sky in more of a howl than anything human. 'Shaaaaarliiiii!' It echoed around the resort, stopping tourists and making workers scurry to find out what was going on.

How could this happen? Nearly everyone he'd ever loved had died. Only Jai, Toby and Hope were left. Were they enough to give him the will to live on without his beautiful wife?

Three months after Sharli's death, Kendwa was barely eating or sleeping. He couldn't look after himself, let alone a small child. He decided it was best to leave Jai with Metra at the homeless mother's shelter. The women would look after Jai while he was powerless. Vedi had relapsed due to the grief of losing her daughter and was incapable of looking after her grandson.

Kendwa's grief consumed him. Even the usual solace he found among the wildlife of Africa couldn't mend his heart. He tried calling Toby, but he was off the grid with Hope, hiding from his vindictive ex-wife. So, alone he hunted the wildlife hunters, ran until he was exhausted, picked fights, got drunk and did it all again.

A couple of months later, he woke up with a massive hangover and instead of his first thought being about Sharli, it was Jai. He'd abandoned his son. How could he do that? He was stronger than this. It was time to find courage. He didn't have Sharli, but he had Jai, Sharli's son—his son.

On his return to Zanzibar, he called into The Curio Shop to find a gift for Jai. Not that it would fix things. He'd been an absent father when Jai needed him most, but there was no use beating himself up about it any more than he already had.

An ancient-looking woman approached him. Her eyes brimmed with tears. 'Samahani,' she said in a croaky voice.

'I am too. But how do you know about my wife?' He recognised the woman from around the markets selling journals and collector lamps from time to time, but they'd never met.

'Najua mambo.'

She knows things. Some say she's a healer and woman of magic and spells. Sharli believed in her strange gifts. 'Did you know she would die?' Kendwa asked, knowing the answer already because of the nightmares Sharli had been having. 'You told her to cut her hair, didn't you?'

The woman nodded. 'Utapata upendo tena.'

'No, I won't. I'll never find love again.' He took a deep breath, feeling his heart twist with grief.

The woman touched his shoulder with boney arthritic fingers.

A zap like an electric shock shimmy through his veins, startling him. She smiled and walked out of the shop.

He stared after her, blinking back tears. Turning away and stepping further into the store, he put the strange encounter to the back of his mind. He needed to find a gift for Jai.

A croaky voice whispered in his ear. 'Third shelf to the left. Behind a big book.'

Kendwa turned, but no one was there. He stepped to the shelf stuffed with curious items.

He moved the volume of Africa's East Coast aside. Behind it was a stack of children's books. The one on the top was *The Complete Adventures of Blinky Bill* by Dorothy Wall. He turned it over in his hand. 'An Australian book in an Africa Curio shop, now that's curious.' Since Jai had been born there, Kendwa liked the idea.

He bought the book, strolled out into the sunshine of Stone Town and smiled for the first time since Sharli had died.

Jai would grow up knowing both his African and Australian connections. He would make sure of it.

Time to mend both their hearts as father and son.

When Kendwa reached the shelter, Metra stood on the rotting deck waving. Jai ran into his arms. He picked him up, hugging him close, sniffing the baby sweetness and tasting both their salty tears on his lips.

'Daddy's home, Jai. Daddy's home.' His heart broke but a couple of the cracks healed at that moment with his precious son.

Dedication

*Dedicated to
my beautiful, kind, loving, handsome,
strong, admirable, compassionate,
dedicated, humorous,
delightful, thoughtful, character-filled sons;
Kris,
Joel
and
Blake.*

*And my second dad,
my father-in-law Colin.
A gem of a man, sadly missed but never forgotten,
especially when a country song is playing.*

282

Author Bio

Donna Munro is an Australian author of women's contemporary fiction and non-fiction. Born in Sydney, Australia, she grew up in the beach-side town of Port Macquarie, the Gold Coast, Queensland, and now lives on the beautiful Sunshine Coast.

Donna never reached five-foot-tall but don't underestimate her for the shortness. She confesses to an addiction to Peanut Butter, Sydney Roosters, sunflowers and exercise. When not at her work desk with a dog snoring beneath it, you'll often find Donna on a beach. She'll have a book in her hands and her toes in the sand.

Find Donna at:

Website   www.donnamunroauthor.com

Blog   www.warmwittywords.com.au

Facebook   https://www.facebook.com/donnamunrowarmwittywords

Instagram   https://www.instagram.com/donnadmunro

Twitter   https://twitter.com/warmwittywords

Pinterest   https://www.pinterest.com.au/donnawritings

Croc Brother Romance series

A Summer in Paradise: Book One

This book was previously published as *The Zanzibar Moon*.

A magical adventure romance to have you wishing you were on a Zanzibar beach.

A Summer Before: Book Two

Kendwa's earlier life is the prequel to *A Summer in Paradise*.
It was previously published as *Kendwa's Secret*.

A thrilling adventure romance to have you wishing you were on a Borneo beach.

A Summer of Hope: Book Three

The sequel to *A Summer in Paradise*.
It was previously published as *Elephant Creek*.

A family adventure romance to have you wishing you were on a Gold Coast beach.

Coming March 2022
a stand-alone contemporary women's fiction
with romantic suspense

Pepper Cassidy can wield a drop saw like most women use a nail file. But when she returns to Blueshell Beach, the last thing she needs is a sexy, unfriendly neighbour to distract her from the family cottage renovations.

Keegan Dallas left the city for a peaceful coastal life—surfing, yoga and a chance to regain custody of his son, Joe. His PTSD is improving, but he's not quite there yet.

She doesn't need or want a quiet, stubborn man who can't even use a hammer, let alone a seemingly damaged guy.

He would rather be alone but can't help falling for the beautiful, clumsy, sunshine-optimistic neighbour.

After a tragic accident renders Joe mute, can they come together to bring back his voice? That's if they don't nail each other to a renovated wall first.

When it seems impossible for love to save them, the past might hold the keys to a happy future after all, but not before a threat to those they love most.

If grief renders you mute can love find the words to save you?

Beach Cottage Haven

'I absolutely loved this book! Thank you for choosing me to read it. The book was well-written with well-rounded and wonderful characters. I was pulled into the story from the beginning and kept hooked throughout. I really didn't want to put it down once I started reading. The backstories of each of the main characters was well-done and gave you clues to the people they became. I really enjoyed how Pepper read her father's diaries and began to understand the man behind her father.' - Darla J Taylor

'A wonderfully rich read, great depth of characterisation, movement, and well-crafted threading of story within story.' - Sally Ryhanen - writer

Buy Donna's books on Amazon,
all good bookstores
or
www.donnamunroauthor.com